SHADOWLAND
YOU HAVE BEEN THERE
...IF YOU HAVE EVER
BEEN AFRAID

PETER STRAUB

BERKLEY BOOKS, NEW YORK

This Berkley book contains the complete
text of the original hardcover edition.
It has been completely reset in a type face
designed for easy reading, and was printed
from new film.

SHADOWLAND

A Berkley Book / published by arrangement with
Coward, McCann & Geoghegan, Inc.

PRINTING HISTORY
Coward, McCann & Geoghegan edition / October 1980
Berkley edition / November 1981

A BERKLEY BOOK ® TM 757,375
Berkley Books are published by Berkley Publishing Corporation,
200 Madison Avenue, New York, New York 10016.
PRINTED IN THE UNITED STATES OF AMERICA

The two schools, old and new, are inventions of the author and should not be confused with any existing schools. Similarly, Shadowland, its location and inhabitants, are entirely fictional.

I owe many thanks to Hiram Strait and Barry Price for their advice and comments about magic and magicians, and to Corrie Crandall for introducing me to them and to the Magic Castle.

For Benjamin Bitker Straub

Contents

Little Red Riding Hood was my first love. I felt that if I could have married Little Red Riding Hood, I should have known perfect bliss.

—Charles Dickens

The key to the treasure is the treasure.

—John Barth

Note

Tom in the
Zanzibar

More than twenty years ago, an underrated Arizona schoolboy named Tom Flanagan was asked by another boy to spend the Christmas vacation with him at the house of his uncle. Tom Flanagan's father was dying of cancer, though no one at the school knew of this, and the uncle's house was far away, such a distance that return would have been difficult. Tom refused. At the end of the year his friend repeated the invitation, and this time Tom Flanagan accepted. His father had been dead three months; following that, there had been a tragedy at the school; and just now moving from the well of his grief, Tom felt restless, bored, unhappy: ready for newness and surprise. He had one other reason for accepting, and though it seemed foolish, it was urgent—he thought he had to protect his friend. That seemed the most important task in his life.

When I first began to hear this story, Tom Flanagan was working in a nightclub on Sunset Strip in Los Angeles, and he was still underrated. The Zanzibar was a shabby place suited to the flotsam of show business: it had the atmosphere of a forcing-ground for failure. It was terrible to see Tom Flanagan here, but the surroundings did not even begin to reach him. Either that, or he had been marked by rooms like the Zanzibar so long ago and so often that by now he scarcely noticed their shabbiness. In any case, Tom was working there only two weeks. He was just pausing between moves, as he had been doing ever since our days at school—pausing and then moving on, pausing and moving again.

Even in the daylit tawdriness of the Zanzibar, Tom looked much as he had for the past seven or eight years, when his reddish-blond curling hair had begun to recede. Despite his profession, there was little theatricality or staginess about him. He never had a professional name. The sign outside the Zanzibar said only "Tom Flanagan Nightly." He used a robe only during the warming-up, flapdoodling portion of his act, and then twirled it off almost eagerly when he got down to serious business— you could see in the hitch of his shoulders that he was happy to be rid of it. After the shedding of the robe, he was dressed either in a tuxedo or more or less as he was in the Zanzibar, waiting patiently to have a beer with a friend. A misty Harris tweed jacket; necktie drooping below the open collar button of a Brooks Brothers shirt; gray trousers which had been pressed by being stretched out seam to seam beneath a mattress. I know he washed his handkerchiefs in the sink and dried them by flattening them onto the tiles. In the morning he could peel them off like big white leaves, give them a shake, and fold one into his pocket.

"Ah, old pal," he said, standing up, and the light reflected from the mirror behind the bar silvered the extra inches of skin above his forehead. I saw that he was still trim and muscular-looking, in spite of the permanent weariness which had etched the lines a little more deeply around his eyes. He held out a hand, and I felt as I shook it the thickness of scar tissue on his palm, which was always a rough surprise, encountered on a hand so smooth. "Glad you called me," he said.

"I heard you were in town. It's nice to see you again."

"One gratifying thing about meeting you," he said. "You never ask 'How's tricks?'"

He was the best magician I ever saw.

"With you, I don't have to ask," I said.

"Oh, I keep my hand in," he said, and pulled a pack of cards from his pocket. "Do you feel like trying again?"

"Give me one more chance," I said.

He shuffled the cards one-handed, then two-handed, cut them into three piles, and then reassembled the pack in a different order. "Okay?"

"Okay," I said, and he pushed the cards toward me.

I picked up two-thirds of the pack and turned the card now on top. It was the jack of clubs.

"Put it back." Tom sipped at his beer, not looking.

I slid the card into a different place in the deck.

"Better watch closely." Tom smiled at me. "This is where the old hocus-pocus comes in." He tapped the top of the deck hard enough to make a thudding noise. "It's coming up. I can feel it." He tapped again and winked at me. Then he lifted the top card off the deck and turned it to me without bothering to look at it himself.

"I can't figure out how you do that," I said. If he had wanted to, he could have pulled it out of my pocket, his pocket, or from a sealed box in a locked briefcase: it was more effective when done simply.

"If you didn't see it then, you never will. Stick to writing novels."

"But you couldn't have palmed it. You never even touched it."

"It's a good trick. But no good on stage—not much good in a club. They can't get close enough. Paying customers think card tricks are dull anyhow." Tom looked out over the rows of empty tables and then up at the stage, as if measuring the distance between them, and while he pondered the uselessness of skills it took a decade to perfect, I measured another distance: that between the present man and the boy he had been. No one who had known him then, when his red-blond head seemed to shoot off sparks and his whole young body communicated the vibrancy of the personality it encased, could have predicted Tom Flanagan's future.

Of course those of our teachers still alive thought of him as a baffling failure, and so did most of our classmates. Flanagan was not our most tragic failure, that was Marcus Reilly, who had shot himself in his car while we were all in our early thirties; but he might easily have been the most puzzling. Others had taken wrong directions and failed so gently that you could still hear the sigh; one, a bank officer named Tom Pinfold, had gone down with a crash when auditors found hundreds of thousands of depositors' dollars missing from their accounts; only Tom Flanagan had seemed to turn his back deliberately and uncaringly on success.

Almost as if Tom could read my mind, he asked me if I had seen anyone from the school lately, and we talked for a moment about Hogan and Fielding and Sherman, friends of the present day and the passionate, witty fellow-sufferers of twenty years past. Then Tom asked me what I was working on.

"Well, actually," I said, "I was going to start a book about that summer you and Del spent together."

Tom leaned back and looked at me with wholly feigned shock.

"Don't try that," I warned. "Nearly every time I've seen you the past five or six years, you've gone out of your way to tease me with that story. You asked enigmatic questions, dropped little hints—you wanted me to write about it."

He smiled briefly, dazzlingly, and for a second was his boyhood self, pumping out energy. "Okay. I thought it might be something you could use."

"Just that?" I challenged him. "Just something I could use?"

"After all this time you must realize that it's more or less in your line. And I've been thinking lately that it's about time I talked about it."

"Well, I'm happy to listen," I said.

"Good," he said, seemingly satisfied. "Have you thought about how you want to start it?"

"The book? With the house, I thought. Shadowland."

He considered that for a moment, his chin still propped on his hand.

"No. You'll get there eventually anyhow. Start with an anecdote. Start with the king of the cats." He thought about it a moment more and nodded, seeing it as a problem in structure, like his act. I had seen him improve it in a dozen ways, revising with a craftsman's zeal, always bending it more truly toward the last illusion, which should have made him famous. "Yes. The king of the cats. And maybe you should really start it at the school— the story proper, I mean. If you look back there, you should find some interesting things."

"Well, maybe."

"If you *look*. I'll help you." He smiled again, and for the space of the smile his thoughtful tough's face was that of a man who had looked, and I thought again that whatever his circumstances and surroundings, it was only a dead imagination that could call him a failure.

"It might be an idea," I said. "But what's all that about the king of the cats?"

"Oh, don't worry about that story. It'll turn up. It always does. Say, I ought to check over some of my equipment about now."

"You're too good for a place like this."

"Do you think so? No, I think we're pretty well suited to each other. The Zanzibar's not a bad old room."

We said good-bye, and I turned away from the bar toward the hazy light rectangle of the open door. A car sped by, a blue-jeaned girl jiggled past in sunlight, and I realized that I was happy to be leaving the club. Tom said that he was suited to the club, but I didn't believe that, and to me it felt—suddenly—like a prison.

Then I turned around again and saw him sitting in the murk with his sleeves rolled up, and he looked like the ruler of that dark empty room. "You're here two more weeks?"

"Ten days."

"I'll only be in town another week myself. Let's get together again before I go."

"That'll be nice," Tom Flanagan said. "Oh. By the way . . ."

I lifted my head.

"Jack of clubs."

I laughed, and he saluted me with his beer glass. He had never once glanced at the card, not even when the trick was over. Casual little miracles like that had nailed him into his life.

The king of the cats?

I hadn't the faintest idea of what this "story" was, but as Tom had promised, it turned up a few weeks later in a reference book. When I had read it, I knew immediately that Tom's instincts had been accurate.

When I set the story down here, I am going to put it in the context in which Tom first heard it.

Anecdote:

"Imagine a bird," the magician said. "Just now—flapping up, frightened, indeed tormented by fear, up out of this hat."

He twitched the white scarf away from the tall silk hat, and a dove the shade of the scarf beat its wings on the brim and awkwardly fell to the table—a terrified, panicked bird, unable to fly, making a loud clatter of wings on the polished table.

"Pretty bird," said the magician, and smiled at the two boys. "Now imagine a cat."

He whisked his scarf once again over the hat, and a white cat slipped over the brim. It came up out of the hat like a snake, flattening itself down onto the table, looking at nothing but the dove. With a slow predatory crawl, the cat went toward the dove.

The magician, who was dressed as a sinister clown in white-face and red wig above black tails, grinned at the boys and abruptly sprang over and backward, landing on his gloved hands. He held himself rigidly still for a second and then folded his legs down and his trunk up in what looked like one flawless motion. Now he was standing where he had been, and he dropped the white scarf over the elongated form of the cat.

When the magician passed his hand into the scarf, it fluttered down onto the flat surface of the table.

Three inches away, the dove still worked its wings and made its terrible clattering noise of panic.

"And that's it, isn't it?" the magician said. "Cat and bird. Bird and cat." He was still grinning. "And since our little friend is still so frightened, perhaps we'd better make her disappear too." He snapped his fingers, twitched the scarf, and the bird was gone.

"Cats remind me of a true story," he said to the mesmerized boys, speaking as if he were merely yarning, as if nothing but entertainment was on his mind. "It's an old story, but the truest stories are very often the oldest ones. This was told by Sir Walter Scott to Washington Irving, and by Monk Lewis to the poet Shelley—and to me by a friend of mine who actually saw it happen.

"A traveler, in other words my friend, was journeying on foot to the house of a companion—not me—where he was going to spend the night. He had been walking all day, and even though it was already late and night was coming on, he was tired enough to rest his feet when he came to a ruined abbey. He sat down, took off his boots, leaned against an iron fence, and began to rub his feet. An odd series of noises made him turn around and peer through the bars of the fence.

"Down below him, on the grassy floor of the old abbey, he saw a procession of cats. They were formed into two long equal lines, and were marching forward very slowly. Now, of course he had never seen anything like that before, and he bent forward to look more closely. It was then that he saw that the cats at the head of the procession were carrying a little coffin on their backs, and were making for, were slowly approaching, a small open grave. When my friend had seen the grave, he looked horrified back at the coffin borne by the lead cats, and noticed that on it sat a crown. As he watched, the lead cats began to lower the coffin into the grave.

"After that he was so frightened that he could not stay in that place a moment longer, and he thrust his feet into his boots and rushed on to the house of his friend. During dinner, he found that he could not keep from telling his friend what he had witnessed.

"He had scarcely finished when his friend's cat, which

had been dozing in front of the fire, leaped up and cried, 'Then I am the King of the Cats!' and disappeared in a flash up the chimney. It happened, my friends—yes, it happened, my charming little birds."

The true beginning of this story is not "More than twenty years ago, an underrated," etc., but, *Once upon a time . . .* or, *Long ago, when we all lived in the forest . . .*

Part One

The School

Arise and sing the praises
Of the school upon the hill
                              —School song

I

He Dreams
Awake

The last day of summer vacation: high cloudless skies, dry intense heat; endings and beginnings, deaths and promises, hover regretfully in the air. Perhaps the regret is only the boy's—that boy who is lying on his stomach in the grass. He is staring at a dandelion, wondering if he should pull it up. But if he pulls that one up, shouldn't he also pull up the one growing three feet away, whose leonine head is lolling and bobbling on a stalk too thin for it? Dandelions make your hands stink. On the last day of summer vacation, does he care if his hands smell like dandelions? He tugs at the

*big tough-looking dandelion nearest him; at least some of
the roots pull up out of the ground. He thinks he hears the
dandelion sigh, letting go of life, and tosses it aside. Then
he slides over to the second weed. It is too vulnerable, with
its huge head and thin neck: he lets it be. He rolls over and
looks up into the sky.*

*Good-bye, good-bye, he says to himself. Good-bye,
freedom. Yet a part of him looks forward to making the
change to high school, to really beginning the process of
growing up: he imagines that the biggest changes of his life
are about to happen. For a moment, like all children on the
point of change, he wishes he could foresee the future,
somehow live through it in advance—test the water there.*

*A solitary bird wheels overhead, so high up it breathes a
different air.*

*Then he must have fallen asleep: later, he thinks that
what happened after he saw the bird must have been a
dream.*

*It begins with the air changing color—becoming hazy,
almost silvery. A cloud? But there are no clouds. He rolls
over onto his stomach and idly looks sideways, where he
can see over four backyards. The swing set in the Trum-
bulls' yard is so rusty it should not stand another year—the
Trumbull children are older than he, but Mr. Trumbull is
too lazy to dismantle the swings. Farther on, Cissy
Harbinger is climbing out of her pool, stepping toward a
lounge chair in such a way that you know the tiles are
burning her feet. She gets to the chair and stretches out,
trying to deepen her already walnut tan. Then there are two
wider backyards, one with a plastic wading pool. Here,
Collis Falk, the gardener the boy's parents have just let go,
is riding a giant black lawn mower around the side of a
white house. No dandelions there: Collis Falk is a ruthless
executioner of dandelions.*

*Way down there, past the houses and the yards, a man is
walking up Mesa Lane. In this old suburb, pedestrians are
not as uncommon as they are in a lavish new development
like Quantum Hills, but still they are rare enough to be
interesting.*

The boy still does not know that he is dreaming.

*The walking man pauses on Mesa Lane—probably he is
a customer of Collis Falk's, and is waiting for the gardener*

to swing back toward him so that he can say hello. But no, it seems he is not waiting for the gardener: he is tilting his head back and looking at the boy. Or looking for him, the boy thinks. The man puts his hands on his hips. He must be three hundred yards away: he shimmers a little in the heat from the pavement. The boy has a sudden overwhelming conviction that the little figure is trying to find him . . . and the boy does not want to be seen. He flattens out in the grass. Unexpected fear sparkles in the boy's chest.

This is an interesting dream, he thinks. Why am I afraid of him?

The air becomes darker, more silvery. The man, who may or may have not seen him, walks on. Collis Falk chugs into sight, appearing to be intent on mowing down the wading pool. Now the boy is blocked from the man's sight, and he can move.

I'm really scared, he thinks: why? The entire neighborhood has turned unpleasant, somehow tainted and threatening. Though he cannot see the little figure way down there on Mesa Lane, the man is somehow broadcasting chill and badness. . . .

(His face is made of ice.)

No, that's not it, but the boy scrambles to his feet, starts to run, and then fully realizes he is in a dream, for he sees a building at the end of his backyard which he knows is not there; nor are the thick trees which surround it. The house is only about twenty feet high and has a thatched roof. Two small windows flank a little brown door. This fairy-tale structure is inviting, not threatening—he knows he is supposed to enter it. It will save him from whatever is pacing up and down on Mesa Lane.

And he knows it is a wizard's house.

When he goes through the trees and opens the door, all of his neighborhood seems to sigh: the rusty swings and the wading pool, Cissy Harbinger and Collis Falk, each brown and green blade of grass, send up a wave of disappointment and regret; and this real regret is from down there, from the man, who knows the boy is blocked from him.

"So here you are," the wizard says. An old man with an extravagantly wrinkled face mostly concealed behind a foaming beard, dressed in threadbare robes, the wizard is leaning back in a chair, smiling at him. He is the oldest

*wizard in the world, the boy knows; and then knows that
he himself is in the midst of a fairy tale, one never written.*
"You are safe here," the wizard says.

"I know."

"I want you to remember that. It's not all like that . . .
being out there."

"This is a dream, isn't it?" the boy asks.

"Everything is a dream," says the wizard. "This world
of yours—a flag in the breeze, a plaything full of meanings.
Take my word for it. Meanings. But you're a good boy,
you'll find out." A pipe appeared in his hand, and he drew
on it and breathed out thick gray smoke. "Oh, yes. You'll
find what you have to find. It'll be all right. You'll have to
fight for your life, of course, you'll have tests to pass—tests
you can't study for, hee hee—and there'll be a girl and a
wolf, and all that, but you're no idiot."

"Like Little Red Riding Hood? A girl and a wolf?"

"Oh, like all of them," the wizard said vaguely. "Tell
me, how is your father doing?"

"He's okay. I guess."

The wizard nodded, blew out another cloud of smoke.
He appeared very feeble to the boy; an old old wizard, at
the end of his powers, so tired he could barely lift his pipe.
"Oh, I could show you things," the wizard said. "But
there's no use in it. I just wanted you to know . . . Guess
I've said it all. This is a deep, deep wood. Wish I weren't so
blamed old."

He seemed to fall asleep for a moment. The pipe
drooped in his mouth and his hands trembled in his lap.
Then his watery eyes opened. "No brothers or sisters,
correct?"

The boy nodded.

The wizard smiled. "You can leave, son. He's gone.
Fight the good fight, now."

The boy has been dismissed; the logic of the dream
compels him outside; the wizard's eyes are closing again.
But he does not wish to leave—he does not want to wake up
just yet. He looks out the windows and sees forest, not his
backyard. Thick cobwebs blanket several trees in dark
grayness.

The wizard stirs, opens his eyes, and looks at the
reluctant boy. "Oh, you'll have your heart broken," he

says. "Is that what you're waiting to hear? It'll be broken,
all right. But you'll never get anything done if you walk
around with an unchipped heart. That's the way of it,
boy."

"Thanks," he says, and backs toward the door.

"That's the way, and there isn't any other way."

"Okay."

"Keep your eyes peeled for wolves, now."

"Right," the boy says, and goes outside. He thinks the
wizard is already asleep. After he goes past the trees which
are not there, he sees his own body asleep on the grass,
lying on its side near a lolling dandelion.

1

For various reasons the Carson School is now no longer
the school it was, and it has a new name. Carson was a
boys' school, old-fashioned and quirky and sometimes so
stern it could turn your bowels to ice water. Later we who
had been students there understood that all of the rather
menacing discipline was meant to disguise the fact that
Carson was at best second-rate. Only a school of that kind
would have hired Laker Broome as headmaster; perhaps
only a third-rate school would have kept him.

Years ago, when John Kennedy was still a senator from
Massachusetts and Steve McQueen was Josh Randall on
television and McDonald's had sold only two million
hamburgers and narrow ties and tab collars were coming
in for the first time, Carson was Spartan and tweedy and a
bit desperate and self-conscious about its status; now it is
a place where rich boys and girls go if they have trouble in
the public schools. Tuition was seven hundred and fifty
dollars a year; now it is just under four thousand.

It has even changed sites. When I was there with Tom
Flanagan and Del Nightingale and the others, the school
was chiefly situated in an old Gothic mansion on the top
of a hill, to which had been added a modern wing—steel
beams and big plates of glass. The old section of the
school somehow shrank the modern addition, subsumed it
into itself, and all of it looked cold and haunting.

This original building, along with the vast old gymnasium (the field house) behind it, was built mainly of wood. Parts of the original building—the headmaster's office, the library, the corridors and staircases—resembled the Garrick Club. Old wood polished and gleaming, oak bookshelves and handrails, beautiful slippery wooden floors. This part of the school always seduced prospective parents, who had the closet anglophilia of their class. Some of the rooms were jewel-box tiny, with mullioned windows, paneled walls, and ugly radiators that gave off little heat. If Carson had been the manor house some of its aspects suggested, it would have been not only haunting but also haunted.

Once every two or three years when I go back and drive past the school's new Quantum Hills site, I see a long neo-Georgian facade of reddish brick, long green lawns, and a soccer field far off—all of it fresh green and warm brick, so like a campus, so *generalized* that it seems a mirage. This cozy imitation of a university seems distant, remote, sealed within its illusions about itself. I know looking at it that the lives of its students are less driven than ours were, softer. Is there, I wonder, a voice still in the school which whispers: *I am your salvation, squirt: I am the way, the truth, and the light?*

I am your salvation—the sound of evil, of that flabby jealous devil of the second-rate, proclaiming itself.

2

Registration Day: 1958

A dark corridor, a staircase with an abrupt line of light bisecting it at one end, desks with candles dripping wax into saucers lined along a wall. A fuse had blown or a wire had died, and the janitor did not come until the next morning, when the rest of the school registered. Twenty new freshmen milled directionlessly in the long corridor, even the exceptionally suntanned faces looking pale and frightened in the candlelight.

"Welcome to the school," one of the four or five teachers present joked. They stood in a group at the entrance to the even darker corridor which led to the administration offices. "It isn't always this inefficient. Sometimes it's a lot worse."

Some of the boys laughed—they were new only to the Upper School, and had been at Carson, down the street in the mansard-roofed Junior School, all their lives.

"We can begin in a moment," another, older teacher said flatly, cutting off the meek laughter. He was taller than the others, with a narrow head and a pursy snapping turtle's face moored by a long nose. His rimless spectacles shone as he whipped his narrow head back and forth in the murk to see who had laughed. He wore the center-parted curling hair of a caricatured eighteen-nineties bartender. "Some of you boys are going to have to discover that the fun and games are over. This isn't the Junior School anymore. You're at the bottom of the pile now, you're the lowest of the low, but you'll be expected to act like men. Got that?"

None of the boys responded, and he gave a high-pitched whinnying snort down his long nose. This was obviously the characteristic sound of his anger. *"Got that? Don't you donkeys have ears?"*

"Yes, sir."

"That was you, Flanagan?"

"Yes, sir." The speaker was a wiry-looking boy whose red-blond hair was combed in the "Princeton" manner, flat and loose over the skull. In the moving dim light from the candles, his face was attentive and friendly.

"You coming out for JV football this fall?"

"Yes, sir."

All the new boys felt a fresh nervousness.

"Good. End?"

"Yes, sir."

"Good. If you grow a foot, you'll be varsity material in two years. We could use a good end." The teacher coughed into his hand, looked behind him down the black administration corridor, and grimaced. "I should explain. This incredible . . . *situation* has come about because School Secretary can't find her key to this door." He banged a heavy arched wooden door behind him with his knuckles. "Tony could open it if he were here, but he doesn't report until tomorrow. Be that as it may. We can all function by candlelight, I suppose." He surveyed us as if it were a challenge, and I noticed that his head was as narrow as the side of a plank. His eyes were so close together they all but touched.

"By the way, you'll all be on the junior-varsity football team," he said. "This is a small class—twenty. One of the smallest in the whole school. We need all of you out on the gridiron. Not all of you will make it through this . . . *crucial* year, but we have to try to make football players out of you somehow."

Some of the other teachers began to look restive, but he ignored them. "Now, I know some of you boys from the good work you did with Coach Ellinghausen in the eighth grade, but some of you are new. *You*." He pointed at a tall fat boy near me. "Your name."

"Dave Brick."

"Dave Brick, *what?*"

"Sir."

"You look like a center to me."

Brick showed consternation, but nodded his head.

"You." He pointed at a small olive-skinned boy with dark liquid eyes.

The boy squeaked.

"Name."

"Nightingale, sir."

"We'll have to put some meat on you, won't we, Nightingale?"

Nightingale nodded, and I could see his legs trembling in his trousers.

"Speak in sentences, boy. *Yes, sir.* That is a sentence. A nod is not a sentence."

"Yes, sir."

"Tackle?"

"I guess so, sir."

The teacher snorted, surveyed us all again. The waxy smell from the candles was beginning to build up, hot and greasy, in the corridor. Suddenly he snaked out one thick hand and grabbed Dave Brick's hair, which was combed into two small curling waves meeting in the center of his forehead. *"Brick! Cut that disgusting hair! Or I'll do it for you!"*

Brick quailed and jerked back his head. His throat convulsed, and I thought he was choking back vomit.

The narrow-faced man snapped his hand back and wiped it on his baggy trousers. "School Secretary is sorting out some papers you will need, forms for you to fill out and things like that, but since we . . . *seem* to have some time, I'll introduce you to the masters who are here today. I am Mr. Ridpath. My subject is world history. I am also the football coach. I will not have any of you in class for two years, but I will see you on the field. Now." He took a step to the side and turned so that his face was in darkness. Oily tendrils of hair above his ears shone in the candlelight. "These men are most of the masters you'll have this year. You will have the pleasure of meeting Mr. Thorpe, your Latin master, the day after tomorrow. Latin is a compulsory subject. Like football. Like English. Like Mathematics. Mr. Thorpe is as tough as I am. He is a great teacher. He was a pilot in World War One. It is an *honor* to be in Mr. Thorpe's Latin I. Now, here is Mr. Weatherbee—he will be your Mathematics I teacher, and he is your form tutor. You can go to him with your problems. He comes to us from Harvard, so he probably won't listen to them."

A small man with horn-rimmed glasses and a rumpled jacket over shoulders set in a permanent slouch lifted his head and grinned at us.

"Next to Mr. Weatherbee is Mr. Fitz-Hallan. He teaches English. Amherst." A rather languid-looking man with a handsome boyish face lifted a hand in a half-wave. He had made the joke about efficiency, and he looked bored enough to fall asleep standing up.

"Mr. Whipple, American history." This was a rotund, bald, cherub-faced man in a stained blazer to which the school crest had been affixed with a safety pin. He put his hands together and shook them before his face. "University of New Hampshire."

Mr. Ridpath glanced back down the black corridor now to his left, where a single dim light wavered behind flat glass. "See if you can help her, hey?" Whipple/New Hampshire padded off into the dark. "We'll have those papers in a minute. Okay. Talk among yourselves."

Of course none of us did, but just jittered in the dark corridor until Mr. Ridpath thought of something else to

say. "Where are the two scholarship boys? Let's see some
hands."

Chip Hogan and I raised our hands. Chip was already
standing with Tom Flanagan and the others from the
Junior School. Everybody looked curiously at the two of
us. Compared to us, all the others, even Dave Brick,
looked rich.

"Good. Good. Call out your names."

We did.

"You're the Hogan who ran seventy-five yards last year
in the eighth-grade championship against St. Matthew's?"

"Yeah," Hogan said, but Mr. Ridpath did not seem to
mind.

"You two boys know the great opportunity you're
getting?"

We said "Yes, sir" in unison.

"All of you new boys?"

There was a general sibilant mutter.

"You'll have to work, you know. Work like you never
have in your lives. We'll make you break your backs, and
then we'll expect you to play harder than you ever have in
your lives. And we'll make men out of you. Carson men.
And that's something to be proud of." He looked around
scornfully. "I don't think some of you are gonna cut the
mustard. Wait till Mr. Thorpe gets his hands on you."

A large old woman in a brown cardigan shuffled out of
the corridor, followed by Mr. Whipple, who carried a
flashlight. She too wore rimless glasses, and toted a large
bundle of papers sorted so that they were stacked
crosswise, in different sections. "Behind the duplicator,
wouldn't you know? Frenchy never washes his cups,
either. He couldn't put these on the counter like anyone
else." While she spoke, she dumped the stack of papers
on the first desk. "Help me distribute these—different
piles on different desks."

The knot of teachers dissolved, each of the men picking
up a separate stack of papers and moving to a different
desk. Mr. Ridpath announced, "Mrs. Olinger, school
secretary," in a parade-ground voice, and the old woman
nodded, snatched her flashlight back from Mr. Whipple,
and marched up the stairs into the light.

"Single file," Ridpath ordered, and we clumsily jostled

into each line and went down the desks, picking up sheets
from each.

A boy behind me mumbled something, and Mr. Ridpath bellowed, "No pencil? No pencil? First day of school
and you don't have a *pencil?* What's your name again,
boy?"

"Nightingale, sir."

"Nightingale," Ridpath said scornfully. "Where are
you from, anyway? What sort of school did you go to
before you came here?"

"This sort of school, sir," came Nightingale's girlish
voice.

"What?"

"Andover, sir. I was at Andover last year."

"I'll loan him a pen, sir," said Tom Flanagan, and we
passed down the line of desks without any more bellowing. At the far end of the corridor, we stood and waited in
the darkness to be told what to do.

"Upstairs, single line, library," Ridpath said wearily.

3

We went, like Mrs. Olinger, up the stairs into sunlight,
which fell and sparkled through the mullioned glass set
beside the high, thick scarred front door. The light was
already dim and gray up here, but across the hall was the
library, which had rows of big windows set between
bookshelves on either side. If the library had not been so
naturally dark, it would have shone. Cordovan-colored
wood and unjacketed spines of books blotted up the
available light, and on normal schooldays the big chan-
deliers overhead burned whenever the library was in use.
Without this light, the library was oddly tenebrous.

Two rows of long flat desks, also of the cordovan-
colored wood, filled the center of the front main section of
the room, and we took our papers to them. Across the
room ahead of us was a waist-high shelf of reference
books behind which sat the librarian's desk and file
cabinets in a kind of well with clear sight lines to all the
tables. Mrs. Olinger watched us file into the library and

take our seats, standing beside a thin woman with tightly permed white hair and gold-rimmed glasses. She wore a black dress and a strand of pearls. The teachers came in last and sat all at one table behind us. They immediately began to mutter to each other.

"Masters?" Mrs. Olinger queried, and the teachers quietened. One of them drummed a pencil in a triplet pattern, and continued to do so as long as we were in the library.

"This is Mrs. Tute," said Mrs. Olinger, and the thin woman wearing the pearls gave a nervous nod like a tremor of the head. "Mrs. Tute is our librarian, and this is her domain. She will be present while you fill out the registration forms and digest some of the information on the other sheets, after which she will provide you with an orientation to the library. If you have any questions, raise your hand and one of the masters will help you."

The pencil continued to rattle against the master's table.

When I had finished, I looked up and saw one or two other boys gazing idly around the murky room. Most of the others were still writing. Dave Brick's two curls had fallen over his forehead, and he looked red and sweaty and confused. He held up a hand, and Mr. Fitz-Hallan slowly lounged up toward his table.

"He's cool," Bob Sherman whispered to me, and both of us watched Fitz-Hallan idly lean over Brick's paper, hands thrust in his pockets holding out at an elegant angle the bottom of his well-cut jacket. Fitz-Hallan was a stylish figure whose elegance seemed so deeply ingrained as to be unconscious, but it was not merely that to which Sherman had referred. He was one of the younger teachers, perhaps not quite thirty, and even his languor was youthful: it seemed detached and kindly at the same time, and separated him from the other teachers as surely as we were separated from them. Fitz-Hallan straightened up, strolled to the librarian's desk, and returned with a ballpoint pen. This he presented to Brick with an abrupt gesture which somehow conveyed both sympathy and amusement. The perfection of this little charade mysteriously contained in it the information that Fitz-Hallan had once been a student at the school, and that he was a kind of living exhibit, a model of what we should try to become.

And that is the first of the three images I retain from the school, less remarkable than the two which followed but which in its way also led inexorably to all that happened. With hindsight I can see that here too was betrayal, delicately implied by the teacher's elegant clothing and manner, his amused sympathy: the way he thrust a cheap ball-point pen toward sweaty, doomed Dave Brick. We were so raw that we could be seduced by civility.

The half-dozen other sheets before the boys contained mimeographed data. The words to the school song *(Arise and sing the praises/Of the school upon the hill)* and the fight song *(Green and gold, gold and green!),* the school motto, *Alis volat propriis.* A translation thoughtfully followed: *He flies by his own wings.* "He" may have been B. Thurman Banter, who had founded the school's first incarnation, the Lodestar Academy, in 1901; Carson began flying under its present name in 1914, under the headmastership of Thomas A. Rowan. "Of Irish extraction and English birth," read the sheet. There followed a list of all headmasters from Rowan to the present, ending with Laker Broome; a list of present faculty, some thirty names, of which the last, Alexander Weatherbee, had been added in ink; the number of books in the library, twenty thousand; of pupils in the Upper School, one hundred and twelve; of football fields and baseball diamonds, two. Another sheet gave the names of all the boys in the senior class, with stars by the names of the prefects.

A commotion at the back of the library made me turn suddenly about. Mr. Ridpath was on his feet behind one of the tables, shouting, "What? What?" His narrow face flamed. With his left hand he gripped Nightingale's collar; with his right he groped beneath the table, trying to capture something which panicked Nightingale was attempting to pass to his table-partner, Tom Flanagan. Both boys looked frightened, Flanagan slightly less so than Nightingale. Mr. Ridpath's question had deteriorated into a series of animal grunts. When his right hand closed over the infuriating object, he withdrew it and held it up, giving his high-pitched snort. It was a pack of Bicycle playing cards. "Cards? Cards?" The flap of the box was still open, suggesting that the cards within had been replaced only a moment before. The three other teachers seated behind Mr. Ridpath looked as startled as the boys, all of whom had by now turned around on their seats. Mr. Ridpath snorted down his nose again. His face was still very red. "Who brought these here? Whose are they? Talk!"

"Mine," Nightingale uttered. He looked like a drowning mouse in Ridpath's grip.

"Well, I'm . . ." The teacher jerked harder on the boy's collar and looked around the room in angry disbelief. "I can't understand this. You. Flanagan. Explain."

"He was going to show me a new card trick, sir."

"A. New. Card. Trick." He tightened his grip on the mouse's collar, twisting it so that Nightingale's necktie slid up toward his ear. "A new *card* trick." Then he released both the Bicycle cards and the boy. When the pack struck the table, he slammed his hand down over it. "I'll dispose of these. Mrs. Olinger?"

She strode down between the tables, Ridpath lifted his hand, she walked back up to her desk. The metal wastebasket rang. She had never even glanced at the deck.

"You jokers," Mr. Ridpath said. "First day. You get away with it this time." He was leaning on the table, glaring at each boy in turn. "But no more. This is the last time we see cards in any room in this school. Hear me?" Nightingale and Flanagan nodded. "Jokers. You'd better stop wasting your time and start memorizing what's on those sheets. You'll need to know it, or you'll be doing card tricks, all right." He had one final threat. "Your Upper School career is getting off to a bad start, Flanagan." He returned to the teacher's table and pressed the heels of his hands into his eye sockets.

"Pass the registration forms to the ends of your rows, boys," said Mr. Fitz-Hallan. I saw that little olive-skinned Nightingale's face was gray with shock.

A few minutes later we were snaking down the dark hall toward a small wooden staircase, on our way to our first glimpse of Laker Broome.

The headmaster's office was at the bottom of the original manor, at the heart of the old building. Mrs. Olinger went before, illuminating her way down the black staircase with her big flashlight. She was mumbling to herself. The other teachers followed her, followed in turn by Mr. Whipple with a wavering candle for the boys' benefit. Whipple's candle was momentarily paled by the light from a window in a door on a small square landing. The light endured until another right-angled bend in the staircase, and after that we followed Whipple's bobbing candle down into an antechamber.

Not a true antechamber, it was formed by the end of the black corridor housing the school offices, from which Mrs. Olinger had first appeared. At that end, a curved wooden arch created the illusion that we were in a room. An oriental carpet lay on the floor. An antique table held a library lamp and a Persian bowl. Opposite the arch was a vast wooden door like the entrance to a medieval church, cross-braced with long iron flanges.

We stood silent in the flickering light of the candle. Mr. Fitz-Hallan knocked once at the big door. Mrs. Olinger said, "Farewell, boys," and took off down the corridor with her characteristic air of irritated urgency, lighting her way with the flashlight. Fitz-Hallan swung open the door, and we jostled into Mr. Broome's office.

Sudden brightness and the smell of wax: on every surface sat at least two candles. The sense of being in a church was much stronger. The headmaster sat behind his desk, his coat off and his hands laced together behind his head. His elbows were sharply pointed triangular wings. He was smiling. "Well," he said. "Step forward, boys. Let me get a good look at you."

When we were ranked in two rough rows before the desk, he lowered his arms and stood up. "Whatever you do, don't knock over a candle. They're pretty, but dangerous." He laughed, a short thin man with gray hair cut down to a bristly cap. Deep grooves beside his mouth cut into the flesh. "Even when school is not in session, the headmaster must slave away at his desk. This means that you will almost always find me here. My name is Mr. Broome. Don't be shy. If you have a problem you want to discuss with me, just make an appointment with Mrs. Olinger." He stepped backward and leaned against a dark wooden bookshelf, his arms crossed over his chest. The headmaster wore horn-rimmed glasses the color of a marmalade cat. His shirt was very crisp. I see now that he was perfect—the final detail in his whole paneled, oriental-carpeted, book-filled office, the detail around which the delicate, deliberate, old-fashioned good taste of the office cohered.

"Of course," he said, "it is rather more likely that your visits here will be in the service of a less pleasant function."

His mouth twitched.

"But that should concern only a small portion of you. Our boys are generally worked pretty hard, and they don't have the time to find trouble. One word of warning. Those who do find it don't last long here. If you want to enjoy the benefits of being a student at this school, work hard, be obedient and respectful, and play hard. Considering the advantages, it is not too much to ask." Again, his taut, measured replica of a smile. "Just what we have the right, not to mention the duty, to ask of you, I should say. It is my intention, it is the school's intention, to leave our mark upon you. Wherever you go in later life, people will be able to say, 'There is a Carson man.' Well."

He looked over our heads at the teachers; most of us too swiveled our heads to look back. Mr. Whipple was leafing through the forms we had filled out. Mr. Ridpath stood at a sort of soldierly ease, his feet spread and his hands behind his back. The other two stared at the floor, as if putting themselves at a private distance from the headmaster.

"You have them, Mr. Whipple? Then please bring them here."

Whipple moved quickly around us to the desk and laid the pile of forms immediately before the headmaster's leather chair. "The two on top, sir," he muttered, and vanished backward.

"Ah? Yes, I see." He uncoiled, the frames of his glasses glowed red for a moment as he passed before a stand of candles, and he lifted the top two forms. "Messrs. Nightingale and Sherman will stay behind a moment. The rest of you may return to the library to pick up your textbooks and schedule cards. Lead them away, Mr. Ridpath.''

Fifteen minutes later Nightingale and Sherman appeared in the door of the library and moved aimlessly toward the now book-covered tables. Sherman's cheekbones were very red.

"Well,'' I whispered to him. "What'd he say?''
Sherman tried to grin. "He's a frosty old shit, isn't he?''
We compared our schedule cards before our lockers in the second-floor front corridor of the modern addition, where the inner walls were tall panes of glass looking out onto a gravel-filled court with a single lime tree.

I heard weeks later from Tom Flanagan why Bob Sherman and Del Nightingale had been kept behind by Mr. Broome. Nightingale had not filled in the blanks for parents' names. He had not done so because his parents were dead. Nightingale lived with his godparents, who had just moved from Boston into a house on Sunset Lane, four or five long blocks from the school. Sherman had been dressed down.

4

New York, August, 1969: Bob Sherman

"Why am I here?'' Sherman asked. "Can you answer that? What the fuck am I doing here when I could be out on the Island sipping a Coors and looking at the ocean?''

We were in his office, and he was speaking loudly to be heard over the rock music pumping out of the stereo system. The office was a suite of rooms in the old German embassy, and all of the rooms had twelve-foot ceilings decorated with plaster molding. Leather couches sat before his long desk and against the wall. A big green Boston fern beside the Bose speakers looked as though it had just taken a vitamin pill. Records were stacked carelessly on the floor, flattening out the deep pile of the carpet.

"You usually have an answer. Why am I in this shithole? You're here because I'm here, but why am I here? It's just another one of those eternal questions. Do you want to take that record off? I'm sick of it."

His telephone rang for the sixth time since I had been in his office. He said, "Christ," picked up the phone, and said "Yeah," and motioned me to put the new record on the turntable.

I tuned out and relaxed into the couch. Sherman ranted. He was a very skillful ranter. He had a law degree. Also he had an ulcer, the nerves of a neurotic cat, and what I assumed was the highest income of anyone from our class. In these days his wardrobe was always very studied, and today he wore a tan bush jacket, aviator glasses tinted yellow, and soft knee-high yellow boots. He clamped the phone under his chin, crossed his arms over his chest, leaned against the window, and gave me a sour grin.

"I'll tell you something," he said when he had put the phone down. "Fielding should bless his soul that he never decided to go into the music business. And he had more talent than most of these bozos we manage. Is he still trying to get his Ph.D.?"

I nodded. "This will sound funny, but when you were leaning against the window like that just now, you reminded me of Lake the Snake."

"Now I *really* wish I was out on the Island. Lake the Snake." He laughed out loud. "Laker Broome. I better clean up my act. What made you think of that?"

"Just the way you were standing."

He sat down and put his boots on the long desk. "That guy should have been locked up. He's not still there, is he?"

"He retired years ago—forced out, really. I wouldn't have worked for him." I had just quit the school myself, after three years of teaching English there. "I never asked you this before, or if I did, I forgot the answer. What did Lake the Snake say to you, that first day? When he kept you and Nightingale in his office."

"The day we registered?" He grinned at me. "I told

you, but you forgot, you asshole. That's one of my favorite party bits. Ask me again after dinner on Saturday night, if you're still coming."

Then I did remember—we had been in his father's "den" one warm day in late fall, drinking iced tea from tall glasses with *Party Time!* embossed on their sides. "I'd come just to hear it," I said. I was in New York on my way to Europe, and Sherman and Fielding were the only people there I cared to visit. And Sherman was a good cook whose dinner parties had a bachelor's haphazard lavishness.

"Great, great." He was already a little distant, and I thought he was thinking again of the grievances given him by his twenty-year-old geniuses. "I saw Tom Flanagan on the street the other day," he said. "He looked really strange. He looked about forty years old. That guy's nuts. It doesn't make any sense, what he's doing. He's working some toilet over in Brooklyn called the Red Hat Lounge. Magic is going to come back when Glenn Miller climbs out of the Channel. When Miss America has . . ."

"Bad teeth?"

"A mastectomy," Sherman said.

On Saturday night there was as much of a lull in the after-dinner conversation as Sherman ever permitted in the days before he moved to Los Angeles. The famous folksinger seated to my left had wiped food from his beard and described a million-dollar drug deal just concluded by two other famous folk singers; the woman with Bob, a blond with the English country-house good looks to which he was always attracted, had opened a bottle of cognac; Sherman was leaning on one elbow, picking bits of bacon out of what was left of the salad.

"My friend across the table wants to hear a story," he said.

"Great," said the folksinger.

"He wants to be reminded of the famous Lake the Snake, and how he welcomed me to his school. On our first day we had to fill in registration forms, and when it asked for my favorite subject, I put down 'Finance.'" The girl and the singer laughed: Sherman had always been good at telling stories. "Lake the Snake was the headmaster, and when a fat little shit named Whipple who taught history showed him my form, he kept me back in his office after he made his welcome-to-the-school speech. Another little kid was kept behind with me, and he sent him out into the hall. I was practically shitting my pants. Lake the Snake looked like an Ivy League undertaker. Or a high-class hired killer. He was sitting at his desk just smiling at me. It was the kind of smile you'd give somebody just before you cut his balls off.

"'Well,' he said. 'I see you are a comedian, Sherman. I don't really think that will do. No, it won't do at all. But I'll give you a chance. Make me laugh. Say something funny.' He braced his hands behind his head. I couldn't think of a single word. 'What a pathetic little boy you are, Mr. Sherman,' he said. 'What is the motto of this school? No answer? *Alis volat propriis.* He flies by his own wings. I presume that now and again he touches ground too. But he does fly, the kind of boy we want here. He doesn't look for cheap laughs and gutter satisfactions. Since you are too much of a coward to speak up, I'll tell *you* something. It's a story about a boy. Listen carefully.

"'Once, a long time ago, this certain boy, who was, let me see, fourteen years old, left his warm cozy little house and went out into the wide world. He thought he was a funny little boy, but in reality he was a simpleton and a coward, and sooner or later he was bound to meet a bad end. He went through a city, and he made little comments that made people laugh. He thought they were laughing at his little comments, but in fact they were laughing at his presumption.

"'It so happened that the king of that country was proceeding through the city, and the boy saw his golden carriage. This was a splendid affair, made by the king's craftsmen, and it was of solid gold, drawn by six magnificent black chargers. When the carriage passed the boy, he turned to the good citizen beside him and said, "Who's the old fool in the fancy wagon? He must weigh as much as all six horses. I bet he got rich by stealing from people like you and me, brother." You see, he was interested in *finance*. He expected his neighbor to laugh, but the neighbor was horrified—all citizens in that country loved and feared their king.

"'The king had heard the boy's remark. He stopped the carriage and immediately bade one of his men to dismount and take the boy by force back to his palace. The men dismounted and grabbed the boy by the arm and dragged him yelling through the streets all the way to the palace.

"'The servant pulled the boy through the halls of the palace until they reached the throne room. The king sat on his throne glaring at the boy as the servant pulled him forward. Two savage dogs with chains on their necks snapped and snarled at the boy, but kept guard by the sides of the throne. The boy nearly fainted in terror. The dogs, he saw, were not only savage, but starved down nearly to madness.

"'"So, little comedian," the king said. "You will make me laugh or you will die." The witless boy could only tremble. "One more chance," said the king. "Make me laugh." Again, the boy could not speak. "Go free, Skuller," snapped the king. The dog on the right flew forward toward the boy. In a second he held the boy's right hand between his teeth. The king told the boy to make a joke *now*. The boy turned white. "Go free, Ghost," the king said, and the dog on the left flew forward and bit down on the boy's left hand.

"'"You see where tasteless remarks get you," said the king. "Begin to eat, my dogs."

"'Begin to eat, my dogs,'" Sherman repeated, shaking his head. "I practically fell on the floor and puked. Lake the Snake just kept looking at me. 'Get out of here,' he said. 'Don't ever come back here again for a stupid reason like this.' I sort of wobbled toward the door. Then I heard something growling, and I looked back and a great goddamned Doberman was getting to its feet beside his chair. 'Get out!' Lake the Snake shouted at me, and I ran out of that office like fiends were after me."

"Holy shit," mumbled the folksinger. Sherman's girlfriend was staring at him limpidly, waiting for the punch line, and I knew he had told this story, which by now I remembered perfectly, many times before.

Sherman was grinning at me. "I see it's all come back to you. When I was nearly at the door, that sadist behind the desk said '*Alis volat propriis*, Mr. Sherman.' I saw a sign on the wall next to his door, where you'd see it every time you left his office. It said, 'Don't wait to be a great man. Be a great boy.'"

"Be a fuckin' son-of-a-bitch bastard," the folksinger said, and then looked up confused because Sherman and I were both laughing. The country-house blond was laughing too: Sherman could always make women laugh. I had learned a long time before that this ability was a large part of his undoubted sexual success.

5

Tom Flanagan and Del Nightingale had picked up their freshman beanies like the rest of us from the carton just inside the library doors, and at the end of Registration Day they stood for a moment together at the entrance to the school, trying them on. "I think they're one-size-fits-none," Tom said. Both boys' beanies were a quarter-size too large and swam on their heads. "Don't worry, we can swap them tomorrow," Tom said. "There were a lot left over in that box. Do you know how to wear these, by the way? This little bill is supposed to be two fingers above the bridge of your nose." Using the first two fingers of his right hand to demonstrate, he adjusted the cap with his right. Nightingale imitated him, and brought the brim down to the level of his topmost finger.

"Well, it's only for the first semester," Tom said. But then, at the beginning, they shared a secret pleasure in wearing the absurd caps: Tom because it meant that he was in the Upper School—the entrance to adulthood. If Tom thought of the Upper School as the realm of beings who were almost men—the seniors did look alarmingly like real adults—for Del it was something simpler and more comprehensive. He thought of it, without being quite aware of the thought, as a place which might become home. Tom at least was at home in it.

At that moment, he wanted Tom Flanagan to befriend him more than anything else in the world.

Of course I am ascribing to the fourteen-year-old Del Nightingale emotions which I cannot be sure he possessed. Yet he must have been very lonely in these first weeks at Carson; and I have Tom's later statement to me that "Del Nightingale needed a friend more than anyone else I'd ever met. I didn't even know, this is how innocent I was, that anyone *could* need a friend as badly as that. And you know how schools are: if you want something, security or affection, very badly, it means that you're not going to get it. I didn't see why that should always be true." The statement shows that Tom was more sensitive than his appearance ever indicated. With his gingery hair, his short wiry athletic body, his good clothes a little scuffed and rumpled, he looked chiefly as though he wished he held a baseball in his hand. But another thing you thought you saw when you looked at Tom Flanagan was an essential steadiness: you thought you saw that he was incapable of affectation, because he would never see the need for it.

I think Del Nightingale looked at him bringing the school beanie down to the level of two fingers balanced on his nose and adopted him on the spot.

"That trick you were showing me isn't in my book," Tom said. "Sometime I'd like to see how it goes."

"I brought a lot of card books with me," Del said. He dared not say anymore.

"Let's go have a look at them. I can call my mother from your place. She was going to pick me up after registration, but we didn't know when it would be over. How do we get to your house? Do you have a ride?"

"It's close enough to walk," Del said. "It's not really my house. My godparents are just renting it."

Tom shrugged, and they went down the front steps, crossed Santa Rosa Boulevard, and began to walk up sunlit Peace Lane. Carson was in a suburb old enough to have imposing elms and oaks lining the sidewalks. The houses they passed were the sort of houses Tom had seen all his life, most of them long and of two stories, either of white stone or white board. One or two houses on every block were bordered by screened-in porches. Concrete slabs gray with age and crossed by a jigsaw puzzle of cracks made up the slightly irregular sidewalk. Tough, coarse grass thrust up between the slabs of pavement. For

Del, who had been raised in cities and in boarding schools
thousands of miles away, all of this was so unreal as to be
dreamlike. For a moment he was not certain where he was
or where he was going.

"Don't worry about Ridpath," Tom said beside him.
"He's always hollering. He's a pretty good coach. But I'll
tell you who's in trouble already."

"Who?" Del asked, beginning to quake already. He
knew that Tom meant him.

"That Brick. He'll never last. I bet he doesn't get
through this year."

"Why do you say that?"

"I don't know exactly. He looks kind of hopeless,
doesn't he? Kind of dumb. And Ridpath is already
shitting hot nickels over his hair. If his father was on the
board, or something like that—or if his family had always
gone here . . . you know." Flanagan was walking with
what Del would later see as the characteristic Carson gait,
which slightly rolled the shoulders from side to side and
wagged neckties like metronomes. This was, as Del
immediately recognized, finally "preppy." Amidst all the
Western strangeness, the strolling, necktie-swinging gait
was familiar enough to be comfortable.

"I guess I do know," he said.

"Oh, sure. Wait till you see Harrison—he's a junior.
Harrison has hair just like Brick's, but his father is a big
shot. Last year his father donated fifteen thousand dollars
to the school for new lab equipment. Where is this house,
anyhow?"

Del had been dreaming along under the ninety-degree
sun, self-consciousness about the beanie melting together
with his sense of unreality and his pleasure in Tom's
company to make him forget that they had a destination.
"Oh. Next street."

They reached the corner and turned into the street. It
seemed impossible to Del that he actually lived there. He
would not have been wholly surprised to see Ricky and
David Nelson playing catch on one of the lawns.

"Mr. Broome wanted to talk to you," Tom said.

"Um-hum."

"I suppose your father is an ambassador or something
like that."

"My father is dead. So is my mother."

Tom quickly said, "Geez, I'm sorry," and changed the subject. His own father had recently begun a mysterious siege of X rays and over-night stays in St. Mary's Hospital. Hartley Flanagan was a corporation lawyer who could chin himself a dozen times and had been a varsity fullback at Stanford. He smoked three packs a day. "Mr. Ridpath isn't too bad, he's just not very subtle"—both boys grinned—"but you ought to watch out for his son. Steve Ridpath. I remember him from the Junior School."

"He's worse than his father?"

"Well, he was a lot worse then. Maybe he's nicer now." Tom's mouth twitched in a pained, adult manner, and Del saw that his new friend doubted his last remark. "He beat the crap out of me once because he didn't like my face. He was in the eighth grade. I was in the fifth grade. A teacher *saw* him do it, and he still didn't get expelled. I just sort of made sure I never got near him after that."

"This is the house," Del said, still unable to refer to it as his. "What does this guy look like?"

Tom took off his beanie and folded it into a hip pocket. "Steve Ridpath? His nickname is Skeleton. But don't ever say it in front of him. In fact, if you can help it, don't ever say *anything* to him. Are we going to go in, or what?"

The door opened and a uniformed black man said, "Saw you and your friend coming, Del."

6

Inside

"Skeleton . . ." Del said, shaking his head, but Tom Flanagan was looking at the tall bald black man who had let them in. He was too surprised not to stare. A few families in this affluent suburb had live-in maids, but he had never seen a butler before. The first impression that the man wore a uniform gradually dissipated as Tom realized that the butler was dressed in a dark gray suit with a white shirt and a silk tie the same charcoal shade as the suit. He was smiling down at Tom, clearly enjoying the boy's startled inspection. His broad face looked young, but the short wiry hair above his ears was silver. "I see young Del is going to get on well at that school if he made such an alert friend already."

Tom blushed.

"This is Bud Copeland," Del said. "He works for my godparents. Bud, this is Tom Flanagan. He's in my class. Are they in?"

"Mr. and Mrs. Hillman are out looking at a house," the butler said. "If you tell me where you'll be, I'll bring you whatever you want. Coke? Iced tea?"

"Thanks," Del said. Tom was still wondering if he ought to shake hands with the butler, and while Del said "Coke," realized that the moment for it had passed. But by then his hand was out, and he said, "Coke please, Mr. Copeland. I'm pleased to meet you."

The butler shook his hand, smiling even more widely. "My pleasure too, Tom. Two Cokes."

"We'll be in my room, Bud," Del said, and began to lead Tom deeper into the house. Cartons and boxes crowded what was obviously the living room. As they passed the dining room, Tom saw that it was nearly filled with a huge rectangular mahogany table.

"If you just moved in, why are they out looking at houses?" he asked.

"They're looking for a bigger place to buy. They want more land around them, maybe a pool. . . . They say this neighborhood is too suburban for them, so they're going to move somewhere even more suburban." They were going upstairs; lighter squares on the wallpaper showed where pictures had hung. "I don't even think they want to unpack. They hate this house."

"It's okay."

"You should see what they had in Boston. I used to live with them most of the time. In the summers . . ." He looked over his shoulder at Tom and gave him an expression so guarded that Tom could not tell if it signified suspicion, fear of being questioned, or the desire to be questioned.

"In the summers?"

"I went somewhere else. But their place in Boston was

really huge. Bud worked for them there too. He was always really nice to me. Ah, here's my room." Del had been walking down a corridor, his black-haired head proceeding along at about the level of Tom's eyes with more assurance than his behavior at the school had indicated that he had in him, and now he paused outside a door and turned around. This time Tom had no trouble reading the expression on his face. He was glowing with anticipation. "If I was really corny, I'd say something like, 'Welcome to my universe.' Come on in."

Tom Flanagan walked rather nervously into what at first appeared to be a totally black room. A dim light went on behind him. "I guess you can see what I mean," came Del's high-pitched voice. He sounded a shade less confident.

7

Ridpath at Home

Chester Ridpath parked his black Studebaker in his driveway and reached across the seat to lift his briefcase. Like the upholstery of his car, it had been several times repaired with black masking tape, and graying old ends of the tape played out beneath the gummy top layers. The handle adhered to his fingers. He wrestled the heavy satchel onto his lap—it was crammed with mimeographed football plays, starting lineups which went back nearly to the year when he had purchased the car, textbooks, lesson plans, and memos from the headmaster. Laker Broome spoke chiefly through memos. He liked to rule from a distance, even at faculty meetings, where he sat at a separate table from the staff: most of his administrative and disciplinary decisions were filtered down through Billy Thorpe, who had been assistant head as well as Latin master under three different headmasters. Sometimes Chester Ridpath imagined that Billy Thorpe was the only man in the world who he really respected. Billy could not ever conceivably have had a son like Steve.

He exhaled, wiped sweat from his forehead back into his hair, temporarily flattening half a dozen fussy curls, and left the car. The sun burned through his clothes. The briefcase seemed to be filled with stones.

Ridpath found his bundle of keys in his deep pocket, shook them until his house key surfaced, and let himself into his house. Raucous music—music for beasts—battered the air. He supposed many parents came home to this din, but was it so loud in other houses? Steve had carried his phonograph home from the store, twisted the volume control all the way to the right, and left it there. Once in his room, he walled himself up inside this savagery. Ridpath could not communicate through a barrier so repellent to him; he suspected, in fact he knew, that Steve was uninterested in anything he might wish to communicate anyhow.

"Home," he shouted, and banged the door shut—if Steve couldn't hear the shout, at least he would feel the vibration.

The house had been in disarray so long that Ridpath no longer noticed the pile of soiled shirts and sweaters on the stairs, the dark smudges of grease on the carpet. He and Margaret had bought the living-room carpet, a florid Wilton, on a layaway plan just after they had mortgaged his salary for twenty years to buy the house. During the fifteen years since his wife had left him, Ridpath had taken an unconscious pleasure in the gradual darkening and wearing away of the nap. There were places—before his chair, in front of the slat-backed couch—where the awful flower-spray pattern was nearly invisible.

Overlaying the piles of dirty clothing were the magazine clippings and pages of comic books which Steve used to make his "things." They had no other name. Steve's "things" were varnished to his bedroom walls. Korea had supplied a surplus of the images Steve preferred in his "things," and by now the room was a palimpsest of screaming infants, wrecked jeeps, bloated dead in kapok jackets. Tanks rolled over muddy hills toward classrooms of dutiful Russian children (courtesy of *Life*). Mossy monsters from horror comics embraced starlets with death's-heads. Ridpath never entered his son's room anymore.

He dropped the briefcase beside his chair and sat heavily, wrenching his tie over his head without bothering to undo the knot. After he had dropped his jacket on the floor beside it, he reached for the telephone set on an otherwise empty shelf. Ridpath shouted, "Turn it down, goddammit," and waited a second. Then he shouted again, louder. *"For God's sake, turn it down!"* The music diminished by an almost undetectable portion. He dialed the Thorpe number.

"Billy? Chester. Just got home. Thought maybe you should get the poop on the new boys. Look pretty good on the whole, but there are a few items I thought you'd want to know about. Sort of coordinate ourselves here. Okay? First off, we got one good, one real good football prospect, the Hogan kid. He might take a little watching in the classroom . . . No, nothing definite, just the impression I had. I don't want to prejudice you against the kid, Billy. Just keep him on a tight rein. He could be a real leader. Now for the bad news. We got one real lulu in the new intake. A kid named Brick, Dave Brick. Hair like a goddamned Zulu, more grease on it than I got in my car. You know what kind of attitude that means. I think we want to crack down on this kind of thing right away, or one bad apple like that could spoil the whole school. Plus that, there's a wiseacre named Sherman. The kid already lipped off, fooled around with his registration form . . . You getting these names?"

He wiped his face again and grimaced toward the stairs. How could a boy listen to that stuff all day long? "One more. You remember our transfer from Andover, the orphan kid with the trust fund? Nightingale. He might of been a big mistake. I mean, Billy, maybe Andover was glad to get rid of him, that's what I mean. First of all, he looks wrong—like a little Greek. This Nightingale kid looks sneaky. . . . Well, hell, Billy, I can't help the way I see things, can I? And I was right, too. I caught him with a pack of cards—yeah, he had the cards out. In the library. Can you beat that? Said he was showing Flanagan a card trick. . . . Yeah, a card trick. *Man.* I confiscated the cards PDQ. I think the kid's some kind of future beatnik or something. . . . Well, I know you can't always tell that kind of thing, Billy. . . . Well, he did have those cards in his fist, big as you please, gave me a little tussle, too. . . . Well, I'd put him in the special file along with Brick, that's what I'm saying, Billy. . . ."

He listened to the telephone a moment, his face contracting into a tight, unwilling grimace. "Sure, Steve'll be okay this year. You'll see a big change in him, now that he's a senior. They grow up pretty fast at that age."

He hung up gratefully. "Grow up"—was that what Steve had done? He did not want to talk to Billy Thorpe, who had two good-looking successful boys, about Steve. The less Thorpe thought about Steve Ridpath, the better.

Skeleton. God.

Ridpath shoved himself to his feet, knocking over the caseful of football plays, took a few aimless steps toward the stairs, then turned around and picked up the case, deciding to go down to his desk in the basement. He had to do some more thinking about the JV team before their first practice. When he walked out of the living room, he glanced into the kitchen and unexpectedly saw the gaunt, looming form of his son leaning over the sink. Steve was pressing his nose and lips against the window, smearing the glass. So he had somehow flickered down the stairs.

8

Universe

"I've only been here three days," Del was saying, now positively sounding nervous, "but I didn't want to just live out of suitcases, the way they're doing. I wanted to get my stuff set up." There came a sound of scuffing feet. "Well, what do you think?"

"Wow," Tom said, not quite sure what he thought, except that wonder played a large part in it. In the dim light, he could not even see all of Del's things. On the wall behind the bed hung a huge star chart. The opposite wall was a frieze of faces—framed photographs. He recognized John Scarne from the photo on a book he owned, and Houdini, but the others were strangers to him. They were men with serious, considering, summing-up kinds of faces in which their theatricality appeared as an afterthought. Magicians. A skull grinned from a shelf at waist level beneath the photographs, and Del hopped around him to light a little candle within it. Then Tom saw all the books held upright by the skull. The middle of the room and the desk were crowded with the paraphernalia of magic tricks. He saw a glass ball on a length of velvet, a miniature guillotine, a top hat, various cabinets filigreed and lacquered with Chinese designs, a black silver-topped cane. Before the long windows, entirely covering them, a big green tank sent up streams of bubbles through a skittering population of fish. "I don't believe it," Tom breathed. "I don't know where to start. Is all this stuff really yours?"

"Well, I didn't get it all at once," Del said. "Some of this stuff has been around for years—since I was about ten. That's when I got involved. Now I'm *really* involved. I think it's what I want to be."

"A magician?" Tom asked, surprised.

"Yeah. Do you too?"

"I never thought about that. But I'll tell you one thing I just thought right now."

Del lifted his head like a frightened doe.

"I think school is going to be a lot more interesting this year."

Del beamed at him.

Bud Copeland brought them Cokes in tall frosted glasses with a lemon slice bumping the ice cubes, and for an hour the two boys prowled through Del's collection. In his eager, piping voice, the smaller boy explained to Tom the inner workings of tricks which had puzzled him for as long as he had been interested in magic. "All these illusions are the flashy stuff, and no one will ever see how they work, but I really prefer close-up magic," Del said. "If you can do close-up card work, you can do anything. That's what my Uncle Cole says." Del held up a finger, still in the dramatic persona he had put on with his top hat at the beginning of the tour. "No. Not quite. He said you could do almost everything. He can do things you wouldn't believe, and he won't explain them to me. He says certain things are art, not just illusion, and because they're art they're real magic. And you can't explain them." Del brought his finger down, having caught himself in a public mood at a private moment. "Well, that's what he says, anyway. It's like he's full of secrets and information no one else knows about. He's kind of funny, and sometimes he can scare the crap out of you, but he's the best there is. Or I think so, anyway." His face was that of a dark little dervish.

"Is he a magician?"

"The best. But he doesn't work like the others—in clubs and theaters and that."

"Then where does he work?"

"At home. He does private shows. Well, they're not really shows. They're mainly for himself. It's hard to explain. Maybe someday you could meet him. Then you'd see." Del sat on his bed, looking to Tom as if he were almost sorry he had said so much. Pride in his uncle seemed to be battling with other forces.

Then Tom had it. The insight which had given him knowledge of the other boy's loneliness now sent him a fact so positive that it demanded to be spoken. "He doesn't want you to talk about him. About what he does."

Del nodded slowly. "Yeah. Because of Tim and Valerie."

"Your godparents?"

"Yeah. They don't understand him. They couldn't. And to tell you the truth, he really is sort of half-crazy." Del leaned back on stiffened arms and said, "Let's see what you can do. Do you have any cards, or should we use mine?"

Years later, Tom Flanagan described to me how Del had then quietly, modestly, almost graciously humiliated him. "I thought I was pretty good with cards when I was fourteen. After my father got sick, I sort of more or less threw myself into the work. I wanted to get my mind off what was happening. I had my card books damn near memorized after a month." We were in the Red Hat Lounge, where Sherman had told me Tom was working—it was not the "toilet" Sherman had called it, but it was only a step above that. "I knew that Del was very accomplished after he had shown me all of the stuff in his room. He had the basis of a professional kit, and he knew it. But I thought I could hold my own in card tricks—the close-up work he especially liked. I found out I couldn't get a thing by him. He knew what I was going to do before I did it, and he could do it better. He didn't like any of the obvious stuff, either—misdirection and forcing. Del had a fantastic memory and great observation, and those faculties have more to do with great card work than you'd believe. He wiped me off the board . . . he blew me away. He must have been the slickest thing I'd ever seen." Tom laughed. "Of course he was the slickest thing I'd ever seen. I hadn't seen much before I met Del."

Del revolved the head of the dim light so that it faced the wall, and darkened the room. Now, with the big tank blocking most of the light from outside, his bedroom was the same tenebrous cloudy gray that the library had been that noon.

"I ought to call my mother," Tom said. "She'll be wondering what happened to me."

"Do you have to leave right away?" Del asked.

"I could tell her to come over in an hour or so."

"If you'd like. I mean, I'd like that."

"Me too."

"Great. There's a phone in the next bedroom. You could use that."

Tom let himself out into the hall and went into the next bedroom. It was obviously the bedroom used by Del's godparents; expensive leather suitcases laden with loose and tumbled clothes lay open on the unmade bed, labeled boxes were stacked on a chair. The phone was on one of the bedside tables. The telephone book sat beside it, its green cover bearing the graffiti of real-estate agents' names and telephone numbers.

Tom dialed his own number, spoke to his mother, and hung up just as he heard a car coming into the driveway. He walked over to the window and saw a boatlike gray Jaguar stopping before the garage doors.

Two people in bad humor got out of the car. Either they had just been quarreling or their bad temper was a moment's paring from a lifelong and steady quarrel. The man was large, blond, and florid; he wore a vibrant madras jacket the gaiety of which was out of key with the petulance and irritation suffused through his neat, puggish features. The woman, also blond, wore a filmy blue dress; as her husband's features had blurred, hers had hardened. Her face, as irritated as his, could never be petulant.

In the hall, their voices rose. Bud Copeland's last name was uttered in a flat Boston accent. In anyone else's house, Morris Fielding's or Howie Stern's, this would be the time for Tom to go to the staircase, announce himself, and speak a couple of sentences about who he was and what he was doing. But Del would never take him down to meet those two irritated people; and the two irritated people would be surprised if he did. Instead Tom went to the door of Del's room—Del's "universe"—and slipped around it, and doing so, helped to shape the character of his own universe.

When his mother arrived, Tom followed Bud Copeland down the stairs to the front door. Tim and Valerie Hillman were standing with drinks in their hands in the box-filled living room, but they did not even turn their heads to watch him leave. Bud Copeland opened the door and leaned out after him. "Be a good friend to our Del, now," he said softly. Tom nodded, then by reflex held out his hand. Bud Copeland shook it warmly, smiling down. An odd look of recognition, disturbing to Tom, momentarily passed over the butler's face. "I see the Arizona Flanagans are gentlemen," he said, gripping the boy's hand. "Take care, Red."

In the car, his mother said, "I didn't know that the house had been sold to a Negro family."

Take care, Red.

9

Tom by Night

In his dream, which was somehow connected to Bud Copeland, he was being looked at by a vulture, not looking himself, but averting his eyes to the scrubby sandy

ground—he had seen vultures from time to time, grotesque birds, on the roofs of desert towns on trips with his
parents. The vulture was gazing at him with a horrid
patient acceptance, knowing all about him. Nothing
surprised the vulture, neither heat nor cold, not life or
death. The vulture accepted all as it accepted him. It
waited for the world to roll its way, and the world always
did.

This was a vulture in vulture middle age. Its feathers
were greasy, its bill darkened.

First it had eaten his father, and now it would devour
him. Nothing could stop it. The world rolled its way, and
then it ate what it was given. The vulture was a lesson in
economics.

So was his father, for his father was dead—that was real
economics. His father was a skeleton hanging from a tree,
having been converted into vulture fuel. The loathsome
bird hopped forward on its claws and scrutinized him.
Yes, it accepted what it saw.

And accepting, spoke to him: as would a snake or a
weasel or a bat, in tones too fast and subtle for his
understanding. It was crucial that he know what the
vulture was saying, but he would have to hear the fast
voiceless voice many times before he could begin to
decipher its message. He hoped he would never hear it
again.

Uncaring, as if Tom were now no more significant than
sagebrush or a yucca tree, the vulture craned its neck and
turned around and began to walk away into the desert.

Heat shimmered around him.

Then, with the suddenness of dreams, he was no longer
in the desert but in a lush green valley. The air was gray
and full of moisture, the valley crowded with ferns and
rocks and fallen trees. Far below him a man in a long coat
continued the vulture's measured indifferent walk. He
went away from the boy, indifferent to him. He became
vague in the gray air. The man disappeared behind a
boulder, emerged again, and vanished.

Where he had been, a large colorless bird flapped
noiselessly away into the dark air.

Tom woke up, sure that his father was dead. His father
was lying beside his mother in their bedroom, dead.

Tom's heart urged him forward, beat in pain and desolation against his ribs, his throat, made him throw off the sheet and walk across his dark room to the door. He groaned, felt that he was doomed to cry or scream. The darkness was hostile, enveloping. He slipped out of his room and went down the hall to his parents' room.

Trembling, he touched the knob. The scream lodged behind his tongue and tried to escape. Tom closed his eyes and gently pushed the door open. Then he opened his eyes and stepped into his parents' room.

He gasped, loudly enough to wake his mother. She was alone in the big double bed. On his father's side, the sheet lay as smoothly on the bed as upon an amputation.

"Tom?" she said.

"Dad."

"Oh, Tommy, he's in the hospital. For tests. Don't you remember? He'll be back tomorrow. Don't worry, Tommy. It'll be all right."

"Had a nightmare," he said thickly, excused himself, and stumbled back to his own bed.

10

Poetry

Before lunch the next day, while Rachel Flanagan drove to St. Mary's to pick up Hartley, Tom sat at his desk and wrote the first and last poem of his life. He did not know why he suddenly wanted to write poetry—he never read it, barely knew what it looked like, thought of it as the sententious verse he had been made to learn in the Junior School. "Breathes there the man, with soul so dead/Who never to himself hath said,/This is mine own, my native land!" His own little terrace of lines seemed so unlike real poetry to him that he did not bother to title it.

This is what he wrote:

> *Man in the air, do you fly by your own wings?*
> *Animals and birds speak to you,*
> *and you in the air understand them.*

Football, magic, dreams trouble
my mind, cards tackle other cards
and scatter in a valley.

Man in the air, were you that bird?
Who magicked himself away in dark?
Man in the air, father me back. Now,
while you and I and he have time.

Two years later, when he struggled to produce an assigned poem for Mr. Fitz-Hallan's junior English class, he found that he was unable, even if he tried to follow Fitz-Hallan's advice. ("You could begin every line with the same word. Or name a color in every line. Or end every line with the name of a different country.") He pulled the old poem from his desk and in despair handed it in. The poem came back with an A and the comment in Fitz-Hallan's cursive hand that *This poem is sensitive and mature, and must have been difficult for you to write. Don't you have a title? I'd like to put it in the school magazine, with your permission.*

Under the title "When We All Lived in the Forest," it appeared in the winter issue of the school magazine for that year.

11

Frosty the Snowman

In the big auditorium down the hall from our homeroom, we filed into the first two rows of seats for our first chapel. Mr. Broome, Mrs. Olinger, and a tall gray-haired man with a long severe face who looked like a bank president were seated on fan-back wooden chairs before us. To the right of them stood a lectern made of champagne-colored wood.

When I looked around I saw Mr. Weatherbee join the rank of teachers leaning against the rear wall. Between the lounging teachers and ourselves the rest of the school was taking its seats: sophomores directly behind us, then the juniors, and the seniors in the last rows. Nearly every boy, I noticed, wore a blue button-down shirt and neatly striped tie under his jacket; many of the boys were wearing suits. Collectively, the juniors and seniors had a raffish look. Privilege encased them, surrounded them like armor. In the cast of their faces was the assumption that they would never have to take anything very seriously. For the first time in my life I saw the truth in the old proposition that the rich were better-looking.

Mr. Broome stood up and went to the lectern. He raked us in the first rows with his eyes, and then his face adjusted to a brisk, dry administrative mask. "Boys. Let us begin with a prayer."

A noise of shuffling, of activity, as a hundred boys bent over their knees.

"Give us the wisdom to know what is right, and the understanding to know what is good. Let us partake of knowledge, and use it to become better men. Let us all spend this new school year with hope, with diligence and discipline, and with ever-renewed application. Amen."

He looked up. "Now. We begin a new year. What does this mean? It means that you boys will be asked to do some demanding things. You will be asked to work as hard as you ever have, and to stretch your minds. College is a bit closer for all of you, and college is not for loafers. Therefore, we do not permit slackers and loafers here. Pay attention to this especially, seniors—you have many hurdles to get over this year. But our school does not attempt to educate the intellect at the expense of the spirit. And I am certain that spirit is shown first and foremost in school spirit. Some of you will not last out the year, and that will not always be due to stupidity. You can, indeed you must, demonstrate your school spirit in your bearing, in your classroom and athletic work, in your relations with one another. In honesty. In dedication. We will test all of these. I assure you, freshmen and seniors and all in between, that we do not hesitate to weed out our failures. Other schools have plenty of room for them. But we will not tolerate them. For it is the boy who fails, not the school. We give you the world, gentlemen, but you must show yourselves worthy of it. That is all. Seniors first, please, on the way out."

"Frosty the Snowman," Sherman muttered to me as we stood. "Wait till you hear the one about the dogs."

12

The tall gray-haired bankerlike man beside Mr. Broome was Mr. Thorpe, and he was already at his desk when we entered his room. This was one of the tiny paneled rooms in the old part of the school, so laden with atmospherics that it seemed to crowd in all around us. A boy with very thick blond hair and black glasses stood beside the teacher. They had obviously been talking, and fell silent as we took our seats.

Mr. Thorpe said, "This is Miles Teagarden, a senior. He will take a few minutes of our time to explain freshman initiation. Listen to him. He is a prefect, one of the leaders of this school. Begin, Mr. Teagarden." Thorpe leaned back in his chair and gazed benignly out at us.

"Thank you, Mr. Thorpe," the senior said. "Freshman initiation is nothing to be afraid of. If you know your stuff and learn the ropes, you'll do fine. You have your beanies and your lists. Wear your beanies at all times when not in class and between school and home. Wear the beanie at all athletic functions and all social functions. Address all seniors as Mister. *Learn our names.* That is essential. And so is learning the songs and the other information on the sheets. If a senior drops his books on the floor, pick them up for him. Carry them where he tells you to carry them. If a senior is standing in front of a door, address him by his name and open the door. If a senior tells you to tie his shoelaces, tie his shoelaces and thank him. Do *anything* a senior tells you to do. On the spot. Even if you think it's ridiculous. Got that? And if a senior asks you a question, address him by name and answer him. Follow the rules and you'll get off to a good start."

"Is that all?" asked Mr. Thorpe. "If so, you may go."

Teagarden picked up a pile of books from Thorpe's desk and hurriedly left the little classroom. Thorpe continued to gaze at us, but the benignity had left him.

"Why is all of this important?" He paused, but no one tried to answer. "What did Mr. Broome particularly stress in chapel this morning? Well?"

A boy I did not know raised his hand and said, "School spirit, sir."

"Good. You are . . . Hollingsworth? Good, Hollingsworth. You listened. Your ears were open. The rest of you must have been asleep. And what is school spirit? It is putting the school first. Putting yourself second to the school. You don't know how to do that yet. Miles Teagarden does know how to do that. That is why he is a prefect."

He stood up and leaned against the chalk tray behind him. He looked immensely tall. "But now we come to your own unfortunate case. Just look at you. Just . . . look . . . at . . . you. Most of you look as though you couldn't find your way home at night. Some of you probably can't even see through the filthy hair on your foreheads. You look slack, boys. *Slack*. That is offensive. It is an insult. If you insult the seniors by looking slack in front of them, I assure you that they will let you know. This is not an easy school. *Not!*" He positively shouted the last word, jolting us upright in our seats. *"Not! Not an easy school*. We have to reshape you boys, mold you. Turn you into our kind of boy. Or you will be doomed, boys, *doomed*, an adjective meaning consigned to misfortune or destruction. *Destruction*, a noun meaning that which pulls down, demolishes, undoes, kills, annihilates. You will be doomed to destruction, *doomed to destruction*, if you do not learn the moral lessons of this school."

Thorpe inhaled noisily, ran a palm across his smooth gray hair. He was a furnace of emotions, this Thorpe, and such terrifying performances were standard with him.

13

Teachers

As the first weeks went by, the personalities of our teachers became as fixed as stars and as dependable in their eccentricities as the postures of marble statues. Mr. Thorpe shouted and bullied; Mr. Fitz-Hallan charmed; Mr. Whipple, incapable of inspiring either terror or love, wavered between trying to inspire both and so was despised. Mr. Weatherbee revealed himself to be a natural teacher, and led us in masterful fashion through the first steps of algebra. (Dave Brick surprisingly turned out to be a mathematical whiz, and took to wearing an ostentatious slide rule in a leather holster clipped to his belt.) Thorpe could freeze your stomach and your mind; Fitz-Hallan, whose family was wealthy, turned his salary back to the school, and doing so, earned the privilege of teaching what he liked—the Grimms' *Household Tales*, the *Odyssey*, *Great Expectations* and *Huckleberry Finn*, and E. B. White for style; Whipple was so lazy that he took great chunks of class time to read aloud from the textbook. His only real interest was in sports, where he functioned as Ridpath's assistant.

Their lives out of the school were unimaginable to us; at dances, we saw wives, but could never truly believe in them. Their houses likewise were mysterious, as if they, like us, had not spouses but parents, and so much homework that their true homes were the old building, the modern addition, and the field house.

14

We had just come out of Fitz-Hallan's classroom, and a small number of seniors were leaving a French lesson in the next room. Bobby Hollingsworth had identified most of the older boys to those of us who were new to the school, and I knew most of their names. They began to look purposeful and superior when they noticed us getting books from our lockers. They sauntered over as soon as Fitz-Hallan had disappeared into his office. Steve Ridpath positioned himself directly in front of me. I had to look up to see his face. I was dimly aware of a prefect named Terry Peters standing before Del Nightingale, and of another senior named Hollis Wax lifting Dave Brick's beanie off his head. The other three or four seniors glanced at us, smiled at Hollis Wax—he was no taller than Dave Brick—and continued down the hallway.

"What's my name?" Steve Ridpath said.

I told him.

"And what's yours, insect?"

I told him my name.

"Pick up my books." He was carrying four heavy textbooks and a sheaf of papers under one arm, and let it all fall to the floor. "Hurry up, jerk. I have a class next period."

"Yes, Mr. Ridpath," I said, and bent over. He was so near that I had to back into my locker to get his books. When I straightened up, he had bent down to stare directly into my face. "You scummy little turd," he said. The reason for his nickname was even more apparent than before. Exceptionally skinny, Skeleton Ridpath from a distance looked like a clothed assemblage of sticks; cuffs drowned his wrists, collars swam on his thin neck. Close up, his face was so taut on his skull that the skin shone whitely; a slight flabbiness under the eyes was the only visible loose flesh. Above these gray-white pouches, his eyes were very pale, almost white, like old blue jeans. His eyebrows were only faint tracings of silvery brown. A strong odor of Old Spice hung between us, though his skin appeared too stingy and tight for whiskers: as though it would begrudge them the room. "You messed up my report," he said, and shoved a bent sheet of paper under my nose. "Five push-ups, right now."

"Oh, hell, Steve," said Hollis Wax. I glanced over and saw that he had "braced" Dave Brick, who was now stiffly at attention, his forearms stuck out at right angles before him and piled with Wax's books.

"Shut up. Five. Right now."

I stepped around Ridpath and did five push-ups in the corridor.

"Who was the first headmaster, jerk?"

"B. Thurman Banter."

"When did he found the school and what was its name then?"

"He founded the Lodestar Academy in 1894." I stood up.

"You zit," he hissed at me, his face twisting; then as he turned away, he reached out a simian arm and smacked the back of my head with his fist—just hard enough to hurt. His knuckles felt like needles. The blow did not surprise me: I had seen a witless hatred in his eyes. He swiveled his bony head on his neck and looked at me gleefully. "Come on. I have to make a class."

But we stopped after only a few steps. "Who's this fat creep, Waxy?"

"Brick," Wax said. Dave Brick was sweating, and his beanie had been pulled down over his eyes.

"*Brick*. Jesus. Look at him." Ridpath took the fold of skin beneath Brick's chin and twisted it between two long fingers. "How many books are there in the library, Brick? What's my name, Brick?" He jabbed one of his bony fingers into Brick's cheeks and pressed it hard against the teeth. "You don't know, do you, fatso?"

"No, sir," Brick half-sobbed.

"Mr. Ridpath. That's my name, dumbo. Remember it, Brick. Brick the Prick. You'd better cut your disgusting Zulu hair, Brick the Prick. There's more grease in it than most guys have in their cars."

Standing beside him with his books, I saw Tom Flanagan and Bobby Hollingsworth coming toward us. They stopped just down the hall.

"And who's this little greaseball?" Ridpath asked Terry Peters.

"Nightingale." Peters smirked.

"Oh! Nightingale," Ridpath crooned. "I should have known. You look like a goddamned little Greek, don't you, Nightingale? Little cardsharp, aren't you, Nightingale? I'll have to take care of you later, Birdy. That's a good name for you. I heard you chirp." He seemed very excited. He turned his ghastly face to me again. "Come on, jerk. Ah, shit. Just give me the books." He and Peters and Wax ran down the hall in the direction of the old section.

"I'm afraid it looks like you've got nicknames," Tom Flanagan said.

15

Dave Brick was doomed to carry the obscene name Skeleton Ridpath had given him, but Del Nightingale's was altered for the worse during football practice on the Friday evening of the first week of October. While Del and Morris Fielding and Bob Sherman and I sat on the bench with several others—freshmen and sophomores— our JV team had lost our first game the previous week. Chip Hogan had made our only touchdown. The final score had been 21–7, and Mr. Whipple and Mr. Ridpath had spent the four practices since the game frenziedly pushing us through exercises and play patterns. Sherman and I hated football, and already were looking forward to our junior year, when we could quit it for soccer; Morris Fielding had little aptitude for it, but suffered it gamely and performed as second-string center with a dogged persistence Ridpath admired; Del, who weighed little more than ninety pounds, was entirely hopeless. In the padded uniform which made the rest of us look swollen, Del resembled a mosquito weighted down with sandbags. All of the exercising tired him, and after we had run through tires and done fifty squat-jumps, Del could scarcely make his legs move through the rest of the practice.

After the squat-jumps, Ridpath lined us up before the tackling dummy. This was a heavy metal frame like a sledge on runners, with the front poles padded to the size of punching bags. We were in two long lines, and in pairs rushed at the padding and tried to move the dummy. Chip Hogan and three or four other boys could make it turn in a circle by themselves. Morris Fielding and I jolted it back a foot or two. When Tom Flanagan and Del hit it, Tom's side moved abruptly and Del's not at all. Both boys fell in the dust.

"Straighten it out and do it over," shouted Mr. Ridpath. "Push it *back*—we need blocking in the line."

Flanagan and Nightingale pulled the cumbersome dummy back where it had been. They rushed the step and a half forward and grunted into the padding. Again Tom's charge pushed it in a jerky sideswiped movement and Del collapsed.

"What the hell are you, Florence Nightingale?" Ridpath screamed.

Florence. That absurdly Victorian name: Ridpath laughed at his own invention, and all of us laughed too: Del had been christened. At that moment Whipple appeared, cherubic and red-faced in his satiny coaching jacket, and Mr. Ridpath ran across to the field where the varsity team was just now beginning to do calisthenics; but the change of coaches had come too late for Del.

"Stand on my shoulders, Florence—I'll move it for you," shouted a muscular, amiable boy named Pete Bayliss. And that sealed the name for Del.

For the rest of the hour we desultorily ran through plays.

We shared a locker room with the older boys, and after practice, when the pads and sweatshirts had been put away and we had just returned from the showers, the varsity boys came noisily into that sweat-smelling, echoing place. Skeleton Ridpath was among them, covered in dirt and with a bruise on his left cheek—he played only because his father made him, and in the last quarter of the varsity game which had followed ours, he had committed two fouls.

The seniors and juniors began throwing their helmets into their lockers, shouting back and forth. Skeleton Ridpath undressed more slowly than the others, and was just untying his pads when most of the other varsity players were already in the shower across the hall. I saw him looking across the room at us, smiling to himself. When he had stripped down to his jockstrap, he stood up, stepped across the bench, and walked halfway over to us. "I guess this is a coed school now," he said, his hands on the bones of his hips.

"He looks like a graveyard," Sherman whispered in my ear. Ridpath glanced at us, irritated that he had missed Sherman's comment, but too inflamed by his hostility to be distracted.

"We take girls now, I guess," he said, staring at Del Nightingale. Del had tucked his chin down and was wriggling into his trousers.

"Hey, Florence. Do you know what happens to girls when they're caught in locker rooms? Huh?"

"Shut up," Tom Flanagan said.

Ridpath raised a hand as if to slap Flanagan—he was at least seven feet away. "You little creep. I'm talking to your date. Is that what you are, Florence? His date?" He stepped forward: he was almost half again as tall as Del, and he looked like an elongated bony white worm. He also looked crazy, caught up in some spiraling private hatred: it was obvious that his remarks were not just casual school insults, and the dozen of us left in the room froze, really unable to imagine what he might force himself to do. For a second he seemed a demented, furious giant.

His bruised face twisted, and he said, "Why don't you suck—"

Tom Flanagan catapulted himself off the bench and rushed toward him.

Skeleton put out a startled fist and jabbed Tom in the chest. Then saliva flew from his mouth, his face worked in fury and bafflement, and he knocked Tom backward into our bench.

Bryce Beaver, one of two juniors who would later be expelled for smoking, came in from the shower naked, with a green school towel around his neck. "Hey, Skeleton, what the shit are you *doing?*" he asked, amazed. "Your old man'll be here in a second."

"I hate these little farts," Skeleton said, his bruised dirty face still a mask of loathing, and turned away. From the back he looked skinned and fragile.

The outside door opened and clanked shut. Mr. Whipple's voice carried to us, saying, ". . . work on all the Y plays, get Hogan to find those receivers . . ." Bryce Beaver shook his head and began toweling his legs.

Mr. Ridpath and Mr. Whipple came into the locker room, carrying with them a scent of fresh air, which lingered only a moment. I saw Mr. Ridpath struggle to keep his smile as he glanced at his son.

16

Two weeks later, when the JV team played the varsity scrubs in a practice game, I saw Tom Flanagan repeatedly bringing down Skeleton Ridpath, bowling him off his feet even when the play was on the other side of the field. The third time it happened, Skeleton waited until Whipple looked away and kicked Tom in the face. On the next play, Tom Flanagan tackled and wrenched him to the ground so savagely that I could hear the noise from the bench.

"Great play! Great play!" shouted Mr. Ridpath. "That's spirit!"

17

Midnight, Saturday: Two Bedrooms

In Del's room, the boys lay on their separate beds, talking in the dark. Tim and Valerie Hillman were making too much noise for them to sleep: Tom could hear Tim Hillman shouting *Bitch! Bitch!* at intervals. Both Hillmans had been drunk at dinner, Tim more so than Valerie. Bud Copeland had served the boys at a table in the kitchen, and clearing up, had said, "Trouble tonight. You fellas jump into bed early and close up your ears."

But that was not possible. Tim's shouts and Valerie's abrupt rejoinders winged through the house.

"Uncle Cole says Tim drinks so much to make himself into another person," Del said in the darkness. "If he's drunk, he's another person. One he'd rather be."

"He'd rather be *that?*"

"I guess so."

"Boy."

"Well, Uncle Cole is always right. I mean it. He's never wrong about things. Do you want to know what he says about magic?"

"Sure."

"It's like what he said about Tim. He says a magician must be apart from ordinary life—he has to make himself new, because he has a special project. To do magic, to do great magic, he has to know himself as a piece of the universe."

"A piece of the universe?"

"A little piece that has all the rest of it in it. Everything outside him is also inside him. You see that?"

"I guess."

"Well, if you do, then you can see why I want to be a magician. Science is all *head*, right? Sports is all body. A magician uses all of himself. Uncle Cole says a magician is in synthesis. *Synthesis.* He says you're part music and part blood, part thinker and part killer. And if you can find all that in you and control it, then you deserve to be set apart."

"So it's about control. About power."

"Sure it is. It's about being God."

Tom knew that Del was waiting for him to respond, but he could not. Though he was not religious and had not entered a church since the previous Christmas, Del's last remark had upset him profoundly.

Across the room, he could *hear* Del's smile. "I saw what you did to Skeleton, you know. You're a killer too."

The subject of these last sentences, who was sure that he was a killer, lay like the two younger boys in a bed in a darkened room. What was going through his mind was surprisingly similar—the similarity would certainly have surprised Del Nightingale—to the content of the boys' conversation. Music, not shouts, filled the air about him— a Bo Diddley record. *Strong:* music so dense and pounding that it seemed to push itself into his skin, force itself between himself and the bed and pick his laden body up and make it float.

Skeleton *knew* that he was a piece of the universe, and that the hatred which was the strongest and best part of him ran through the universe like a bar of steel. Skeleton too had seen desert vultures, and violent bands of color in the desert sky; and he had seen the sand far out of town turn purple and red when night came on. Even in his baffled and empty childhood, he had known that such things were in his key, that they struck the same note as the deep well of black feelings within himself. Other people were blinkered, self-deluded rabbits: they looked at the desert and saw what they called "beauty," walling themselves off from it. Other people were afraid of the truth in themselves, which was also the truth at the world's heart. Every man was a killer—that was what Skeleton knew. Every leaf, every grain of sand, had a killer in it. If you touched a tree, you could feel a wave of blackness pumping through it, drawn up from the ground and breathed out through the bark.

And lately, as he worked more and more on his "things," as he varnished images of pain and fear onto his walls, he had come closer and closer to that truth. Skeleton had begun to have new ideas about his "things," ideas he could scarcely bear to peep at. They were a unity, they were the unity which was Skeleton Ridpath, but there was something more.

And lately . . .

lately . . .

he had, peeping at his new ideas, seen glimpses of their power. A man was showing him how right he was, and how little he still knew. It was as if the man had stepped off his walls, walked out of the "things" and lifted his broad-brimmed hat from his head to show the face of a beast. The man, who was everywhere and nowhere, in his dreams and hovering just out of sight as he prowled from one room to another, was animal, tree, desert, bird . . . he wore a long belted coat, his hat shaded his face—he was what was real. He spoke to Skeleton when Skeleton thought about him: and what he said was: *I have come to save your life.* He wanted something of poor Skeleton, his will drove out at poor Skeleton, and poor Skeleton would have cut off all the fingers of one hand for him. He had power to make a king's look feeble. He was like the music at the heart of the music, what the musicians would play if they were twelve feet tall and made of thunder and rain.

He is *me,* Skeleton thought. *Me.* He grinned up in the darkness at a picture of a giant bird.

18

"Goose Girl"

"'There was once an old queen, whose husband had long been dead, and she had a beautiful daughter,'" Mr. Fitz-Hallan read. "First sentence of the story 'Goose Girl.' What does that tell you the story is going to be about?"

"The beautiful daughter," Bobby Hollingsworth said, his arm up in the air.

"Right. Old queen, dead king, young and beautiful daughter. Shortly to be all alone in the world, we suspect. After all, she's half an orphan already. If this story is typical, soon she's going to be off on some sort of quest—and there it is, in the second sentence. She's sent to marry a prince, far away. What happens to her?"

"She has a wicked servant who terrorizes her and makes her take her place," Howie Stern said.

"Exactly. Remember when we were talking about identity in these stories? Here we are again. The servant girl steals the heroine's identity. The magic talisman, the cloth with three drops of blood, is lost, and the wicked servant gains power over the princess. She takes her clothing and makes the princess dress in her rags. Clothing can masquerade as identity—it's how we signal who we are. So the servant marries the prince, and the true princess is sent off to work with Conrad, who takes care of the geese. Could this ever really happen?"

"No," Bob Sherman said. "Never. There'd be a million ways you could tell a princess from her servant. They wouldn't talk the same way. They wouldn't even wear the same clothes in the same way."

"Lots of little social differentiations," said Fitz-Hallan. "Right. But the story says that identity can be stolen from you, and even though you're right, that goes deeper than class. In other stories, men's shadows replace their owners and make the men act like shadows. That's even more absurd, but also more terrifying. If identities can be stolen, someone, even some *thing,* can steal yours." He paused to let this sink in. "How does the beautiful princess become reinstated?"

Del said, "The prince's father makes her tell her story to a stove and listens through the stovepipe. Then he finds out who she is."

"Yes, but what has made him suspicious?"

"Falada," Tom said.

"Falada. The horse her mother gave her."

"It's magic—she's reinstated through magic," Del said. He was smiling.

"You'll go far," Fitz-Hallan said. "Magic. The bad

servant has Falada's head cut off and nailed to a wall, and Conrad, the goose boy, hears her talking to the horse's head and hears the head answer. *Oh, poor princess in despair,/ If your dear mother knew,/ Her heart would break in two.* The natural world of common sense and social differentiation is set aside, and magic takes charge of things. It speaks in poetry. It alters the world. Remember that first sentence? *There was once . . .* It doesn't matter what comes after that; when you hear words like that, you know the ordinary rules don't work—animals will talk, people will turn into animals, the world will turn topsy-turvy. But at the end . . ." He raised his hand.

"It turns back again," Del said. "Magically right."

"You do put things well sometimes, Nightingale," Mr. Fitz-Hallan said.

The bell rang; the class ended; I was admiring Mr. Fitz-Hallan's timing when I witnessed something that at first seemed more a part of the world we had been discussing than it did of the world of school. Mr. Fitz-Hallan and the others were picking up their books. I was sitting next to Tom Flanagan, and I heard him utter a little grunt, more of displeasure than of astonishment. I looked, and saw his pencil floating in the air about a foot above his notebook. He grabbed at it and tore it out of its place. I saw (thought I saw) it momentarily resist, as if it were glued to the air.

Flanagan blushed and jabbed the pencil in his shirt pocket. When he saw me gaping, he scowled and shrugged: *What the hell's so funny?* I decided that what I had seen had been a pointless but clever mime: he had thrown the pencil up, and I had looked just as it stopped rising and started to fall.

19

Two-thirty, that school night: suddenly and irrevocably awake, Skeleton Ridpath threw back his covers. The house was oppressively hot. Through the side wall he could hear his father snoring: a choked rattling inhalation

followed by a long wheezing, grinding, somehow moist
noise that made his skin shrink. He grimaced with
loathing and switched on the light beside him.

And nearly shrieked, for directly above him, eight feet
from his eyes, was the last image he had seen before being
jolted awake—a large gray bird, opening its wings and
spreading its talons. No, not quite the image. The bird
whose image he had varnished onto his ceiling was an
eagle, but the bird which had troubled his sleep was . . .
He did not know, but not an eagle. It had been outside
the window, battering at the frame with its wings. It had
been trying to come in, ordering him to let it enter, and
the terror of what was about to happen had jerked him
from sleep. The savage bird outside had been making a
noise—speaking to him, commanding him—which he now
recognized came from his father's awful snoring.

Calming, letting that other bird diminish in his mind, he
took in the comforting matter surrounding the eagle. Rifle
barrels, many blood-streaked corpses, a baby hoisted
aloft on a spear. These gradually faded into an area
dominated by automobiles and household appliances and
women's photographs from which he had removed the
faces. In their place he had glued animals' masks, foxes'
and apes'.

Different areas of his walls were different "things,"
now gradually melting into one comprehensive "thing."
He had known it would turn that way—long ago, years
ago, when he had given up all his other hobbies and begun
putting pictures on his walls, Skeleton had foreseen a day
when, guided by a powerful impulse, all the pictures
would form a single epic statement.

He had begun by selecting pictures of the objects he
hated, things that represented the Carson way of life: new
cars and grotesquely large refrigerators piled with food;
manor houses, well-dressed suburban women, football
players. Because he hated these things, because his father
and his father's colleagues accepted them as values,
because they were elements of a world he wished would
blow to pieces, they gave him a perverse thrill: hating
them, he liked looking at them. Now he cut out every
grotesque picture he saw, and welded horrors onto the
representations of the suburban life he detested. In some

places, four separate layers of photographs had been fixed to the wall. From the old, milder "things" had crawled forth his true imagery. Skeleton knew he was getting better.

A year ago, he had been delighted by the notion that what he was doing was surrounding his room with *himself:* so that he stood within it as he stood and revolved within his own mind. When he had come to this thought—eating tasteless meatloaf and averting his head from his father's perpetual monologue about sports—he had twitched so violently that he had knocked his Coke off the table.

But during the following summer, this vision of his room had been overtaken by a vision even more commanding and dangerous. About this he rarely allowed himself to think at length, but the essential element burned in his mind every time he shut the door behind him.

The room did not open inward, but out.

It was not a mirror.

The room was a window.

It was a casement opening out onto the sky, and showing in fragmented, only gradually revealed form what actually lay outside. Lately the man in the dark coat, a man like the dark kings and wolves scheming at the door in Fitz-Hallan's fairy tales, had been appearing on his walls. When he found the right man (or when the right man found him?), the brim of his hat shading his face and his finger pointing, it would all lock together.

Skeleton jumped out of bed and began to rustle through the heap of magazines beside his bed.

Tom said: "*You see, there was a mystery in our school, and the end of the mystery was the awful thing that happened when Del and I were doing our magic show. But that wasn't the answer to the mystery, just its conclusion. The answer was at Shadowland; or the answer was Shadowland.*

"*Skeleton was having visions of a man in a long coat and hat—the man I had seen in a dream. Of course I didn't know about Skeleton's visions, and it wouldn't have done me any good if I had. You saw what happened that day in Fitz-Hallan's class, when my pencil got stuck somehow in*

*midair—and I could see you decide immediately that your
eyes had been fooled somehow. Despite what I had seen
myself, I would have decided the same thing. After all, it's
always best to look for the most rational explanations for
irrational-seeming occurrences. Any magician would tell
you that—look at how they universally discount people like
Uri Geller.*

"But you saw me blush. Funny things had been happening to me. I hardly had the vocabulary to express them.
'Nightmare' was one way, but that didn't get the atmosphere. And is there such a thing as a 'daymare'?
Anyhow, I never let anybody know about it, not even Del,
but queer things were happening to me—some days, it was
like I never woke up at all, but went through school and the
rest of the day in some sort of dream, full of terrible hints
and omens.

"You want examples? For one thing, sometimes I
imagined that birds were looking at me—observing me,
keeping track of me. On the walk down to lunch, I'd see a
flock of sparrows, and all of them would be looking
straight at me. Every one, drilling into me with those quick
little eyes. At home, I'd look out of the window in the living
room, and a robin on our lawn would swivel its head and
stare at me through the glass, just as if it had something to
say to me. Now, that's pretty mild. It made me think I
might be going nuts, but it was still mild.

"Other things were less mild. I remember one day a
week or two before our nine-week exams, when I went in
the front door of the school and almost fainted. Because I
didn't see what I knew was there—the steps going up, and
the corridor and the library doors. For a second, maybe
two or three seconds, I saw what looked like a jungle. The
air was hot and very humid. There were more trees than I'd
ever seen before in my life, crowded together, leaning this
way and that, snaked around with vines. I had the sense of
a tremendous energy—as if the whole crowded scene was
humming and buzzing away. Then I saw an animal face
peering at me through the leaves. I was so scared I almost
fell over. And I came out of it. There were the steps, there
were the library doors, there was Terry Peters pushing me
in the back and ordering me to get a move on.

"Things like that happened maybe once a month after I

made friends with Del. Those were the 'daymares.' But then, my friend, there were the nightmares. I was way ahead of the rest of the school. Every night I had terrible dreams—I was lost in a forest, and animals were trying to hunt me down, or I was floating way up high in the air, knowing I was going to fall . . . but the oddest feeling I had in these dreams, no matter how bad they were, was that I was somehow seeing how things really were. It was like the world had split open, and I was seeing part of the engine of things—or not seeing as much as feeling it there. As scared as I was, there was this funny kind of satisfaction, the satisfaction of knowledge. As if without at all understanding it, I was at least seeing how the mystery worked. Suppose the skies opened and you saw a great wheel turning around, the wheel that turns us around the sun— that's the kind of feeling I had.

"I didn't always have that feeling of mysterious insight, though. In some dreams I saw a black figure coming toward me—gliding toward me, like we were both suspended in the air. He held a knife. Or a sword. Something long and dangerous. He glided closer and closer, filling my vision . . . and then he cut off my hands. Or the pain in my hands was so great that it felt like he'd cut them off."

I looked at his hands on the bar, at the round pads of scar tissue.

"We'll get to that," he said.

20

Over the next few weeks, Skeleton Ridpath seemed to us to skulk backward into himself. His face grew odder, the flabby skin beneath his eyes darkening to a deeper gray. Once, on a Saturday in early November, he jumped out of his car at a stop sign, ran onto the sidewalk outside a candy store on Santa Rosa Boulevard, and slapped Dave Brick hard enough to make him stagger because he had neglected to wear his beanie. But the seniors' minds, like ours, were on other things. The nine-week examinations were coming soon, and these, designed to show students and masters how well we would likely do on the half-term exams in January, were notoriously tough. Also, just a week and a half before the examinations, the JV and varsity football teams were to play their homecoming games against Larch School, our traditional rival. On the evening after the homecoming games the first big dance of the year took place in the field house. In white jackets and beanies, six boys from the freshman class were to wait on the seniors. We were all aware that Skeleton was in danger of failing his exams; some of us vainly hoped that he would flunk out of the school. And all of us who were to serve as waiters at the dance hoped that there was no girl so desperate to attend the Carson homecoming dance that she would go out with Skeleton.

All of us were united by our loathing for Skeleton Ridpath, and by our fear of him. We thought Tom Flanagan a hero for what he had done during the football game when Ridpath kicked him in the face. That more than anything else demonstrated how events could be magically right. Once during these two or three weeks while Skeleton's attention wandered off into other kinds of unpleasantness, Tom and Bobby Hollingsworth saw him standing in the anteroom to the headmaster's office. He jerked back and out of sight behind the arch, and they assumed he was waiting to be flayed by Lake the Snake; two days later, Tom saw him there again while he was bringing Mr. Weatherbee's attendance forms to the office. This time Skeleton did not jerk back behind the arch, but flapped one bony paw urgently, dictatorially—clear off. Tom turned away from lurking Skeleton in the shadowy arch, and nearly bumped into Bambi Whipple, who carried the mimeographed pile of his nine-weeks exams.

Later that day we learned that Bryce Beaver and Harlan Willow had been expelled for smoking in the field-house turrets, and the enigma of Skeleton Ridpath skulking outside of the offices was swallowed by the shocked excitement the expulsions caused. Laker Broome canceled after-school practices to hold a special school meeting; while Mr. Ridpath fumed in the back row at the loss of an hour and a half's preparation for the game, Broome dryly, meticulously said that he wanted to forestall gossip by explaining that a "tragedy" had occurred in the life of the school, that two able boys had disgraced themselves. They might well have ruined their prospects. That this was a tragedy, no one would dispute. But he had no choice: they had given him no choice.

In his face was no regret, only a tidy satisfaction. The entire school could hear Chester Ridpath loudly coughing from the back of the auditorium, but perhaps only we in the first two rows could see the long creases in Laker Broome's face deepen in self-congratulation.

21

Ridpath made our practices savage and grinding during the four days before the game, running through the same simple plays ten, then a dozen times; in his mind we had become the X's and O's of his diagrams, capable of unending and painless manipulation. Each session ended with three laps of the field, normally punishment for only the worst duffers. But this too was punishment—for the loss from the varsity team of Beaver and Willow, who had been on his first string. From these practices we limped home, bruised from blocking and tackling, nursing bloody noses, too tired even to do homework or watch Jackie Gleason and Art Carney in *The Honeymooners*.

On the day of the game the football field had been freshly limed, and the yard lines shone chalky white. Under an utterly cloudless sky, in air only beginning to carry autumn's snap, a crowd of parents in crew-neck sweaters and chino pants, plaid skirts and blazers, streamed from the visitors' parking lot toward the bleachers. It was obvious that most of these casual fathers in their blue sweaters and brown Weejuns had been Carson students; none of them had the weathered, experienced faces I thought of as typically "Arizona." They had grown up here, but they could have come from anywhere urban and knowing.

While Sherman and Howie Stern and Morris Fielding and I sat on the bench, our junior-varsity team lost by three touchdowns. We had managed only a single field goal. The varsity team ran out to cheers and school yells—most of the parents had flasks—and cheerleaders from a nearby girls' school flounced and cartwheeled and spelled out the school's name. The Larch School made two touchdowns in the first half, one more in the second. We made none. Ridpath had committed an elementary error and worn us out.

22

I saw something anomalous during the varsity game. Most of our JV team was seated in the last row of the stands, and from there we could look across the field to the grassy rise on its opposite side. When the visitors' lot outside Laker Broome's private entrance had filled, the parents had driven past it over the grass and parked their cars all along the yellow-green length of lawn which we often took as our way down to the Junior School for lunch. The snouts of Buicks and Lincolns and a few MG's pointed across and above the field toward the stands. Toward the end of the first half of the varsity game, I looked up at the row of grilles and bumpers facing us from the rise and saw a man standing between two of the cars.

He did not look like a Carson School parent. No chinos, no lamb's-wool Paul Stuart sweater, no Weejuns. The man was dressed in a long belted raincoat and an old-fashioned brown fedora hat pulled down low on his forehead. His hands were deep in his pockets. At first he reminded me of Sheldon Leonard in the television series *Foreign Intrigue*—in the fifties, way out there in the dry West, belted trench coats carried a whiff of glamour; they stood for spies, travel, Europe. Nothing about this exotic character suggested an interest in prep-school athletics.

Then I saw Del Nightingale's reaction to the man. Del was sitting beside Tom Flanagan three rows beneath me, and he looked up toward the rise a moment after I did. The effect on Del of the man dressed like Sheldon Leonard was startling: he froze like a bird before a snake, and I was sure that if you touched him you'd feel him quiver. He uttered a wordless noise—almost like an electronic beep. It was purely the sound of astonishment. Skeleton Ridpath, seated on the bench in uniform, also appeared to be affected by the man's appearance on the rise. I thought he nearly fell off the bench. The man retreated backward between the cars and disappeared. Skeleton turned around and glared back at the stands. His head looked fleshless, the size of a grape above his shoulderpads.

23

"Sometimes I'm Happy"

Streamers hung from the auditorium ceiling, tied up around the dim colored spots; in place of the metal chairs was a vast empty space for dancing, ringed by tables covered by dark blue cloths. At ten minutes to eight the only people in the room were the freshman waiters and the chaperons, Mr. and Mrs. Robbin. Mr. Robbin taught physics and chemistry, and was slight and gray-haired, with thick inquisitive glasses. His wife was taller than he, and her own hair was screwed up into a bun. The Robbins were seated together along the outside wall and looked dated and "scientific," like Dr. and Madame Curie; flecks of brilliant yellow and cadmium blue, then of orange and red, revolved over them, cast by the color wheel hung in the middle distance.

When the Robbins had entered, they had nodded vaguely to us—he taught only upperclassmen. Then Mr. Robbin had turned his radium-seeking gaze on Del and said, "You're Nightingale, aren't you? New boy? Getting on all right?" Gossip had informed all of the school that Del Nightingale was a fabulously wealthy orphan, one of whose legal guardians was a bank he in fact owned. Robbin sat beside his wife and held up an arm. With the other hand he indicated his wristwatch. "Satellite tonight. Five to ten. An artificial star. A miracle."

Besides Tom, Del, and myself, the waiters were Bobby Hollingsworth, Tom Pinfold—still grouchy about the game—and Morris Fielding. Morris, who played piano, had volunteered on the chance that the band might be worth hearing.

Shortly after eight the musicians arrived, carrying their instrument cases. Several carloads of sophomores and juniors followed them into the auditorium. The ones with dates went for paper cups of punch, the ones without leaned against the wall and watched the musicians setting up on the cavernous stage.

Dwarfed on the immense apron of the stage, the eleven men in the band sat down in their chairs and began riffling through sheet music. Morris and I had great hopes for one of the tenor saxophone players, who wore dark glasses. They put their horns in their mouths and began to play "There's a Small Hotel."

Hollis Wax and a prefect named Paul Derringer came in with their dates just after eight-thirty; seeing that no one had yet begun to dance, they moved to the senior tables and began looking around for our white coats. "This is going to be a great homecoming dance," Wax said to his date as I approached. "After a fiasco like today." Then to me: "Gin and tonic. For all of us." He tilted his head to look at the band. "Look at those guys. Bunch of oompah shoe salesmen. One of 'em's blind." I went off to get the punch. "Bring us the Everly Brothers too, while you're up," Wax called out.

Within the next twenty minutes most of the seniors arrived, dressed as their fathers had been at the game; at most of the dances, the school relaxed its rule about ties and jackets. The first brave couples went out into the big empty space and began to dance. Mr. and Mrs. Robbin got up wearily from their table and meandered around the dance floor. Bobby Hollingsworth and I made up another batch of punch by pouring grape juice, sparkling water, and root beer into a cut-glass bowl. The band began on "Polka Dots and Moonbeams," and Mr. Robbin's head twisted back and forth as he computed distances between the couples nearest him. Like Dave Brick, he generally wore a slide rule slung from his belt, and he looked as though he missed it. The tenor player in the sunglasses stood up to solo, and proved that he had been worth waiting for. Bobby Hollingsworth turned smiling to me as we ladled out the terrible punch, and nodded toward Terry Peters, who was standing near one of the large doors on the outside wall. Beside him was a stunning girl.

Peters was unscrewing the cap off a silvery flask and making sure that Mr. Robbin was looking the other way. He poured from the flask into his date's cup and his own.

Morris Fielding rushed up to me carrying a tray and said, "Six cups. Isn't he great? He really blows! Who do you think influenced him, Bill Perkins or Zoot Sims?"

Just as Morris was leaving with his six cups of punch, Terry Peters wheeled his date out the door, moving so quickly that almost no one saw him go. Bobby Hollingsworth started laughing, and then abruptly stopped. I too stopped what I was doing. Skeleton Ridpath, in a black sweater and black trousers, slipped in through the closing door and eased it shut behind him. His awful fleshless face was exalted. He crept along behind the tables, going toward the stage. Our tenor player was emoting on the chord changes of "Sometimes I'm Happy," but I barely heard him. I watched Skeleton lift a cup of punch from an unattended table and move closer to Del Nightingale, finally drawing near enough to reach out and touch his shoulder. Instead he poured the awful stuff down Del's collar.

Del jumped and uttered a noise like the squeal of a month-old puppy. He whirled around and saw Skeleton before him and promptly backed into a table. "Gee, I'm sorry, Florence," Skeleton said, showing the palms of his hands in a false gesture of sympathy. I could barely hear his words, but I took in straight and clear the taunting mock-humility in which they were encased. The two boys, the small one in the white jacket and the one like a black worm, circled around, each walking backward. Only Bobby Hollingsworth and I saw this, apart from two or three amused seniors at a nearby table. When Skeleton and Del had circled completely around, Skeleton opened his mouth and I saw his lips move: *Catch you later, hey, Florence?* Del started backpedaling away, butted up against the same table, then turned his back on Ridpath and went for the side door into the hallway. Skeleton slumped into one of the camp chairs near the steps. He ran a bony hand over his face and grinned up at nothing in particular. On his face was still that look of abstract, unearthly good cheer.

When the band took an intermission I watched Skeleton climb up the steps and disappear behind the instrument stands.

Mr. Robbin kept checking his watch after the band's return, and when he was satisfied the satellite was visible, he stood, cupped his hands to his mouth, and said, "Anybody wants to see a miracle, come out now." His wife dutifully stood up beside him, but no one else paid any attention. He shouted, "Come on! This is more important than dancing." Finally he waved the band to a sputtering halt. "You guys too," he said. "Take a break. Get some fresh air."

"Shit, man," said the bass player, inspiring some laughter from the students on the dance floor. Two of the trumpet players immediately plugged cigarettes into their mouths. Most of the other musicians shrugged and set down their horns.

24

Tom Said Later

When the rest of the school and the band filed out into the cold air—Tom said later—Skeleton stole away from whatever he had been doing at the back of the stage and took a chair fifteen feet from the hall door, to one side of the refectory table. He was leaning back smiling at them when Tom and Del returned from the bathroom. "Cleaned up now?" he asked. "Must have been pretty uncomfortable, all that crap going down your shirt."

"Leave him alone," Tom said. Both boys skirted Ridpath and went to the far side of the long table.

"Shut up, stupid. You think I'm talking to you?" Ridpath twisted his chair so that he was looking directly at them again. A few musicians smoked on an otherwise empty stage; a few couples bent toward each other at the far end of the auditorium. "You're afraid of me, aren't you, Florence?"

The question was devastatingly simple.

"Yes," Del answered.

"Yes, what?"

"Yes, Mr. Ridpath."

"Yeah. That's good. Because you'll do anything I tell you to, just the way you're supposed to. I get sick looking at you, you know that. You look like a little *bug*, Florence, a shitty little *cockroach*. . . ." Ridpath stood up, and Tom saw flecks of white at the edges of his mouth. He had somehow strolled up to the front of the table without their seeing him move: he threw out a stabbing punch, and Del jumped backward to avoid it.

Tom opened his mouth, and Skeleton whispered fiercely: "Keep out of this, Flanagan, or I'll tear you apart." He turned his shining gaze toward Del again.

"You saw him too."

Del shook his head.

"I know you did. I saw you. Who is he? *Come on, runt. Who is he? He wants me to do something, doesn't he?*"

"You're crazy," Del said.

"Oh no I'm not oh no I'm not oh no I'm not," Skeleton said softly, all in a rush, leaning over the table toward Del. "See, nobody's watching. We might as well be all alone here." He snatched at Del's hand and clamped his fingers around the wrist. "Who was he?"

Del shook his head.

"You saw him. You know him."

Del's whole being constricted with revulsion, and he tried to wrench himself away. Skeleton changed his grip with a wrestler's quickness and began to squeeze Del's hand in his. "Little girl," he muttered. "Trying to hide from me, aren't you, little girl?" Ridpath did his best to break the bones in Del's hand.

Tom lunged at Skeleton's wrist.

Skeleton jerked his hand aloft, nearly lifting Del off the floor. Then he looked at Tom in fury and despair and still with that sick gladness and swung his arm down hard into the side of the punch bowl. At the last second he released his fingers and used his palm to smack Del's hand against the heavy bowl.

Del screamed. The bowl shattered, and purple-brownish liquid gouted into the air. The two boys were instantly soaked, Skeleton less so because he had jumped back immediately after the impact; Del half-fell into the mess on the table.

"I want to *know*," Skeleton said, and ran out through the hall door.

When the rest of us came back into the auditorium, after seeing a red speck drift far above over the field house, Tom and Del were mopping the floor. Del's hand, not broken, bled in a straight line across his knuckles: his face stricken, he wielded the mop with one hand while awkwardly holding his torn hand out from his side, letting it bleed into a bucket.

"Jeez, you monkeys are clumsy," Mr. Robbin said, and ordered his wife to get cotton and tape from the first-aid box in the office.

25

Night

"But why not tell *me?* I'm your best friend."
    "There's nothing to tell."
    "But I bet I know who it is already."
    "Dandy."
    "What's the big mystery?"
    "Don't ask me, ask Skeleton. I don't even know what he's talking about."

26

Alis Volat

The next weekend we had an away game at Ventnor Prep, which was just over a hundred miles to the north, in a suburb even more affluent than our own, and was indisputably a first-rate school: unlike Carson, Ventnor was known all over the Southwest. It was the only school for three states around with a crew team. They also had a fencing squad and a rugby team. We thought of Ventnor as a school for intolerable snobs. It owned a famous collection of antique porcelain and glassware which was supposed to exert a refining influence on the students there.

The bus ride took two and a half hours, and when we arrived we were soon given refreshment—presumably we needed Cokes and watercress sandwiches to toughen us up for the game. Members of the Ventnor Mothers' Committee served the waferlike sandwiches in a reception room that appeared to have been modeled on Laker Broome's office. This was a "pregame mixer," to be followed by a "postgame tea," but there was no mixing. The Ventnor boys clustered on one side of the reception room, we on the other.

Skeleton Ridpath spoke to no one on the way down and in the reception room drank five or six glasses of Coke and prowled around looking at the ornaments on the shelves. These were a display of some of the famous antiques, but Skeleton remained unrefined. He grinned whenever he looked at Del. He looked ghastly, ready for a hospital bed.

Del's hand was still bandaged, and the white gauze flashed like a lamp against his olive skin. He wore a tailored blue blazer, a white shirt, a blue-and-red-striped tie. In this sober outfit he somehow appeared prematurely sophisticated. The dazzling whiteness of new gauze against his skin was dashing as a medal—romantic as an eyepatch. He suddenly appeared to already-novelizing me in the role of one destined to be famous.

Mr. Ridpath coughed into his hand, said, "Well, boys," and began to herd us toward the locker room.

Once again, both games ended in disaster. The JV's lost by three touchdowns; the varsity made a touchdown in the first quarter, but the Ventnor quarterback snapped off two passes which brought them ahead, and in the second half a fullback named Creech recovered a fumble and ran thirty yards. After that our defense fell to bits. Ventnor simply marched down the field every time they had the ball.

"This place is so rich they *buy* athletes," Chip Hogan

told me as we filed out of the stands to walk across several hundred yards of manicured field to return to the reception room and the tea. "Did you see those two huge guys in the line . . . and that enormous fullback? I know those guys from the city. They get scholarships and living allowances, *and* uniform allowances. They even get a training table at meals. Nobody stuffs *them* full of veal birds." He gritted his teeth. "See you at the shitty tea," he said, and began to run because he could not bear to move more slowly.

At the bottom of the stands, I could go either the way Chip was running, directly across the football field and over a hill to the main building, or along a path which followed the landscaped contours of the grounds and trailed up and down the little rises past the artificial lake. About half my class was visible on this path, too embarrassed by our failure to want to appear at the tea before they had to. I turned away from the school buildings and went down the path toward my friends.

"Jesus, I don't want any of their tea," Bobby Hollingsworth said after I had caught up with them.

"We don't have any choice, really," said Morris. "But to tell you the truth, I'd rather lie down here and go to sleep."

"Maybe we'll have some fun on the bus going home," Tom suggested.

"With Ridpath on the bus? Get serious." Bobby jammed his hands in his pockets and ostentatiously surveyed the grounds. "Can you believe this place? Have you ever seen anything more *nouveau riche?* It makes me sick."

"I think it's kind of pretty," Del said.

"Well, shit, Florence, why don't you buy it?" Bobby flamed out. "Give it to somebody for Christmas."

"Don't jump down his throat," Tom said. "You're just mad because we lost again."

"I guess," Bobby said. Of course he would not apologize. "I suppose you like losing. Lose a game, horse around on the bus. Right? Get your jollies. Why not get Florence to buy the bus, then we could kick Ridpath off. *Jesus.*"

Del had begun to look extremely uncomfortable, and said something about getting cold. He obviously intended that all of us start walking again and join the team in the reception room.

From where we stood, backed by the big trees shielding the lake, we could see across all of the school's grounds to the gymnasium and the other buildings. Most of the varsity players had showered and changed and were walking in small slow-moving groups toward the administration building. It was too dark and they were too far away for us to really see their faces, but we could identify them by their various gaits and postures. Miles Teagarden and Terry Peters slouched along between the two buildings. Teagarden, who had fumbled, was bent over so far he appeared to be policing the grass. "Ugh," Tom said when Skeleton Ridpath lounged through the door of the gym—his was a figure no one could mistake. Skeleton ambled toward the rear door of the administration building. Defeat held no embarrassment for him.

Then I heard Del, already six or seven feet ahead of us, moan softly: just as if he'd been lightly punched in the gut. The man in the *Foreign Intrigue* costume was walking, very erect and unselfconsciously, down into one of the sculptured hollows between ourselves and the school. His back toward us, he was moving toward the grandstand and football field. Around him the darkening air was granular, pointillistic. The brim of his hat pulled down, the belt of his coat dangling, the ends swinging.

"Let's move it, Del," Tom said.

But Del stood frozen in position, and so all of us watched the man receding into the hollow.

"The janitor works late around here," said Bobby Hollingsworth. "I hope he breaks his neck."

Del held his bandaged hand chest-high, as if flashing a signal or warding off a blow.

"I don't see the point of watching the janitor," Morris Fielding said. "I'm getting cold too."

"No, he's a Ventnor parent," said Bob Sherman. "Those coats cost about two hundred bucks."

"See you there," Morris said, and resolutely turned his back and set off down the path.

"Two hundred bucks for a coat," Sherman mused.

By now all of us were watching the retreating figure as if mesmerized. The ends of his wide belt swung, the tails of the coat billowed. The dark air glimmered around him and seemed to melt into his clothing. For the second time that day, I fantasized that I was seeing not an ordinary mortal but a figure from the world of Romance.

He disappeared around the side of the grandstand.

"Oh, let's move," Tom said. "Maybe we can catch up with Morris."

More than a hundred yards away, Skeleton Ridpath let out a wild shriek—a sound not of terror but of some terrible consummation. I looked over at him and saw his gaunt arms flung up above his head, his body twitching in a grotesque jig. He was positively *dancing*. Then I faintly heard the beating of wings, and glanced back over my shoulder to see a huge bird lifting itself up over the grandstand.

"Yeah, let's go," Del said in an utterly toneless voice. He yanked at Tom's arm and pulled him down the path in the direction Morris Fielding had gone.

One more event of that day must be recorded. When we joined the tea, the reception room was much more crowded than it had been during the mixer. Ventnor fathers leaned patronizingly toward men in wrinkled gabardine jackets who were surely Ventnor teachers, Ventnor mothers poured lemon tea from the Ventnor silver to other Ventnor mothers. They all looked understandably smug. I was given a cup of the delicate tea by a woman with the elastic, self-aware beauty of a model and went to stand beside Dave Brick. He too had never left the bench. "I just worked it out," Brick said, flipping his slide rule into its holster. "Two-point-three-six of our school would fit into what they've got here. I'm talking about land mass." "Terrific," I said. Skeleton Ridpath drifted past holding a cup of tea in a swimming saucer. He looked crazy enough to levitate. Brick and I backed away, but Skeleton was not paying attention to us. He went a few paces toward one wall, then moonily shifted off at an angle. His mousy hair was still slicked down from the shower. I saw Ventnor parents stare at him, then look quickly away. Skeleton drifted up to the shelves of things where he had browsed before the games. Dave Brick and I, not believing, saw him lift a small glass object from a shelf and slide it in his pocket.

27

Tom's Room

Here there were no star charts, skulls, exotic fish; no photographs of magicians, only of Tom and his father on horseback, sitting in a rowboat with fishing poles, toting shotguns across a Montana field. The only other picture was a reproduction of one of the Blue Period Picasso's sad-faced acrobats. One side of the room held a built-in desk and a rank of shelves: after returning from Ventnor, both boys had eaten dinner with Tom's parents and then gone into the bedroom to study.

At ten-thirty Del said his eyes hurt and closed his books and flopped down onto the guest bed.

"You're going to flunk math."

"I don't care." He burrowed deeper into the white pillowcase. "I'm not like Dave Brick."

"Well, if you don't care, then I don't either. But the exams start on Wednesday." Tom looked interrogatively over his shoulder, but his friend's small form still lay face down on the guest bed. Suffering seemed to come from him in waves; for a second this emotion pouring from his friend confused itself in Tom's mind with bereavement, and he thought that he would be unable to keep from crying. Hartley Flanagan had gone through dinner like a man concentrating on a mountain several miles off. There had been another long session with his doctor that afternoon. All Tom's instincts told him that soon his mother or his father would say that they had to have a long talk: after the talk, nothing would remain unchanged. Tom stared at the wall before him, almost seeing his own face looking back from the cream-painted plaster, a face about to record an alteration, a shock; he saw himself ten, twenty years hence, as isolated as Skeleton Ridpath.

As isolated as Del—that suddenly came to him.

He turned around, pushing his books back with his elbows. "Don't you think you ought to talk about it?"

Del relaxed slightly. "I don't know."

"I damn near bit my tongue in half on the bus, but I knew you wouldn't want to talk there."

Del shook his head.

"And we couldn't talk during dinner."

"No." He rolled over and looked up at Tom.

"Well, we've been sitting in here for three hours. You read some of those pages four times. You look terrible. I'm so tired I could drop off right here. Isn't it about time?"

"Time for what?"

"For you to tell me about that guy."

"I don't know anything about him, so I can't."

"Come off it. That can't be true."

"It is true. Why do you think I'd know anything about him?" Del brought up his knees and dropped his head onto them. To Tom he looked as though he were decreasing in size, knotting himself up into a disappearing bundle.

"Because . . ." Tom plunged on, now unsure of himself. "Because I think it was that guy you talk about all the time. Your uncle."

"Can't be." Del was still huddling into himself.

"You say."

Del looked up. "You want to talk about my Uncle Cole? Okay. He's in New England. I know he's in New England. He's studying."

"Studying magic?"

"Sure. Why not? That's what he does. And that's where he is. Why didn't you know? Because you never asked. Because you never seemed that interested before." His face trembled.

"Hey, Del . . ." Now Tom was in a morass. "I didn't . . . I didn't know what . . ." *I didn't know what you would tell me.* And from that first day, heard Bud Copeland's warning: *Take care, Red.* "Well, sure, I was interested," he lamely said.

"Yeah, you and Skeleton." Del dropped his head onto his knees again. "Everything's changing," he said in a muffled voice.

"Well. . . ?"

"Just changing. I think everything should always be the same. Then you'd always know . . ."

Where you were. What was going to happen.

Del lowered his legs and sat absolutely upright on the bed. "I get this feeling," he said. He was as rigid as an Indian on a bed of nails. "Did you ever read *Frankenstein* or *The Narrative of A. Gordon Pym?* No? I get this feeling I'm headed toward something like the end of those books—ice all around, everything all white, freezing or boiling, it doesn't matter, no . . . towers of ice. No way out—nothing. Just towers of ice. And something real bad coming. . . ."

"Sure," Tom said. "And then a prince will come along and say the magic words and three ravens will give you the magic tokens and a fish will carry you on his back." He tried to smile.

"No. Like what Mr. Thorpe says if someone can't answer a question. *Hic vigilans somniat.* He dreams awake. That's how I am. Like I'm dreaming, not living. I don't believe anything that's happening to me. How would you like to try living with Tim and Valerie Hillman?"

"I didn't think . . ."

"You're right. That's not what we were talking about."

"Okay. So let's go back to the towers of ice and the prince and the three ravens and the magic fish."

"By all means, let us leave the Hillmans behind. I have an idea."

"It's about time."

"You were talking about rescue. Prince—ravens—that stuff."

"I guess. Sure. I guess."

"Why don't you come to visit Cole Collins with me over Christmas? I'm supposed to go see him. Come with me. Then you could meet him."

Tom felt an extraordinary mix of emotions, fear and pleasure and dread and anticipation, protectiveness and weakness. He looked at Del, and wanted to embrace him. He saw Del all alone in an Arctic landscape. Then he thought of his father and said, "I can't. I just can't. I'm sorry."

It took him a second to realize that Del was crying.

"Sometime I will. I will, Del. Jesus, stop that. Let's do some card tricks or something—that shuffle you were showing me."

"I don't have to be awake to shuffle cards," Del said. "Whatever you want, Master."

II

The Magic
Show

1

On the Monday before the nine-week exams, Laker
Broome announced frigidly in chapel that an eighteenth-
century glass owl had been stolen from the refectory room
at Ventnor School, and that the Ventnor headmaster had
told him that the theft must have occurred during the
afternoon of our football game. "Mr. Dunmoore is a
tactful man, and he did not directly accuse our school of
harboring the thief, but there are certain inescapable

facts. The Ventnor collection is regularly dusted. Last
Saturday the pieces on open shelves were dusted by the
school housekeeper at eleven-fifteen, shortly before our
arrival at the school. *They were doing their best to give us
a good impression of Ventnor, gentlemen.* After our
departure it was noticed that the piece was missing, and
the matter was immediately reported to Mr. Dunmoore.
It represents a serious loss, not only because the piece in
question is valued at something like twelve hundred
dollars, but because its theft renders the collection in-
complete. Therefore, the value of the entire Ventnor
collection is affected. And that is a matter of several
hundred thousand dollars."

Mr. Broome whipped his glasses from his head and
took a step back from the lectern. "It is also a matter of
the honor of this school, which is beyond any value. I do
not wish to believe that any of our boys would do anything
so disgraceful, but I am forced to believe it. It is
abhorrent to me, but I must accept that looking at me this
moment is the boy who stole that owl. Ventnor is a
boarding school. Over the weekend, extensive searches
were undertaken in the quarters of both students and
staff—not a single person at the school failed to cooper-
ate. So you see where that puts us, gentlemen."

The glasses went back on the taut face. "We have only
a few boys at this school capable of such a disgusting act,
and we know who they are. *We believe we know the
identity of the thief.* I want him to come forward. I want
the boy to identify himself to me personally sometime
during the school day. Things will go much easier for him
if he voluntarily accepts the responsibilities for his actions. If the boy has the courage to confess his deed, we
will be able to limit his punishment to expulsion. Otherwise, more serious measures will be called for."

Mr. Broome inclined his head to look directly at us in
the first two rows. He stared almost pugnaciously at Dave
Brick, then at Bob Sherman, then at Del Nightingale. "I
promise you," he said, "that the culprit will be found out.
Dismissed."

As we filed out, Dave Brick bulked up beside me. He
grabbed my elbow. "He thinks I did it!"

"Quiet," I said.

"What do we do?"

I knew what he meant. We both turned to look for Skeleton Ridpath, and saw him slouching out of the seniors' row, hands in pockets, smiling faintly. We were both too afraid of him to report what we had seen. We went up the stairs in silence.

"But they must *know,*" Dave moaned. "He's the only one who . . ."

We had reached the door of Thorpe's classroom, and Dave Brick exhaled loudly, a sound of pure despair. His skin had suddenly gone white and oily—terror made him look like a thief.

Inside, Mr. Thorpe began to shout almost at once. Of the tirade I can remember only a few words, one of the Latin tags which peppered his classroom rejoinders. *Mala causa est quae requirit misercordiam.* It is a bad cause which asks for mercy. Ostensibly he was speaking of the exams in two days, but all of us knew that he meant the theft as well. Several times he used the word "vermin." It was a harrowing session, and it left all of us shaken.

As we left Thorpe's classroom to go to our lockers, I looked down across the glassed-in court and saw Skeleton sneaking out through the big doors at the back of the stage. Damn you, I thought, damn you, damn you, damn you. Do us all a favor and flunk out.

2

On the Monday the exam grades were posted outside the library, I shoved my way up to the board with the freshman list. I read down it to find my name, and saw that I had more or less the same grades as my rivals. We could hear the seniors shouting and groaning before their own board.

Mrs. Tute struggled through us to get to the library door, muttering, "Heavens! Heavens!" Her palsied head looked pained and angry—all of the staff had looked irritated since the theft at Ventnor.

Back at the Upper School after lunch, I saw that only Hollis Wax was standing before the seniors' grade list, and I crossed the hall and stood beside him. "You never gave me those gin-and-tonics," he said. "Freshman labor is unreliable this year." "Yes, sir," I answered, and searched out Ridpath, S., hoping for a row of F's. When I found his name I was amazed to see that he had three A's and two B's. Hollis Wax had nothing better than a C. "Nosy maggot," he said, and dropped his books on the floor. I picked them up and did ten push-ups and tied his shoes.

3

Dave Brick had been summoned to Laker Broome's office. The note was delivered to Mr. Thorpe's class in the hands of Mrs. Olinger, who looked as bruising and chill as an iceberg: even Mr. Thorpe submitted quietly to her presence. He unfolded the note, looked both stern and pleased, and said, "Brick, see the headmaster." Poor Brick the Prick shuffled his books into his briefcase and trembled toward the door. He'd had a particularly brutal haircut just before the exams, and on his cannonball head all the visible flesh turned bright pink. After that he was not seen for the rest of the morning. His frightened ghost seemed to wail from his empty desks during the two remaining classes before lunch.

"Actually, it's neat," Sherman told me. "This way, Snake proves that he runs a taut ship, and everybody else is off the hook."

Brick's absence from classes and later from his table at lunch affected the teachers much as it did Sherman. They were more relaxed; and most of us, seeing their new ease, realized with a little shock that the staff had also decided that Brick was the thief. I decided that if Brick had been expelled, I would see Mr. Fitz-Hallan privately and tell him what I knew.

But Brick was sitting on the stone back steps of the Upper School as we came up from lunch, and he saw us and stopped tapping his slide-rule case against the concrete. The five or six of us walking together stalled for a moment, unsure of how to treat him. But then we realized that he would not still be at the school if Broome had expelled him during the first period, and we surged forward, full of questions.

He did not want to answer most of them. "Hey, guys, all he wanted was just to talk to me—honest. That's all he wanted." Close up, it was obvious that he had been crying, but he said nothing about it and we were too embarrassed to ask; though I saw Bobby Hollingsworth revving himself up to say something truly vile, he had the sense to check it before someone punched him. Dave Brick had been given the complete Lake-the-Snake treatment, and he had not deserved it and he had come through it well; at that moment he had more goodwill than he'd ever known at Carson.

4

After the next class we had a free period, and Brick sat next to me in the library. "Let's go down to the stage," he whispered. "Too many people here." We got permission to leave from Mrs. Tute, picked up our books and walked around the perimeter of the school, down the wide stairs, and went through the big doors to the shadowy cavern behind the dark curtains.

Morris Fielding was working something out on the piano, but he was concentrating so hard that he scarcely nodded at us. Brick drew me over to the other side, where it was even darker.

I could hear the clip on his slide-rule case rattling against the metal ring. "I didn't tell him anything. Honest. I didn't. He kept *at* me and *at* me—he's so scary, I thought . . ." He began to snuffle, but cut it off, afraid that Morris would hear. Big and pudgy, with his Hollywood hairdo shorn down to a black fuzz, he looked like an enormous infant, and I realized how brave he must have been not to tell everything to Broome. "I just kept telling myself that I didn't do it, *I* didn't do it—and I couldn't tell him about Skeleton, could I?"

"So he just let you go?" I asked.

"Finally. He said he believed me. He said he hoped I

knew how necessary it was to find whoever was guilty. Then he gave me something to give to Mrs. Olinger and Mr. Weatherbee." He took two identical papers from his jacket pocket. His fingers had left damp stains on them. "It's some kind of announcement."

"Well, you have to hand it to that guy," I said. "At least he apologizes."

But when we looked at the papers, we saw that Mr. Broome was simply using Dave Brick to pass out an announcement that students would be able to form clubs in the second semester. "That's all?" Brick said. "That's it?" His legs wobbled, and he sat down heavily on a heap of curtain material, relief and disappointment clanging together violently in him. After what he had been through, I think he could not believe that Broome had simply dispatched him as an errand boy.

"It's okay," I yelled. "He's just relieved."

"So he's relieved," someone purred from the dark area inside the door, and all three of us snapped our heads around to see who it was.

Skeleton Ridpath walked forward into the dim light: he had come around the door so softly he might as well have come through the keyhole, like a ghost or a wisp of smoke.

"So Brick the Prick is relieved, huh? Get out of here, you freshman creeps. Don't ever come back here again." He swiveled on one hip and bent toward Morris. "Fielding. You leave that goddamned piano alone."

"I have a right to play it," Morris said quietly.

"A right? *You* have a right? *Shit.*" Skeleton shook himself like a wet dog, sudden rage making his nerves twitch, and darted across the stage to the piano. He closed his bony hands around Morris' neck and started to pull him off the bench. "What I say, you do, you hear that, you twerp? Keep your filthy hands off that piano." Morris resisted at first, but then decided that broken pride was better than a broken neck. Skeleton heaved him off the bench and onto the floor. "None of you little shits come back here in the future, hear me? Keep off. Stay away. This is out of bounds." He rubbed a long hand over his hideous face. "What are you gawping at?" he asked Brick.

Brick was still clumsily seated on the pile of curtain material. "Gah," he said.

"I said, what are you gawping at?"

"I hate you," Brick said. "And you . . ." The first sentence had come out in one thoughtless passionate rush; the second expired.

"And I what?" Skeleton floated up toward us again.

"Nothing."

"Nothing." Skeleton looked around, appealing to an invisible audience. His arm went out like a striking snake, and he drove his fingers into Brick's neck. "You get out now," he ordered. "Right fast. And stay out."

We left. Dave Brick rubbed his neck; he croaked rather than talked during the next two lessons, but his voice was nearly back to normal by the time we went home after practice. "If he does that once more, I'll tell on him," he swore to me as we went toward the locker room. "Then he can kill me. I don't care."

5

During the weeks leading up to Christmas break and the semester examinations which shortly followed it, two minor, almost secretive currents ran through the school— certainly through the freshman class. The first of these was Laker Broome's private search for the thief of the glass owl. The week after Dave Brick had been interrogated for three hours, Bob Sherman was summoned away from Latin class just as Brick had been. This time there were none of the immediate assumptions that had been made about the unfortunate Brick; only a few boys, Pete Bayliss and Tom Pinfold and Marcus Reilly among them, assumed that now the theft had been cleared up and could be forgotten. They were athletes and could not stand Sherman, who did not even pretend to respect Paul Hornung and Johnny Unitas.

As Brick had been, Bob was sitting in the cold outside the rear entrance to the Upper School when the rest of us came back from lunch. He looked tough and cynical and tired, and a little abashed to play the role of celebrity.

"Congratulations," I said.

"He needs his head examined," Bob said. "If I wanted to grab something valuable, I'd kidnap Florence and never have to think about money again."

Two days before Del was called into Broome's office for his own three-hour session, the applications were due for club proposals. That was the second underground stream which went through our class in the weeks before Christmas break. Most of the school treated the idea of clubs as a joke, and proposed a Gourmet Club (which would eat in restaurants instead of the dining room), a Loafers' Club, a Playboy Club, a Hardy Boys Club (devoted to discussion of the works of F. W. Dixon), an Elvis Presley Club (more or less the same thing). The frivolous applications were weeded out by Mr. Weatherbee and the other form advisers, and I think only a handful reached Mr. Broome. He gave his approval to three, and one of these, a J. D. Salinger Society, never met—the two seniors who proposed it identified too closely with Holden Caulfield to submit to meetings. Morris Fielding's Jazz Society was passed, and in time a drummer and a bassist with more enthusiasm than skill were discovered in the sophomore class. Broome undoubtedly saw in the club a cheap source of entertainment for school dances. Tom thought that Broome approved the Magic Circle because it sounded like a harmless diversion, even after Del told him about his interrogation in Broome's office.

One circumstance—really an image—suggests otherwise: after Del had been called from Thorpe's class in the usual manner, the first thing he saw in the artfully bookish office was the proposal he had typed six days before—it lay alone on the polished desk. Del immediately assumed that Broome wanted to talk to him about it, and most of his fear left him. After all, why would anyone think that *he,* of all the boys at Carson, would want to steal a glass bauble?

"So your interest in magic goes deeper than card tricks," Broome said, smiling enigmatically.

"Much deeper, sir," Del replied.

"Just how deep does it go?"

Del thought he was being honestly questioned, that

Broome was interested in him. He said, "It's what I care about most."

"I see." Broome leaned back in his chair and put the soles of his shoes on the edge of his desk—the model, in his striped shirt sleeves, horn-rims, and posture, of a concerned academic and administrator. Even the dozing dog beside the chair fitted this picture. "It's what you care about most. Do you intend to pursue a career in that rather, uh, unusual field?"

"I'd really like to," Del said. "I'm pretty good already."

"Yes, I bet you are." Broome smiled. "And what do you think about magic—about tricks and all that?"

"Oh, it's a lot more than just tricks," Del answered happily. "It's entertainment, and it's surprises, and . . ." He hesitated. "And it's about a whole way of looking at things."

"I see that you are indeed serious," Broome said. He took his feet off the edge of his desk and pushed the proposal a half-inch to one side. "Have you been happy here, during this first semester?"

"Pretty happy," Del said. "Most of the time."

"I gather that you've been given an unfortunate nickname."

"Oh, well," Del said. "It's pretty bad, yes, sir."

"I could think of better ones for you."

This put Del off guard, and he asked, "What are they, sir?"

"Thief. Sneak. Coward. Wasn't that clear?"

From this point the questioning proceeded in the familiar manner.

6

Economics Lesson

While his father cut his time at the office in half, and then to a third, Tom dreamed of the vulture again. By the time of the last dream, Hartley Flanagan had lost forty pounds, and even if he had felt like pretending to be a healthy man

and going through his routine of legal work and workouts
at the Athletic Club, he would have been embarrassed by
the way the skin hung on his cheeks, his suits on his
bones. Finally he had energy enough only for the hospital
and home.

By now, we are in basketball season—one week into
winter weather. Tom is not his usual energetic self in
school these days, and his work has fallen off: he is afraid
of failing his exams, afraid he is going crazy, of being
kicked off the JV basketball team; mostly he is afraid of
what is happening to his father. Death has never been so
real to him as it is now, and when he thinks of a future
without his father, without *a* father, he sees a black valley
bristling with threats.

Yes, the vulture says to him. So now he can understand
it.

*Yes. That is so. A black valley full of threats. But, dear
boy, what else did you expect. To be a child forever?*

No, but . . .

You did.

I did.

The vulture, still in that hot sandy place where there are
no shadows, nods intelligently.

*And you know what happens when you go into that
valley?*

Tom cannot answer: a fear as large as himself has
slithered into his skin.

*Why, you die, boy. It's that simple. Without protection,
you die.*

His father's corpse swings around on a rope to face him.

*I am your father now, boy. Me. I'm your old man now,
me and everything else in the valley.*

The fear inside him began to shake.

The vulture came toward him, looking him brightly and
intelligently in the eye.

Foul thing. Carrion-eater. Maggot.

Enough, little bird. The vulture rustled its wings,
stabbed its great yellow beak forward, and impaled his
hand. His own screams woke him up.

Skeleton Ridpath, that same night, is dreaming of an
anthill in which the ants have the faces of the freshmen—
they are scurrying around on little plots and errands,

rushing through corridors and passageways, twittering to each other. He has a rake, and is about to shatter the anthill when he hears a loud booming noise, a crashing like huge waves. For an instant he sees a nondescript brown hat pulled down to shade a probing inhuman face, and terror fills him, and then he wakes up and the booming, crashing sound is all about him. He knows what it is, and is almost afraid to look at the window; but finally he does look, and tastes vomit backing into the chamber behind his tongue. An enormous white owl, weirdly bright against the black window, is opening its shoulders and battering the glass. He can see every feather of the big wings. The owl wants *in*, it demands to enter, and Skeleton knows perfectly well that if he opens the window it will tear him to pieces. Its head is almost the size of his own. Poor Skeleton shudders back against the wall, a primitive part of his mind afraid too that the eagle on his ceiling will come to life and swoop down to take his eyes. He covers his eyes with his fists and shoves his face into the pillow.

7

Two days before Christmas break, it was my turn to take the attendance sheet to the administrative office before chapel. Mrs. Olinger, dressed as always in her lumpy gray cardigan, was conducting one of those standoffish fights between the teachers and the staff common at any school. Her victim was Mr. Pethbridge, the French teacher. Pethbridge was languid and effete, with blond hair and a large handsome mouth. He always wore tweed suits slightly tucked at the waist—French, like his thin, elegant eyeglasses. Mrs. Olinger had little time for him, and she took so much grim delight in their dispute that she did not want to interrupt it for me.

"Well, I don't see why it has to be in a different place every time," Mr. Pethbridge complained. He was carrying a big stack of his examination papers, and his physical attitude, chin lifted, belly thrown out, seemed to express one word: *Women!*

"You don't."

"I'm afraid not, my dear."

"This is a working office, Mr. Pethbridge. Our files are in constant use. Our files are *growing*. There is also a security aspect."

"Oh, my dear."

"Does it cause you any inconvenience, Mr. Pethbridge?"

"Yes, Mrs. Olinger. Instead of simply putting my exams in a file I can easily find, I have to wait for you to determine where they should go, using random-number theory, I am certain, which takes valuable time—"

"And when you do not wash your coffeecups, Mr. Pethbridge, it sets a bad example for the others and costs me valuable time."

Skeleton Ridpath came up beside me, holding some change in his fist. He scowled at me from deep inside his bony, bruised-looking face, took a step to one side, and knocked a heap of textbooks to the floor.

As I stooped to pick them up, silently cursing both Mrs. Olinger and Skeleton, the school secretary began to rattle away in a calm, dogged, infuriated way about the relative merits of her lost time as compared to the French teacher's, and finally moved to the counter to take Skeleton's money and push a notebook toward him. Skeleton contemptuously took the textbooks from me and drifted off to the side. Mrs. Olinger accepted my list and said, "Why will you boys insist on hanging around the office when you must have better things to do?"

When I left, Skeleton was still idling at the back of the corridor, pretending to adjust his watch.

Later that afternoon Mr. Broome passed word down through Mrs. Olinger and Mr. Weatherbee that he wanted Morris' Jazz Society and the Magic Circle to demonstrate their skills to the entire school in an hour-long program to be scheduled in April. Mr. Weatherbee read the memo to us at the end of the day: Morris looked nervous, Tom and Del were obviously excited.

8

Christmas break was the usual happy respite from school, except for one boy in our class. We went to visit my grandparents in Los Angeles; Morris and his parents went for a skiing holiday in Aspen, and Morris used the long slopes to work out in his head which songs his trio might play least badly during their half-hour. Everyone else stayed home for the traditional Christmas. When my family returned from California, I took a bus to Tom Flanagan's house and was told that Tom was out. There was no tree, no Christmas decoration, merely an enormous random-looking pile of books and games on the living-room floor. His mother was very haggard. The evident worry on her face, the lack of seasonal decoration contrasted with the job lot of presents: desolation.

9

The semester examinations, held over four days in the drafty field house beneath ancient photographs of football players with their arms about each other's shoulders, the uniforms, stances, and even the faces dated, were difficult but fair, proving that what the school appeared to be and what it was could occasionally mesh. Long, staggered rows of boys wearing crew-neck sweaters scribbled, blew their noses and sucked at lozenges, scratched their heads and gazed at the dead youthful football players. Mr. Fitz-Hallan and Mr. Ridpath, reading *The Far Side of Paradise* and *Quarterbacking* respectively, sat at a long table at the head of the rows. For Tom Flanagan the long exams in the field house seemed like hours entirely out of time, perhaps out of space as well—the world beyond the rows of desks and sneezing boys could have changed seasons, been taken by hurricane to Oz, or gone dark at midday and turned to ice.

The results, in most cases similar to those of the

previous examinations, contained a few surprises. When
we thronged around the notice boards outside the library
two weeks later, Tom saw that he had managed one B,
but otherwise had his usual C's; Del had failed nothing,
had in fact done astonishingly well—a row of B's. And
when Tom and Del risked a glance at the seniors' list,
they saw that Skeleton Ridpath had five A's.

10

Fads

Things returned to superficial normality when the half-
dozen suspected juniors and seniors, none of them Skeleton Ridpath, had been quizzed; school narrowed down
into a tunnel of work. A few minor sartorial fads swept
through the school in February and March. After a few
seniors began wearing their cowboy boots to school,
everyone appeared in them until Mr. Fitz-Hallan started
addressing students as "Hoss" and "Pecos" and "Hoot";
one week, everybody wore the collars of their jackets
turned up, as if they had just stepped in out of a strong
wind.

Closer to the bone was the wave of sick jokes: these
were some sort of release from what I now see was the
hysterical illness at work in the school's unconscious.
What did Joey's mother say when he wouldn't stop
picking his nose? Joey, I'm going to saw the fingers off
your wooden hand. What did Dracula say to his children?
Quick, kiddies, eat your soup before it clots. What did the
mother say when she had her period? Same thing. We
actually laughed at these awful jokes.

Even closer to the bone was the "nightmare" fad which
took over the school in the hiatus between the quizzing of
the last senior and Laker Broome's outburst in chapel at
the end of March. Much more than grisly so-called jokes,
this demonstrated that something ill was growing at the
school's heart, and fattening on us all—that what was
happening secretly to Tom Flanagan was not exclusive to
him.

Bambi Whipple released this fad in the course of his free-association chapel talk. Each of the teachers took one chapel a year. Mr. Thorpe's had been the week before Bambi's, and that too may have contributed, being overheated and inflated with Thorpe-ish emotions. Thorpe's speech began with references to a mysterious "practice" which undermined boys' strength and un-manned those who gave in to it. Thorpe grew more vehement, just as he did during class. Saliva flew. He raked his hair with his fingers; he referred to Jesus and the Virgin Mary and President Eisenhower's boyhood in Kansas. Finally he mentioned a boy who had attended Carson, "a boy I knew, a fine boy, but a boy troubled by these desires *and who sometimes gave in to them!*" He paused, drew in a noisy breath, and bellowed, *"Prayer! That's* what saved this fine boy. One night, alone in his room, the desire to give in grew on him so fiercely that he feared lest he commit that sin again, and he went on his knees and prayed and prayed, and made a vow to himself and to God . . ." Thorpe reared back at the podium. "And to have a permanent reminder of his vow, he took a knife from his pocket . . ." At this point Thorpe actually removed a pocketknife from his own pants pocket and brandished it. ". . . and he opened the knife and gritted his teeth and put the blade to the palm of his hand. Boys, this fine young fellow *carved a cross in the palm of his right hand! So the scar would always remind him of his vow! And he never* . . ." And so on. With gestures.

Bambi Whipple's effort on the following week was considerably less forceful. As in the classroom, he spoke with little preparation; the effect of Whipple's rambling monologue may have been as much due to Thorpe's horror story as to what he himself said. But in the course of his ramble, something reminded him of dreams, and he said, "Gee, dreams can take you to funny places. Why, I remember dreaming last week that I had committed a terrible crime, and the police were looking for me and eventually I holed up in a kind of big warehouse or something, and suddenly I realized that I didn't have anywhere else to go, that was it, they were going to get me and I was going to spend the rest of my life in jail. . . . Boys, that was a terrible feeling. Really terrible."

That afternoon a sheet of paper appeared on the notice board outside the library which read: *Last week I dreamed that a fat bore from New Hampshire was beating me to death with a pillowcase. That was terrible. Really terrible.* Mrs. Olinger tore it down, and another appeared: *I dreamed about rats moving all over my bed and crawling up and down my body.* When Mrs. Tute emerged from the library and shredded that note, the board was clear only until the next morning, when someone put up the sign: *I was looking into a snake's eyes. The snake opened his mouth wider and wider until I fell in.*

That was how the fad began. The notice board became an array of such notes; as soon as Mrs. Tute or Mrs. Olinger ripped them down, dozens more appeared, opening the door to what lay behind all of those well-fed suburban faces.

. . . wolves were ripping at me, and I knew I was dying . . . all alone in the middle of icebergs and huge mountains of ice . . . a girl with long snaky hair and blood on her fingers . . . I was up in the air and no one could get me down and I knew I was going to blow away and be lost . . . something like a man but with no face was chasing me and he was never going to get tired . . . and directly inspired by William Thorpe, *a man was cutting at my hand with a knife, swearing at me, and he wouldn't listen to what I was screaming at him . . .*

There must have been faculty meetings about it. Poor Bambi Whipple appeared one day looking very cautious and chagrined. Mr. Thorpe thundered on in his usual way—no one would have dared to rebuke him. Mr. Fitz-Hallan quietly led us into a discussion of nightmares, and spent fifty minutes relating them to the Grimms' stories we had read.

But the real sign that the faculty was distressed by the "nightmare" fad was Mr. Broome's chapel.

He was a surprise substitution for Mrs. Tute, and when we saw him twitching at the podium instead of the librarian, the entire school knew that whatever was going to happen would be explosive. Laker Broome resembled a wrapped package full of serpents. After his short peremptory order to God ("Lord. Make us honest and good. And lead us to righteousness. Amen"), he whipped off his glasses and started twirling them by one bow.

The shouting began in the second sentence.

"Boys, this has been a bad year for the school. A TERRIBLE year! We have had indiscipline, smoking, failures, and theft—and now we are cursed with something so sick, so *ill,* that in all my years as an educator I have never seen its like.

"NEVER!

"There is a poison running through the veins of this school, and you all know what it is. Some of you, perhaps led on by a certain ill-considered remark from this podium"—here a freezing glance at Whipple—"have been indulging morbid fantasies, giving rein to that poison, exactly in the way that Mr. Thorpe preached against a month ago.

"Now, I know what causes this. Its cause is nothing more or less than guilt. Nightmares are caused by *guilt.* Caused by a guilty mind and soul. And a guilty mind and soul are dangerous to all about them—they *corrupt.* All of you have been touched by this disease.

"First of all, I am going to order you to stop this sick indulgence in a corrupt practice."

Behind me, in the second freshman row, I heard Tom Pinfold whisper to Marcus Reilly, "Does he mean beating off?" Reilly snickered.

"There will be no more—*no more*—talk of nightmares in this school. If some of you continue to be troubled in this way, I suggest that you see our school psychologist. If anyone continues to trouble us by bragging about bad dreams or by putting accounts of them up in a public place, that boy will be expelled. That is that. *Finis.* No more."

The glasses went on again, and his face settled into a grim, lined hunter's mask.

"Secondly. I am going to root out the corruption in our midst and expose it here and now. The boy at the bottom of this perverse craze does not deserve to stay among us a minute longer. We are going to rid ourselves of him during this chapel, gentlemen, we are going to expose him. The boy who stole from Ventnor School will be cleaning out his locker by the end of the hour."

I risked a glance back at the seniors' rows, and saw the
face of Skeleton Ridpath, tilted back, moony and empty.

Mr. Broome darted forward from the podium and
pointed at Morris Fielding, who was seated at the right-
hand end of the first row. *"You.* Fielding did you steal
that owl?"

"No, sir," Morris got out.

"You." The finger moved to Bobby Hollingsworth.

Astonished, by the time he had passed me and reached
the second row of freshmen, I realized that he was going
to question every one of the hundred boys in chapel.

He finished with the freshmen and moved on to the
sophomores. The rows were close together, and as he
swept through the aisles, he bumped against the backs of
seats in front and sometimes cracked against them so hard
as to jolt them sideways; he took no notice. Our class had
turned around on its seats to watch. Each time, the
jabbing finger, the accusing shout.

"You. Shreck. Did you steal it?"

I could see his shoulders tremble beneath the fabric of
his blue worsted suit.

Mr. Thorpe, who had been sitting at the front in the
second wooden chair, stood and walked quickly down the
side of the auditorium to confer with Mrs. Olinger. As
with the boys whose chairs he had knocked aside, Mr.
Broome took no notice. The other teachers clustered
around the Latin teacher and Mrs. Olinger.

"You. King. Admit that you stole it. . . . *You.*
Hamilton. You're guilty. Admit it."

Finally he got to the seniors, leaving a maze of twisted
chairs to show where he had been. The trembling in his
shoulders was more pronounced, and his voice was ragged
from all the shouting.

"You. Wax. Wax! Look at me! Did you?"

"No, sir."

"Peters! You, Peters. Was it you?"

"Uh-uh, sir, No."

I watched with dread as he approached Skeleton, half-
hoping, half-fearing that Skeleton would begin to shriek.
As Broome worked down the aisle toward him, Ridpath
never looked his way but kept his dazed, empty face
pointed toward the ceiling, fixing it on the spot where the

color wheel had revolved during the homecoming dance.

Then Broome was there. *"You. Ridpath! Ridpath! Look at me! Did you steal it?"*

" . . ."

"ANSWER ME!"

". . ." Still that weird silence.

"DID YOU?"

Then we all heard Skeleton's drawling answer. "Not me, Mr. Broome. I forgot all about it."

"AAAAH!" Mr. Broome raised his fists in the air and wailed. The teachers at the back of the auditorium leaned forward, afraid to move—all except Mr. Thorpe, who took a brisk two steps toward the headmaster. Broome waved him back.

"Okay. Next boy. You, *Teagarden*. Was it you?"

And it went on until the last senior had said no. Mr. Broome stood at the end of the aisle with his back turned to the school. The cloth of his jacket shook. I was afraid that he would turn around and start all over again with the freshmen, and looked at my watch and saw that the whole first period had disappeared. Just then a bell rang in the hall. *"Okay,"* Mr. Broome said. "We're not finished yet. One of you has lied to me twice. I am not through with him. Dismissed."

During the next class I looked through the windows onto the parking lot and saw Mr. Thorpe driving Mr. Broome out onto Santa Rosa Boulevard. An hour later Mr. Thorpe drove back in alone. Mr. Broome did not appear back at Carson for two days.

11

Hazing

After English class the next day we had a free period. Morris and his trio had permission to practice on the stage, and so did Del; the club performances were now only three weeks away. Morris immediately set off around the back of the school and down the stairs—we could see the two sophomores who struggled with bass and drums already swinging open the big door off the downstairs corridor. Del hung indecisively by his locker for a few minutes, wondering how he could work on his act without his partner. Tom had stayed home—gossip told us—because his father had been taken to the hospital "for good." Then Del muttered to the rest of us, "Oh, well, it's better than study hall," and wandered away after Morris.

"I think that guy's a homo," Bobby Hollingsworth said. Sherman told him to shut his trap.

After five or ten minutes in the library, I realized that I had left one of the books I needed in my locker. Dave Brick was across the table from me, but he too had forgotten to bring the book—it took a long time to extract this information. Ever since Laker Broome's astonishing chapel performance, Brick had begun to look dopey and half-awake everywhere but in algebra class. "Hey, I have to look at that too," he whispered, surfacing out of his daze. "You can have mine when I'm done," I whispered back, and got permission to leave the library.

I found the book in the jumble at the bottom of my locker and turned around. The halls were empty. A lively conversational buzz came from Fitz-Hallan's room, a disgruntled roar from Whipple's. A door to the Senior Room at the end of the back corridor cracked open, and Skeleton Ridpath edged around it, still with that moony look on his face. Then he stiffened and turned toward the far corner; a second later he began to run down the empty hall. *What the dickens?* I thought. Through the thicknesses of glass I saw him round the corner and race down the stairs. Finally I realized that he had heard the piano. "Oh, no," I said out loud, and began to go quickly down the corridor. I had just reached the Senior Room when I saw the top-left-hand corner of the door to the stage—all that was visible to me—swing out.

I ran down the stairs and opened the door again just in time nearly to be knocked down by Brown and Hanna, the sophomores working with Morris. "Don't go in there," Hanna said, and sprinted up the stairs. Brown was leaning his bass against the wall just inside the door and trying to get outside at the same time, and he just stared at me as if I were nuts. I could hear Ridpath's voice but not his words. Brown left the bass rattling from side to side like a heavy pendulum, and flashed around the door.

I went into the gloom. ". . . and don't come back or I'll cut your balls off," I heard Skeleton curse. "Now for you two."

The first thing I saw was Morris' pale face far off above the piano, looking both frightened and obstinate. Then I saw Del standing beside a table covered in black velvet. He had turned in my direction. He just looked frightened, and about ten years old. Skeleton's long back hovered before me, about ten feet away. From the way his head was turned, he was looking at Del.

"They have a right to be here," I said, and was going to continue, but Skeleton whirled around and stopped the words in my throat. I had never seen anything like his face.

He looked like a minor devil, a devil consumed by the horror of his ambition—the shadowy light hollowed his cheeks, somehow made his lips disappear. His hair and his skin seemed the same dull color. He might have been a hundred years old, a skull floating above an empty suit. In the monochrome face, his eyes smoked. They were screaming before he did, so loudly and with such pain that I was silenced.

"Another one? Another one?" he yelled, and jerked himself forward toward me. The light shifted, and his face returned to normal. The purple badges below his eyes looked as though they itched. "Damn you," he said, and his eyes never altered, and before he hit me I had time to think that I had seen the real Steve Ridpath, the one his face and nickname concealed. He flailed out and clouted me in the ribs, and dreamily grabbed my lapels and twisted us both about and pushed me back between Del and Morris.

The blood pounded in my ears. I faintly heard the sound of wood on wood—Morris quietly closing the lid of the Baldwin. "Now, wait a second," came Fielding's voice.

"Wait? Wait? What the hell else have I . . ." Skeleton raised his bony fists up to his head. "Don't you tell me to wait," he hissed. "You don't belong here." He was speaking to Morris, but looking at Del Nightingale. "I warned you," he said.

Then he swiveled his head toward Morris. "Get away

from that fucking piano." He began to move spastically toward Morris, and Morris smartly separated himself from the bench. Nearly sobbing, Skeleton said, "Goddammit, why can't you *listen* to me? Why can't you pay attention to what I say? Now, stay away from . . . Christ!" He pushed his fists into his eyes, and I thought perhaps that in fact he was sobbing. "It's too late for that. Oh, Jesus. You *crappy* freshmen. Why do you have to hang around here?"

"To practice, you dope," Morris said. "What does it look like?"

"I'm not talking to you," Skeleton said, and took his hands away from his eyes. His face was wet and gray.

Morris' mouth opened.

"You think you know everything," Skeleton said quietly to Del.

"No," Del said.

"You think you own him. You'd be surprised."

"Nobody owns anybody," Del said, rather startling me.

"You *shitty* little bastard," Skeleton erupted. "You don't even know what you're talking about. And you're the one who thinks I should wait. *Damn.* I know as much as you do, Florence. He helps me. He wants to know me."

By now Morris and I were sure that Ridpath was literally insane, and what happened next only confirmed it.

As scared as he was, Del had the courage to shake his head.

This enraged Skeleton. He began to tremble even more than Laker Broome during the chapel interrogations the day before. "I'll *show* you," he shouted, and went for Del.

Skeleton slapped him twice, hard, and said, "Take off your jacket and your shirt, goddamn you, I want to see some skin."

"Hey, come on," Morris said.

Skeleton whirled on us and froze us to the boards with his face. "You're not in it anymore. Stay put. Or you're next."

Then he jerked at the back of Del's dark jacket and pulled it off. Del hurriedly began to unbutton his shirt, which glimmered in the dim light. As if having something to do helped his fear, he seemed calm, despite his haste. His cheeks burned where Skeleton had slapped him.

Morris said, "Don't do it, Del."

Skeleton twisted toward us again. "If you dare to say one more thing, either of you, I'll kill you, so help me God."

We believed him. He was bigger and stronger, and he was crazy. I glanced at Morris and saw that he was as terrified, as incapable of helping Del, as I was.

"You fucking Florence," Skeleton moaned. "Why did you have to *be* here? I'm going to initiate you, all right." His face constricted and blanched, then went a dull shade of red. "With my belt. Bend over that piano bench."

Morris groaned and looked as if he might faint or vomit.

Del dropped his glimmering shirt—it was silk, I realized—on the dusty floor and went to the piano bench. He knelt before it and leaned over, exposing his pale boy's back. Skeleton was already breathing oddly. He unfastened his belt, drew it out through the loops, and doubled it.

For a moment he simply looked at Del, and I saw on his face that expression I had seen before, of a devil's desperation and need and distrust, of a hungry certainty all mixed up with fear. I too groaned then. Skeleton never paused. He moved slightly behind Del, to one side, and raised the doubled belt and sliced it down on Del's back.

"Oh, Jesus," he said, but Del said nothing. An instant later, a red line appeared where the belt had struck.

Skeleton raised his belt again, tightening his face with effort.

"No!" Morris shouted.

The belt came whistling down and cracked against Del's skin. Del jerked backward a bit and closed his eyes. He was silently crying.

Skeleton repeated his odd, painful prayer—"Oh, *Jeesus*"—and raised the belt and cut down with it again. Del gripped the legs of the piano bench. I saw tears dripping off his chin and breaking on the floor.

And that is the second image which stays with me most strongly from Carson. The three lines blistering in Del Nightingale's white back, Skeleton twisting over him in his agony, his face twisted too, the belt dangling from his hand. The first image, of Mr. Fitz-Hallan ironically proffering a ball-point pen to Dave Brick—that picture of the school's health—jumped alive in my mind, and I thought without thinking that the two were connected as two points on a single graph.

"You rich little freak," Skeleton wailed. "You have everything." He broke away from Del, looked wildly at Fielding and me from out of his tortured face, broke toward us and we scrabbled backward toward the heavy curtains. Skeleton uttered a word, "bird," as one speaks without realizing it, broke direction again, and threw the belt at the curtains and began to lunge toward the door.

We heard it slam; then heard a loud silence.

12

It felt as though a cymbal had been struck in that cavernous dark space, the shattering sound cutting us free from whatever had held us up, held us in place. Morris and I, already sitting, collapsed onto the boards. Del slipped off the piano bench and lay beside it.

I began to go toward him on all fours. Morris followed. Del's face was streaked with what looked like mud; finally I saw that it was the dust melting on his wet face. "It doesn't matter," Del said. "Get my shirt."

"Doesn't matter?" Morris said as he stood up and went for the discarded shirt. "We can get him expelled now. He's done. And he hurt you. Look at your back."

"I can't look at my back," Del said. He raised himself up on his knees and put one hand on the piano bench. "May I please have my shirt?"

Morris came up white-faced and handed it over. Del's face was red, but composed. The wet dust looked like thick warpaint. "Do you need help standing up?" Morris asked.

"No."

All three of us heard the door opening again, and

Morris hissingly drew in his breath; Del and I probably did the same.

"You in here?" came a familiar voice. "Hey, I can't find you." Expecting Skeleton's return, none of us could identify the speaker.

"Hey, I was looking all over for you," Dave Brick said, walking slowly toward us out of the gloom. "You get that book? Holy cow." This last because now he could see the way we were staring at him, Morris and I fearfully, Del with the warpaint on his face.

"Holy *cow*," Brick repeated when he was close enough to see Del's back just before Del struggled into his shirt. "What have you guys been *doing?*"

"Nothing," Del said.

"Skeleton hit him with a belt," Morris said, standing up and dusting off his knees. "He's out of his mind."

". . . a belt . . . ?" Brick made as if to help Del put on his jacket, but Del waved him away.

"Really out of his mind. Are you okay, Del?"

Del nodded and turned away from us.

"Does it hurt?"

"No."

"We can actually get rid of Skeleton now," Morris hammered on.

Brick went ". . . geez . . ." and sat down on the piano bench. "Right here?" he asked stupidly. "In school?"

Morris was looking thoughtfully at the piano and the bench. "You know what I think," he said.

"Uh?" Brick said. Del, who was still facing the curtains, and I said nothing.

"I'm thinking that's the second time Skeleton went nuts when he saw me playing that piano."

"No kidding," Brick said, gazing in wonder at the piano.

"Why would he do that?" Morris inquired. "Because he put something there he wants to keep hidden. Sound good?"

Brick and I looked at each other, finally understanding. "My God," I said. "Get off that bench, Brick." He jumped away from the piano bench, and he and I lifted the lid as Morris folded his arms and peered in.

Brick screamed. Something small and crystalline flew

up out of the bench, a silvery mothlike thing that rattled like a beetle. Dave Brick's scream had jolted Del out of his trance, and he turned around and watched with the rest of us as the small silvery thing flew in a wide arc across the apron of the stage and fell with a soft thud into the pile of old curtains.

"What was *that?*" Morris asked.

Brick ran heavily, echoingly, across the stage to the pile of curtains. He bent to touch what lay there, but pulled back his hand. "That owl. From Ventnor."

"But it flew," Morris said.

"It flew," I repeated.

"Yes," Del said. I glanced at him, and was startled by the shadowy smile I saw lurking in his face.

"You shook the bench," Morris said. Brick leaned down and picked up the owl. "That's what happened. You shook it."

"No," said Del, but no one paid any attention.

"Yeah," Brick said. "We both did, I guess."

"Sure you did," Morris said. "Glass owls can't fly." He leaned over again. "Well, what else do we have here?" And pulled out copied exam after copied exam. "Well, now I know why he used to sneak back up here all the time. He wanted to make sure it was all still where he put it. When we tell people about this, he won't last another five minutes at this school."

"We've got him by the short hairs," Brick said, suddenly stunned by joy.

Del looked at all of us and said, "No." He extended his right hand toward Dave Brick, and Brick came toward us and put the owl in his hand. "Wait a second there," Morris said, but Del was already raising his arm. He hurled the owl at the stage. It made a noise like a bomb and flew apart into a million shining pieces. Dave gawped at him in sheer dumb amazement for a moment, and— you have already guessed it—wept.

Del walked out after that, just before the bell rang for a new period. "What do we do?" Brick asked, wiping his face on his sleeve. "We go to our next class," Morris said firmly. "And after?" I asked. "We find someone to tell all this to," Morris said. "I get a funny feeling about all this,"

I said. "Like maybe Del won't help us." Morris shrugged, then looked uncomfortable. "The owl," Brick blubbed. The three of us looked at the fragments on the stage— nothing faintly owllike remained. "We didn't shake the bench," Brick said. "You had to," Morris said. "No," I said, and heard myself echoing Del—*no* was about the extent of what he had said ever since Skeleton had run out. I could still hear the rattling noise it had made as it flew. "Darn," Morris said. "We have to go. Look." He faced me, still believing that something reasonable could be extricated from a scene in which one student insanely beat another with a belt and glass owls flew thirty feet across stages. "Fitz-Hallan likes you. He eats you up. Why don't you talk to him about this?" I nodded.

On the way to my next class, I passed the Senior Room. A student was laughing in there, and all of my insides tingled. I knew with a cave dweller's atavistic knowledge that it was Skeleton Ridpath, all alone. During a free period, I did go to see Fitz-Hallan, but he was no help; Carson closed ranks, denied the mystery.

13

Thorpe

"I have spoken to Mr. Fitz-Hallan," he said, "and last night I communicated with Nightingale and also with his godparents, Mr. and Mrs. Hillman. This morning I spoke privately to Morris Fielding. Now I must ask you, is there anything in your story you would care to change, in the light of its quite extraordinary nature?" Mr. Thorpe glared at me. He was controlling his anger very well, but I could still feel its heat. We were in the office Thorpe used as assistant headmaster, a bare cubicle on the other side of the corridor from the secretary's offices. Mr. Fitz-Hallan was sitting in a typing chair beside Mr. Thorpe; I stood before the metal desk. Mr. Weatherbee, my form adviser, stood beside me.

"No, sir," I said. "But may I ask you a question?"
He nodded.

"Did you also speak to Steve Ridpath?"

His eyes flickered. "We shall come to that in time." He arranged three pencils before him, the sharpened points toward me like a row of tiny stakes. "Firstly, boy, whatever aim you may have in concocting a preposterous story like this is quite beyond me. I have told you that I spoke to young Nightingale. He completely denies that he was beaten with a belt. He did admit that Mr. Ridpath's son, a senior, found you in an area normally off limits to frosh, and rebuked you for being there." He held up a hand to shut off my protest. "It is true that two of you, Morris Fielding and young Nightingale, had permission to be on stage. Steven Ridpath of course had no way of knowing that. He may have acted imprudently, but he acted in the interest of discipline, which is in line with the general improvement in his work this year. I requested Mr. Hillman to inspect his godson's back, and Mr. Hillman reported to me that he found no indications of any such beating as you—and Fielding, regrettably—claim took place."

"No indications," I said, not believing.

"None whatsoever. How do you account for that?"

I shook my head. Those welts could not have disappeared so soon.

"I can explain it to you, then. None took place. I believe Steven Ridpath when he says that he made young Nightingale do several push-ups and slapped his back, which was covered by shirt and jacket, when the push-ups were performed sloppily. Initiation is officially over, but in unusual circumstances the school has turned a blind eye to its continuance. When we felt that it was done to preserve order."

"Order," I said.

"Something it seems you know little about. To proceed. Of course we found no traces of the Ventnor owl backstage. Because it was never there. We did find written-out examinations in young Ridpath's handwriting, to be used by him as a study aid after the examinations took place."

"That doesn't make sense. He used the exams as study aids when he'd already taken them?"

"Precisely. To keep his grasp of the older material. A very wise thing to do, I might add."

"So he's going to get away with it," I said, unable to keep from blurting it out.

"*Quiet!*" Mr. Thorpe banged the metal desk and made the pencils jump crazily. "Consider, boy. We are going to be lenient with you. Because young Fielding's family has attended the Carson School for fifty years, and he thinks he saw what you also think you saw, Mr. Fitz-Hallan and I agree that perhaps you are not consciously trying to mislead us. But you leaped to conclusions and substituted your imagination for what you actually saw—a typical example of the irrationality which has been sweeping through this school, and which Mr. Broome has worked so hard to combat." The thought of this seemed to deepen his rage. "Such fantastification as we have had here in the past month is beyond my experience. Perhaps some of our English people should stick to factual texts in the future." A burning sideways glance at Fitz-Hallan. "A school is no place for fantasy. The world is no place for fantasy. I have already said this to Morris Fielding. Mr. Weather-bee . . ."

The adviser straightened up beside me. "Perhaps you can keep a closer eye on incipient hysteria in the freshmen. Teachers must do more than teach, here at Carson."

When our class went to the locker room to undress for an intramural basketball game, I looked at Del Nightingale's back as he pulled off his shirt. It was unmarked. Morris Fielding noticed that at the same time I did. I remembered the glass owl flying or seeming to fly out of the bench, making a whirring beetlelike noise, and knew from Morris' expression that he remembered it too. And though I had planned to use the minutes before the intermural game to talk to Del, I backed away, as if from the uncanny.

Tom's father died at the end of March.

14

I Hear You

Chester Ridpath switched off Ernie Kovacs on the old twelve-inch Sears television in the living room and covertly looked at his son, who had eaten only half of his Swanson TV Chicken Dinner. The kid was starving himself—half of the time he forgot the food was there in front of him, and stared off into space like a zombie. Or like something from those movies he liked, something that only pretended to be normal and okay. . . . Chester immediately banished these thoughts and sent them into the limbo where he had consigned everything he had thought or imagined about the "hazing" incident two weeks earlier. Old Billy Thorpe had stuck up for Stevie, but Ridpath could see that despite his loyalty to a colleague, Billy wasn't quite sure in his own mind that he had done the right thing—every now and then he looked like a quarterback fourteen points down. Of course they had all felt like that lately, with Laker Broome cracking up in chapel the way he had and nobody knowing from one minute to the next if the head would keep his job. What a terrible year it had turned out to be. . . . He picked up the TV dinner's aluminum pan from the footstool in front of him and on his way out of the room took Steve's half-eaten dinner too. The kid smiled faintly, as if half-thanking, half-mocking him.

Thank God Billy Thorpe had never seen Steve's room.

Because that was the problem. Any kid who wanted to surround himself with garbage like that was the kind who could use a belt on a freshman or cheat on his exams.

Hell, Steve didn't cheat.

Did he?

Ridpath balled up the two crinkly pans and dumped them into the bin. Waste. His own father would have belted him from here to kingdom come for throwing away food. Just look at him now. If a fly landed on his nose, he wouldn't brush it off.

So talk to him. You talk to kids all day long.

Talk at them.

Better than nothing.

No, nothing was better. He'd seen Steve's face some-times when he was in the middle of a story. Indifference. Blank as the face of a corpse. Even when he was just a short-pants kid, sometimes he'd crack him one and see that same expression on the little shit's mug . . . *Jesus,* he was glad Billy Thorpe had never seen that awful crap up in Steve's room. If that was the kind of stuff the kid had on his mind . . .

"Hey, Steve," he said, and went back to the kitchen door. "Isn't that Kovacs kind of strange? Bet those cigars cost . . ." He stopped the sad attempt at conversation. Steve's chair was empty. He had gone back up to do whatever the hell it was he did in that room.

Should go in there and rip out all that evil junk—just rip it out. Then tell him why—tell him why it's for his own good. Should have done it long ago.

No: first tell him why, then rip it out.

But of course it was too late for that. How long had it been since he and Steve had really talked? Four years? More?

Chester finished wiping the silverware dry and crossed the untidy living room and stood at the bottom of the stairs. At least that savage music wasn't on; like his good grades, it could be a sign that Steve was growing up, and getting old enough to know that all you had to do was burn the damn ball *back,* just forget the pain and return the fire. Wasn't that what a father had to teach his son? If you don't land the first punch, be goddamned sure you land the second.

"You busy, Steve?" he called up the stairs. There was no answer. "How about a talk?" And surprised himself—his heart beat a little faster.

Steve was not listening: he was pacing around the bedroom, his feet going *bang bang* on the linoleum. Praying to the pictures, or whatever he did when he wasn't varnishing.

"Steve?" *Bang, bang,* went the footsteps, echoed by his heart. Ridpath went halfway up the stairs and reached the step from which he could see his son's door, which was closed. Through the crack at the bottom of the door, with his eyes right at the level of the floor and looking through the posts of the railing, Ridpath could see the bottoms of Steve's loafers, pacing past. *Bang, bang, bang, bang.* Steve was patrolling from one end of the room to the other, metronomically, wheeling around when he reached a wall and marching back in a straight line. Marching, he was mumbling something to himself: it sounded like *I hear you, I hear you* to Chester. *I bang hear bang you bang I bang hear . . .*

"Okay, you hear me," he said. "How about coming out and having a beer with the old man?" His throat was dry—hell, you'd almost think he was afraid of Steve. "A beer sound good?" he asked, and was pathetic even to himself.

I bang hear bang you bang I bang hear bang you bang I bang . . . The black bottoms of the shoes appeared in the crack at the bottom of the door, one, two, hayfoot, strawfoot, came back in five or six seconds, vanished. "Beer?" Chester muttered, realizing that whatever Steve was hearing, it was not his father.

Sometimes Steve acted like he was tuned in to another world, somewhere out in space where all you heard was the far-off metallic voices on a lost radio beam.

"Aaah," Steve uttered, a single private moan of pleasure or insight, and his feet went by the door again—it was as if someone had just finished explaining something to him.

Then Ridpath, his face glued to the newel posts of the half-railing on the second floor, remembered a terrible dream, what must have been a dream, from the winter before—a huge bird fighting against Steve's window, breaking the glass, whapping its big wings against the side of the house and tearing with its talons. . . . "Oh, my God," he whispered.

Steve was going *aaah* now, but Ridpath could not see the black bottoms of the loafers as he went past the door.

Beating, beating, thundering at the house, whipping that awful beak from side to side . . . Ridpath had a sudden irrational notion that now that nightmare bird was upstairs in Steve's room . . .

bang, went one foot on the left side of the room, where

the window was, and then *bang, bang,* both feet on the right-hand side of the bedroom.

Bang. Just as if he had touched down back on the window side of the room—just as if that nightmare bird was ferrying him back and forth, the joy of flight causing *aaah aah* to bubble out of his throat

—couldn't be, he wasn't hearing right, there was some reason why he could no longer see Steve's loafers move past the door . . . some reason . . . those damn kids and their endless talk about bad dreams. *I was up in the air and no one could get me down.* Ridpath felt his whole body go cold. *Whisper,* went Steve's loafer on the right side of the room, and—an instant later—*whisper,* on the left.

"Come talk when you're ready," Ridpath said, but only to himself.

That was on a Friday night. Chester Ridpath fled into the basement and uncorked a bottle of Four Roses he kept hidden under his workbench.

15

Two Saturdays after that, Tom Flanagan left his mother's side for the first time since the funeral. From the morning of Hartley Flanagan's death, his son and wife had been as if welded together: they had gone together to the funeral director and made the burial arrangements, had eaten every meal together, lingered together in the living room at night, talking. Mr. Bowdoin, the insurance man, had explained to both of them that Hartley Flanagan had left enough to pay all the bills for years to come. Together they had conferred with the Reverend Dawson Tyme, planned the funeral—Tom sat beside Rachel while she made all the telephone calls. He sat beside her while she cried, sat beside her and said nothing when she said, "It's better he's gone, he was in so much pain." Sat across the room in an uncomfortable Victorian chair when the fat Reverend Mr. Tyme returned and crowded beside his mother on the couch and blew out little minty breaths and said, "Every tragedy has its place in his plan." Saw that she, like himself, doubted the plan and mistrusted any man who would invoke it. Shopped with her; with her opened the front door to their visitors; stood beside her in the crowded funeral parlor during what the director called "the visitation"; stood beside her finally at the grave on a warming Sunday and realized that it was April first—April Fool's Day. And watched the crowd of Hartley's fellow lawyers and their wives and Hartley's friends and cousins and saw grief on some faces, restlessness on others, even embarrassment on others; there was no time to talk to any of the mourners, not even Del. They had to get back to the house and serve the food keeping warm in the oven. *Chin yourself up out of that grave,* he said to his father, *just get out of there and be like yourself again,* but the dry sun came down on them, the Reverend Mr. Tyme talked too much and pretended that he had been a friend of his father's, an April wind blew sand onto the graves and stirred the flowers. The grass looked sharp enough to inflict wounds. When it was over, he too cried and did not want to leave the grave. He looked at fat, minty Dawson Tyme and the lawyers—all of them were sleek, well-fed beasts, carnivores. A wall had crumbled, an anchor had snapped; he was without protection. The vulture had won and now it was Tom's turn to begin the walk into that long valley.

"You don't have to go to school for a while, do you?" asked his mother once they were back in the spiritless house. No. He did not.

After the fourth day his mother said, "Don't you want to get out of the house, Tom?" and he said *no*. After the fifth day she repeated her question and said that they had to think about his going back to school and making up his lost work: again he said *no*. Resuming his normal life seemed a betrayal of his loss. When Rachel Flanagan repeated her question after the sixth day, he recognized that he was now no longer a temporary adult. "You haven't seen your handsome little friend Del since the funeral," she said. "Don't you want to practice for your show? And anyhow, it'll do you good to get away for a while."

"He lives in Quantum Hills now," he said. "The

Hillmans finally bought a house. It has a pool and a tennis court."

"Quantum *Hills*." Her voice was faintly ironic. "Isn't that nice? And the suburban bus line goes right to the shopping center."

"Yeah," he said. "Maybe I'll go out there."

She embraced him.

Once out of the shopping center, he walked for half an hour along a street so black it shone. Enormous houses, some on landscaped hills and others in landscaped valleys, hovered like dream palaces far back on endless lawns. Whipping sprinklers whirred and sprayed, making rainbows which kept the grass green. Striped awnings shaded the vast windows. It was a suburb where no one ever walked. What was Del doing here, in the city's most artificial and dream-struck setting, this place of pools and tennis dresses? It suited the Hillmans, but it could not possibly be what Del wanted for himself. But—this came to him as he turned into the curving banked street—it was what Carson wanted for them: already many of their classmates lived here. Howie Stern and Marcus Reilly, Tom Pinfold and Pete Bayliss, six sophomores, took the bus the school sent out to Quantum Hills. All the stringency of life at Carson was meant to lead them to a place like this. If he had not met Del, if his father had not died, he would never have seen its absolute remoteness from him. He would have (he imagined) slid toward Quantum Hills as if on greased rails. He could not, now. He could only invent his future as Del was doing; he had been shaken from his frame.

Then just for an instant it seemed to Tom as if the shining blackness of the street was lapping at the cuffs of his trousers, the pale sky dark with witches. From a thin branch a starling screeched and fixed him with its black eyes. The world tilted.

This passed as quickly as it had come. The street subsided, the air cleared, the houses righted themselves. None of it could give a warning, because it represented a way of life in which warnings were obsolete. Tom realized that he was directly before the house Del's godparents had bought.

It was the classic Quantum Hills house, and the largest on the street, set far back on a rising treeless lawn. A wide asphalt drive curved up before it, marked by carriage lamps on tall dark poles. Where the drive met the two wide steps up to the entrance, the iron figure of a small black jockey held out a bright metal ring toward the rear bumper of a Jaguar. Modern, vaguely Moorish in design, the house sprawled behind these signs of a new Arizona prosperity.

Tom began to trudge up the drive, walked past the Hillmans' car and the sightless boy holding out his shining ring, mounted the steps. Something in his chest seemed to be trembling. He pushed the bell and jerked back his hand as if he had expected a shock.

The white door swung open, and Bud Copeland was looking down at him, smiling. "Hello, son. You here to see Del? Come on in, I'll take you up. You don't exactly need a map, but the first time, you might need a guide."

"Hello," Tom said tonelessly.

"You get yourself in here, young man, you look like you need a friend. Come on, get yourself through this doorway."

Tom moved through the doorway and into a wide entry which revealed half of an enormous living room, a stone fireplace nine feet high, furniture and boxes dumped here and there before a window the size of a wall. That it looked much as he had imagined it was reassuring—the odd unplaceable fear subsided.

"I heard about your father, son," Bud's velvet voice said beside him. "Terrible thing for a boy to lose his dad. If there's anything I can do to help, just ask."

"Thanks," Tom said, surprised and moved by the real sympathy in the man's face and voice. "I will."

"You do that. I'll do anything I can. Now. What do you think of our new quarters?"

"It's a big place," Tom answered, and thought he saw buried amusement in Bud's civilized face.

"My mother always told me to be careful too, Tom Flanagan," Bud said, and took him up a floating staircase at the side of the living room. "You and Del should have your tricks all polished up by now for your performance. If you still plan on giving it."

"Yeah, sure, but we still have to do some work," Tom said, following Bud's enormous back down an eggshell-white hall. "Oh, yeah, we're going to give it. You bet we are."

"Happy to hear it, son."

"Say, Bud," he said, and the black man heard something in his voice and turned around to face him. "You don't have to answer if you don't want to."

"I'll remember that," Bud said, smiling.

"Why do you stay here? Why do you do work like this?"

Bud's smile broadened, and he reached out to rasp Tom lightly on the top of the head. "It's a job, Red. I don't mind it. If I was twenty years younger, I'd likely be doing something else, but this berth suits me fine, the way I am. And I think maybe I can do some good for your friend in there." He nodded toward a door at the end of the hall. "Maybe I can do some good for you sometime too. Reason enough?" He raised his eyebrows, and again there was that unsettling look of recognition, as if Bud knew all about the birds and the visions.

"I'm sorry for prying," Tom said. His ears burned.

"I'd say you were interested, not prying. Don't look so embarrassed. You want a Coke or anything?"

Tom shook his head.

"Then I'll see you on your way out." Bud smiled again and went past him back toward the floating staircase.

Tom hesitated a second, dreading the conversation about his father he would have to have with Del before they could get to work. He heard Bud moving swiftly down the stairs, from an open window heard a far-off splash as someone dived into the pool. He went the rest of the way down the hall and stopped at Del's door.

No noises, no sound at all came from behind it. Through the unseen window floated the drawling voice of Valerie Hillman. Del's room was so quiet Tom thought his friend must be asleep. Tom raised his fist, lowered it, then raised it again and knocked.

Del did not respond, and Tom thought at first that his friend must be out by the pool with his godmother. But Bud would have known that. "Del?" he half-whispered, and knocked again.

Over or under a ripple of laughter from outside, he heard Del very quietly saying, "Come in." Del too was nearly whispering, but the quiet in his voice was that of effort—of concentration and force.

Tom turned the handle and gently pushed the door. The room was so dark as to be nearly black, and Tom again had the sense of being drawn into that separate world which was Del's—of stepping from sunlight and Arizona directly into mystery.

"Del?"

"*In.*"

Tom walked slowly into the darkness. His first glance around the room showed him only the big fish tank before drawn curtains, the looming faces of the magicians up on a shadowy wall. He saw that it was nearly twice the size of Del's old room; looking to the right, he saw a jumble of boxes and wooden things that must have been the kit. He turned his head to the left and saw shadowy space.

"*Look,*" Del commanded from the center of the shadows.

"Hey," Tom said, for at first he could see only the outline of a bed.

Then he could not say anything, for he had suddenly seen Del's rigid body, and it was suspended in the empty air four feet above the bed. Del snapped his head sideways. He was grinning like a shark.

Tom could not imagine what expression his own face wore, but it sent Del off into gleeful laughter. Laughing, he descended, first falling nearly a foot and stopping sharply, as if he had hit a ledge, then slipping down more slowly another eighteen inches. Tom held out a hand as if to catch him, but was not capable of moving nearer. Del's laughter bubbled up again; his feet dropped onto the bed, and the rest of his body followed.

Tom watched, so scared he thought he might faint or vomit, as Del's face drew back into itself and his body lifted up off the bed again and hovered a handbreadth above it.

"Now, that's how we end our magic show," Del managed to say, and this time could stay up while he laughed.

16

"The next day was Sunday," Tom said to me in the Zanzibar, the third time I went there to talk to him, "and I was still dazed. What had really struck me was the utter wrongness of it. Because I knew it was real. That little son of a bitch was actually levitating. It was real magic, and it seemed like the moment everything, all the craziness, had been leading to, the birds and the weird visions and everything else. I felt sick to my stomach. I was being frog-marched into magic, and I scarcely knew what was true and what was false anymore.

"I went outside. Sparky, my dog, woke up and started dancing around, asking me to throw his disgusting old tennis ball. I picked up the soggy ball and pegged it toward the fence. Sparky tore after it. Just then, before Sparky got to the ball, the air started to go funny—dark and grainy, like an old photograph. Sparky spun around and looked around; he whimpered. He started to race back toward the kitchen door. His ears were all flattened out—I remember seeing that, and I remember being relieved: I wasn't crazy, it was actually happening.

"That fairy-tale house was in front of me, where the fence should have been, that house with the little brown door and the trees all around it and the thatched roof. Through one of the little windows beside the door I could see the old man looking at me, running his hands through his beard. I went up the path. Now, now, now, I thought— now I can find out. I don't know what I thought I was going to discover, but I had that feeling. The old man, the wizard, if that's what he was, was going to clear everything up for me. When I reached his door, I looked through the window again, and got a shock. He looked terrible—as sick and scared as I had been that morning. On his face these feelings looked frighteningly out of place—you expected a face like that to be incapable of showing such things. He backed away from the window. I pushed the door open.

"The house was completely black. In midair, a candle was burning—it must have been on the mantel, but it didn't *illuminate anything around it, just shone out. Like a cat's eye.*

"The door banged shut behind me. I turned around to get out, pretty badly scared, but I couldn't see the door. Then I heard something coming toward me, and I turned back around to face it.

"And then I almost dropped dead of fright. I realized that it wasn't just one thing, it was a lot of things, and they were sick somehow, sick and wrong . . . it could have been four or five, it could have been a hundred. I couldn't tell. But I knew they were from him, that man I had seen or dreamed of seeing on Mesa Lane on the day before school started. It was like that whole world I had sensed before, in the house, the magic world, had been warped into evil.

"A face flickered in front of me, grinning like a devil, and then other faces jumped into life around it—cackling and grinning, the ugliest faces I had ever seen. They were there only for a moment; then they disappeared.

"Behind the candle there was now a spot of brightness. In the circle of light I saw the shadow of a pair of hands making a dog's head. The ears lifted. The tongue lolled. Shadow play, that's called: making pictures with your hands' shadows. I'd seen it before, of course, but never done as well—those fingers seemed almost triple-jointed— and never so that it seemed sinister. The dog's face turned toward me. Now, that's impossible in shadow play, you know. But I could see the ears sticking up, and the neck. Then the fingers parted to let the eyes shine through. That was as bad as the faces. The eyes were just empty light, and they looked completely malevolent. It wasn't a dog, I knew. It was a wolf's head.

"Then the eyes widened out, the hands fluttered and folded and melted together into a bird. A bird with huge wings and a tearing beak.

"It flew straight toward me, still in its circle of light, claws out—not hands, a shadow-bird. I ducked down, and heard laughter from all over the room.

"The shadow-bird disappeared into the blackness. I heard it beating away, and turned my head to follow it, and saw another sort of shadow play. A gang of men was kicking a boy, killing him by kicking him to death. They were in a ring around him—I heard them grunting, I heard

*their feet landing. One of them kicked the boy's head, and
I saw blood flying, spattering out. This was taking place in
the circle of light, but no fingers could have been making it.
The men kicked the boy's body aside, fluttered apart just as
if they were hands after all, and reformed as a word:
SHADOW. Then another series of letters flew together.
LAND. Shadowland. The laughter built up around
nasty and knowing, and I didn't know if all those twisted
faces watching me were laughing because they were warning me away from Shadowland, or because they knew I
would identify the dead boy with Del and would know I
had to go there."*

"Had to?" I asked.

"Had to," Tom said.

17

On the morning of the day we were to have the club
performances, I arrived at school an hour early: my
father, who drove me in, had a seven-thirty appointment
in the center of town. He dropped me off across the street
from the Upper School and I crossed the street and went
up the steps. The front door was locked. I peered in
through the leaded glass and saw an empty, murky entry,
stairs ascending to the library in darkness.

For a short time I sat on the steps in the early sun,
waiting for the janitor or one of the teachers to arrive and
let me in. Then I got bored and went back down the steps
to the sidewalk. When I looked back, the school had
changed; seeing it empty, I saw it anew. Carson looked
peaceful, well-ordered, and at one remove from the rest
of the world, like a monastery. It looked beautiful. Under
the slanting light, Carson was a place where nothing could
ever go wrong.

Down the street, I slipped through the bars of the gate
across the headmaster's private entrance. I moved up the
private drive and then stepped onto the grass. From this
side I could see only the original old buildings of the
Carson School. This view too seemed mysteriously
touched by magic. For a second my heart moved, I forgot

all the bad things that had happened, and I loved the place.

Then, after I had moved farther around toward the rear of the building and gone through a gap in the thick hedges, I saw a form lying facedown in the grass beside a briefcase, and knew I was not alone. Cropped head, meaty back straining the fabric of a jacket: it was Dave Brick. My euphoria drained off on the spot. Brick was stretched out disconsolately on the grassy slope where Mr. Robbin had summoned us all to look for the satellite. The ludicrously tight jacket was Tom Flanagan's. Brick had borrowed it because he had absentmindedly left his own at home two days before, and Flanagan was the only boy who had a spare in his locker. Brick was tearing up handfuls of grass slowly and methodically. When he saw me he began to rip out grass at a faster pace.

"You're early," he said. "Eager beaver."

"My father had an early appointment downtown."

"Oh. I always get here early. Get more time to study. Janitor's late this morning." He sighed and finally stopped pulling up grass. Instead he rolled his face into it. "It's going to start all over again."

"What is?"

"The questions. The Gestapo stuff. With us."

"How do you know?"

"I heard Broome talking with Mrs. Olinger last night when I left school. He wanted me to hear."

"Oh, God," I said, as much with impatience as with apprehension.

"Yeah. I almost stayed away this morning." Then he lifted himself up onto his forearms. I feared for Tom's jacket. "But I couldn't, because then he'd know why, and he'd come at me harder when I finally came back."

"Maybe he'll leave you out this time," I said.

"Maybe. But if he calls for me, I'm going to tell him this time. I can't take that anymore. And now it'll be worse."

"I already told Thorpe, and it didn't do any good."

"Because you didn't tell him I saw Skeleton too. That was nice. I'm, you know . . . grateful. But I don't care about Skeleton anymore. If Broome calls me out of Latin, I'm telling."

"I don't think he'll believe you."

"He will," Brick said simply. "I know he will. I'll make him believe me. I don't care if the whole school blows up."

When the janitor appeared, I followed Brick inside with the feeling of walking into a maze where a deranged beast with the head of a bull crouched and waited.

Five minutes after the start of Latin class, Mrs. Olinger appeared with a folded note in her hands. Dave Brick looked at me with flat panic in his eyes. Mr. Thorpe groaned, restrained himself from bellowing, and tore the note from Mrs. Olinger's hands. He unfolded and read it and wiped a hand over his face. His reluctance was as loud as a shout. "Brick," he said. "Headmaster's office. On the double."

Brick was trembling so uncontrollably that he dropped his books twice trying to ram them into his case. Finally he stood up and blundered through the center of the classroom. He looked at me with a white face and raisin eyes. Flanagan's jacket made him look like Oliver Hardy.

Then I again had that sense of a secret life running through the school, beating away out of sight, humming like an engine. After Latin class, Mrs. Olinger was waiting outside the room. She looked uneasy, like all messengers with bad news. Mrs. Olinger touched Mr. Thorpe's elbow and whispered a few words in his ear. "Blast," Mr. Thorpe said. "All right, I'm on my way," and sped down to the headmaster's staircase. We went to Mr. Fitz-Hallan's room and found a note chalked on the board telling us that class was canceled and that we should use the free time to read two chapters in *Great Expectations*.

"What's up?" Bobby Hollingsworth asked me as we settled down and opened our books. "I can't explain it," I said. "I bet they're finally getting around to throwing out Brick the Prick," Bobby said happily.

I finished the chapters and went out to my locker for another book. On the way I passed the Senior Room and heard a voice I thought was Terry Peters' uttering a sentence with the word "Skeleton" in it. I stopped and tried to hear what he was saying, but the door was too thick.

After I got the book from my locker, I looked down

across the glassed-in court and saw Mr. Weatherbee rush out of his room and tear down the hall, moving in a kind of agitated scuttle. Mrs. Olinger moved after him.

Mr. Fitz-Hallan, Mr. Weatherbee, Mr. Thorpe—it was the cast that had heard my original accusations.

Out in the hall, a few older boys ran past, lockers slammed, bells went off at irregular intervals.

18

The air of a general but unacknowledged disruption was still present as we trooped into the auditorium. Below the stage on which a piano faced a drum kit and a recumbent bass, the students were standing up in the aisles, moving into little talkative groups, breaking up again, calling to each other. Many of the morning's classes had gone teacherless. Morris saw Hanna and Brown standing together on the far side of the auditorium, and went around to join them in waiting for an announcement. I saw Mr. Thorpe shake his head at Mr. Ridpath, then curtly turn away. His eyes snagged mine, and he pointed at a spot beside the door. Mr. Ridpath too glared at me, but Mr. Thorpe seemed far angrier.

He reached the door before me and expressionlessly watched me come toward him. He looked like a gray-haired icicle—the Mount Rushmore of icicles. He waited a few seconds, making me sweat, before he spoke. "Be in my office at three-fifteen sharp." That was all he had intended to say, but he could not keep from releasing some of his rage. "You caused more trouble than you will ever know." When I could not reply, he made a disgusted puffing sound with his lips and said, "Get out of my sight until three-fifteen."

He was going to expel me, I knew. I went weakly to the first row of seats and sat down beside Bob Sherman. Most of the school was still standing and talking.

"Boys," shouted Mrs. Olinger. "Be seated, please." She had to repeat herself several times before anybody took any notice. Gradually the buzz of conversation died out, and was replaced by the sound of chairs scraping the floor. Then a few voices picked up again.

"Quiet," shouted Mr. Thorpe. And then there was silence. Morris, standing on the side of the room with the other members of his trio, looked crippled with stage fright.

Only then did I think to look for Skeleton Ridpath: if he was in the audience, it would mean that he too would be in Thorpe's office at three-fifteen. I turned around and saw that he was not in the seniors' two rows. So perhaps Broome had already expelled him.

From the podium before the stage, Mrs. Olinger was saying, "We are privileged this morning to witness the first performances by our two clubs. To begin with, please give your full attention to the Morris Fielding Trio, with Phil Hanna playing drums and Derek Brown accompanying on the bull fiddle."

Morris smiled at her because of the old-fashioned term and I knew that he at least was going to be all right. The three of them filed up the stairs to the stage. Brown picked up his bass, Morris said, "One . . . one . . . one . . . one," and they began playing "Somebody Loves Me." It sounded like sunlight and gold and fast mountain springs, and I switched off everything else and just listened to the music.

During Morris' last number I heard a startled buzzing and whispering. I turned around to see what had caused it. Laker Broome had just come into the auditorium. He had one hand clamped on Dave Brick's shoulder. Brick was white-faced, and his eyes were swollen. Morris also turned his head to see what was happening, and then went determinedly back to his piano. I heard him insert a quote from "Hail, Hail, the Gang's All Here" into his solo.

He was having, under trying circumstances, the best time he could, which is one definition of heroism; but looking at Laker Broome's rigid posture and assassin's face, I thought that the bomb I had been expecting all morning had just been tossed into the auditorium.

19

The headmaster applauded with everyone else when Morris nodded and stood up from the bench. Dave Brick had been parked on an empty chair far at the back of the room, apart from the rest of the students. Mr. Ridpath stared at him with loathing for a moment, then began to sidle toward Mr. Broome, hoping for one last word, but Mr. Broome looked straight into the center of his narrow vain face, and Mr. Ridpath froze solid to the floor. "Attention, boys," Mr. Broome called out.

When we were all turned around in our seats to face him, he began speaking and walking up the side of the auditorium to the bottom of the stage, and we swiveled to watch him—it was a display of power. "I hate to interrupt these interesting proceedings, but I want you to bear with me and share a fascinating story. I promise that this will only take a moment of your time, and then we can enjoy the second part of this excellent show. Gentlemen, we have finally been given the answer to the single greatest problem this school has faced since its founding, and I want all of you personally to witness the final act of that problem." He smiled. By now he was at the podium, and with mock casualness, he leaned one elbow on the blond wood: he was tense as a whippet. "Some of us will be meeting at three-fifteen in the assistant headmaster's office. That will be a private meeting. At four-fifteen I want the entire school reassembled here just as you are now. This school has been unwell, and it is time to cut back the diseased branches." He gave that taut, creased smile again, and I saw in him the same devil who had burned in Skeleton Ridpath's face just before he had beaten Del. "And now I believe we have some magic from two members of the first year."

It sounded like Broome wanted to stage a full-scale spectacular after school, with limbs lopped off in public and Christians thrown to lions. He wanted to answer the student performances with his own. That devil who had shone from his eyes was a devil of ambition and jealousy, who could not accept being upstaged. Tom and Del quietly left their seats and walked past Mr. Broome to go up the steps to the stage.

Broome drifted off to the side and leaned against the far wall beside one of the big doors, crossing his arms over his chest. He was smiling to himself. Tom and Del pulled the curtains shut, and for several moments we could dimly hear footsteps and the shifting of equipment. The piano, on casters, rolled back with a rumbling like a truck's. For some time we heard the rustling of material. Then the curtain twitched and pulled smoothly back, revealing a painted sign on a stand.

FLANAGINI AND NIGHT
ILLUSIONISTS

Most of the students seated below the stage began to laugh.

White smoke poured across the stage, billowed and hung, then began to drift up toward the beams and lights, and we could see that the sign had gone. In its place stood Tom Flanagan, dressed in what looked like an Indian bedspread and a turban of the same material. Beside him was the high table draped in black velvet, and on the other side of the table stood Del. He wore black evening dress and a cape. Deep laughter erupted again, and the two boys bowed in unison. When they straightened up, the smoke now entirely gone, their faces revealed their nervousness.

"We are Flanagini and Night," Tom intoned, sticking to his script in spite of the laughter. "We are magicians. We come to amaze and entertain, to terrify and delight." He flicked the velvet cover off the table, and something that looked like a fiery ball or shooting star lifted off from beneath and burned up six feet above their heads and winked out. Laker Broome watched it as if it were as ordinary as a horsefly. "And to amuse, perhaps." Del twitched the cape from his shoulders, twirled it over the table, and a four-foot-high stuffed white rabbit bounded off, so lifelike and grotesque that a few boys gasped. We were all in shock for a second, and then Del grasped it by one tall ear, bounced it off his foot, and threw it over his shoulder into the blackness behind him. There was an instinctive professional grace in his movements, and that (and the realization that the rabbit was a stuffed toy) made us all laugh, with them now, not against them.

They did several clever card tricks using boys from the audience; a series of tricks using scarves and ropes, including one in which Night proved that he could escape in three minutes from a rope knotted by two football players; they produced a dozen sprays of real flowers from the air.

Then Flanagini put Night into a cabinet and pierced it with swords, and when Night emerged whole, he pushed forward another cabinet—this one black and covered with Chinese patterns—and put Flanagini inside it. "The speaking head, or Falada," Night announced, banging the cabinet on all sides to demonstrate that it was solid. He shut a lacquered panel and hid Flanagini's body. The turbaned head looked out impassively. "Are you ready?" Night asked, and the head nodded. The top panel was shut. Night produced a long sword, took an orange from some pocket of the table, tossed the orange in the air, and swung the sword around to slice it in half. "A well-honed samurai sword," he said, and flexed it. "A deadly fighting instrument." He whistled it through the air again, and then slotted it sideways into the seam where the two panels met. He wrapped both his hands in black hand-kerchieves and pushed the flat sword deeply into the notch, where it seemed to meet an obstruction. Night paused to wrap the handkerchieves more tightly around his palms, put his hands again on the sword, and pushed. He grunted, and pushed again. The sword slid through to the other side of the cabinet, and Night yanked it out and wiped it with one of the handkerchieves. Then he pushed the bottom section of the cabinet away so that it no longer supported the top portion. He opened the panel of the bottom section to show Flanagini's body from the neck down. "The dance of death," he said, and rapped the side of the cabinet with the flat of the sword. For a moment the body in the Indian garment convulsed and trembled. "The speaking head." He moved to the left of the top section and opened the panel. Flanagini's head stared out from beneath the turban. "What is the first law of magic?" Night asked, and the floating head answered, *"As above, so below."* "And what is the second law of magic?" Night asked. *"The physical world is a bauble."* "And what is the third law of magic?" *"Reality is extremity."* "And how many books are in the library?" "I don't remember," came the indisputable voice of Tom Flanagan, and laughter jolted us as if we had been in a spell. Night closed both panels and moved the lower portion of the cabinet back beneath the upper section. When he swung open the panels, Tom stepped out, intact.

Wild applause.

"An illusion only," Night said, "a titillation, an amusement."

(A few sniggers, provoked by the syllable "tit.")

Night drew himself up and was black and serious as a crow's wing.

"But what is illusory can be true, which is magic's fourth law, like lightning here and then gone, like the smile of a wizard."

(White smoke began to billow across the stage again.)

"And man's dreams and deepest fantasies, these truthful illusions, are magic's truest country. Like the dream of—"

(The big doors on the side of the auditorium suddenly clicked open and swung wide. One of the boys in the back, several rows behind me, shouted.)

"—opening the doors of the mind."

(He spread his arms wide.)

"The mind opens, the shoulders open, the body opens. And we can . . ."

Smoke, not white but yellow and greasy, puffed in through the doors.

Del stopped intoning his magical gibberish and looked at the doors. His face went rubbery. The pose of professional mumbo-jumbo fell away, and he was a confused fourteen-year-old boy. In the second just before the auditorium went crazy, I had time to see that Tom, Flanagini, was also looking at something, and that he too was stricken. But he was not looking at the open doors: he was staring straight back up at the rear of the auditorium—so high up that he must have been nearly looking at the ceiling back there.

Mr. Broome took a step across the opening of the doors, saw what there was to see, and then turned around and pointed at the small, now insignificant pair on stage. He screamed, "You did this!"

"You're right," Tom said to me at the Zanzibar. "I never even saw what was outside until a couple of seconds later. I was standing there, waiting for Del to say that last word.

*"Fly." He'd said the whole speech except for that, and then
he was going to float up and amaze everybody. We'd
worked out a way to get those doors open weeks before,
and if Del could make it, he was going to try to get as far as
the first door and then just walk out, and that would be the
end of the show. I kept waiting to hear that last word,
"fly," and I was scared stiff—but then I looked back at that
end of the auditorium and I saw two things that scared me a
hell of a lot worse. One of them was Skeleton Ridpath. He
was terrible. He was grinning. He looked like a big bat, or
a huge spider—something awful. And the other thing I saw
jumped into being a fraction of a second later, as if Ridpath
and I had jointly summoned it up. It was a boy engulfed in
flames—swallowed up in fire, fire that couldn't be there, fire
that just seemed to stream out of him. I looked at him with
my mouth open, and the burning boy disappeared. I don't
know how I stayed on my feet. When Laker Broome
started shouting at us, I looked down and saw what Del
saw, the whole Field House blazing away. All that smoke
pouring out, and the fire jumping and jumping. I looked
back toward Skeleton, but he was already gone—maybe he
was never there in the first place. Then the whole place
went nuts.*

20

Laker Broome's scream paralyzed everybody, magicians
and audience alike, for a second, even the boy who had
shouted a moment earlier. And then this second of silence
broke—during it we had heard that awful whooshing,
snapping noise of a monstrous fire. Everybody stood and
ran toward the two doors, throwing chairs aside. Laker
Broome was shouting: "Everybody out! Everybody out!"

Maybe five boys got out the doors before Mr. Thorpe
yelled, "Stop in your tracks!" Already, the doors were a
pandemonium: all of us crowding and shoving to get out,
and the boys who had left screaming to get back in. "Back
away," Mr. Thorpe yelled, and started to throw boys
bodily back into the auditorium. Then we could feel the
heat, and the crowd surged back, knocking down the
smaller boys at the rear.

When the doors were cleared, we saw that the flames were leaping within six or seven feet of the auditorium—the outside looked like a solid world of fire. The old wooden field house was completely blanketed in flames. One of the stocky little turrets was leaning sideways, poised over the huge body of the fire like a diver.

The boys who had got outside and then forced their way back in stood beside the doors looking dazed and flushed and scared. I saw with amazement that one of them, a sophomore named Wheland, no longer had eyebrows—his face was a pink peeled egg.

"You *fool*," Thorpe hissed at the headmaster. "Didn't you see? You almost got all of them killed."

Broome just stared at him ferociously, then grabbed the sophomore's shoulder. "What did you see out there, Wheland?"

"Just fire, sir. We have to get out in front."

Mr. Thorpe was sending Mrs. Olinger to the office to call the fire department—"Move it!"

"Couldn't you get down the side?"

"The bushes are burning. On both sides. You can't get out that way."

At Wheland's words, everybody broke and ran toward the hall door. This was much narrower than the auditorium's side doors, and in seconds it was buried under a crowd of brawling boys. I saw Terry Peters knock down a sophomore named Johnny Day, and then throw Derek Brown down on top of him. "My *bass!*" squalled Brown. He ran straight into a line of tall upperclassmen, trying to get to the stage. Many boys were screaming. Mrs. Olinger, I saw with horror, was stuck in the middle of the battling crowd, unable to get to the telephone.

Then I realized that the auditorium was filling with smoke.

"We have to close those doors," Tom called from the stage. He unwound himself from the Indian garments and jumped down. Mr. Thorpe ran up to help him.

Mr. Ridpath was shouting useless orders. The other teachers ran up, seeing what Tom and Mr. Thorpe were doing. A senior was clubbing boys with a metal chair, trying to hack his way to the doors, and I ducked around him to try to help them close the doors.

The smoke was already very thick on that side of the

auditorium. I brushed against Mr. Thorpe, who said, "Grab this and pull." It was the metal bar on the door, and it was uncomfortably hot. "Ropes," Mr. Fitz-Hallan muttered, and Tom said, "We used them . . . so we could pull from backstage: they come in the window in back—"

"Blast," muttered Mr. Thorpe, and for a time we searched on the ground immediately outside the door and pulled lengths of rope inside. All of us were having trouble breathing: the smoke got in our eyes and throats and burned like acid. "That's all of them," Tom said. Through the boiling smoke we could see the wall of fire that once had been the field house: both turrets were gone now, and a column of blacker smoke rose directly up from the center of the burning mass. We slammed the doors shut on a row of advancing flame.

I turned and stumbled into Del, who was reeling through a thicket of upturned chairs. "Can't see," he said. Boys in the blocked doorway continued to scream. Del collapsed over the raised legs of a chair.

Then Tom was miraculously beside me, lifting Del. "No one's going to make it through the door," he shouted in my ear. "They can get out by going over the stage."

"The equipment," Del said. "We have to get it out."

"We will," Tom said. "Here, you get up there—you'll be able to see better. The smoke won't be so bad." He half-carried Del to the stage and hoisted him up. Del scrambled forward and groped around until he found whatever it was he wanted to save.

"Where's Skeleton?" Tom said close to my face. His own face was greasy and strained, and his eyes looked white.

"Not here."

"We have to get them away from that door," he shouted. Mr. Broome and Mr. Ridpath were yelling on the other side of the auditorium, peeling boys off the pile around the door. Mr. Fitz-Hallan loomed up out of the smoke beside me, carrying a boy in his arms. "Stage door," he said. "Some of them are passing out. A few of them are hurt." Mrs. Olinger was clutching the flap of his jacket. "I'll be back," Fitz-Hallan said, and crawled up onto the boards. He set down the boy and unceremoniously yanked Mrs. Olinger up.

Hollis Wax was running screaming across the auditorium. I saw Derek Brown picking himself out of a tangle of chairs, weeping. Wax caromed into the doors Flanagan and the teachers had managed to close and banged his fists against them. "They're *hot!*" he screamed. "They're going to burn!"

Tom ran toward him, seeing in the smoke like a bat, and Wax immediately broke for the stage. Then I dimly saw Tom picking up Brown and dragging him across the floor toward me.

"Get him onto the stage," he ordered, and I got my arms under Brown and pulled his shoulders onto the stage. Then I lifted his legs and sprawled him onto the wood. "Carry him out," Tom yelled from somewhere. I could see Mr. Fitz-Hallan coming toward me with another boy: a crocodile of sobbing students clung on behind him, as Mrs. Olinger had. I got up on the stage beside the English teacher and hauled Brown out and through the door to the hall. Even out there, wisps and trails of smoke drifted in the sunny corridor. "Bass," Brown sighed, straightening up and grinding at his eyes. Hollis Wax hovered far down the corridor, looking back. Tom and Fitz-Hallan came out beside me, and Wax saw us and turned and sprinted as soon as Fitz-Hallan waved at him. "All of you," Fitz-Hallan called, "follow Wax outside and wait in the parking lot."

Doubled up, Mr. Ridpath lurched out into the hall just as we were going back inside. A little crowd of coughing boys and teachers burst out after him. "Can't . . ." Ridpath uttered, and then bent over further, coughing. "Outside," Fitz-Hallan ordered. Tom was already back through—I saw him slipping across the dark stage. Brown took Mr. Ridpath's hand and began to move as quickly as he could down the corridor Wax had taken. The boy who had tried to hack his way out with a chair jumped through the door just as Tom disappeared off the apron of the stage back into the smoky chaos of the auditorium.

I walked slowly across the stage, not breathing. My eyes burned with smoke. *The bass,* I thought, and then noticed that the stage was empty of everything except the piano. The field house was making an end-of-the-world rushing roar. Mr. Broome vaulted up onto the stage beside me. "You," he said. "I order you to leave this building immediately."

I looked out into the auditorium and saw that the doors were burning. It was hotter than a steam room. A deadweight of maybe twenty boys lay in a heap before the hall exit: Mr. Weatherbee was bent over in the smoke, dragging two boys toward me. I jumped down and helped get them onto the stage. "Can't stay in here anymore," he croaked, and rolled onto the platform and grabbed the boys' wrists and went for the back door. He was crawling by the time he reached it.

Tom and Mr. Fitz-Hallan were pulling unconscious boys from the pile. I jumped down, and the outside doors gave way at the same instant. Fire streamed in as though shot from a flamethrower. Black spreading scars instantly appeared on the auditorium floor.

"Get up off the floor, Whipple," Mr. Broome sang out. I looked up, surprised to see him poised on the edge of the stage like a ham actor. "You'll burn like bacon. Get up off the floor."

Over the noise of the fire I heard the wailing of sirens.

Mr. Broome shouted, "Everybody out! This instant! All out!" Mr. Whipple was too heavy to lift. I inhaled a gulp of burning smoke; my knees turned inside out and I fell over his jellylike stomach. Tom appeared beside me, carrying one of the unconscious boys.

"Out! Out! Out!" screamed Mr. Broome.

Fire caught the curtains of the stage, and lying on the ground I saw them crackle up and disappear like tissue paper. Mr. Fitz-Hallan went on his knees twenty feet away. Mr. Whipple's stomach roared and he rolled over and threw up a yard from my head. I could see Tom holding an arm over his mouth and hear him wheezing as he pulled at Mr. Fitz-Hallan's arm. Then an enormous form in black shiny clothing leaned over and picked me up. He smelled like smoke.

21

The Making of a Hero

The fireman carried me out into the parking lot, where four trucks sprayed arcs of water on the shell of the field house and into the side of the auditorium. He put me on the grass beside one of the trucks, and I crawled half-upright. Mr. Fitz-Hallan was being led out of the parking-lot exit, hauling Tom behind him. Both of them looked like mad scientists in a comic book, their faces smeared with black, their clothing smoking. Behind them came a line of firemen carrying the last of the boys: not twenty any longer, only five or six. One red-faced fireman staggered beneath Mr. Whipple.

An ambulance squealed down the rise into the lot and pulled up short by the side door. The attendants jumped out and opened the rear doors to pull out stretchers. I managed to stand up. Morris, Sherman, Bobby Hollingsworth, and the others were bunched together on the grass below the parking lot, watching the arcs of water disappear into the field house. I could see lines of red on Morris' face—someone had hit him with something and cut his scalp. He looked gallant and unperturbed with blood all over his face, and the shock hit me and I started to cry.

"It's okay," Tom said. Once again he was miraculously beside me. "I just looked around, and I think everybody's okay. Did you see Skeleton Ridpath?"

I wiped my eyes. "I don't think he's here."

"Well, I think he is," Tom said. He turned away and went toward the teachers, who were in a group at the back of the parking lot, clustered around Mr. Broome. The headmaster looked as though he had been in the auditorium longer than anyone—his face was nearly black. Ashy smudges blotted his seersucker jacket. He looked straight through Tom and continued to harangue Mr. Thorpe. His Doberman lay beside him, exhausted and also matted with ash. The dog reeked of smoke and burning wood and twisting metal—I caught it from where

I stood—and I realized that I probably did too. "You can't tell me a boy wasn't smoking," Mr. Broome was saying. "It started in one of the turrets. I saw it clearly. What else have we been warning these boys about day after day?" He wobbled a bit, and Mr. Thorpe grabbed his elbow to keep him upright. "I want a list of every boy in the auditorium. That way we'll find our guilty man. Get a list, tick them off—"

"Mr. Broome," Tom said.

One fireman rushed by, then another.

"Men are working here," Mr. Broome said. "Stay out of their way."

"Was Steve Ridpath in school this morning?" Tom asked.

"Sent him home."

"He's at home," Mr. Ridpath coughed out. "He took the car. Thank God."

"Were you going to kick Del out of school?" Tom asked.

"Don't be an ass," Broome said. "We have work to do. Now, leave us alone."

A big man in a suit like a policeman's came across the gravel and stood beside Tom and me. A badge on his shoulder read *Chief*. "Who is the principal here?" he asked.

Mr. Broome stiffened. "I am the headmaster."

"Can I see you for a second?"

"Any assistance," Mr. Broome said, and followed the chief out into the center of the lot.

"Where's Del?" Tom asked. "Did you see Del?"

"A *deceased?*" Broome said loudly, as if he had never heard the word.

The two firemen who had rushed past us earlier were coming out of the side door carrying a body on a stretcher.

"The label in his jacket says Flanagan," the fire chief said.

"Flanagan is not deceased," Mr. Broome said airily. "Flanagan is very much with us. I helped him out of the auditorium myself."

"Oh, no," Tom said, but not in contradiction to the headmaster's lie. Mr. Fitz-Hallan and Mrs. Olinger, closely followed by Mr. Thorpe, were already at the ambulance door. Four boys who had passed out in the smoke groaned from bunk-bed-like stretchers in the white metal interior. I heard a crash as the last of the field house collapsed. The boys watching yelled as they would at fireworks. Mr. Fitz-Hallan leaned over and gently lifted the top of the blanket. I could not hear the two or three soft words he uttered.

"Let these men get on with their work, Flanagan," Mr. Broome shouted.

As they lifted the covered body into the ambulance, the slide rule in its charred leather holster slipped over the edge of the cot and bounced against the white steel.

Which is the last of the three images that stay with me from the first year at Carson—a composite image, really. Dave Brick's slide rule banging against the bottom of the ambulance doors, the boys cheering at the last gasp of the field house, Mr. Broome yelling impatiently: that was what all the ironic civility had come down to. A dead boy, a few shouts, a madman's yell.

Tom and I found Del sitting on the lawn at the front of the school. He was guarding the magic equipment, the bass, and Phil Hanna's drums, all of which he had managed to get out while Tom had been saving lives. He had watched the arrival of the fire trucks and the ambulance, but had not come down into the lot himself because he had been afraid that someone might steal Brown's bass. "It seemed awfully important to him," he said. "And anyhow, I could hear everybody coughing and yelling, so I knew they were all right." He looked at Tom's face, then mine. "They are all right, aren't they?"

Tom sat down beside him.

22

Graduation

Four teachers, including Mr. Fitz-Hallan and Mr. Thorpe, stayed overnight in the hospital because of smoke inhalation; so did twenty-four boys. The morning edition of the city's biggest paper bore the headline "SOCIETY SCHOOL HEADMASTER LEADS 100 BOYS TO SAFETY." *"Freshman Lost,"* was the subhead. Nobody ever mentioned expulsion or theft again, as if the fire had solved that question.

In any case, there was no one to whom to mention it: the rest of the year's classes were canceled, and teachers made up their final grades by averaging all the work up to the day of the fire. Many boys half-believed Laker Broome's story of saving most of the school single-handedly because the newspapers made a chaotic event seem clearer than it had been to any of those involved. But they remembered what Tom Flanagan had done; only the board of directors and most of the parents assumed that the newspapers were absolutely correct. They wanted to believe that the school's administration had behaved in a crisis the way they themselves would like to.

A news photographer snapped Mr. Broome's picture at the reception on the lawn after commencement. When we looked up the hill toward the Upper School we could see the enormous hole in the landscape where the Field House had been. Parents and students moved around on the grass, taking sandwiches from the long tables attended by the dining-room maids. I had just left my parents, who stood in a little group with Morris and Howie Stern and their parents near the impromptu stage where a member of President Eisenhower's last Cabinet had implored us to work hard and build a better America. I happened to be beside Mr. Broome when the photographer took his picture, and when the man walked off, Broome looked indulgently down at me. "What do you think of our school?" he asked. "You'll be a sophomore in a few months. That entails more responsibility."

We looked at each other for a moment.

"You will all be great men. All of you." Even the long creases in his face were different, less defined. Many years later I realized that he had been heavily tranquilized.

I said good-bye to him and went back to my friends and parents. Tom and his mother walked past, accompanied by Del and the Hillmans. In the middle of the crowd, even with a parent and godparents beside them, Tom and

Del looked alone. Laker Broome stared straight through them and smiled at a tray of sandwiches.

"Remember?" Tom said in the Zanzibar. "Of course I remember what we were talking about. We were working out the arrangements for me to go with Del to Shadowland. My mother didn't want me to fly, so we were going to take the train. It sounded like fun—getting on a train in Phoenix and taking it all across the country."

"Why did you want to go?" I asked.

"Only one reason," Tom said. "I wanted to protect Del. I had to do it."

He swiveled around on his bar stool and surveyed the empty room. Light from the windows fell like a spotlight on the stage at the far end. He did not want to look at me while he said the rest of it.

"I knew I couldn't keep him from going, so I had to go with him."

He sighed, still watching the yellow ray of light on the vacant stage as if he expected to see a vision there.

"There was one thing I really didn't know. But should have. The school was Shadowland too."

And for months, for nearly two years, in other bars or in hotel rooms, other cities, other countries, wherever we caught up with each other: *Let me tell you what happened then.*

Part Two

Shadowland

We are back at the foot of the great narrative tree, where stories can go . . . anywhere.
      —Roger Sale, *Fairy Tales and After*

I

The Birds Have Come Home

Del was quiet the whole first day of the trip. . . .

1

Del was quiet for the first day of their journey, and Tom eventually gave up trying to make him talk. Whenever he commented on the vast, empty scenery rolling past the train's windows, Del merely grunted and buried himself deeper in a two-hundred-page mimeographed manuscript which Coleman Collins had mailed him. This was about

something called the Triple Transverse Shuffle. Apart
from grunts, his only remark about the desert landscape
was, "Looks like a million cowboy hats."

During this time Tom read a paperback Rex Stout
mystery, walked through the cars looking at the other
passengers—a lot of old people and young women with
babies around whom buzzed talkative soldiers with drawling, suntanned accents. He inspected the bar and dining
car. He sat in the observation bubble. There the desert
seemed to engulf everything, changing colors as the day
and the train advanced. It moved through yellow and
orange to gold and red, and in the instant before twilight
threw blue and gray over the long distances, flamed—
dyed itself a brilliant rose-pink and burst thunderously
into brilliance. This endured only a heart-stopping second, but it was a second in which the whole world seemed
ablaze. When Tom came hungry back to their seats, Del
looked up from a page full of diagrams and said, "Poor
Dave Brick." So he had seen it too.

Night came down around them, and the windows gave
them back their faces, blurred into generalities.

"Booger," Tom muttered, almost in tears: the complex
of feelings lodged in his chest was too dense to sort out.
He had somehow missed Dave Brick in the smoky
pandemonium of the auditorium, must have gone right
past him half a dozen times and left him back there,
behind them, in the country they were leaving a little
more with each *click* of the wheels. The sensation of
moving forward, of being propelled onward, was as strong
as the sense of threat outside Del's house that noon
before Del had risen into the air—it was the sense of
being mailed like a parcel to a destination utterly unknown. He met his mild blurred eyes in the dirty window
and saw darkness rocking past him in the form of a
telegraph pole's gloomy exclamation point.

"You did a lot," Del said.

"Sure," Tom growled, and Del went back to his pages
of diagrams.

After twenty more minutes in which Del fondled cards
and Tom held tightly to his feelings, fearing that they
would break and spill, Del looked up and said, "Hey, it
must be way past dinnertime. Is there anywhere to eat on
this train?"

"There's a dining car up ahead," Tom said. He looked at his watch and was startled to see that it was nine o'clock: they had been rocked past time, while they had been busy leaving *behind* and *back there.*

"Great," Del said, and stood up. "I want to show you something. You can read it when we're eating."

"I don't get any of that stuff you're looking at," Tom said as they started walking down the aisle toward the front of the car.

Del grinned at him over his shoulder. "Well, you might not get this either. It's something else," leaving Tom to wonder.

Any stranger looking at them would have known that they went to the same school. They must have looked touchingly young, in their blue Gant shirts and fresh haircuts; they were unlike anyone else on the train. Cowboys with dusty clothes and broken hats and cardboard suitcases had climbed on at every stop. With names like Gila Bend and Edgar and Redemption, these were just brown-board shacks in the desert.

In the dining car Tom first realized how odd he and Del appeared, here on this train. As soon as they walked in, he felt exposed. The women with their children, the soldiers, the cowboys, stared at them. Tom wished for a uniform, for ten more years on his body. A few people smiled: being cute was hateful. He promised himself that for the rest of the trip he would at least wear a shirt a different color from Del's.

Del commandeered a small side table, snapped the napkin off his plate, and accepted the menu without looking at the waiter. Intent on some private matter, he had never noticed the stares. "Ah, eggs Benedict," he said. "Wonderful. Will you have them too?"

"I don't even know what they are," Tom said.

"Then try them. They're great. Practically my favorite meal."

When the waiter returned, they both ordered eggs Benedict. "And coffee," Del said, negligently proffering the menu to the waiter, who was a glum elderly black man.

"You want milk," the waiter said. "Coffee stunt your growth."

"Coffee. Black." He was looking Tom straight in the eye.

"You, son?" The waiter turned his tired face to Tom.

"Milk, I guess." Del rolled his eyes. Tom asked, "Do you drink coffee?"

"In Vermont, I do."

"And the princes and the ravens bring it in gold cups every morning."

"Sometimes. Sometimes Rose Armstrong brings it." Del smiled.

"Rose Armstrong?"

"*The* Rose Armstrong. Just wait. Maybe she'll be there, maybe she won't. I hope she is."

"Yeah?" Now it was Tom who smiled.

"Yeah. If you're lucky, you'll see what I mean." Del adjusted the cloth on his lap, looked around as if to make sure no one was eavesdropping, and then looked across the table and said, "Before you get your first taste of paradise, maybe you ought to see what he sent me."

"If you think I'm old enough."

Del plucked a folded sheet of typing paper from his shirt pocket and passed it to Tom. He was positively smirking.

Tom unfolded the sheet.

"Don't ask any questions until you read all of it," Del said.

Typed on the sheet was:

SPELLS, IMAGES & ILLUSIONS
(For the Perusal of My Two Apprentices)
Know What You Are Getting Into!

Level 1	Level 2	Level 3
Trance	Theatrics	Flight
Voice	Rise	Transparence
	Silence	Altered Landscape

Level 4	Level 5	Level 6
Window of Flame	Collector	Ghostly Presence
Window of Ice	Mind Over Matter	Living Statue
Tree Lift	Mind Control	Fish Breathing

Level 7	*Level 8*	*Level 9*
Altered Time	Put A Hurting	Wood Green
		Empire
Created	Conjure Minor	
Landscape	Devils	
	Desired Fireworks	

Tom looked up when he had read it.

"Read it again."

Tom glanced down the lists again. "I don't get it."

"Sure you do." Del's whole being was alight.

"Do you get one of these every summer?"

Del shook his head. "This is the first time. But when I saw him at Christmas, he said that if I came back with you, he'd send me a description."

"Of what? Everything he can do?"

"He can do a lot more than that. But I guess what he means is a description of what a magician ought to be able to do."

"He can turn statues into people? He can . . . ?" Tom searched the list. "Alter the landscape?"

"I guess so." Del laughed. "I've seen a lot of that stuff. Not all of it, but a lot."

"So if Rose Armstrong brings you coffee, she might come in upside down? With upside-down coffee in an upside-down cup?"

Del shook his head, still laughing.

"I don't like that business about 'Know What You Are Getting Into.'"

"I told you he was scary sometimes."

"But it's like a threat." And then his mind gave him an image he had a month ago decided was false: that of Skeleton Ridpath hovering two inches below the ceiling of the auditorium, hanging like a spider, exulting in the coming destruction.

"It's not really a threat," Del explained. "Sometimes up there, everything is normal, and at other times . . ." He waved at the paper. "Other times, you learn things. Oh, great, here comes dinner."

Tom gingerly cut into one of the eggs on his plate, saw yolk flood out into the paler yellow of the sauce, and lifted a dripping fork to his mouth. "Wow," he said when he swallowed. "How long has this been going on?"

"The hollandaise comes out of a bottle," Del said. "But you get the general idea."

2

As they ate, the train slowed into a station—Tom could see only a metal water tower and a peeling shed. The usual men in curling hats waited to get on.

Del said, "With these levels, I guess you can sometimes do something on a higher one without being able to do everything on the lower ones. Like I can rise, you know, but Uncle Cole says everybody can learn to do that, if they concentrate the right way. But I'm really Level One—I can't even do voice, throw my voice yet. I'm still trying to learn. "Trance" is just like hypnotism. An idiot can do it. Theatrics, now . . ."

Tom watched the lonely cowboys filing past. They looked thirsty. Nobody ever saw cowboys off, nobody ever greeted them.

". . . it's just the ordinary stage stuff, all you have to know is how to do it, how the mechanics work . . ."

They were like spacemen, so loosely tied to earth, but where they orbited was towns like this, the name of which was Lone Birch.

Then he saw a face that violently took his mind off cowboys. All the pleasure in him went black and cold.

"*Theatrics*, see, he thinks it's all junk, just the word shows it." Del looked at him curiously. "You lose your appetite all of a sudden?"

"Don't know," Tom said. He craned over the table, trying desperately to see the bruised face among the half-dozen men waiting outside.

"You think you saw a friend? In Lone Birch?"

"Not a friend. I thought I saw Skeleton out there. Waiting to get on the train."

Del laid down his knife and fork. "Oh. I just lost my appetite too." He looked perfectly composed. "What do we do?"

"I don't want to do anything."

"I think we ought to take a look. That way we'll know. How sure are you?"

"Pretty sure. But I just saw him for a second—just a glimpse."

The train began to *snick-snick* out of the station.

"But a face like that . . ."

"It's pretty hard to miss," Tom said. "Yeah."

"Let's go." Del pushed himself away from the table. "I'll pay the waiter. I'll go forward, and you go back. We're about halfway in the train." Del took a deep breath and swayed a little with the train's motion. "If it's him . . . I don't mean to give you orders—and he could be sitting facing the way you come in—but maybe he's just traveling . . ."

"And maybe I'm wrong," Tom said. Part of him was happy that Del's nervousness had emerged. "And maybe if I see him, I'll kick him off the train." Now that Del had shown his own fear, his could turn to anger. "I guess we'd better start."

"That's what I said," Del reminded him over his shoulder, and held out a folded ten-dollar bill to the waiter.

Tom entered the next car and looked over the passengers. Many slept—babies sprawled over their mothers sprawled over two seats. Soldiers slept with caps pulled over their eyes, snoring like a yard full of pigs. A few wakeful ones glanced at him over the tops of magazines. Skeleton Ridpath was not there.

He went quickly down the aisle, pushed aside the heavy door, and for a moment stood in the rocking space between cars and peered through the gritty window. This was their car—Tom felt an angry certainty that if Skeleton were on the train, he would be sitting near them. The thought made his bowels liquefy. But the seat behind theirs was empty; the people he could see from the window were those to whom he had spoken or nodded. He pushed the door aside and went in.

One of the sleepy mothers smiled at him. The long car felt warm and comfortable. Tom imagined that if Skeleton were actually seated there, his nerves would have screamed, alarms howled.

Three cars remained. Since Skeleton had got on Tom's half of the train, there was a thirty-three-percent chance he was in the next car. Tom left his own carriage and pushed open the door to the next.

Here all the lights were off. Tom closed the door behind him. His eyes adjusted slowly. This car is almost empty, which is why the few in it were able to enforce their unanimous opinion that nights on trains were for sleeping. One of the men, mustached and blue-jeaned, grunts in his sleep and digs his face deeper into the untender material of the seat. Tom has seen at once that none of them is Skeleton. He wishes that he could curl up like this, grind his face into a seat, and be somewhere else, safe—and then he feels that he is walking straight through their dreams, trespassing in them.

This man who lifts a shoulder before him, is he dreaming of the snake that circles the world and rests with its pointed tail in its mouth?

And the man two rows back who sleeps like a child, his head thrown back and knees asplay, does he dream of some Rose Armstrong, some perfect girl who haunts him? Or of a flame-girdled toad with a jewel in its forehead and a key in its mouth?

And does this one dream of being a hunter in a starry wood—Orion with his drawn bow?

Or of a man become a hunting bird?

Then he feels that he does not trespass through their dreams, but *is* them; that he is a dream being dreamed. His feet do not quite touch the ground. Their snores and stirrings carry him to the end of the dark carriage, and the door floats to the side under the pressure of his hand. He sweats, his head full of cobwebs . . . hunting birds . . . blazing toads . . .

He was sweating, that is, sweating and dizzy on the swaying platform between carriages, and it seemed to Tom that his mind was floating out of his control, prey to any fancy that came along. He has been someplace he has never been before. *Being dreamed?* Him, steady Tom Flanagan? The thought of Skeleton was somehow the cause of that. And as he put his hand on the door to the next carriage, he realized that by his earlier reckoning, there was a fifty-percent chance of seeing Skeleton in this car.

He marched up the aisle, looking rapidly from side to side, checking the faces even though he was sure that if his enemy were present, he'd be so visible as to be fluorescent. Two ten-year-old girls flouncing up the aisle in identical calico dresses separated to let him pass.

Tom pushed his way out into the breeze again. By his reckoning, the odds were a hundred percent that Skeleton was in this last car.

He had to pee—it was like pre-exam panic. He swallowed, and hoped that Del was already safe in his seat, thinking that Skeleton was out of their lives for good. Tom grasped the handle and pushed the door. He knew Skeleton was there.

But there it was again, that shock, even though he had thought he was prepared. For down at the end of the carriage, the very back of Skeleton's head met him, narrow and matted with mouse hair.

He has no power now, Tom told himself; he can't do anything to us. There was no reason to fear him. In that case, maybe Del was right. Don't let him see you, just make sure and go away and hope he gets off the train at the next station.

Tom almost did it. What stopped him was the thought of going back to Del and saying, yes, he is here, and then spending the next two days and nights in fear. He imagined himself and Del in their sleeping car, heeding every sudden noise. He would not allow himself to be so childish.

He took a step nearer the hated head.

Tom closed his mouth on a breath, took a quick step around Skeleton's side, and dropped himself into the facing seat. Adrenaline blasted his good intentions, and he blurted out, "What are you doing here, anyway?"

Then crumbled—another shock. The face was Skeleton's at fifty, not Skeleton's now. It was the same skinned, reptilian visage with smudgy pouches beneath the same colorless eyes, but with a lot of extra years on it. "I got a right to be here," the man said. Then the stingy flesh colored. "Who the hell are you, anyway? Get outta here." The man's thin hand trembled against the side of his face, went to his tie. "Geez, get this kid." He appealed to empty seats for witness. "Get lost, kid. Lemme alone."

This moment was truly like being trapped in a dream—the man was eerily like Skeleton, was, if anything, even more hideous than Skeleton. But he was certainly not Skeleton. He looked one step elevated from trampdom.

"You're tryna mess with me, ain't ya, kid? Just get outta here before I cut you to pieces." The man was like an angry, bewildered dog.

Tom was already up out of the seat, stuttering apologies. He saw a conductor down at the other end of the car, and fled.

From movies he knew that little balconies rode at the end of trains, and he darted out through the rear door. Yet here was another puzzle. Another car swayed before him. He was not at the end of the train. *What the . . . ?* The car had not been on the train when they boarded that morning. He and Del had entered the fourth car from the end: he remembered that absolutely. This car had somehow been magicked onto the end of the train.

Tom reeled.

"Get this kid," the man said to the conductor.

The door heaved to one side, and he slipped through, ignoring the conductor's shout.

But the next car—now here was real disorientation. He had gone fifty years back in time. Gas lamps flickered on flocked walls, a thick patterned carpet glowed. Hunting prints shone down from the walls. A knot of men dressed in old-fashioned checked and belted suits regarded him. Most were bearded, some smoked long cigars. He could smell the whiskey in their glasses.

"You have made a mistake," a tall burly man with a stand-up collar and a Vandyke said quietly. "Please leave." He looked stonily at Tom through a thin gold pince-nez.

The conductor banged the door open and fastened a rough hand on Tom's upper arm. "I couldn't stop him in time, Mr. Peet."

"All right, yes, understood. Remove him."

The conductor hauled Tom out into the next carriage. The old defeated Skeleton Ridpath turned on his seat in a grotesque parody of snobbery and faced the window.

"Don't ever go back there again," the conductor said in Tom's ear. He did not sound angry. "They might look crazy, but that's their business."

"What is that, anyway?"

The conductor released Tom's arm. "Private party—own their own car. Food? Liquor? You never seen anything like it. You gotta be rich to live that good. They hooked up a couple stations back, going all the way to New York. Just leave 'em alone, son. You got plenty of train to walk around in."

When Tom got back to his seat, he sat down beside Del, who stared. "Is he there?"

"Just an old guy who looks like him."

"Aaaah." Del slumped back into his seat, sighing. "Thank God." He smoothed his glossy hair, looked at Tom, grinned. "You know, we were both scared shitless. But what could he do to us, really? Even if he was on the train?"

"Maybe he's the Ghostly Presence," Tom said, and Del tried to smile.

That night, rolling through Illinois on his upper bunk, Tom dreamed of lying by a campfire in a deep wood. The moon was a huge eye. A snake whispered up to him and spoke.

3

A morning of French toast dripping maple syrup, hard little sausages that tasted of hickory smoke, tomato juice: Ohio just ending outside the dining-car windows, an epic of grain-filled plains separated by dark smoky cities. By now nearly everybody who had joined their train in Arizona was gone, and churchy, singing Midwestern voices had replaced the sunburnt drawls. The most important new passengers were four middle-aged black men dressed in conspicuously handsome suits—they had supervised the loading, late at night in Chicago, of a trove of instrument cases into the baggage car and were supposed to be famous musicians. The conductors treated them like heroes, like kings, and they looked like kings: they had an extra charge of authority and no need of anyone else. Morris Fielding would have known their names.

"One of them's called Coleman Hawkins," Del said. "The conductor told me. And you'll never guess the name of the quiet one without any hair."

"You're right. I can't guess."

"Tommy Flanagan. He plays piano, and the conductor says he's fantastic."

"Tommy *Flanagan?*" Tom put down his silverware and looked at every table in the dining car.

"I don't think they get up this early," Del said wryly. "Don't look that way. If someone has to have your name, it might as well be a fantastic piano player."

"Yeah, it's sort of neat . . . but I'd rather have him be a fantastic third baseman," Tom said. For a second he had felt that the man, as modest and civilized as an Anglican priest, had stolen his name from him.

4

"I wonder what he's going to do this time," Del said.

"Play the piano somewhere, dummy."

"Not your namesake, Jell-O Brains. Uncle Cole. I wonder what it'll be this summer."

"Is it always different?"

"Sure it is. One summer it was like a circus—clowns and acrobats all over the place. That was when I was a little kid. Another summer, it was like movies. Cowboy movies and cop movies. That was a year I went to movies all the time—I was twelve. Saw a double feature every Saturday. And when I got to Shadowland, every day was like a different movie. I never knew what was going to happen. There was Humphrey Bogart and Marilyn Monroe and William Bendix and Randolph Scott—"

"Right *there?* That's impossible."

"Well, it looked like them. I know it wasn't them, but . . . sometimes it was pieces of their movies. He has projectors all over the place. He can make it look like anything is happening. Every summer is like a different performance. I just wonder what it'll be this time." He paused. "Because it's always tied in with what's going on

before you get there. That's all part of magic, he says—
working with what's in your mind. Or on your mind. And
with all the stuff that went on this year . . ." Del looked
decidedly worried for a moment.

"You mean it might be about school?"

"Well, it never has been. Uncle Cole hates schools. He
says he's the only person he knows who should be allowed
to run a school."

"But it might be Skeleton and our show and . . ."

"The fire. Maybe." Del brightened. "Whatever it is,
we'll learn something."

"I guess there are some things I'd rather not learn,"
Tom said, making the only truly conservative statement of
his life.

"Just listen to whatever he says first. When he meets us
at the station. That's the clue to everything."

Tom said, "The Case of the Famous First Words."

Del looked uncomfortable again. "Hey, breakfast is
over, huh? Let's get out of here." He rattled his fork
against his plate, looked at the window. The filthy brick
backs of office buildings and warehouses slid by, en-
crusted with fire escapes—some bleak Ohio city. He
finally came out with what he had been planning to say.
"Listen, Tom. You have to know . . . I mean, I should
have said before. My uncle—everything I said about him
is true. Including that he's half-crazy. He drinks. He
drinks one hell of a lot. But that's not the reason, I don't
think. He just *is* half-crazy. Except for the summers, I
think he's alone all the time. Magic is everything he's got.
So sometimes he gets kind of wild . . . and if he's been
drinking . . ."

"That's what I thought," Tom said.

Take care, Red.

"Does Bud Copeland know him?" Tom asked.

Del nodded. "He met him once—once when he came
to Vermont to get me. I, uh, I broke a leg. It was just an
accident. But they met, yeah." Tom did not have to ask
the question. "Bud wanted me never to go back. I had to
talk him into it. He didn't like Uncle Cole. But he didn't
understand, Tom. That was all."

"I get it," Tom said.

"He's not all crazy," Del pleaded. "But he just never

got the recognition he should have, and he spends all that time alone. It's okay, really. It's not even half. That's just an expression."

"But you broke your leg because he got carried away."

"That's right. But people break their legs skiing all the time." This had the air of something Del had said many times before—to Bud Copeland and the Hillmans. "It was just a little break, a hairline break, the doctor called it. I was only in a cast about three weeks, and that's nothing."

"Did your uncle get the doctor?"

Del colored. "Bud did. My uncle said it would heal by itself. And he was right. It would have. Maybe not as fast, but it would have healed."

"And how did it happen?"

"I fell down a sort of a cliff," Del said. Now his face was very red. "Don't worry. Nothing like that is ever going to happen again."

5

They changed trains in Pennsylvania Station; during the two hours before the departure of the Vermont train, the boys put their bags in lockers and walked around the station.

"Just a couple more hours," Del said as they stood in a doorway and looked at people coming in and out of the Statler Hilton across the street. "This is going to be what people call an adventure."

"I feel like I'm already having an adventure," Tom answered. The musicians, Hawkins and the man with Tom's name and the other two, were hailing cabs, joking, already going in different directions.

"Someday we'll be like them," Del said. "Free. Can't you see what that'll be like? Traveling, performing . . . going wherever we like. I love the thought of the future. I love the whole idea."

Suddenly Tom saw it as Del did: lone-wolfing around the world, carrying an airline ticket always in his pocket, living in taxis and hotels, performing in one club after another . . . A layer of self deep in his personality trembled, and for the first time he really said *yes* to a life so different from any his parents or Carson School would have chosen for him.

6

The afternoon saw them stalled north of Boston, far out in the green Massachusetts countryside. Brindled cows swung their heads and regarded them with liquid eyes; people strolled along the tracks, sat on the slope of the line and looked back at the cows. "Will we be here much longer?" Tom asked the conductor.

"Could be a couple more hours, way I hear it."

"That long?"

"You boys jus' got lucky."

At intervals a bored, half-audible voice broadcast over the loudspeakers: *"We regret the inconvenience of this delay, but . . . We anticipate resumption of service in a short . . ."* Lively rumors traveled through the train.

"Big mess-up at the next junction," their porter finally told the boys. "First thing like it in a lot of years. A train clear over on her side, people all bust up—terrible day for the railroad."

"What can we do?" Del asked, almost frantic. "Someone's waiting for us at a station in Vermont."

"Wait is all you can do," said the porter. "Nobody goes anywhere till the line's clear. If your daddy's waiting for you in Vermont, he'll know all about this—they got TV in Vermont too."

"Not in that house," Del said in despair.

Tom looked outside and saw a few men in suits and ties passionately hurling rocks at cows.

As the hours went by, Tom felt his energy flicker like a dying candle. His eyes were heavy enough to drop from their sockets. All the colors in the train seemed lurid. Twice he went to the toilet and in a stink so concentrated that it was nearly visible allowed his stomach to erupt and leave him weightless. "I've got to get some sleep," he said when he had staggered back after the second time, and saw that Del was already there, folded up into himself like an exhausted bird.

When they finally moved again, the jolt of the carriage snapped Tom into wakefulness. Del still slept, curled in stationary flight.

The junction where the wreck had occurred was twenty miles down the track. For a moment the boys' carriage, the entire train, silenced: passengers crowded in the aisle to look out the windows but did not speak. A train the size of their own lay sprawled like a broken snake on the left side of the tracks. A gout of sparks blew into the air and died before the brilliant dots could fall on the few who still lay, covered up to the neck with blankets, on the sloping ground. One of the toppled carriages had been folded as neatly as paper; others were battered. Over the half-dozen policemen standing about, heavy gray smoke shifted in the humid air. Tom thought he could *smell* the wreck: oil and metal, the smell of heat and the smell of blood. The screams too. That was a smell like a taste in his own mouth, familiar and rancid.

7

Hilly Vale

Late that evening they reached a town called Springville, and Del said, "It's the next stop." He stood and pulled their suitcases off the luggage rack and arranged them in the aisle—he was being very businesslike and concentrated. Del sat up straight in his seat for fifteen minutes, not speaking, and for the last ten minutes stood by the door, looking straight ahead.

"Hey, what . . ." Tom said, but Del did not even blink.

"Hilly Vale," the metallic voice said. *"Hilly Vale. Please watch your step while leaving the train."*

Del shot him a glance, but Tom was already hauling his suitcase toward him.

They went down into hot, humid night. For a second Tom heard insect noises, a drumming and creaking and scratching and singing as loud as if they stood in the midst of jungle, and then the train started up and the insect noises disappeared. The station was so small it looked like a cartoon; yolky yellow light from overhead bulbs hugged it close. The train sailed into blackness and became a red dot vanishing around an invisible bend. Insects scratched and banged and whistled.

"Well?" Tom said. He felt as if he had been put down by the side of the road in Alaska or Peru.

Then the cacophony of insect sounds increased: drills, hammers, wrenches on pipes, musical saws, penny whistles, piano strings, whole boxes of tools dropped from a great height, doorbells, breaking bottles, miniature kamikaze aircraft, blows against flesh.

Del *shushed* him. For a second the two boys stood embraced by the yellow light in what should have been silence.

Mr. Thorpe stepped out of the blackness.

8

But no, it was not Mr. Thorpe, any more than the man on the train had been Skeleton Ridpath. He was tall, white-haired, dressed in a dark blue suit with wide chalky pin stripes. He had the sort of slight, elegant limp that makes limping look desirable. His nose was long and curved: the whole long squared-off face was powerful. Coleman Collins looked like an ambassador or an aged actor become so grand that he was offered no parts but those of financial pirates, grand dukes, and rascally Nazi generals. He smoothed down the longish white hair at the side of his head, and Tom thought that if you saw him playing a Latin teacher in a movie, you would know that his students would begin dying of a mysterious ailment late in the first reel. The limp became a definite waver, and Tom saw that the man was drunk.

"So the birds have come home," the magician said.

II

The Erl King

Del just picked up his bag and went straight for the car, the biggest, blackest Lincoln you ever saw. . . .

1

Wordlessly Del picked up his suitcase and began to walk toward the steps down into the station parking lot. In confusion so great it was almost like pain, Tom watched the smaller boy advancing away from him, and then looked back at the magician. Coleman Collins' icy face flickered a smile at him. *I didn't think he'd be so old,* Tom thought. *He's even older than Mr. Thorpe.*

"Say hello to your uncle," Collins said. Even slightly slurred by alcohol, his voice was resonant and cultured. "He has waited long enough to hear it."

Del stopped moving. In the instant of silence after he dropped his case, the insects began their symphony again. "I know. I'm sorry." Del half-turned to look at his uncle. "I *am* sorry. There was a big accident—a train went off the track . . ." Del turned savagely away again, and Tom recognized with astonishment that his friend was either in tears or on the verge of them.

"A big accident. A big big *big* accident, was it? Not just a teeny-weeny little one? Not just a little spilled coffee, a little bump on the tracks, a little messy commotion? Didn't stain your clothes, all that coffee flying about?"

"It wasn't our train," Tom said.

The magician focused his icy eyes on Tom—who was relieved to see, way down under all the layers of real and assumed anger, a layer of amusement. "Ah. The mystery deepens." He lolled back against the railing. "Surely one of you two boys can explain why an unrelated accident, all that coffee flying about on some *other* train, led to my sitting here for most of the day. Is that in your power, Del?"

Del turned and explained. Haltingly, badly, with what looked almost like stage fright—but he was explaining, he was talking to his uncle, and Tom felt the strange tension about them wilting from the air.

When Del was done, his uncle said, "And did you not see the spot, child? Didn't you sight the site? No visions of blood, or wrecked carriages, of dazed and crippled survivors, eager-beaver reporters, hard-eyed *Polizei?*" He startled both the boys by laughing. "No corpses, no—"

"Uncle Cole," Del said.

The magician glittered at him. "Yes, dear one?"

"Is Rose Armstrong here this summer?"

Collins pretended to consider the question. "Rose. Rose Armstrong. Now, I think I heard . . . was it a sick cousin in Missoula, Montana? Or was that some other Armstrong? *Yess.* Some dreary Armstrong person, not our little Vermont Rose. Yes, I do think that the girl should be taking part in our exercises. If we can ever get them begun, that is."

"She *is* here."

"She is. The real Rose."

"Uncle Cole," Del said. "I'm sorry we were so late."

"So it's come to that," Collins said. "Oh, dear. Let's have a look at something." He held out one palm, and a silver dollar appeared between his first and second fingers. He revolved his hand, and the coin had moved to the space between the next two fingers. When he turned the palm back to the boys, the coin had vanished. He showed the back of his hand: not there. But then it was in the other hand, moving itself so quickly between his fingers it seemed to have a life of its own. He tossed the coin in the air and caught it. "Can you do that yet?"

"Not as fast as you," Del said.

"Let's get home," said Coleman Collins.

2

The magician's car was the only one in the lot: a black Lincoln without a mark on it, long as a bank, and all the more impressive for being at least ten years old. Their bags went in the enormous trunk, the boys in the front seat beside Del's uncle. The interior of the Lincoln smelled of whiskey and cigarettes and, less strongly, of leather. Collins looked over Del's head at Tom as he rolled out of the lot. "So you are *the* Tom Flanagan."

"I'm Tom Flanagan, anyhow. *The* Tom Flanagan plays the piano."

"And modest and good—and very good at the work, I gather. Welcome to Vermont. I hope we'll give you a summer to remember."

"Yes."

They were gliding into an area of dark little shops, vacant gas stations. The magician seemed to be grinning at him. "I live for these summers, you know. It could have been different—Del might have told you something about me. But I had only one ambition. Can you guess? To be the best magician in the world. And to *stay* the best magician in the world. Which is what I have done. Letters—I get mail from all over the world, asking for my advice. Can they meet me? Can they study with me? No, no, no, no. I have only one pupil. Two, now. That, and the knowledge—it's enough."

"The knowledge?"

"Oh, yes, the knowledge. You'll see. You'll *experience*. And that is all I will say at present."

Now they were on a wide main road, cutting through the center of the small darkened town; soon they swerved off onto a narrow road which led directly into deep wood. Collins held a bottle between his thighs, and lifted it now and then to sip. Before long the trees blotted out the stars.

3

The narrow road twisted through the forest, and when it began to ascend, split into two forks. Collins took the left fork—this was unpaved, and rose sharply. After a few minutes, Tom was dimly aware of a field on his side of the road: a gray horse, nearly invisible in the murk, drifted up to a fence, followed by two black shapes that must have been horses also. Then the trees closed in again.

"What's it like here in the winter?"

"Snowed in, little bird. Very beautiful."

They continued to rise on the narrow bumpy road.

Tom asked, "Do you have neighbors?"

"All of my neighbors are in my head," Collins said, and laughed again. He glanced at Del. "And is it good to be back, accidents and upsets notwithstanding?"

"Oh, yes," Del breathed.

"Ah."

After perhaps twenty minutes, Collins turned the car into a paved drive which looped back and then made a wide descending curve interrupted by big iron gates set into high brick gateposts. From the posts, a wall fanned into the trees on either side.

"You'll excuse my precautions, Thomas," Cole Collins said, gently stopping the car. "I am an old man, all alone in these woods. Of course vandals can still come across the lake in the winter, to get at the summer houses." He

propped the bottle on the seat and got out to punch a
series of numbered buttons on one of the posts. The gates
slid open.

The car moved forward, rounded a bend, and they
could see the house. It looked like a Victorian summer
house which had been added on to by generations of
owners: a three-story frame building with gables and
corbels and pointed windows, flanked by more modern
wings. It took Tom a moment to see why these were
odd—the lines of white board were unbroken by windows. Lights hung on the wood illuminated bright circles
on the windowless facades; lights hung in the trees on
either side of the house. It looked faintly like a compound—faintly like something else.

"The school," Tom said. "I mean . . . it sort of reminds
me of our school."

Del looked at him in surprise.

"Lucky boy," Collins murmured. He opened the door.
"Leave your things in the car. Someone will bring them in
later." He staggered a bit, getting out of the car, but
tucked the half-empty bottle under his arm with an almost
soldierly snap. "Step lively, step lightly, but step inside.
We can't hang around outside all night."

Tom got out and saw Collins' tall figure outlined against
the vast house. Strings of lights shone from widely
separated trees deep in the woods; others were so close
together as to remind him of the circles of light through
which Jimmy Durante walked at the end of his show, just
after saying, "Good night, Mrs. Calabash, wherever you
are." There were many more lights than he had seen from
the car.

"Why do you light up the forest like that?" he asked.

"Why? So I can see what's coming and what's going,"
Collins said. "And what big eyes you have, Grandmother.
Ready?"

Collins opened the front door and stood to one side to let
them enter. Del walked in before Tom, and when Tom
went through into the dim interior, his friend faced him
with a shining, exalted face. Then he saw why. Candles
blazed all over the entry: candles burned on the little table

stacked with newspapers, candles burned on the shelf where Coleman Collins dropped his car keys.

"The fuse for this part of the building blew, I suppose," Collins said. "Someone's probably fixing it now. Nice of them to get out these candles for us. They give a welcoming glow, don't you think? Or do you think they look too much like Halloween?"

"You knew," Del said. "Just like Registration Day— like Tom said, at school. You *knew*."

"I don't know what you are talking about," Collins said. "I must take a bath and lie down for a bit. There will be some food in your rooms." He leaned against the wall of the entry, supporting his shoulders on the shelf, and crossed his arms over his chest. Tom got another shining glance from Del. "Wash up in the bathroom down here. Then go up. Tom's room is right next to yours, Del. He will be in the connecting room. When you have eaten, come downstairs and I will see you in the Little Theater. Can you still find it?"

"Sure I can."

"Stupendous. I'll see you there at . . ." He looked at his watch. "Shall we say eleven?"

Del nodded.

"Fine. Tom, there will not be much of a view of the lake at this hour, but tomorrow you should be able to see it. A very tempting vista." Again there was a suggestion of mockery and unstated meanings in his voice. He nodded and began to mount the stairs. Halfway up, he wobbled backward, and the boys stood nailed to the floor, fearing that he was about to topple down, but he righted himself with a hand against the wall, said, "Oops," and continued upward.

Del shook his head in relief. "Let's go wash our hands."

He led Tom to a small bathroom just off the entry. While Del lathered his hands in the sink, Tom waited in the doorway. "Are the woods always lighted up like that?"

"First time. But those candles! I was right."

"About it being like school this time."

"We'll see," Del said. "Your turn."

"Well, I hope it isn't like school." Tom edged around Del in the little bathroom.

"Hey, did you know this was a haunted house?" Del asked playfully.

"Come on, Florence."

Del pushed a button beneath the light switch, and the radiance in the bathroom abruptly turned purple. In the sink, Tom's hands shone a lighter, more vibrant purple. He looked in the mirror—Del was laughing—and saw his face, the same shade of purple, disappearing under a hideous mask which seemed to stretch forward from the glass. The effect was half-comic, half-frightening. The face, with distorted rubbery lips and dead skin, the very face of greed, of acquisitiveness sucked down into pure hunger, looked at him with his own eyes. It pushed forward slowly, slowly, and became the only thing in the room. Tom finally jerked backward, unable to face the ugly thing down, and banged into Del. The face hung vibrating in the air.

"I know." Del laughed. "But it just comes up close and then melts back down into the mirror. It's a great trick. The first time I saw it, I howled like hell." He pushed the button, and Tom was again standing in an ordinary wallpapered half-bath. His face was itself, familiar but pale.

"Uncle Cole calls it the Collector," Del said. "Don't ask me how it works. Let's go up and eat."

"The Collector," Tom echoed, now really shaken. That was just how it had looked.

Their rooms, in the left wing of the house, were windowless, bright, incongruously modern and "Scandinavian": they could have been rooms in an expensive motel. Creamy off-white walls hung with colorful but bland abstract paintings, neat single beds covered in blue corduroy, thick white carpets that showed their footprints. White louvered doors swung open onto deep closets where their clothes had already been hung or folded, their suitcases packed away at the back. White desks with lamps stood against the walls. In Del's room, connected to Tom's by sliding wooden pocket doors, a table had been set for two. A crystal decanter half-filled with red wine stood beside covered dishes and a salad bowl.

"Boy," Tom said, smelling the steaks.

Del marched to the table and sat down, snapping his napkin onto his lap. He poured from the decanter into Tom's glass and his own.

"He lets you drink wine?"

"Of course he does. He can hardly be puritanical about drink, can he? And besides that, he really believes dinner isn't complete without wine." Del sipped, and smiled. "He used to put water in it when I was younger. There isn't any water in this."

"Well, this isn't much like school," Tom said.

The steaks were still warm, bloodred in the center and delicately charred on the outside. Other covered dishes concealed a little hill of spinach, mounded mushrooms, french fries. Tom lifted his glass and sipped: a dusty, stony, slightly grapy flavor, intensely pleasing—the more it sat in his mouth, the more taste it gave him. "So that's what good wine is like," he said.

"That's what Margaux is like anyhow," said Del, busily chewing. "He's giving us something good because this is our first night." A moment later he said, "He *knew*. He knew about the candles. I couldn't be sure before. But he knows everything that happened."

"Anyhow, your Rose Armstrong will be around," Tom said, and Del's face flushed with an increase of pleasure.

"This is going to be the perfect summer," he said.

When they left Del's room to go downstairs, they paused a minute to look out one of the big windows in the hallway. These gave a view of a long expanse of wood; the spotlights or torches illuminated a congregation of branches or slabs of boulder, holes into the wood. Where the wood ended, a black non-thing that must have been the lake began. Tom saw iron railings dripping down a cliff behind the house. Far off in the woods bordering the other side of the lake, similar lights burned—fuzzy as Japanese lanterns. "Time to get downstairs," Del said, and moved away from the window. To Tom it looked like the setting for a party yet to begin, full of promises and anticipations. "Come on," said Del, eager to be down-

stairs, and Tom gave it one last look and saw the party's
first guest. A wolf, or what looked like a wolf. It came
into one of the circles of light, tongue lolling, and stared
toward the house. Far off, centered in the light, the wolf
seemed staged, posed as for a picture. It seemed like a
signpost, a hint. "Hey!" Tom said.

"Come *on*," Del said from the staircase. "We have to
get to the Little Theater."

"Coming," Tom said. The wolf was gone. But had it
been there at all? A wolf, in Vermont?

Going back down, he noticed that the house was more
complicated than it looked. At the top of the staircase an
old-fashioned swinging door barred them from a large
black space in which Tom made out the shape of a tall
door. "What's back there?"

"Oh, my uncle's room. We have to get down."

They rattled down the stairs and turned back into the
body of the original house. They passed a living room
where a lamp burned on a table between two couches
covered in an unexpectedly feminine fabric, passed the
entrance to a galleylike kitchen. Del pushed open another
door which Tom had assumed led outside; but it took
them into another "motel" corridor, carpeted dark
brown, its ceiling illuminated by indirect lighting. At the
beginning of this corridor, another hall jutted off to the
rear and ended at a crossbarred wooden door as impressive as Laker Broome's. "And what's back there?"

"I don't know. He never lets me go in there."

Del bustled down the corridor until he came to a black
door set in a recess lighted by a single downspot. A brass
plate had been screwed into the door just above the boys'
heads, but it was blank. Del quickly checked his watch.
"God. A whole minute to spare."

Now what? Tom wondered. An office like Lake the
Snake's? A concrete-block classroom overlooking Santa
Rosa Boulevard?

But what he saw when Del opened the door was at first
a steeply banked jewel-box theater with perhaps fifty
seats. Though empty, it still seemed full of life, and a half-
second later Tom saw that the walls had been painted with
ranks of people in chairs—people with rapt faces, one of
them drinking from a cup through a straw, one pawing a
box of chocolates. Then there was something grotesque in

their midst . . . But Del was pushing him into the first row and turning him around.

"This is wild," he said. They faced a tiny stage. A polished table and a Shaker chair stood before brown velvet curtains. He looked quickly over his shoulder to find what had briefly caught his eye, and saw it immediately. It was the Collector, black-suited, a few rows back and to the side of the man drinking through a straw: pushing his rapt, greedy face forward, wishing to devour whatever he saw on the tiny stage; a grotesque joke. Then Tom was startled by the thought that the grotesque figure resembled Skeleton Ridpath.

His eye caught another surprise just as he heard the clicking of a door behind the velvet curtains: a few seats away from the Collector, a group of men with outdated but elegant clothing and neat beards, cigars stuck in their mouths, a group of raffish bucks out on the town . . . Del jabbed him in the ribs, and he snapped his head back just as Cole Collins parted the curtains and sat in the Shaker chair. His handsome, slightly hooded blue eyes were glazed, but his face was pink. Instead of the suit, the magician wore a dark green pullover from the top of which frothed a green-and-red scarf, beautifully fitted to his neck. He smiled, taking in the whole room, and Tom felt the presence of the painted men behind him. The back of his neck prickled.

"The magician and his audience," Del's uncle said with the air of one who opens a treasure chest. "A subject you should consider. What is their relationship? That of an actor and those he seeks to move, to entertain? That of an athlete and those before whom he demonstrates his skill? Not quite, though it has elements of both." His smile had never left his face. "An audience always fights a magician, boys. It is never truly on his side. It feels hostility toward him: because it knows that it is being fooled."

No, it can't be, Tom thought. They left the train in New York, they are part of some other story. And that awful joke can't have anything to do with Skeleton.

"The magician must make them relish it. He is the storyteller whose only story is himself, and every man jack in the audience, every drunk, every dolt, every clever skeptic, every doubter, is looking for the chink in his story that he can use to destroy him."

Tom forced himself to look straight ahead: he had to

keep his neck rigid by willpower. He felt as though Mr.
Peet and the others were moving in their seats.

"The magician is a general with an army full of
deserters and traitors. To keep their loyalty, he must
inspire and entertain, frighten and cajole, baffle and
command. And when he has done that, he can lead
them."

In the midst of his tension, Tom felt a growing area of
tiredness, and realized that the wine and Collins' tirade
were making him sleepy.

The smile was taut now, and directed straight at Tom.
"I am saying that the practice of magic is the courting of
self-destruction—that is one of its great secrets. The
closer you allow yourself to come to that truth, the greater
you may become. Listen: magic is used only to inspire
fear and to grant wishes—even those you do not wish to
have. In itself it is not important. Enough."

He gave Tom that smile like a glare. "Do you want to
learn to fly? Would you like to leave the earth behind,
boy?"

"You called us birds," Tom said. And thought for the
first time in months of the Ventnor owl.

Collins nodded. "Are you afraid?"

"Yes," Tom said. He had a terrible urge to yawn, and
felt his lips stretching.

"You don't have the *beginning* of an idea what magic
is," Collins hissed.

Tom thought: I can't spend all summer with this
crazyman.

"But you will learn. You are a unique boy, Tom
Flanagan. I knew it when I first heard about you.
Shadowland will give you every gift it has, because you
will be able to accept them. And you are exactly the right
age. *Exactly!*"

He looked from Tom to Del, back again, his eyes like
marbles. "What experiences you two have before you. I
envy you—I would chop my hands off to have what you
take for granted. Now. A few, ah, ground rules. Do you
remember everything I have said so far? Do you understand what I said?"

They nodded simultaneously.

"The magician is a general in charge of what?"

"Traitors," Del said.

His eyes full of triumph and the windy spaces of drunkenness, the magician looked at Tom alone. "Ground rules. The rules you obey, in this house. Did you see the wooden door set back in a little half-hallway on the way to this theater?"

Tom nodded.

"You are forbidden to open that door. You are free to wander where you like, except for that room and my room. Which is in back of the swinging doors at the top of the stairs. Understood?"

Tom nodded again, felt Del beside him nod his head.

"That is number one, then. In this theater we practice cards and coins, the close-up work. Tomorrow we will see Le Grand Théâtre des Illusions, and that is where you will learn to fly. If, that is, you give yourself entirely to me." Then, abruptly: "Your father is dead?"

"Yes," Tom whispered.

"Then for the summer I am your father. That is number two. In this house I am the law. When I say you cannot go outside, you stay in. And when I tell you to stay in your rooms, you will obey me. There will always be a reason, I assure you. Okay. Questions?"

Del sat as silent as a stone; Tom asked, "Are there any wolves in Vermont? Have you ever seen one?"

Collins tilted his head. "Of course not," and gave an equivocal, playful glance. Then he relaxed back into his chair. "Did you ever hear the story about how all stories began?"

Both boys shook their heads. In Tom, there was a sudden, strong resistance to all about him. This man was not his father. His stories would be lies: there was nothing about him that was not dangerous.

"This story," Collins said, plucking delicately at a fold of the scarf and exposing another quarter-inch of its pattern above the green velour, "is—might be, rather— yes, *might* be about treachery. And it might be about coming close to the destructiveness of magic. You decide."

4

"The Box and the Key"

"A long, long time ago, in a northern country where snow fell eight months of the year, a boy lived alone with his mother in a little wooden house at the foot of a steep hill. There they lived a decent, purposeful, hardworking life. Chores always demanded to be done, provisions to be salted away, cords of wood to be cut and stacked. There was endless work, little of what boys today would call fun, but much joy. The boy's entire world was the snug wooden house with its wood fires and waxed floors, the animals he cared for, his work and his mother and the land they inhabited. The life made a perfect circle, a perfect orb, in which every action and every emotion was useful, in tune with itself and each other action and emotion.

"One day the boy's mother told him to go out and play in the snow while she did her baking. I imagine that she did not want him dodging around her skirts, pestering her for a taste of what she was mixing. She dressed him warmly, in heavy sweaters and thick socks and boots and a big blue coat and a woolen cap and said, 'Go out now and play for an hour.'

"The boy asked, 'May I climb the hill?'

"'You may go all the way to the top if you like,' said his mother. 'But give me an hour to do my baking.'

"So out he went—he loved to climb the hill, though sometimes his mother decided that marauding animals made it dangerous. From the top he could see his little house, its chimney and windows, and the entire little valley where it sat, that cozy little house in a deep northern valley where dark firs grew straight out of the snow.

"It took him half an hour, but finally he had struggled up to the top of the hill. Looking one way, he could see hill after hill stretching away into a cold northern infinity. And when he looked the other direction, he saw right down into his own valley. There, now looking like a dollhouse, was his home. Smoke puffed from its chimney, drifted and blew, and his mother crossed and recrossed the kitchen window, carrying mixing bowls and trays for the oven. It looked so warm, that little house with its busy woman and its drifting, blowing column of smoke.

"The boy alone on the snowy hill decided to dig. Perhaps he thought he would build a fort under the snow. He scooped out a handful of snow, then another, and all the time he was conscious of what lay down in the valley—the warm house, his mother moving back and forth across the kitchen window.

"He dug for a time, looking back and forth from his hole in the snow to his house and his mother, and soon realized that he had little time left in which to play. He looked back down at his house and his mother in the window, and dug a few more cold wet handfuls out.

"It was time to begin going back. He watched a curl of smoke lift from the chimney.

"Then he heard a voice in his mind saying: *Dig out another handful.*

"He looked back at his warm house, and he put his hand deep into the snow.

"His fingers touched something hard and smooth and colder than ice. He looked back at the house, where his mother was taking hot cakes from the tray with a long-handled baker's spatula; and then he looked back into the hole he had made, and dug quickly around, feeling for the sides and edges of whatever he had found.

"It was a box—a silver box, so cold it burned his hands right through his gloves. That voice in his mind, which was his own voice, said: *Where there is a box, there is a key.*

"So he looked back at the house and knew its warmth . . . saw the smoke lazing from the chimney . . . saw his mother glance toward the window. And he took one hand and just delicately scraped his fingers across the bottom of the hole.

"His fingers turned over a little silver key.

"Where there is a key, there is a lock, his own voice said within its head.

"He revolved the cold silver box in his hands and saw

how the lock was set into a complicated pattern of scrollwork just before the lip of the top. He looked back once more at the warm house, his mother wiping her hands on her apron before the window. And he put the little key into the lock.

"The box clicked.

"Then for the last time he looked back at his warm house and his mother, at all he had known, and he raised the lid of the box."

Coleman Collins lifted his hands, palms facing about a foot apart, and suddenly swooped them upward. "Every story in the world, every story ever told, blew up out of the box. Princes and princesses, wizards, foxes and trolls and witches and wolves and woodsmen and kings and elves and dwarves and a beautiful girl in a red cape, and for a second the boy saw them all perfectly, spinning silently in the air. Then the wind caught them and sent them blowing away, some this way and some that."

He put his hands back on the table, smiling; he looked drunk as an owl to Tom, but the resonant voice coiled in the sleepy spaces of his mind, echoing even when Collins was not talking. "But I wonder if some of those stories might not have blown into other stories. Maybe the wind tumbled those stories all together, and switched the trolls with the kings and put foxes' heads on the princes and mixed up the witch with the beautiful girl in the red cape. I often wonder if that happened."

He pushed himself away from the table and stood up. "That was your bedtime story. Go up to your rooms and go to bed. I don't want you to leave your rooms until tomorrow morning. Run along." He winked, and disappeared through the curtains, leaving them momentarily alone in the empty theater.

Then he poked his disembodied-looking head through the join of the curtains. "I mean now. Upstairs. Lead the way, Mr. Nightingale." The head jerked back through the curtains.

A moment later it reappeared, thrust forward like a jack-in-the-box. "Wolves, and those who see them, are shot on sight. Unless it is a *lupus in fabula*, who appears when spoken of." The head opened its mouth in a soundless laugh, showing two rows of slightly stained and irregular teeth, and popped back through the curtain.

"Lupus in fabula?" Del said, turning to Tom.

"Mr. Thorpe used to say it sometimes. The wolf in the story."

"Who appears when . . ."

"Spoken of," Tom said miserably. "It doesn't mean real wolves, it means . . . Oh, forget it."

5

The Wolf in the Story

"This isn't like any other summer," Del said as they passed the short hall which ended at the crossbarred door. "He never told me a story before. I liked it. Didn't you?"

"Sure, I guess," Tom said, pausing. "Weren't you ever curious about what was behind that thing?"

Del shrugged, looked uneasy. "You mean, I should have looked just because he told me not to?"

"Not exactly. But what's so important that we aren't even allowed to see it? I just wondered if you were curious."

"I never had time to be curious," Del said. "He said upstairs. We're supposed to stay in our rooms."

"Does he do that a lot, order you to stay in your room all night?"

"Sometimes." Del firmly pushed open the door to the older part of the house and began to march past the kitchen and living room.

"But wouldn't you anyway? I mean, why make it an order? Why would we get out of bed in the middle of the night, go wandering in the dark? . . . If he makes it an order, he's just making us think about doing it. See what I mean?"

"Well, I'm going to sleep," Del said, going up the stairs.

"And what if you want a glass of water? What if you have to take a leak?"

"There's a bathroom attached to your room."

"What if you want to look outside? We don't have any windows?"

"Look, aren't you tired?" Del said furiously. "I'm

going to sleep. I'm not going to parade around and look at stuff I'm not supposed to see, I'm not going to look at the stars, I'm just going to bed. You do what you want to."

"Don't get so angry."

"I am angry, damn you," Del said, and moved away from Tom to open his door and disappear inside.

Tom went to his door. Del was tearing his shirt off over his head, not bothering to unbutton it. Their beds had been turned down. "So why are you so all-fired hot all of a sudden?"

"I'm going to bed."

"Del."

His friend softened. "Look. I'm tired enough to drop. It's our first night." Del sat on his bed and kicked off his shoes. He undid his belt, stood up, and pushed his pants down. "And I'm going to close these doors so I don't have to know if you're going to get into trouble."

"But Del, he *wants* us to think about—"

"You're tired, aren't you?" Del said, tugging one of the pocket doors out of the stub wall.

"Yes."

"Then go to bed and forget it." He went to the other stub wall and pushed its door across, cutting off his room from Tom's.

"Del?" Tom said to the door.

"I'll see you in the morning. I'm too tired to think about anything."

Tom turned away. His own room glowed: bed so neat it appeared to have been opened by can opener, soft lights. The second Rex Stout book he had brought in his suitcase lay on the bedside table. He touched the switch beside the door, and the overhead lights darkened. The light beside the book made that end of the room, the book and the bed and the lamp, as inviting as a cave.

He undressed quickly to his underpants and slipped into bed. Tom picked up the Rex Stout book and turned to the first page. After a few minutes the print swam, and then seemed to make unrelated but pointed comments about some other story. He realized that he was dreaming about reading. Tom turned off the light and rolled into his cool pillow.

An indeterminate length of time later the barking of

dogs brought him back up to consciousness. First one dog, then two. Sounds of a fight followed. A door slammed somewhere, men cursed, one dog screamed in rage or pain. A man shouted *"Bastard!"* and the dog's sound of agony turned into a yelp. Tom sat up in bed. His hand was asleep, and he rubbed it until it throbbed. Downstairs, men were moving with heavy footsteps across the floor, going in and out. A glass broke, the other dog began to growl. "Del?" Tom said. Several loud male voices raised at once.

Tom went to the pocket doors and pushed one a few inches back into the wall. Del lay face down in the dark, breathing deeply. Tom slid the door to again and groped across the room to the hall door, expecting that it would be locked.

But it was not: he opened it a crack. The lights in the hall dimly glowed. Now he could hear the voices and the dogs more clearly. The men sounded as brutish as the animals. Tom opened the door wide and saw himself reflected in the big window opposite. The lights in the woods shone through his body. He stepped out into the hall. Downstairs, at the back of the house, a man shouted, "Get that mutt over—*god damn*—shake that damn . . ." It was not the voice of Coleman Collins.

A pool of light suddenly appeared on the flagstone terrace beneath his window, outlining a man's tall shadow. Tom stepped back from the window. A burly man in an army jacket stepped into view, hauling a large black dog on a chain. The dog turned to snarl at him and the man jumped forward and cuffed its mouth. "Jesus!" the man bawled. Protruding from one of the pockets of the green army jacket was the neck of a bottle. He dropped the chain, vanished back under the window for a moment, and reappeared with a shovel. He feinted at the dog with it, set it down, and vanished into the house again. When he came back he carried a set of long-handled tongs with metal-banded clamps at the end. This too clattered down onto the flagstones, and the man swaggered back toward the house, shouting something. He had a short bristly brown beard. One of the men from the train: Tom's heart nearly stopped, and his eyes jumped up to the illuminated woods.

Oh, no.

On a flat boulder directly under a light, so far away Tom could not see details of face or clothing, a slight figure in a long blue wrap and red cap set on blond hair was holding up a small glittering box. The little figure wonderingly turned the box over in its hands. Then the head turned and looked directly at him. He backed away in panic, and the boy's head looked aimlessly away, first to one side, then to the other. *"Del,"* Tom whispered. He looked back at the boy on the rock. *"Del!"* The boy was still turning the box over and over in his hands. Tom sidled over to Del's door and rapped his knuckles against it twice. "Get out here," he said, only just not whispering. He knocked again—the noise downstairs was so loud they would not hear him if he took a hammer to the door. The blond boy set the box down on the slab and dreamily brushed his fingers along the rock. "You have to see this," Tom said, speaking almost normally.

The door opened a crack. "Go away. Go in your room."

"Look," Tom said.

Now the boy held up an object that must have been a silver key.

"Oh," Del said, and opened his door all the way and came a step out into the hall. The men downstairs roared.

On his little stage of rock, the boy held the key to the box.

"He wanted us to see it," Tom whispered. In his pajamas, Del hugged himself beside him. One of the black dogs screeched again—had the bearded man struck it with the tongs? He did not want to get close enough to the window to find out.

The boy in the blue coat put the box to his ear and then held it out at arm's length. He must have used his thumbs to pop open the lid.

Evil black smoke gouted from the box. They were able to see the figure on the rock dropping it, then the smoke obliterated the entire scene in a coiling, billowing mass.

"Like our show," Tom murmured. "When the smoke blows away, no boy."

"That wasn't a boy," Del said, going back into his room.

"It was a *girl?*" Tom asked.

"That was Rose Armstrong. Now go to bed." Del turned around and closed his door.

Tom glanced back at the light: the last vestiges of black smoke drifted over a deserted rock. The leaves around it shook. Down below the windows, the dogs continued their argument.

A man's loud voice rose: "Get that *fucking . . .*"

Another answered: "Goddamn soon. Okay with you?"

"Oh, everything's dandy with me."

Coleman Collins, very clear: "Are you finally ready?"

The downstairs door slammed open and shadows sprang across the flags, immediately followed by a crowd of men, most of them carrying shovels, two of them pulling the chained dogs. Coleman Collins came behind, now wearing a bright plaid shirt, wash pants, and laced boots; a lumberjack. "Give me that bottle," he ordered. The man in the army jacket pulled the bottle from his pocket. Collins tilted it over his mouth and handed it back. "Okay. I'll be back after I . . ." *Check on my guests?* Tom hurried back into his bedroom.

He jumped into bed, pulled the sheets over himself, and waited. *I might even go to sleep,* he told himself, *and not have to do anything else.* But his heart drummed, his nerves simmered. He heard the sounds of men moving randomly around on the flags, then the sound of boots coming up the stairs.

Tom stiffened. The boots came along the hall to Del's door and paused. Del's door opened. A second's silence; Del's door closed and the boots moved along to his own door. It opened, and light filtered into his room. "Keep your head under your wing," Collins said softly: it sounded almost tender. The door closed, and the room was black again. Tom heard Collins moving back down the hall, down the stairs.

He waited only a second, then jumped out of bed and groped for his shirt and pants. His feet found his loafers. When he opened the door and went on his knees to the window, he saw the men and the dogs heading out across the flagstones to the woods. Some of the men held flaming torches. Behind them, Collins strode along, carrying a knobbly walking stick. As soon as they had left the flagstones, he trotted to the staircase and began to descend.

6

In the entry the candles still burned, now only inches from their holders. When he turned back toward the body of the house, he saw weak light spilling from the living room into the hall. He saw that he was passing a row of tall posters in frames—a series of theatrical bills behind glass, like time capsules. They loomed beside him, the glass reflecting a little of the dim light from the living room, a little more of Tom's own outline. In the silence, he felt observed.

Chairs in the living room had been shoved here and there, cigars still burned in ashtrays, glasses stood empty on the wooden tables beside the couches and on the coffee table.

The glass doors at the far side of the living room were open onto the flagstone patio. Across the clutter of the wide room, Tom saw the lights of the men's torches winding through the woods. He stepped onto soft thick carpet. Cigar smoke drifted through the air.

Would he keep his head under his wing? He dodged furniture, going toward the open glass doors, and caught beneath the cigar smoke the odors of trees, earth, and night. Head under your wing, Tom?

"Nuts to that," he whispered, and stepped through the open glass doors onto the flagstones.

7

The torches bobbed through the woods a hundred yards ahead, appearing and disappearing as the men who held them skirted trees. Tom could hear their loud voices melting into the snarling of the dogs, and sensed their anticipation without hearing their words. They were going off to the left side of the lake, along the curve of the hill where he and Del had seen Rose Armstrong.

He left the flags, wondering if they were looking for her. On his right a long rickety iron staircase cut straight down the hill to where the moon laid a silvery path across the lake. Tom descended as the men had, his heart stopping when the iron ladder shook and trembled, to a small beach. A building that must have been a boathouse hovered black against the dark water; a few feet from the shape of the boathouse, a white pier thrust out into the lake. No, that scene on the illuminated stage of rock had been public: whatever Mr. Peet and the others were doing now was not.

Still, he wondered what men like that would do if they caught a girl. Then he wondered what they would do if they caught him.

Fortunately, he could follow the torches and keep far enough behind so that they would never see him. He looked back as soon as he got into the woods and saw that the lights of the house gave him a clear beacon for his return.

Twice he walked straight into trees, scraping his forehead and nearly knocking himself down. The moon, sometimes so bright that he could see the blades of rough grass as silvery individual waves in a leaning, breathed-upon ocean, at times abruptly receded behind tall black trees and left him wandering in a black vastness punctuated only by the weaving torches up ahead.

Like Hansel, he kept looking back, seeing the house retreat into a dense, dreamy integument of branches and bushy leaves. Before long the house was less a beacon than a half-dozen scattered points of light chinking the forest.

This was nature of a kind he had met only in books—nature fighting for its own breath, crowded and tangled, populated with a hundred thrusting and bending shapes. Every step brought him near fingers and arms of wood reaching out for him; his loafers slipped on wet moss. The third time he walked into a tree, the moon having temporarily departed, the tree did knock him down.

Then the lights of torches disappeared. Tom stood absolutely still, afraid to turn around—if he lost his direction, he would be lost indeed. He thought: *Insects.* Since leaving the house, he had not heard one; just hours ago, at the station, their noises had crowded the darkness.

From over the rise where the men had disappeared with the dogs and torches, indistinguishable shouts erupted.

Very slowly he went forward, his hands out before his face. Something, an animal or bird, chattered at him from far up: he bent back his neck, and furry needles brushed his forehead. The thought that it was a spider sent him vaulting forward. His foot snagged a root immovable as an anvil, and Tom went sprawling face and elbows first into mushy loam.

He was conscious of a thudding heart, a muddy face, and a drenched shirt. He rubbed his hands over his face and crawled the rest of the way forward.

Finally the voices were very near. He was on his belly, inching up the little slope behind which the torches had vanished. A man said, "Buster's ready." The dogs grumbled; some of the men laughed. Coleman Collins said in a sharp voice, "Take care with that fire, Root. You want to be able to see."

"Umz plug whuzza right place?" asked someone in a thick voice—presumably Root, for Collins answered, "I said it was, didn't I? Just watch your tinder. *Be careful where you squirt that stuff!* We want a blaze, not a conflagration."

Crawling forward, so scared of being seen that his breath froze in his throat, Tom could now see the lights of the torches—or of Root's conflagration—reddening the trees before him.

"Herbie, you sure this is the set?" asked Mr. Peet.

"Of course this is it," Collins said.

Herbie?

Tom crawled to the top of the rise and peeked around the trunk of a red maple set glowing by the fire.

Mr. Peet and Coleman Collins stood together beside a leaping fire tended by a thick-bodied man in a yellow T-shirt and baggy carpenter's pants—Root. His head was shaved nearly down to the skull. The others had jabbed their torches into the soft ground and were furiously digging. Dirt flew. "There's your set right there," said Collins, pointing to a grassy mound on the other side of the fire. In his lumberjack shirt, his face ruddied by the fire, the magician looked extravagantly healthy, muscular as Mr. Peet. "Where'd you get the dogs this time, Thorn?" he asked.

The man in the army jacket came from the other side of the mound, holding both black dogs by the chains around their necks. "Same old shit. Paid 'im fifty-five apiece—claims they're the strongest he had. Couldn't get no bulls." Thorn's face had been battered into a Halloween jack-o'-lantern. "Bulls is best, for this."

"Bulldogs or terriers," Collins said.

"Bulls is best," Thorn repeated.

"Thorn, you're an idiot. Give me that bottle again." Thorn sulkily fetched the whiskey from his pocket. Collins drank and passed the bottle to Mr. Peet. "Those two will work out fine. I'm pleased. Now, give the chains to Root and help with the pit."

"Yeah," Thorn said. He swaggered away to do as he was told.

"Hey, let's send the little one in," Root called.

"Jesus *Christ*," one of the men shoveling dirt said. "Why not give us a break, huh? Or come over here and shovel for yourself, shithead."

"Now, . . ." Mr. Peet said warningly but too late.

Root had wrapped the chains around a tree and was charging the man who held a shovel. The others stopped digging and watched the man plant his feet and swipe at Root with the flat of the shovel. Hit in the side, Root went down. "Shithead," the man said.

"Okay, Pease," Mr. Peet said calmly. "Root, just hold the dogs. It's too early to try them out. Keep that fire stoked up."

"Fucking animal asshole," muttered the one called Pease, taking up his shovel and digging so hard that dirt flew nearly all the way to Root.

Half an hour later, the four men digging had opened up a pit almost five feet deep and four feet long. Root sullenly jerked at the dogs' chains whenever he inexpertly tossed more wood on the fire. Tom watched all this, now and then nearly dozing, mystified. What was it the dogs were to be tried out on? What was the long trench for? It looked uncomfortably like a grave.

Finally the magician said, "Let's get them stirred up.

Seed, you and Rock go to work on the set for a while."

"*Yeah*," said one of the diggers, a fat bearded man who resembled a depraved Burl Ives. He grinned, showing a hockey player's gap where his front teeth should have been.

Seed sprang up out of the trench, followed by another man. They carried their shovels to the mound and immediately began pitching earth from it.

"Faster, faster," ordered Mr. Peet. "We want them to know you're there."

"Shit, they hear us okay," said Seed, displaying the gap in his teeth.

"You know how many there are, Herbie?" asked Rock.

"One is enough," Collins answered. "Look, let's get that other man out of the pit. Snail, you go over to the other side."

Snail, Seed, Rock, Pease, Thorn, Root: were those names?

The one called Snail crawled from the pit, went to the mound, hefted his shovel and slammed the flat of the blade down onto the earth. "Shake 'em up good," he said, and began to pitch dirt as earnestly as Seed and Rock.

They resembled three monstrous dwarfs, these heavy-set men. Snail and Rock had vast tattooed biceps; and when Snail pulled off his shirt, Tom saw that tattoos blanketed his chest: a white skull with black eyeholes housed the tail of a glittering, scaly dragon with eagle's wings.

"Mr. Snail, move those wings for me," ordered Cole Collins, and the tattooed man laughed and dug more ferociously.

"A goddamned *hole*," Snail shouted. "Here's one of the goddamned *holes*."

Thorn jumped out of the pit, bellowing like a lunatic, and charged toward Snail; instead of attacking him, as Tom feared, jolted fully awake by the man's din, Thorn jabbed his shovel in the earth next to Snail and began to peel back the earth over the entrance to the burrow.

"Get that little one in there, Root," said Mr. Peet.

"Wish we had a bull," Thorn said from his jack-o'-lantern face. Root pulled the smaller dog up, untied its chain, and pointed it to the uncovered hole. "Get in there, mutt," Root said, but the dog needed no command: it streaked into the hole.

"Now, get the other one ready," said Mr. Peet. "I'll bet anybody twenty it comes out in under a minute." He looked at his watch, and Thorn said, "Twenty."

Snail's tattoos widened and trembled in the firelight. The effect was so distracting that it was a moment before Tom realized that he was laughing. "Ground-pounder."

"A minute," Thorn said, shrugging his shoulders.

Yelps, growls, barks came from the hole. Then the sound of screaming that Tom had heard in the bedroom.

"Watch your tail, boy," said Mr. Peet, and a second later the dog came boiling out of the hole. Bright red lines bisected its head.

"Twenty from Thorn," said Mr. Peet. "Send in the other one," and Root positioned the second quivering dog. Pease and Seed, the fat one like Burl Ives, began scrabbling with their shovels on the top of the mound.

For hours it seemed—Tom lay at the base of the red maple, dozing off and waking to some new horror—the dogs nipped into the tunnels Pease and Seed uncovered in the "set," emerged whining and bleeding, were sent back in. Money flowed among the eight men, most of it going to Root, Mr. Peet, and Collins. During one of his spells of wakefulness Tom saw Collins grab a shovel from tattooed Snail and attack the "set" as fiercely as any of the younger men. He realized that Collins was not limping, and was so tired he thought only that in front of these men he would not limp either. "Paydirt! Paydirt!" the one called Rock kept screaming.

There was another thing, Tom told himself, something else you would not think to notice unless you looked at these men for a long time: they were all very white. Their skin looked compressed, like cheap unhealthy meat, smudgy; they were strong, but they were indoor men.

Indoors, late-night men toiling outside, the ferocity of their labor and their shouts, the guttering torches and the leaping fire, the yells and the exchanges of bills and the bloody dogs—this phantasmagoric scene unrolling before Tom sometimes seemed so unreal he thought he was back in his bed in the windowless room . . . then he was truly

asleep, and dreamed that Del was lying on the little hill
beside him, explaining things. "Mr. Snail is the treasurer
of a big corporation in Boston, Mr. Seed and Mr. Thorn
are both lawyers, Mr. Pease and Mr. Root are major
stockholders in U.S. Steel and race in the America's Cup
every year—Mr. Peet is the United States Secretary of
Commerce."

"Get those tongs ready!" someone was shouting. *"Get
hold of those goddamned tongs!"*

Tom groaned and rolled over, brushing the bottom
branches of the maple with his elbow; then he remembered where he was, and compressed himself down as
small as he could and went back on his belly. His neck
hurt, his knees ached, his head sparkled with pain; but as
he looked down at the men, the dream stuck to him, and
so he saw the Secretary of Commerce gripping the
handles of the metal tongs, swearing at the corporation
treasurer to back away. One of the major stockholders in
U.S. Steel held a dog at the ready over the pit. A
pumpkin-faced lawyer in an army jacket was yelling *"Gid
'im! Gid 'im!"* Another lawyer waved a fistful of folded
bills: deep in the mound, the second dog wailed like a soul
tormented in hell.

"Soon," said the Secretary, and the Boston treasurer
crouched over, grinning tensely like an ape.

Then two shocking things happened, so close together
they were nearly simultaneous. Spouting blood, a tortured dog windmilled out of the mound; a lawyer whose
body was covered with a glittering, moving dragon tattoo
took one look at it and raised his shovel over his head.
Tom saw one front leg hanging by a bloody thread, ribs
opened up to shine like painted matchsticks, and then the
lawyer brought down the shovel and crushed the dog's
head. The lawyer kicked the dog's body into the trees.

The second shocking thing, like the first, was a succes-
sion of images so brightly colored they might have been a
series of slides. A furry, stubby head wet with blood
poked into visibility for a second; the Secretary of
Commerce jabbed with the metal tongs, and all the
financiers howled gleefully; the Secretary jerked his arms
powerfully upward like a man making a home run in
another language, and the metal bands of the tongs
clasped the belly of a squalling, crazed, bleeding badger

and carried it in a wide arc through the firelit air. The Secretary pivoted, whirling the heavy body in the tongs, and dropped the animal into the pit. The U.S. Steel stockholder loosed the foaming dog and it too went headfirst into the pit. Instantly the financiers began shouting out bets.

The bets, Tom suddenly knew, were on how long the badger would live.

The shouting men closed around the pit, passing money back and forth, and Tom could not see what was happening inside it. But he could imagine it, which was worse. At times, when a spray of blood flew up, one or another of the financiers backed away, cursing, and Tom saw rolling hair. The dragon bled on its iridescent scales; a florid rose bled on a bicep; miraculous blood appeared on a yellow T-shirt, dazzling and unexpected as stigmata.

After twenty minutes one man raised his arms and crowed. Money came to him in loud waves. Then there was only the sound of breathing, the ragged breathing of hard-worked men and the punctured, frothy breathing of a badly wounded dog. The Secretary of Commerce took a pistol from his pocket and fired it once into the pit.

Tom shuddered back, rustling along the ground like a leaf. "All right. You've had your blood," said Coleman Collins; but it was too late, because the magician was looking up the hill right into his eyes, and saying, "There's another one for the pit. Go to sleep, boy."

A thick, slobbering man spun around and ran toward him; and Tom passed out.

8

Go to sleep, boy. Tom found himself back on the train going north from Boston. Coleman Collins, not Del, sat beside him, saying, "Of course, this isn't your train. This is Level One."

"Trance," Tom said. "Voice."

"That's right. Wonderful memory. While we're here, I want to thank you for all you've done for Del. He's needed someone like you for a long time."

A wave of sick feeling, disguised as friendliness, flowed

from the magician, and Tom knew he was in deeper trouble than any the troll-like men could have caused him.

"Would you like to see Ventriloquism? That's fun. I always enjoy Ventriloquism." He smiled down at the boy as they swayed along in the crowded train. "This is all very elementary, of course. I hope you'll stay long enough for me to show you some of the more difficult things. It's all within *your* power, I assure you."

"We'll be with you all summer."

"Two and a half months is not long enough, little bird. Not nearly. Now. Where should that voice come from? Up there, I fancy." He lifted his distinguished face and nodded at a grille set in the car's ceiling.

Instantly a hysterical voice crackled out: *"EMER-GENCY! EMERGENCY! BRACE YOURSELVES AGAINST THE SEAT IN FRONT OF YOU! BRACE YOURSELVES . . ."*

The magician was gone. A fat woman in the aisle beside Tom's seat shrieked; she had been holding a paper carton containing several cups of coffee. As she shrieked, the coffee sailed upward, spinning into the air.

Now many were shrieking. Tom folded his head down between his knees and felt hot coffee spattering his back.

The jolt knocked him off the seat entirely, and the noise of the wreck was a nail driven into his eardrums. He could see the woman staggering backward down the aisle, her face caught in an expression between terror and dismay. The railroad car lifted its nose into the air and began to tilt sideways. "They broke my leg!" a man yelled. "Jeeesus!" His yell was the last thing Tom heard before the sound of an explosion going off loud as a bomb a short distance down the track.

"Light," came the voice of the magician.

A shattering burst of whiteness, caused by another explosion, flashed through the car. Inches from Tom's head, a Dixie cup shot up into flame. Tom batted it away, but could not see where it went. *"Jeesus!"* screeched the man with the broken leg. The uptilted car swayed far over to the right and began to topple.

All about Tom, who was now lying faceup in the aisle, the burns on his back singing like an open wound, people groaned and screamed: the car sounded like a burning zoo.

He gripped one of the seat supports and thought: *I'm going to die here. Didn't a lot of people die?*

When the car struck the ground, the screams intensified, became almost exalted.

9

Tom opened his eyes. He was lying in the hollow where Pease and Thorn and the others had labored over their badger-baiting. Coleman Collins, looking ruddy and healthy and ten years younger in his outdoorsy clothes, took a pull off a bottle and winked at him from where he sat beside the shredded mound.

"That wasn't just magic," Tom said.

"What is 'just magic'?" The magician smiled at him. "I'm sure there is no such thing. But you went to sleep. I imagine that you were dreaming." He lifted a knee and extended an arm along it. He looked like a scoutmaster having a chat around the fire with a favored boy.

"I was up there—" Tom pointed. "You said, 'All right. You've had your blood.' Then you saw me. And you said, 'There's another one to throw in the pit. Go to sleep, boy.'"

"Now I know you are tired," Collins said, leaning against what was left of the mound. "You have had a very long day. I promise you, I never said any of those things."

"Where are all the others?" Tom sat up and looked around the clearing. Firelight showed a mound of earth where the pit had been.

"There are no others. There is just you and me. Which is, I assume, what you wanted."

"Mr. Peet," Tom insisted. "He was here. And a lot of others—with funny names, like a bunch of trolls. Thorn and Snail and Rock and Seed . . . You were all trying to get a badger to come out of its house. There were two dogs—Mr. Peet shot one of them."

"Did he, now?" The magician shifted his position against the mound and looked indulgently toward Tom.

"I assumed that you followed me because you wanted to talk. You disobeyed me, that is true. But any good magician knows when to break the rules. And in doing so you demonstrated courage and intelligence, I thought— you were curious, you wanted to see what the terrain was like."

Terrain meant more than the land they sat on. Tom nodded.

"I think also you must have read some of my posters— relics of my public career. Isn't that right?"

"I noticed them," Tom admitted. He thought he trusted Coleman Collins less than anyone else on earth.

"You will hear all about it—this is to be the summer of my unburdening." Collins drew up his knees and looked soberly at Tom over their tops, where he had knit his hands together. Suddenly he reminded Tom of Laker Broome. "As for now, I want to say something about Del. Then there is a story I want you—only you—to hear. Then it will finally be your bedtime.

"My nephew has had an unsettled life. He was on the verge of flunking out of Andover when the Hillmans moved. Now, you may not think much of the Hillmans— you see, I am being very frank with you—but for all their faults, they want to protect Del. And he does need protection. Without a good anchor, without a Tom Flanagan, he will pound himself against the rocks. He needs all my help, all your help too. Watch out for him. But also watch him."

"*Watch* him?"

"To make sure he does not go off the deep end. Del does not have your healthy relationship with the world." He drew his knees in tighter. "Del stole that owl from Ventnor School. Had you guessed?"

"No," Tom said.

"I heard about the theft from the Hillmans. They know he took it, too. But they did not want him expelled from yet another school."

"Another boy took it. Some kids saw him do it."

"Del wanted another boy to take it. Del is a magician too: a better one than he knows, though nothing like the magician you could be. Del stole that owl, no matter whose hands were around it. Watch out for Del. I know my nephew."

"That's plain crazy," Tom said, though a tiny area of doubt had just opened up within him. "And here's something else that's crazy—all that stuff about my being better than Del. Del is better than I'll ever be. Magic is all he really cares about."

"He is better at things you will learn very quickly. But you have within you powers you know nothing of, my bird." He looked at Tom with a kind of fatherly omniscience. "You are not convinced. Would you like proof, before your story? You would?" He turned his head. "There is a fallen log over there—see it? I want you to pick it up." When Tom began to stand, he said, "Stay where you are. Pick it up with your mind. I will help you. Go on. Try it."

Tom saw the edge of the log just protruding into the clearing. It was one that Thorn had not thrown on the fire, perhaps three feet long, dry and gnarled. He thought of a pencil on his desk, jerking itself upward, at the end of one of Mr. Fitz-Hallan's classes.

"Are you afraid to try?" Collins asked. "Humor me. Inside yourself, say, *Log, go up.* And then imagine it lifting. Please try. Prove me wrong."

Tom wanted to say, *I won't,* but realized how childish it would sound. He closed his eyes and said to himself, *Log, go up.* He peeked: the log reassuringly sat on the grass.

"I didn't know you were a coward," said the magician.

Tom kept his eyes open and thought about the end of the log rising. Still it did not move. *Log, go up,* he said to himself. *Log, go up!* The end of the log twitched, and he stared at Collins' amused face. "A mouse?" said the magician. *Up!* Tom thought, suddenly full of rage, and knowing that it would not move. *UP!*

But the log obediently stood on end, as if someone had pulled a wire. *UP!* It rose and wavered in the air; then Tom felt a wave of helpless blackness invading his mind like nausea, and the log began to spin over and over, accelerating until it blurred. *No. Enough,* Tom said in his mind, and the log thumped back down on the grass. He looked at it in dumb shock. His eyes hurt; his stomach felt as though he had eaten spiders. He wanted to run—he feared that he would be sick. He heard handclaps, and saw that Collins was applauding. "You did that," Collins said, and Tom's mouth tasted black.

"I just gave you the tiniest nudge, remarkable boy. Now, listen to the story. One day in a forest, a sparrow joined another sparrow on a branch. They discussed sparrow matters for a time, brightly, inconsequentially, as sparrows do, and then the second sparrow said, 'Do you know why frogs jump and why they croak?' 'No. And I don't care,' said the first sparrow. 'After you know, you'll care,' his companion promised. And this is what he told him. But I shall tell it my way, not the sparrow's."

Tom saw the log whirling wildly, sickly, in midair.

10

"The Dead Princess"

A long time ago, when we all lived in the forest and none of us lived anywhere else, a group of sparrows was flying across the deepest and darkest part of the wood, aimlessly flying far from their normal haunts until they began their search for food.

As sparrows do, they paid little attention to anything, and were content to wrangle and chatter with each other, zipping here and darting there, commenting. "It's quiet," said one sparrow, and another answered, "Yes, but it was much quieter yesterday," and another promptly disagreed—and soon they were all agreeing or disagreeing.

Finally they circled through the air above the trees, listening to see how quiet things really were, in order to argue about it more accurately. The sparrows were now, as they had not properly realized before, almost over the palace of the king who ruled all that part of the forest. And there was no noise at all.

Which was odd indeed. For if the forest was normally full of noises the sparrows had known all their lives, the palace was a virtual beehive—horses trampling in their stables, the dogs woofing in the courtyards, the servants gossiping in the open spaces. Not to mention the pots rattling in the kitchen, the banging from the palace workshops, the *bing bing bing* of the blacksmith . . . Instead of all these sounds the sparrows should have heard, only silence met their ears.

Now, sparrows are as curious as cats, so naturally they all flew down to have a look—they had forgotten all about their argument. Down they came, and down, and down, and still they heard no noise. "Let's get away," said one of the younger sparrows. "Something terrible has happened here, and if we get too close, it may happen to us as well."

Of course no one paid any attention. Down they came, down, down, until they were within the walls of the palace. Some sat on the windowsills, some on the cobblestones, some on the rain gutters, some on the stable doors; and the only sounds they heard were those they made themselves.

Then they saw why. Everything else in the palace was asleep. The horses slept in the stables, the servants slept leaning against walls, the dogs slept in the courtyards. Even the flies on the doorknobs slept.

"A curse, a curse!" shouted the young sparrow. "Let us go, let us go now, or we shall be just like them."

"Stop that, now," said one of the oldest sparrows, for he had finally heard something. This was the faint sound of a human voice, and not just anybody's, but the king's. *Woe is me, woe is me*—that was what the king was saying to himself far up in one of the turrets, so despairingly that all of the sparrows immediately felt sad in sympathy.

Then another, very brave sparrow heard another sound. Someone was pacing up and down in the long building beside them. He slipped around the door to see who besides the king was left awake. The sparrow saw a long dusty room with an enormous table right in its center. Beams of light filtered down from the ranks of high windows, each falling in turn upon the back of a woman in a long rich gown who was slowly moving away from him. When she reached the rear of the dining room, for that was what the brave sparrow had entered, she turned about all unseeing and came back toward him. She wrung her hands together; she worked and knotted her brows. The sparrow's whole little heart went out to her, and he thought that if he could help this distraught beautiful lady in any way, he would do it on the spot. Of course, he knew that she was the queen—sparrows are intensely conscious of rank. When she saw him standing before the door, he cocked his head and looked at her with a glance so intelligent and kindly that she stopped in her tracks.

"Oh, little sparrow," the queen said, "if you only understood me." The sparrow cocked his head even farther. "If you understood me, I would tell you of how our daughter, Princess Rose, sickened and died. And of how her death took all the life from the palace—from our kingdom too, little sparrow. I would tell you of how all the animals first fell asleep, so soundly that we could not awaken them, and then of how all the people but the king and I succumbed to the same illness and fell asleep where they stood. And most of all, little sparrow, I would tell you of how the death of my daughter is causing the death of the kingdom, for as you see us now, we are surely all dying, every one, in palace and in forest, king and commoner, wolf and bear, horse and dog. Ah, I almost think you understand me," she said, and turned her back on the sparrow and continued her sad pacing.

The sparrow nipped around the heavy oaken door and joined his fellows. He whistled to them all to be quiet, and then told them exactly what the queen had said. When he had finished, one of the older sparrows said, "We must do something to help."

"*Us? Us? Help?*" the younger sparrows all began to twitter, hopping about in agitation. For it was one thing to witness interesting and entertainingly tragic events, another to try to do something about them.

"Of course we must help," said the oldest sparrow.

"*Help? Us?*" the youngest sparrows twittered. "What can we do?"

"There is only one thing we can do," said the oldest sparrow. "We must go to the wizard."

Now, that really pitched them into consternation, and there was a lot of hopping about and quarreling. Even the youngest sparrows had heard of the wizard, but they had

certainly never seen him. Besides that, the very mention
of him frightened them. One thing everybody knew about
the wizard was that while he was fair, he always made you
pay for any favor he did you.

"It is the only thing," said the oldest sparrow.

Where does he live? Is it far? Can we find him? Does he
still live? Will we get lost? A thousand chirping questions.

"I once saw where he lived," said the oldest sparrow.
"And I believe that I can find it again. But it is a long way
away, clear across the forest and on the other side."

"Then let us follow you now," said the brave sparrow,
and they all lifted up and circled away from the dreadful
quiet of the palace.

For hours they flew over the thick trees and wide
meadows of the forest, over foaming rivers and wandering
valleys. Over the caves of bears and the dens of foxes,
over hollow logs where ants dozed, over packs of wild
ponies asleep on rock cliffs.

Finally they saw a little curl of smoke coming up
through the heads of the trees, and the oldest sparrow
said, "That is the wizard's house." And they began to
circle down, down, down through the trees. And finally
saw a nondescript little wooden house with two little
windows set beside the front porch.

One by one the sparrows landed on a branch outside
one of the windows; when the branch was so full of
sparrows it bent, they landed on the next higher; and so
on, until sparrows filled the entire tree. Then they all
began to sing at once.

The door of the little wooden cottage opened, and the
wizard stepped out into the light. He was an old, old man,
with skin the color of milk. The dark robes he wore were
covered with the moon and stars; once they had been
impressive, but now the robes were so threadbare you
could see the fabric right through the stars. He looked up
at the tree with his clear old eyes and said, "I see that the
sparrows have come to visit. What do they want, I
wonder?"

Then the oldest sparrow looked at the brave sparrow,
and this fellow spoke up—his voice may have trembled,
because the wizard frightened him, and now that they

were actually here he wished they were somewhere else, but he told the wizard the entire story, just as the queen had told it to him.

"I see," the wizard said. "And you wish me to give life back to Princess Rose?"

"That is right," said the sparrows.

"It is not difficult," said the wizard, "but you must agree to sacrifice something before I will do it."

Then all the sparrows began to chirp and protest.

"Would you give up your wings?"

Another loud wave of twittering. "No, that is impossible," said the oldest sparrow. "Without our wings we could not fly."

"Would you give up your feathers?"

The sparrows' noises were even louder after this question. "No, we cannot," said the oldest sparrow. "Without our feathers, we would freeze to death in the winter."

"Would you give up your song?"

The sparrows were quiet for a moment, and then burst out louder than before. "Yes," the sparrows said. "That will be our sacrifice."

"It is done," said the wizard. "Return to the palace."

As one bird, their nervousness giving them added speed, they lifted off the tree and wheeled about over the wizard's cottage and began the long flight across the forest.

Hours later, when they reached the palace, all was as it had been—all the inhabitants of the palace save the queen and king still slept. The sparrows looked at each other uneasily, wondering if the wizard would take their sacrifice but give nothing in return.

Then, from down under the palace, they heard a dusty little voice calling: *Momee! Daddee! Momee! Daddee!*

And a great wooden door set right down into the ground opened up, and a little girl wandered out, rubbing her eyes.

So the horses woke up in the stables, the dogs woke up in the courtyards, the flies spun awake off the doorknobs, the servants stirred and yawned; and in the deep forest, foxes too yawned and stretched, bears shook their massive heads, wolves stirred beneath trees.

At that instant every sparrow in the palace began to feel

a transformation within himself: just as if a cold hand had thrust itself down in their innards and were moving bits and pieces about. Their minds grew fuzzy; their bodies plumped out, altered in substance, their beaks softened and spread, their feet grew.

And instead of birds, now there were frogs on the windowsills, frogs on the railings, frogs hopping on the stones.

Fortunately the king witnessed this transformation and understood what had happened. He raised his arms in thanksgiving and said that from that day forth all frogs in his kingdom would be protected, for once they had been sparrows who had gone to the wizard to return the life of his daughter.

"'And that is why frogs croak, and why they hop,' said one sparrow to another on a branch in the wood. 'They were once birds, but were tricked by a great wizard, and now they are still trying to sing and still trying to fly. But they can only croak and hop.'"

11

"Well, that's your second bedtime story," the magician said. "Now I am afraid I must leave you. You'll be able to find your way back to bed soon enough, I'm sure." He began to stand up on the matted grass, but the expression on Tom's face stopped him. "What are you thinking, Tom?"

"On Registration Day in our school," Tom began, his face flushed angrily, "the headmaster kept Del and another boy in his office. He told each of them a kind of fairy tale. You knew about that."

The magician stood, put his hands in the small of his back, and stretched from the balls of his feet. "Think about one thing, Tom. What would you give to save a life? Your wings, or your song? Would you be a sparrow . . . or a frog?"

He grinned dazzlingly at the boy, lifted both arms in the air, and vanished.

"*No!*" Tom yelled, and jumped forward—on hands and knees, he scrabbled to the spot where Collins had been standing, and felt only grass and earth. He looked wildly around, expecting to see Collins running through the forest, but saw only the dying fire and the trees. Far off in the woods he saw one of the lights burning over an impromptu stage. There was no sign of Collins. Tom let himself down on the coarse grass, groaning: his mind spun. A dead Rose, sparrows into frogs, the old wizard, what he had done with the log . . . *While you are here I am your parent.*

Tom picked himself up off the grass; he supposed he could stumble back to the house. But with the first step he took, the forest around him seemed to melt.

At first he thought he was going to lose consciousness again, and find himself in the wrecked train with screams and the rending of metal thick and palpable in the air about him—

and the coffee scorching his back—

(Didn't stain your clothes, all that coffee flying about?)

and he realized that the magician had known at the Hilly Vale station that he was going to put him on the wrecked train *(Not just a little spilled coffee, a little bump on the tracks, a little messy commotion?),* and in the second before the forest disappeared as finally as Coleman Collins, Tom had time to think that Collins had somehow caused that wreck in order to put him inside it six hours later.

This is Level One. Any good magician knows when to break the rules.

He could have screamed as loudly as any poor soul on the train, but his fear pinned his screams to his tongue. The trees had blurred like watercolors held under a tap; everything slid and dissolved into a pane of meltingly pale green. Green mist enveloped him, abstract and cool, and he felt as though he were falling from an airplane.

White fluted pillars took shape as suddenly as if blown into being. The ground shifted, became harder, less resilient. With his next step forward, he whanged his leg against the metal back of a padded chair.

"Oh, my God," he whispered. He was standing in a

large vaultlike room with a curtained stage at one end. Tom himself was halfway up a pitched bank of seats, in the middle of a row. Misty green walls inset with white pillars led down to the stage. A few lights burned high above him.

He was in the big theater where Collins was going to teach them to fly.

"Oh, God," he said. "I wasn't even outside."

Tom blindly went down the side of the rows of seats and let himself out into the hall. Here too a few lights burned. He was only five feet from the entry to the Little Theater. He clicked the door behind him and looked for its brass plate: Le Grand Théâtre des Illusions. Beneath it was a white sheet of paper on which had been written: *Go to bed, son.*

He weaved down the hall and the lights clicked off behind him. All he wanted to do was to roll into sleep as fast and hard as he could: now he could not begin to puzzle out the hoops within hoops through which Collins had made him jump. *And that is why frogs croak and why they hop. They were once birds, but were tricked by a great wizard, and now they are still trying to sing and still trying to fly.*

12

"You answer my question first."

"No, you answer mine. Tell me about Rose Armstrong."

"Not until you tell me what you did last night."

"I can't."

"Did Uncle Cole tell you not to?"

"No."

"Then you can tell me. Did you go downstairs? Did you go outside?" Del pushed his spoon back and forth in a bowl of oatmeal. "Did anyone see you?"

"All right. I went downstairs. Then I followed all those guys outside."

"You did *what?*" Del had completely lost his self-possession. He virtually goggled at Tom.

"I went out. I think I did. Then everything went funny.
I wound up back in the big theater."

"Oh." Del relaxed. "So you were supposed to go out."

"You know that right off?"

"Sure," Del said. They were eating breakfast in Del's
room. A tray had appeared outside the door at nine. "I've
been through this about a million times, remember? He
did some magic on you. You can't even really tell me
what happened because it's all mixed up in your head.
That's normal. That's part of what we're here for. So now
I can relax. I thought you might get us both kicked out."

"Well, now that you're relaxed, tell me about Rose
Armstrong."

"What do you want to know about her?"

"Why does she do what your uncle wants her to do? I
mean, why would she go out there and sit on a rock in the
middle of the night? Doesn't she have better things to
do?"

Del pushed his plate away. "Well, I guess she wants to
help Uncle Cole. Why else?"

"But why would she want to?"

"Because he's great." Del looked at him as if he had
confessed an inability to multiply six by two. "She
respects him. She likes working for him."

"Does he pay her?"

"Look, I don't know, okay? I know that her parents are
dead. She lives in town with her grandmother. You have
to know that Uncle Cole is famous up here—he used to
travel all around, a long time ago, and up here they still
remember that. He's Hilly Vale's celebrity. They love
him. Did you read his posters downstairs?"

"No," Tom said. "I want to look at them today."

"Well, you'll see. He went everywhere. Then he
decided he was wasting his talent, and he came here."

"How old is she?"

"About our age. Maybe a year older."

"Do you like her?"

"Sure I like her."

"Do you like her a lot?"

"What do you mean, a lot?"

"You know what I mean."

"Okay. I like her a lot."

"Do you ever go out with her?"

"You don't understand," Del said. "It's not like that."

"Well, is she ever around so you can just talk to her? Can she tell you what your uncle is up to?"

"Yes, she's around and you can talk to her. But she doesn't know the reasons for the things he asks her to do. It's like . . . a big puzzle. She's just one of the little pieces."

"Well, do you kiss her and stuff like that?"

"That's my business," Del said.

"Do you make out with her? She's a year older, huh? Does she let you make out with her?"

"I guess," Del said. "Sometimes."

"Is she good-looking?"

"You can decide for yourself."

"You're a real snake in the woodpile, Nightingale," Tom said. He was delighted. "All this time you never told me? She's your girlfriend? You spend all summer making out with a girl a year older than us? Wow."

"We have to go downstairs," Del said sternly. "Didn't you ever make out with Jenny Oliver? Or with Diane Darling?" These were girls from Phipps-Burnwood Seminary; Tom had taken both of them to school dances.

"Sometimes," Tom said. "Sure, sometimes."

"Okay," Del said, and stood up.

"You old snake in the woodpile," Tom said. He rose too, and they went out into the sunny hall. As they went down the stairs, he said, "Tell me what she looks like. Is she a blond?"

"Yep."

"Well?"

"She's a blond, she has two eyes and a nose and a mouth. She's about as tall as you are. Her face is . . . oh, how do you describe someone's face?"

"Try."

They stopped together just outside the living room. It was immaculate, Tom saw, as if Mr. Peet's trolls had never been in the house.

"Well, she looks kind of . . ." Del hesitated. "Kind of . . . well, hurt."

"Hurt?" This was far indeed from anything Tom had expected, and he laughed.

"I knew I couldn't explain it," Del said. "Let's go. He'll be waiting."

Tom glanced over his shoulder at the series of posters on the wall, saw only that they were printed in a variety of old-fashioned typefaces and that none of the names immediately visible were familiar. Then he set off after Del. His mood had risen: full of breakfast, rested, and on a sunny morning he could see the fun of what Shadowland offered, a game more challenging than any he had ever played. He had not been threatened or injured the night before: he had merely been tricked, and tricked in a way only a great illusionist could have managed.

The handwritten sheet of paper was gone from the door. But had it been there at all? Tom wondered, and thought that now he was getting into the spirit of Shadowland.

"Have you ever heard the name Herbie—does it mean anything special to you?" he asked.

"Herbie? You'll see Herbie," Del promised from ahead of him.

Inside the long theater, the walls hung misty and green between the fluted pillars, the seats stood like rows of open mouths; the lighting had been dialed low. Del, in his seat in the front row when Tom entered, laughed at whatever was on stage. Tom turned to see, and was startled by the spectacle of a department-store dummy propped stiffly on a tall chair. The arms jutted out, the legs stuck forward. The mannequin had been dressed in black evening clothes; its face had been powdered or painted white. A curly red wig sat on its crown.

"That's Herbie," Del said as Tom slid into the seat next to him. "Herbie Butter."

"A doll?"

"Shh."

One of the doll's hands jerked forty-five degrees up. The movement was a robot's, not human. The head swiveled, blank and perfect, first to one side, then the other. The other arm jerked up with the same robot's angular suddenness. Tom relaxed into his seat, enjoying this.

"The Amazing Mechanical Magician and Acrobat," Del whispered.

One leg, then its fellow, bent; the robot-mannequin came out of the chair, and Tom could almost hear the working of gears. It began to slide ridiculously about the stage, at one moment almost tumbling off the edge, then walking with great dignity into the curtains and grinding away in place until the gears shifted again and spun it away.

"Is that your uncle?"

"Of course it is," Del whispered.

"He's great."

Del rolled his eyes. The greatness was beyond question.

For some minutes, Coleman Collins, Herbie Butter, moved hilariously about the stage, always on the verge of destruction, or surely, it seemed, on the way to it. His eyes were perfectly round and blank, his movements those of a wound-up toy: the face, covered with powder, was sexlessly young—but for the male formal dress, the white face and red hair could have been those of a pretty young woman in her twenties.

Collins then demonstrated another of his capacities.

He strode jerkily to a halt in the middle of the stage, swiveled to face the boys, and remained stock-still for no longer than a second and a half.

"Get this," Del said.

Before Del had finished, the robotlike figure was whipping up into the air: it turned over in midair and landed on its hands. Then it ticked over to one side, spread its legs, and executed a series of flawless cart-wheels.

Landing on its hands again, the figure sprang over backward and came down on its feet; then over again, turning in the air, blindingly fast. Then Collins came out of a crouch and fell face forward on the stage—a robot turned off by remote control. With what must have been a terrific effort of muscular skill, he seemed to bounce back upright, arms and legs never changing their position, so slowly it was like a fall in reverse slow motion.

"Boy," Tom muttered.

Herbie Butter bowed and twinkled offstage; a second later he was back, pushing a magician's table on which rode a tall silk hat.

"Imagine a bird," he said, and the voice was not Coleman Collins', but lighter, younger.

A pass of a white silken scarf, and a white dove came out of the hat.

"Imagine a cat"; a white cat slipped over the brim of the hat. The cat began immediately to stalk the terrified bird.

Herbie Butter did one of his astounding backflips, coming to rest on his fingertips, then flipped forward to land where he had been, and dropped the white scarf over the cat.

The scarf fluttered to the surface of the table.

"And that's it, isn't it? Cat and bird. Bird and cat."

It was that first morning that he told Tom and Del the story which ended with the words *"Then I am the King of the Cats!"*

"Can I ask you a question?" Tom said, his arm up as if he were back in Latin class.

"Of course." The magician sat on a little table; the voice was still light and sexless.

"How can you do those things—those gymnastic things—when you limp?"

He felt Del's disapproval pouring from him, strong as a scent, but the magician was not ruffled.

"A good question, and too frank to be rude, nephew, so don't take offense. The real answer is 'because I have to,' but that won't be specific enough for you. I intend to tell you more completely, Tom, in a short while—because I will expect you to do something very similar. I promise you. You will know. Is that all?"

Tom nodded.

"Come on up and shake my hand. Please."

Mystified, Tom stood and went toward the magician, who slipped off the table and went to the edge of the stage. Herbie Butter bent down to take his hand; but instead, his fingers closed about Tom's wrist. Tom jerked his head up and looked into the white anonymous face. He could see nothing of Coleman Collins in it.

"For your benefit." The fingers tightened around his wrist. "Everything you will see here, and you will see many odd things, comes from your own mind—from within you. From the reaction of your mind with mine. None of it exists elsewhere."

Herbie Butter released Tom's wrist. "For three months, for as long as you stay, *this* is the world for you. Which you will help to create." He smiled. "That is one of the meanings of the King of the Cats."

Yes, Tom thought.

"Give yourself to it. I ask you because you are one of the rare ones who can."

Yes I am, Tom thought. He was aware of Del giving him a sharp look.

"And you are alone this summer. Your mother goes to England tomorrow. Her cousin Julia is getting married to . . . a barrister, is it? And after the wedding, your mother will travel in England? Isn't that right?"

"But how . . . ?"

"So this is the summer of Tom Flanagan's growth as well as the summer of my unburdening. You are a very special boy, Tom. As you showed me last night."

He would have been worried by the expression now on Del's face, which was dark and considering, but he was looking into the white asexual face and seeing Coleman Collins there—the robust Collins of the night before. "Thank you," he said.

13

"Shall we have some fun?" the magician said. "It will be necessary to close your eyes."

Tom shut his eyes, still feeling the roughness of Collins' fingers about his wrist, still glowing from the praise, and heard the magician say, "This is Level Two."

He snapped his eyes open, remembering the wrecked train and angry with himself for being duped so easily: Del, he supposed, had opened his eyes too. He turned to see, but Del avoided his eyes.

They were still in the big theater. On the stage before

them was not the single table, but a large complicated wooden construction like an illustration from a book—so foreign, it seemed to Tom. Some tinny happy music played over them: to two fifteen-year-olds in 1959, this peppy simple jazz was irresistibly like the soundtracks to the old cartoons they saw on television on Saturday mornings. The building was at once complicated and comfortable, full of odd angles and tiny windows. On the big front window had been painted in black: APOTHE-CARY.

"Well, let's look inside," Collins said; now he wore half-glasses and a striped apron. His face shone bare of powder—he looked like everybody's favorite old uncle.

The building swung open, turning itself inside out. The sides pulled back and revealed rows of bottles and jars, a serving counter, a high black register.

"You wouldn't happen to require any cough medicine, my young men?"

A row of jars labeled *cough syrup* coughed and bounced on their shelf.

"Sleeping pills?"

Another row of bottles snored loudly—almost sending up *zzzz* in white balloons.

"Reducing tonic?"

Two bottles shrank to half their size.

"Rubber bands?"

A box of rubber bands on the counter stood up and played cheery music: the same tinny happy jazz that had begun as soon as they had closed their eyes. Tom saw the bell of a trumpet, the slide of a trombone . . .

"Vanishing cream?"

A jar next to the rubber bands slowly disappeared. Del was giggling beside him; and he giggled too.

"Greeting cards?"

The corny joke fulfilled itself: A rack of cards before the counter shouted "Hi!" and "Hey, how you doin'?" "Hello, neighbor!" "God be with you!" "Get well soon!" "Have a good trip!" "Take it easy!" "*Bonjour!*" "*Shalom!*"

"Come on up and take your seats for the boxing match," the kindly old pharmacist called to them.

As they left their seats, the yelling cards and trumpet-playing rubber bands and coughing jars and snoring bottles swung outward. In the middle of the stage a roped-in boxing ring was occupied by a fat cartoon man with bristling jowls and a flat, malevolent head. Boos erupted from the persistent soundtrack. The man grimaced with cartoon ferocity, beat his chest, bulged his tattooed biceps.

"Bluto," Del said in delight, and Tom answered, "No, I think . . ." He could not remember what he thought.

A bell rang with a clear commanding insistence, and the kindly old pharmacist, now wearing a flat tweed cap and a vibrant checked jacket, called out, "Hurry and take your seats for the first round." They scrambled up onto the stage and got into metal camp chairs placed just outside the ring.

"It's the big fight, you know, the dirty scoundrel's comeuppance," said the boxing fan. He had a monocle and protruding teeth, and a voice faintly, ridiculously English. "Now, our hero is somewhere about . . . ah, yes. Chap's a trifle late."

A very familiar rabbit bounded into the ring and clasped his hands together over his head to the sound of mass cheering. The villain glowered. He spat on his gloves and smacked them together. The rabbit, who was nearly as tall as the man, darted toward the villain and clasped his arms around the obese waist. He bounced a couple of feet off the canvas, then rebounded once, and then took off so powerfully that he and the villain sailed straight into the air. Tom craned his neck: the pair of them were still going up. They were just a dot in the sky. Now they were plummeting down. They were going to crash. The rabbit produced a frilled parasol and floated back to the canvas; the villain splatted down and was as flat as a dime.

He rose up and shook out his two-dimensional body. His flesh miraculously plumped. He slavered with rage, with the brute need to punish. The rabbit circled round him, lightly dancing on his big rear paws, landing short but stinging blows. The tattooed villain cocked back a fist suddenly as large as a ham, and brought it around in a whooshing haymaker. All his upper body bulged with effort. The breeze flattened the rabbit's ears; and the wind from the punch tore at Tom's hair, tugged at his shirt.

More than the villain's upper body must have bulged.

The rear of his boxing shorts split with an awful rending sound, revealing polka-dot underpants. The man's face flashed bright red, red as a stop sign, and he bent forward and clasped his gloved hands over his outthrust bottom; he minced pigeon-toed around the ring, face flashing like a neon sign.

"Bit cheeky, what?" asked the boxing fan. "But I fancy . . ."

Bugs, who had momentarily disappeared, now returned astride a bicycle. He wore a frock coat, a topper like the Mad Hatter's, and swung a bell in his hand. The bicycle bobbed from side to side in rhythm with the ringing of the bell. A sign around his neck read: Stychen Tyme, Instant Tailor.

Tyme. Tom thought. Now, who . . . ? He remembered. The Reverend Mr. Tyme, speaking pompous nonsense at his father's funeral. April; the brisk wind blowing sand over the graves, bobbling the flowers. His body went cold. He was aware, as if a great distance from his own feelings, that he was horrified. It could not have been an accidental reference.

Bugs wheeled around the tattooed man, weaving a large needle this way and that. Occasionally he touched his fingers before his face and nodded, just as the Reverend Dawson Tyme had done: Tom's outrage broke. As Bugs sewed up the villain in a cocoon of thread, he was giving a running parody of the minister's manner. He bobbed his head, shook his fuzzy jowls, looked chummy and superior and pontificating all at once—almost, Tom could smell the little minty puffs of breath.

When the tattooed Bluto *(Snail?)* was invisible, tied up like a wriggling worm, Bugs jumped from his bike and set to work on it with whirring, flying hands; in a second, it stood upright in a single column, the seat supporting an open book: a lectern. Bugs bowed, knitted his hands, preached a silent sermon over the bound body—his gestures were hilariously oily. Tom felt a vast and subversive relief, seeing the Reverend Mr. Tyme parodied so deliciously.

"Awful old bore, isn't he?" asked the boxing fan.

"Yes. Yes," Tom said. *This* is what magic can do, it came to him: magic existed in the teeth of all the hypocrites and bores, in the teeth of all the proprieties too. He had scarcely ever felt so good.

Bugs's hands went a-flurrying over the bicycle again: a hammer rang, nuts and bolts flew out. Sparks sprayed comically overhead. When he raised it up, he held a rifle. Bugs ripped off the frock coat, turned it inside out, and it was a military uniform. A bugle zipped from a side pocket, and Bugs blew taps. The rifle went to his shoulder, he sighted over the bicycle seat, and fired a salute. Then he jammed the rifle barrel-first into the ground, jerked it sharply toward him, and the wrapped body fell through a trapdoor.

The rabbit danced clog-footed for a moment, shook the rifle until it became a bicycle again, mounted and rode off until he was a speck in the misty green distance.

"Hope you enjoyed it," Cole Collins said.

Tom turned euphorically toward the boxing fan and saw that now he was the magician again, in his striped suit. He looked tired and jovial: any elderly uncle showing nephew and nephew's friend a good time.

"I see you did," Collins said. He extended his hand and set it carefully on Tom's head. "You wonderful child."

Tom's expression of joy turned rigid.

"Do you know what day it is?"

Tom shook his head, and the magician gently lifted his hand.

"It is Sunday. I would be very remiss if I did not include some religious instruction in this little show. On Sundays, it is always best to display a little piety."

He clapped his hands, and the wing of the set before them began to revolve. The music which had buzzed cheerily about them altered; settled into a smoother, still pumping rhythm. Tom began to tap his foot, and the magician nodded approvingly.

The set revolved completely, showing a long refectory table with wine goblets and plates; the table sat before a window showing a long green Italian distance, a brilliant sunset. Thirteen robed men sat behind the table, their heads and bodies in attitudes as familiar as the rabbit, but not as immediately recognizable.

Del laughed out loud. Then Tom did recognize the scene and the postures—eleven men leaning or looking toward the tall bearded man in the middle, one self-consciously looking elsewhere.

"It's that painting," he said. Collins smiled.

The music tightened up, became a fraction louder. A piano hit a rolling stride. The men at the table began moving their hands in unison, then rose, danced in front of the table and sang:

> La ba la ba, la ba la *ba!*
> La ba la ba, la ba la *ba!*
>
> We got *fish* for suppah,
> First one *thing,* then anothah,
> We got *fish* for suppah,
> First one thing, then anothah.
>
> We ain't *got* no menu,
> But our *fish* will send you.
> We got *fish* for suppah,
> First one thing, then anothah.
>
> Last night we had bread and fish,
> Tonight we got fish and bread.
> Tomorrow night we gonna change the dish,
> And have plain fish instead.
>
> Ah!
>
> We got *fish* for suppah,
> But first one thing, then anothah,
> We got *fish* for suppah,
> First one thing an' anothah.

A saxophone slipped out from beneath a robe as easily as Bugs's bugle from his military jacket. The squat bearded man holding it breathed out a solo while others waved their hands and did a buck-and-wing. Another disciple produced a trumpet and blasted. Strutting and hand-waving from the disciples: after the chorus they all showed their teeth and shouted:

AH!

We got *fish* for suppah,
But first one *thing,* then anothah,

[the stage began to revolve again]

We got *fish* for suppah,
But first one thing an' anothah.

[men and table now out of sight]

The music had ended. They were looking at a flat black
wall. "Simple pyrotechnics," Collins said. "Now, would
you like to advance to Level Three and fly?"

"Oh, yes," both boys said at once.

14

*Then all blew away like dust, like a dream, and it was
night, much colder than before—*

and he was skimming, naked and wrapped in a fur
blanket, along in a sleigh with Coleman Collins. Snow
blew in a tempest about them, half-obscuring the horse
ahead. They were following a track through dark trees,
going up; plunging blindly on, the horse flickered gray
against the surrounding white.

The magician turned his face to Tom, and the boy
shrank back against the cold metal edge of the sleigh. The
face was bone, hard and white as a skull. "I have taken
you aside," were the words that came from this apparition. "Everything is just as it was, but we have stepped
aside for a moment. For a private word." The face was no
longer bone, but animal—the face of a white wolf. "I
forbid you nothing. *Nothing,*" uttered the awful face.
"You may go anywhere—you may open any door. But,
little bird, remember that you must be prepared to accept
whatever you find." The long jaws spread in a smile filled
with teeth.

The horse drove madly on through the buffeting wind and snow.

"What night is this?" Tom cried out.

"The same, the very same."

"And did I fly?"

The wolf laughed.

You may open any door.

Uphill into deeper night and tearing cold; the horse working against the snow.

"It is the same night, but six months later," said the wolf. "It is the same night, but in another year," and laughed. Tom's whole body suffered with the cold, tried to flee back into itself.

"Did I *fly?*"

Collins said through his wolf's face, "You are mine. Nothing that is in magic will be unknown to you, boy. For you are no one else's but mine."

The trees fell behind them, and they seemed to streak upward through an utter barrenness.

We got fish *for suppah:* Jesus doing a buck-and-wing.

The wolf said: "Once I was you. Once I was Del." He turned and grinned at the freezing boy wrapped in fur. "But I learned from a great magician. The great magician became my partner, and together we toured Europe until he did an unspeakable thing. After he did the unspeakable thing, we could no longer remain together—we had become mortal enemies. But he had taught me all he knew, and I too was a great magician by then. So I came here, to my kingdom."

"Your kingdom," Tom said.

The wolf ignored him. "He taught me to do one thing in particular. To put a hurtin' on things. His words. He spoke that way. And finally I put a hurtin' on him." The long teeth glittered.

"Did you put a hurtin' on the train?" Tom asked.

The wolf lashed the horse: not a wolf, but a man with a wolf's head. "No one but you will understand your future. You will be as the man who brings forth diamonds, and they say, is this pitch? You will be as he who brings forth wine, and they say, is this sand?" The long snout swiveled toward Tom. "When that happens, boy, *put a hurtin' on them.*"

The horse reached the top of the rise and halted. It

steamed in the frigid air, hanging its neck. Tom saw foam spring out on the horse's flanks.

"Look down," the figure beside him commanded.

Tom looked over the steaming, foaming horse into a long white vista. The land dropped, the green firs resumed. At the bottom of the valley lay a frozen lake. Above it, on the far end, Shadowland sat on its cliff like a jeweled dollhouse. Its windows gleamed.

"Pretend that is the world. It is the world. It can be yours. Everything in the world, every treasure, every satisfaction, is there.

"Look."

Tom looked toward the shining house and saw a naked girl in an upper window. She raised her arms and stretched: he could not see her anything like as clearly as he wished, but what he saw was like a finger laid against his heart. Shock and tenderness vibrated together in his chest. Seeing the girl was nothing like looking at nude photographs in a magazine—those acres of spongy flesh had only a fraction of the voltage this girl sent him.

"And look."

At another window men gambled: one player raked in a huge pile of bills and coins. Tom looked back to see the girl, but where she had been was only incandescent brightness. *Are you his too, Rose?*

"And look," the man with the wolf's face commanded.

Another window: a boy opening a tall door, hesitating for a moment, outlined in light, then suddenly engulfed in light. Tom understood that this boy—himself?—was undergoing an experience of such magnitude, such joy, that his imagination could only peer at its dimmest edge; swallowed by light, the boy, who might be himself, had found an incandescence and beauty greater than the girl's—so great that the girl must be a part of it.

"And now look," he was commanded.

In the gleam of another window he saw only an empty bright room with green walls. The column of a pillar. The big theater.

Then he saw himself flow past the window, many feet above the ground. His body sailed past, must have turned in the air, floated before the window again and spun over as easily as a leaf.

"I did," he breathed, not even feeling the cold now.

"Of course you did," the magician said. *"Alis volat propriis."*

Laughter boomed from the magician, from the hillside, from the valley, from even the steaming horse and the frigid air.

"Don't wait to be a great man . . ." came the magician's floating voice, and Tom lapsed back and fell *through* the fur and metal, falling through the hillside and the laughing horse and the wind.

". . . be a great bird."

He remembered.

In the big green room. Coleman Collins before himself and Del, saying, "Sit on the floor. Close your eyes. Count backward with me from ten. 10, 9, 8, 7, 6, 5, 4, 3, 2, 1. You are at peace, totally relaxed. What we do here is physiologically impossible. So we must train the body to accept the impossible, and then it will become possible.

"We cannot breathe in water. We cannot fly. Not until we find the secret muscles that enable us to do so.

"Spread your hands, boys. Spread your arms. I want you to see your shoulders in your minds. See those muscles, see those bones. Think of those shoulders opening, opening . . . think of them opening out."

Tom remembered . . . saw what he had seen. His muscles flaring and widening, something new and reckless moving in his mind.

"When I say *one,* you will inhale; when I say *two,* you will exhale and think very calmly about rising an inch or two above the floor. *One.*"

Tom remembered filling his chest with air: the new sensation in his mind began to burn bright yellow.

"Two."

Within the memory of the theater, another memory bloomed: Laker Broome crazily sweeping through aisles of boys in chapel, jabbing his finger, shouting. Hatred filled him, and he pushed all the air from his lungs. The wooden floor had seemed to tremble beneath him.

"Just let your mind roam," came the strong quiet voice.

He had seen himself floating up like a helium-filled balloon: then he had again seen Laker Broome standing like an actor before the smoke-filled auditorium, giving him useless orders; seen the Reverend Mr. Tyme prancing at his father's funeral; seen Del, levitating in a dark bedroom. Then he had seen the most disturbing images of all, tanks and soldiers and bloody corpses and women with the heads of beasts all lacquered on a ceiling above him, images filled with such horror and disgust that they seemed to whirl about the image of a man in belted raincoat and wide-brimmed hat who made them dance. . . .

Why, yes, he had thought. *Like that.* And suddenly weightless, had rolled over on his back and not touched the ground. His mind felt like fire.

Then another image rammed into his mind, even more horrifying than the last: he saw the auditorium full of boys and masters, himself and Del onstage as Flanagini and Night. He was far above them all, and his eyes hurt, his head was bursting with pressure. His long spidery body felt as though needles had pierced it. He was seeing with Skeleton Ridpath's eyes, and his body was Skeleton's, just before the fire.

He had collapsed heavily onto the wooden floor. Blood burst from his nose.

"So now you see," Collins had whispered to him.

"Don't you know now that you could breathe in water?" Collins said. Tom's whole body ached; the cold tore at him.

"The secret is hate," Collins said mildly. "Rather, the secret lies in hating well. You have the germ of quite a good hater in you."

Tom tugged the fur robe more tightly about him. His ears were cold enough to drop from his head.

"I want to show you one thing more, little friend."

"But I didn't really fly," Tom said. "I just went up . . . and I rolled over—"

"One thing more."

The icy wind ripped at them, and pulled Collins' face back into the wolf's visage. He snapped his whip up into the air, hauled at the reins with his other hand, and cracked the whip down as the horse plunged around in the snow.

When the whip landed, the horse screamed and took off downhill like a cannonball. The wolf-face turned and

grinned at him just as the wind blurred Tom's eyes, and
the world turned as misty as the walls of the big theater.
Tom pulled the fur robe up over his face and inhaled its
cold, dusty, slightly gamy aroma until he felt the sleigh
begin to slow down.

They were on level ground. A wide plain of snow lay in
moonlight like a room without walls. In the center of the
plain stood a tall burning building.

Tom stared at the blazing building as they drew nearer
to it: burning, it seemed to diminish in size. They trotted
ten feet nearer, close enough now to feel the heat pouring
from the blaze.

"Do you recognize it?"

"Yes."

"Get out of the sleigh," the magician ordered. "Walk
closer to it."

He did not move at first, and Collins clutched one of his
elbows through the robe and yanked him across his body
and dumped him out into the snow. The robe slithered,
and Tom snatched at it to keep its warmth about him. He
stood up; his burning feet barely cracked the snow's hard
surface.

"Are we really here?" he asked.

"Go closer and *really* look." His voice made a joke of
the word.

Tom limped toward the edge of the fire. It was no taller
than himself. There was Fitz-Hallan's room, there was
Thorpe's. Metal beams curled in the midst of the flames.
He could hear the glass panels cracking and shattering
around the enclosed court. And would there be a dwarf
lime tree, shriveling and blackening? The building tightened down into itself a notch. Was it just a film—a
projection from somewhere? It warmed him like a fire.

He began to weep.

"What does it say to you?" Collins asked, and Tom
whirled around to see him. He looked like a Russian
nobleman in his fur-collared coat.

"It's too much," Tom managed to get out, hating himself
for crying.

"Of course it is. That's part of the point. Look again."

Tom turned again and looked at the burning school.

"What does it say to you? Open your mind to it and let it speak."

"It says . . . get out of here."

"Does it really?" The magician laughed: he knew better.

"No."

"No. It says, *Live while you can. Get what you can when you can.* You haven't been bad at that, you know."

Tom began to shake. His feet were frozen, his face blazed like the fire. Coleman Collins seemed about to see straight inside him, and to cynically dismiss what he saw there. Like any young person, Tom was adept at intuiting other people's attitudes toward him, and for a moment it occurred to him that Coleman Collins hated both Del and himself. *The secret lies in hating well.* He was trembling so violently that the robe would have slipped from his shoulders if he had not gripped it with both hands. "Please," he said, asking for something so large he could not encompass it in words.

"It is night. You must go to bed."

"Please."

"This is your kingdom too, child. Insofar as I make it yours. And insofar as you can accept what you find in it."

"Please . . . take me back."

"Find your own way, little bird." Collins cracked the whip, and the horse lunged forward. The magician swept past without another glance. Tom flailed out for the bar at the end of the sleigh, missed it, and fell. Cold leaked up his thighs, slithered down his chest. He pulled up his head to find the fire, but it too was gone. Collins' sleigh was just disappearing into the firs.

Tom got his knees under him and awkwardly stood up, gripping the robe. From the other side of the snowy plain a wind approached, made visible by the swirl of snow it lifted and spun. The trace of the wind arrowed straight toward him; he turned to take it on his back and saw flecks of green just before the wind knocked his legs out from under him and deposited him—

on nothing, on green air through which he fell without falling, spun without moving. He threw out his arms and caught the padded arm of a chair.

15

He was back in Le Grand Théâtre des Illusions. One light burned gloomily down at him, revealing in semi-chiaroscuro his strewn clothing. Tom yanked his trousers on and shoved his feet into his shoes; he balled up his socks and underwear and thrust them into a pocket. Then he put on his shirt. All this he did mechanically, numbly, with a numb mind.

He looked at his watch. Nine o'clock. Nine or ten hours had vanished while Coleman Collins played tricks with him.

He went down the darkened hall. What had Del been doing all this time? The thought of Del revived him—he wanted to see him, to have his story matched by Del's. That morning, he had been almost joyful, being at Shadowland; now he again felt endangered. Warmth was just beginning to return to his frozen toes.

Tom had reached the point in the hallway, just before it turned into the older part of the house, where the short corridor led to the forbidden door. Tom stood at the juncture of the two corridors looking at the cross-beamed door. He remembered Collins' words: *This is your kingdom too, child.* He thought: Well, let's see the worst.

And as he had said to Del the first night, wasn't the very commandment not to open it a disguised suggestion that he look behind the door?

"I'm going to do it," he said, and realized that he had spoken out loud.

Before he could argue himself out of his mood of defiance, he moved down the short hallway and put his hand on the doorknob. The brass froze his hand. He thought back to the third thing Collins had shown him, back in the wintry sleigh: a boy opening a door and being engulfed by lyric, singing brightness.

Your wings, or your song?

He pulled open the forbidden door.

16

The Brothers

"Look, Jakob," a man said, looking up from a desk. He smiled at Tom, and the man who sat at another desk facing him lifted his head from the papers before him and gave a similar quizzical, inviting smile. "Do you see? A visitor. A *young* visitor." His accent was German.

"I have eyes, I see," said the other man.

Both were in late middle age, clean-shaven; glasses as old-fashioned and foreign as their dress modified their sturdy faces, made them scholarly. They sat at their desks in a little pool of light cast by candles; high bookshelves loomed behind them.

"Should we invite him in?" said the second man.

"I think we ought. Won't you come in, boy? Please do. Come in, child. That's the way. After all, we are working for you as much as for anyone else."

"Our audience, Wilhelm," said the second man, and beamed at Tom. He was stockier, deeper in the chest than the man with the kindly face. He stood and came forward, and Tom saw muddy boots and smelled a drifting curl of cigar smoke. "Please sit. There will do." He indicated a chesterfield sofa to the right of the desk.

As Tom advanced into the dark room, the crowded detail came clear: the walls covered with dim pictures and framed papers, a stuffed bird high up on a shelf, a glass bell protecting dried flowers.

"I know who you are. Who you're supposed to be," he said. He sat on the springy chesterfield.

"We are what we are supposed to be," said the one called Wilhelm. "That is one of the great joys of our life. How many can claim such a thing? We discovered what we were supposed to be young, and have pursued it ever since."

"We shared the same joy in collecting things," said

Jakob. "Even as children. Our whole life has been an extension of that early joy."

"Without my brother, I should have been lost," said Wilhelm. "It is a great thing, to have a brother. Do you have one, child?"

"In a way," Tom said.

Both brothers laughed, so innocently and cheerfully that Tom joined them.

"And what are you doing here?" Tom asked.

They looked at each other, full of amusement which somehow embraced and included Tom.

"Why, we are writing down stories," Jakob said.

"What for?"

"To amaze. To terrify. To delight."

"Why?"

"For the sake of the stories," Jakob said. "That must be clear. Why, our very lives have been storylike. Even the mistakes have been happy. Boy, did you know that in our original story it was a fur slipper which the poor orphan girl wore to the ball? What an inspired mistranslation made it glass!"

"Yes, yes. And you remember the strange dream I had about you, my brother: I stood in front of a cage, on top of a mountain . . . it snowed . . . you were in the cage, frozen . . . I had to peer through the bars of the cage—so much like one of our treasures . . ."

"Which we were determined to show the world the wonder we felt in discovering, yes. You were terrified—but it was a terror full of wonder."

"These stories are not for every child—they do not suit every child. The terror is there, and it is real. But our best defense is nature, is it not?"

Tom said "Yes" because he felt them waiting for an answer.

"So you see. You learn well, child." Jakob set down the quill pen with which he had been toying. "Wilhelm's dream—do you know that when Wilhelm was dying, he spoke quietly and cheerfully about his life?"

"You see, we embraced our treasures, and they gave us treasure back a thousandfold," Wilhelm said. "They were the country in which we lived best. If our father had not died so young—if our childhood had been allowed its normal span—perhaps we could never have found what it is to live in that country."

"Do you hear what we are saying to you, boy?" Jakob asked. "Do you understand Wilhelm?"

"I think so," Tom said.

"The stories, our treasures, are for children, among others. But . . ."

Tom nodded: he saw. It was not the personal point.

"No child can go the whole way with them," Wilhelm said.

"We gave our wings," Jakob said. "For our song was our life. But as for you . . ."

Both brothers looked at him indulgently.

"Do not idly throw away any of your gifts," said Jakob. "But when you are called . . ."

"*We* answered. We all must answer," Wilhelm said. "Oh, my, what are we saying to this boy? It is late. Do you mind stopping work until tomorrow, brother? It is time to join our wives."

They turned large brown eyes toward him, clearly expecting him to leave.

"But what happens next?" Tom asked, almost believing that they were who they appeared to be and could tell him.

"All stories unfold," Jakob said. "But they take many turns before they reach their ends. Embrace the treasure, child. It is our best advice. Now we must depart."

Tom stood up from the chesterfield, confused: so much of what happened here ended with a sudden departure! "Where do you go? According to you, where are we?"

Wilhelm laughed. "Why, Shadowland, boy. Shadowland is everything to us, as it may be to you. Shadowland is where we spent our busy lives. You may be within a wood . . . within a storied wood . . ."

"Or fur-wrapped in a sleigh in deep snow . . ."

"Or dying for love of a sleeping princess . . ."

"Or before a dwindling fire with your head full of pictures . . ."

"Or even asleep with a head full of cobwebs and dreams . . ."

"And still you will be in Shadowland."

Both brothers laughed, and blew out the candles on their desks.

"I have another question," Tom said into the lively blackness.

"Ask the stories, child," said a departing voice.

A flurry of quiet rustling, then silence: Tom knew they were gone. "But they never give the same answers," he said to the black room.

He felt his way to the door.

17

When he turned the corner back into the main hallway, Coleman Collins was standing before him in the semi-darkness, blocking his way. Tom felt an instant ungovernable surge of fright—he had broken one of the rules, and the magician knew it. He must have seen him turn out of the short corridor.

Collins' posture gave him no clues; he could not see his face, which was shadowed. The magician's hands were in his pockets. His shoulders slouched. The entire front of his body was a dark featureless pane in which a few vest buttons shone darkly: tiger's eyes.

"I went in that room," Tom said.

Collins nodded. Still he kept his hands in his pockets and slouched.

"You knew I would."

Collins nodded again.

Tom edged closer to the wall. But Collins was deliberately blocking his way. "You knew I would, and you wanted me to." He bravely moved a few inches nearer, but Collins made no movement. "I can accept what I saw," Tom said. He heard the note of insistence, of fear, in his voice.

Collins dropped his head. He drew one heel toward him along the carpet. Now Tom could see his face: pensive, withdrawn. The magician tilted his head and shot a cold glance directly into Tom's eyes.

There might have been some playacting in it; Tom could not tell. All he knew was that Collins was frightening him. Alone in the hallway, he was scarier than in the freezing sleigh. Collins was more authoritative than a dozen Mr. Thorpes. The expression which had jumped out of his eyes had nailed Tom to the wall.

"Isn't that what you said? Isn't that what you wanted?"

Collins exhaled, pursed his lips. Finally he spoke. "Arrogant midget. Do you really think you know what I *want?*"

Tom's tongue froze in his mouth. Collins reared back and propped his head against the wall. Tom caught the sudden clear odor of alcohol. "In two days you have betrayed me twice. I will not forget this."

"But I thought—"

The magician's head snapped forward. Tom flinched, feared that Collins would strike him.

"You thought. You disobeyed me twice. That is what I think." His eyes augered into Tom. "Will you wander into my room next? Ransack my desk? I think that you need more than cartoons and amusements, little boy."

"But you told me I could—"

"I told you you could *not.*"

Tom swallowed. "Didn't you want me to see them?"

"See whom, traitor?"

"The two in there. Jakob and Wilhelm. Whoever they were."

"That room is empty. For now. Get on your way, boy. I was going to give your friend a word of warning. You can do it for me. Scat. Get out of here. Now!"

"A warning about what?"

"He'll know. Didn't you hear me? Get out of here." He stepped aside, and Tom slipped by him. "I'm going to have fun with you," the magician said to his back.

Tom went as quickly as he could to the front of the stairs without actually running. He realized that he was dripping with sweat—even his legs felt sweaty. He could hear Collins limping away down the hall in the direction of the theaters.

The next second brought a new astonishment.

When he looked up the stairs, he saw a nut-faced old woman in a black dress at their top, looking down at him

in horror. She lifted her hands sharply and scurried away
out of sight.

"Hey!" Tom said. He ran after her up the stairs. He
could hear her moving frantically as a squirrel, trying to
escape him. When he reached the head of the stairs, he
ran past the bedrooms and saw the hem of a black dress
just vanishing around a corner at the end of the hall. To
his side, through the glass and far away, lights burned
deep in the forest and sent their reflections across the
black lake.

He reached the far end of the hall and realized that he
had never been there before. The old woman had opened
an outside door, one Tom had never seen, and was
starting to descend an exterior staircase that curved back
in toward the patio and the house. Tom got through the
door before it closed and clapped a hand on the old
woman's shoulder.

She stopped as suddenly as a paralyzed hare. Then she
looked up into his face with a compressed, dense mixture
of expressions on her dry old face. A few white hairs grew
from her upper lip. Her eyes were so brown as to look
black, and her eyebrows were strongly, starkly black. He
understood two things at once: she was foreign, and she
was deeply ashamed that he had seen her.

"I'm sorry," he said.

She jerked her shoulder away from his hand.

"I just wanted to talk to you."

She shook her head. Her eyes were cold flat stones
embedded in deep wrinkles.

"Do you work here?"

She made no movement at all, waiting for him to allow
her to go.

"Why weren't we supposed to see you?" Nothing. "Do
you know Del?" He caught a glimmer of recognition at
the name. "What's going on around here? I mean, how
does all this stuff work? Why aren't we supposed to know
you're here? Do you do the cooking? Do you make the
beds?"

No sign of anything but impatience to get away from
him. He pantomimed breaking an egg into a pan, frying
the egg. She nodded curtly. Inspired, he asked, "Do you
speak English?"

No: a flat, denying movement of the head. She stabbed him with another black glance, and turned abruptly away and flew down the stairs.

Tom lingered on the little balcony for a moment. From the bottom of the long hill, girdled by woods, the lake shone enigmatically up at him. He tried to find the spot where Coleman Collins had taken him in the sleigh, but could find no peak high enough—had all that really taken place only in his head? Far off in the distance he heard a man crying out in the woods.

His room had been prepared for the night. The bed was turned down, the bedside lamp shone on the Rex Stout paperback. That, and the clear-cut puzzles it contained, seemed very remote to him—he could not remember anything he had read the night before. The sliding doors between his room and Del's were shut.

He went to the doors and gently knocked; no response. Where was Del? Probably he was out exploring—imitating Tom's actions of the night before. Probably that was what the "warning" was about. Tom sighed. For the first time since getting on the train with Del, he thought of Jenny Oliver and Diane Darling, the two girls from the neighboring school; maybe it was Archie Goodwin and his strings of women that brought them to mind, but he wished he could talk to them, either of them. It had been a long time since he had talked to a girl: he remembered the girl in the window the magician had shown him— shown him as coolly as a grocer displays a shelf of canned beans.

His room was barren and lonely. Its cleanliness, its straight angles and simple colors, excluded him. He hated being alone in it, he realized; but now he did not feel that he could go anywhere else. Loneliness assailed him. He missed Arizona and his mother. For a moment Tom felt utterly bereft: orphaned. He sat on the hard bed and thought he was in jail. All of Vermont felt like a prison.

Tom stood up and began to pace the room. Because he was fifteen and healthy, simple movement made him feel better. At that moment, in one of those peculiarly adult mental gestures which I see as characteristic of the young Tom Flanagan, he arrived at both a recognition and a decision. Shadowland, as much as he knew of it, was a test harder and more important than any he had ever taken at Carson; and he could not let Shadowland defeat him. He would use Collins' own maxim against him, if he had to, and discover how to do the impossible.

He nodded, knowing that he was arming for a fight, and realized that he had lost the desire to cry which had come over him a moment before. Then he heard a noise from behind the sliding doors. It was a light, bubbling sound of laughter, muted, as if hidden behind a hand. Tom knocked again on the doors.

The sound came again, even more clearly.

"Del . . . you there?"

"For God's sake, be quiet," came Del's whisper.

"What's going on?"

"Keep your voice down. I'll be right there."

A moment later the left half of the door slid an inch back, and Del was scowling out at him. "Where were *you* all day?" Del asked.

"I want to talk to you. He made me think it was winter—"

"Hallucinatory terrain," Del said. "He's spending a lot of time with you, letting me knock around by myself . . ."

"And I remember flying." Tom felt his face assume some expression absolutely new to him, uttering this statement. He half-expected Del to deny it.

"Okay," Del said. "You're having a whale of a time. I'm glad."

"And I met an old woman. She doesn't speak English. I had to practically tackle her to get her to stop running away. And your uncle . . ."

His voice stopped. A girl had just walked into the tiny area of Del's room he could see. She wore one of Del's shirts over a black bathing suit. Her hair was wet and she had moth-colored eyes.

Del glanced over his shoulder and then looked irritatedly back at Tom. "Okay, now you've seen her. She was swimming in the lake just after dinner, and I asked her up here. I guess you might as well come in."

The girl backed away toward the slightly mussed bed, stepping like a faun on her bare legs. It was impossible for Tom not to stare at her. He had no more idea then if she were beautiful than he did if the moon were rock or powder: she looked nothing at all like the popular girls at Phipps-Burnwood. But he could not stop looking at her. The girl's eyes went down to her tanned bare legs, then back to him. She tugged Del's shirt close about her.

"You probably guess already, but this is Rose Armstrong," Del said.

The girl sat down on the bed.

"I'm Tom Armstrong," he said. "Oh, Jesus. Flanagan, I mean."

III

The Goose Girl

Just looking at her had me so rattled—I saw right away what Del had meant about her looking "hurt." You couldn't miss it. That face looked like it had absorbed about a thousand insults and recovered from each one separately. But if she'd ever had them, she was recovering, all right. Honestly, I couldn't believe that Del had been seeing this amazing girl every summer; and watching her sit down on Del's bed with her knees together, I knew, knew, knew, that my whole relationship with Del had just changed.

1

Miami Beach, 1975

But before we can really look at Rose Armstrong through Tom Flanagan's eyes and travel with these three young people through their final convulsive months at Shadowland, I must introduce a seeming digression. Up to this point, this story has been haunted by two ghosts: of course one is Rose Armstrong, who in a black bathing suit and a boy's shirt has just now sat down on Del's suggestively mussed-up bed, badly "rattling" Tom Flanagan. The other ghost is far more peripheral; certainly the reader has forgotten him by now. I mean Marcus Reilly, who was mentioned less than half a dozen times in the first part of this story—and perhaps Marcus Reilly is a persistent "ghost" only to me. Yet suicide, especially at an early age, makes its perpetrator stick in the mind. It is also true that when I last saw Marcus Reilly, a few months before he killed himself, he said some things that later seemed to me to have a bearing on the story of Del Nightingale and Tom Flanagan; but this may be mere self-justification.

At the beginning of this story, I said that Reilly was the most baffling of my class's failures. As a Carson student, he had a great success, though not academically. He was a good athlete, and his closest friends were Pete Bayliss and Chip Hogan and Bobby Hollingsworth, who was on the same terms with everyone. A burly blond boy with a passing resemblance to the young Arnold Palmer, Marcus was bright but not reflective. His chief characteristic was that he took things as they came. His parents were rich—their house in Quantum Hills was more lavish than the Hillmans'. He could have been taken as one kind of model of the Carson student: someone who, though clearly he would never become a teacher, could be expected to have some slight trace of Fitz-Hallan about him always.

After our odd, limping graduation, Reilly went off to a private college in the Southeast; I cannot remember which one. What I do remember is his delight in finding a place where suntans and a social life were taken to be as critical as grades. After college he went to a law school in the same state. I am sure that he graduated in the dead center of his class. In 1971 Chip Hogan told me that Reilly had taken a job in a Miami law firm, and I felt that small, almost aesthetic smack of satisfaction one gets when an expectation is fulfilled. It seemed the perfect job and place for him.

Four years later a New York magazine commissioned me to do an article on a famous expatriate novelist wintering in Miami Beach. The famous novelist, with whom I spent two tedious days, was a self-important bore, turning out of his hotel onto sunny Collins Avenue in a flannel suit and trilby hat, with furled umbrella. He had consciously given two months of his life to Miami Beach in order to fuel his disdain for all things American. He pretended an ignorance of the American system of coinage. "Is this one really called a quarter? Dear me, how *unimaginative*." When I had sufficient notes for the article, I put the whole project into a mental locker and decided to look up Bobby Hollingsworth. I had not seen Bobby in at least ten years. He was living in Miami Beach, I knew from the alumni magazine, and owned a company that made plumbing fixtures. Once, in an Atlanta airport men's room, I had looked down into the bowl and seen stamped there "HOLLINGSWORTH VITREOUS." I wanted to see what had become of him, and when I called him up he promptly invited me to his house.

His house was a huge Spanish mansion facing Indian Creek and the row of hotels across it. Moored at his dock was a forty-foot boat that looked like it could make a pond of the Atlantic.

"This is really the place," Bobby said during dinner. "You got the greatest weather in the world, you got the water, you got business opportunities up the old wazoo. No shit, this place is paradise. I wouldn't go back to Arizona if you paid me. As for living up North—wow." He shook his head. Bobby at thirty-two was pudgy, soft and a sponge. A diamond as big as a knuckle rode on one sausagy hand. He still had his perpetual smile, which was not a smile but the way his mouth sat on his face. He wore a yellow terry-cloth shirt and matching shorts. He was enjoying his wealth, and I enjoyed his pleasure in it. I gathered that his wife's family had given him his start in the business, and that he had rather surprised them by his success. Monica, his wife, said little during the meal, but jumped up every few minutes to supervise the cook. "She treats me like a king," Bobby said during one of Monica's excursions to the kitchen. "When I get home, I'm royalty. She lives for that boat—I gave it to her for Christmas last year. Squealed like a puppy. What do I know from boats? But it makes her happy. Say, if you play golf we could go out to the club tomorrow. I got an extra set of clubs."

"I'm sorry, but I don't play," I said.

"Don't play *golf?*" For a moment Bobby seemed totally perplexed. He had taken me into his world so completely that he had forgotten that I was not a permanent resident there. "Well, hell, why don't we go out in the boat? Laze around, have a few drinks? Monica would love that."

I said that I might be able to do that.

"Great, kiddo. You know, this is what that school of ours was all about, wasn't it?"

"What do you mean, Bobby?"

His wife came back to the table and Bobby turned to her. "He's coming out on the boat with us tomorrow. Let's toss some lines overboard, catch dinner, hey?"

Monica gave a wan smile.

"Sure. It'll be great. Now, this is what I'm saying—our old school had one goal, right? To get us to where I am now. And to know how to live once we get here. That's the way I see it. To make us into the kind of people who could fit in anywhere. I want to write in to the alumni magazine and say that you can travel all over the Southeast and see my name whenever you stop to take a leak. And that's almost true."

Monica looked away and turned over a lettuce leaf on her salad plate to peer at its underside.

"Do you ever see Marcus Reilly?" I asked. "I understand he lives here."

"Saw him once," Bobby said. "Mistake. Marcus got involved in some bad shit—got disbarred. Stay away from him. He's a downer."

"Really?" I was surprised.

"Oh, he was a big deal for a little while. Then I guess he got weird. Take my advice . . . I'll give you his phone number if you like, but stay away from him. He's a failure. He has to stick his nose above water to suck air."

The next morning I called the number Bobby had given me. A man at the other end of the line said, "Wentworth."

"Marcus?"

"Who?"

"Marcus Reilly? Is he there?"

"Oh, yeah. Just a second."

Another telephone rang. It was lifted, but the person at the other end said nothing.

"Marcus? Is that you?" I gave my name.

"Hey, great," came the breezy, husky voice of Marcus Reilly. "You in town? How about we get together?"

"Can I take you to lunch today?"

"Hell, lunch is on me. I'm at the Wentworth Hotel on Collins Avenue, just up on the right side from Seventy-third Street. Tell you what, I'll meet you outside. Okay? Twelve o'clock?"

I called Bobby Hollingsworth to say that I would not be able to go out on his boat. "That's fine," Bobby said. "Come back next time, and we'll go out with a couple of girls I know. We got a date?"

"Sure," I said. I could see him lolling back on a deck chair, propping a drink on his yellow-terry-cloth belly, telling a good-looking whore that whenever you took a leak in the Southeast, you could read his name just by looking down.

There was nothing splendid about Collins Avenue up where Marcus Reilly lived. Old men in canvas hats and plaid trousers below protruding bellies, old women in baggy dresses and sunglasses crawled beneath the sidewalk awnings of little shops. Discount stores, bars, cut-rate novelty shops where everything would be an inch deep in dust. At the Wentworth Hotel, the motto *Where Life Is a Treat* was painted on the yellow plaster. The lobby seemed to be outside, in a sort of alcove set off the sidewalk.

At five past twelve Marcus came bustling out, wearing a glen-plaid suit, walking quickly past the rows of old people sitting in aluminum-and-plastic chairs as if he were afraid one of them would stop him.

"Great to see you, great to see you," he said, pumping my hand. He no longer resembled the young Arnold Palmer. His cheeks had puffed out, and his eyes seemed narrower. The moisture in the air screwed his hair up into curls. Like the expatriate novelist's, his suit was much too warm for the climate, but he had none of the novelist's internal air conditioning. Marcus snapped his fingers, smacked his palms together, and looked up and down the street. I could smell violence on him, as you sometimes can on a dog. "Jesus, hey, here we are. What is it, fifteen years?"

"About that," I said.

"Let's move, man. Let's see some sights. You been here long?"

"Just a couple of days."

Marcus rolled away from me and began bustling down the street. "Too bad. Where you staying?"

I named my hotel.

"A dump. A dump, believe me." We rounded the corner and Marcus opened the door to a green Gremlin with a big rusting dent on its right-rear fender. "A word I could use to describe this whole town." We got into the Gremlin. "Just toss that stuff into the back." I removed a stack of old Miami *Herald*s and a ball of dirty shirts. "You want lunch first, or a drink?"

"A drink would be fine, Marcus."

"Beautiful." He raced the motor and sped away from the curb. "There's a good joint a couple of blocks away." We raced around the corner, Marcus talking like a man possessed the entire time. "I mean, it's got its good points, and I'm not counted out yet, but a dump is what you'd call a place full of ingrates, right? Am I right? And that's what we got here—wall to wall. People I brought along, got started right, did everything for . . . you know I was disbarred, don't you? You must have got my number from Bobby?"

"Yes," I said.

"The shit king. 'In six states, you can take a dump on my name,' right? Bobby's so goddamned cute these days. And I helped *him* when he first came to Miami." Marcus was sweating, moving the car as if it were heavy as a truck. His curls tightened up a notch. "You don't get contracts like he got, no matter what kind of rich dopefiend gash you married, without help from people who know people. Not in Miami. Not anywhere. And now he treats me like scum. Ah, screw Bobby. The way he puts on flab, he'll drop dead when he's forty. Here we are."

Marcus banged the Gremlin against the curb and rocketed out of the seat. He half-ran into a bar called the Hurricane Pub. It was so open to the street it seemed to be missing a wall.

"Counselor!" the bartender shouted.

"Jerry! Give us a couple beers here!" Reilly bounced onto a stool, lit a cigarette, and started talking again. "Jerry, this guy here's an old friend of mine."

"Real nice," Jerry said, and put the beers down before us.

Marcus drained half his glass. "In this town, you see, it helps to know everybody. That way you know where the bodies are buried. I'm not through yet. I got deals cooking like you wouldn't believe. Hell, I'm still a young guy." I knew his age because it was mine. He looked at least ten years older. "And I got the right mental attitude—you're not counted out until you count yourself out. And believe it or not, I get a bang out of being here—I even get a bang out of the Wentworth. Collins Avenue addresses are gold in this town. Two, three years, I'll have my license back. You'll see. And what do you bet friend Bobby will come around looking for a favor? I know everybody, *everybody.* I can get things done. And that's one thing people in this town respect, a guy who can deliver." The rest of his beer was gone. "How about something to eat?" He slapped two dollars down on the bar and we rushed back out onto the street.

A few blocks down, he opened the door of Uncle Ernie's Ice Cream Shop. "You get great sandwiches here." We sat at a table in the rear and ordered our sandwiches. "That school we went to—that *place*—boy, I can't get it out of my mind. For one thing, Hollingsworth's always talking about it—like it was Eton or something." Even sitting and eating, Marcus was a congeries of small agitated movements. He worked his elbows, drummed his fingers, unscrewed his hair, rubbed his cheeks. "You remember Lake the Snake and that chapel?"

"I remember."

"Stone crazy. Wacko. And Fitz-Hallan and his fairy tales. Man, I could tell him a few fairy tales. Last year, when I still had my license, I got involved with these people—*heavy* people, you know? These were serious people. Maybe I wasn't too swift, who knows, but people like that always need lawyers. And if I want somebody to get hurt, he'll get hurt, you know what I'm saying. And at the same time, through connections of these serious people, I got next to some folks from Haiti. This city is full of Haitians, illegals most of them, but these people were different. Are different. You done with your sandwich yet?"

"Not quite yet." Marcus' had vanished as if he had taken it in one gulp.

"Don't worry. I want to show you something. It's in your line—I know your work, remember. I want to show you this. It's connected to these people from Haiti."

I finished off my sandwich and Marcus jumped up from his seat and tossed money on the table. Out on the sunlit, shabby street, Marcus' big florid face came up an inch away from my own. "I'm in tight with them right now, these guys. Disbarred, who cares if you're a Haitian? They got a flexible notion of the law. We're going to do big things. You know anything about Venezuela?"

"Not much."

"We're into buying an island off the coast—big old island, classified as a national park. One of these guys knows the regime, we can get it reclassified in a minute. That's one of the things we're talking about. Also a lot of *odd* stuff, you know, *odd*?" He took my elbow and hauled me across the street. "Mind if we stop at McDonald's? I'm still hungry."

I shook my head, and Marcus led me into the bright restaurant. We had been standing directly in front of it.

"Big Mac, fries," he told the girl. "Next time you're here, we'll go to Joe's Stone Crab. Fantastic place." He took his order to the window and began to bolt the food standing up. "Okay, let's talk. What do you think about that stuff Fitz-Hallan used to say?"

"What stuff?"

"About things being magically right? What does that mean?"

"You tell me."

"Bobby thinks that's what he's got. The boat, the house, the two-hundred-dollar shoes. I helped him get a rock-bottom deal on a Jacuzzi. That's what he thinks it is. You probably think it's a good paragraph."

"At times," I said. The Big Mac was gone, and the fries were following it.

"Well, I think it's a crock. I've seen a lot of stuff, being with these guys. They . . . got a lot of strange beliefs." The fries were gone, and Marcus was moving out of the restaurant, wiping his fingers on his trousers. "They can make you go blind, make you deaf, make you see things, they think. Magic. I say, if it's magic, it can't be right. There's no such thing as good magic, that's what I learned."

"You know about Tom—"

"Flanagan. Sure. I even went to see him once, down here. But . . ." His face suddenly fell apart. It was like watching the collapse of an intricate public building. "You see a bird over there?"

I looked: a few peeling storefronts, the ubiquitous old men.

"Forget it. Let's go for a ride." He belched, and I smelled meat.

I looked at my watch. I wished I had gone out on Bobby's boat and were sitting on wide seamless water, listening to Bobby gab about the toilet business. "I really have to go," I said.

"No, you can't," Marcus said, and looked stricken. "Come on. I want to show you something." He pulled me toward his car by the sheer force of his desperation.

Back in the Gremlin, we drove aimlessly around upper Miami Beach for half an hour, Marcus talking the entire time. He took corners randomly, sometimes doubling back as if trying to lose someone, often cutting dangerously in front of other cars. "See, there's the library . . . and see that bookstore? It's great. You'd like it. There's a lot of stuff in Miami Beach for a guy like you. I could introduce you to a lot of the right people, get you material like you never dreamed existed, man. You ever been to Haiti?"

I had not.

"You ought to go. Great hotels, beaches, good food . . . Here's a park. Beautiful park. You ever been to Key Biscayne? No? It's close, you want to go there?"

"I can't, Marcus," I said. I had long since suspected that whatever he wanted me to see did not exist. Or that he had decided I should not see it after all. Finally I persuaded him to drive me back to my hotel.

When he dropped me off, he took one of my hands in both of his and looked at me with his leaky blue eyes. "Had a hell of a good time, didn't we? Keep your eyes open, now, pal. You'll read about me in the papers." He roared off, and I thought I saw him talking to himself as his battered car swung back out into Collins Avenue. I went upstairs, took a shower, ordered a drink from room service, and lay down on the bed and slept for three hours.

Two months later I heard that Marcus had shot himself—he had named me as executor of his estate, but there was no estate except for a few clothes and the Gremlin, in which he had killed himself. The lawyer who rang me said that Marcus had put the bullet in his head around six in the morning, in a parking lot between a tennis court and the North Community Center. It was about three blocks from the McDonald's he had dragged me into.

"Why would he name me as his executor?" I asked. "I barely knew him."

"Really?" asked the lawyer. "He left a note in his room that you were the only person who would understand what he was going to do. He wrote that he had shown you something—while you were visiting him here."

"Maybe he thought he did," I said. I remembered him asking me if I had seen a bird as little tucks and dents appeared in his face, just as if someone were sewing him up from the inside.

2

Tom and Rose

The girl would not meet his eyes. She sat on Del's bed, looking at her feet as if he had embarrassed her. Tom saw that she thought he had been making fun of her—Del was staring at him in amazement—and he said, "I'm sorry. That just popped out. I didn't mean anything by it."

"I know who you are," she said. Then she lifted her face and gave him a look from her pale iridescent eyes which nearly blew him across the room. "Everybody says you're going to be a great magician."

"Look, I'm a little sick of hearing that," Tom said, speaking with more heat than he had intended. Rose Armstrong looked as though a strong word would melt her. The silk shimmered about her arms. "Who is everybody, anyhow?"

"Del and Mr. Collins. Especially Mr. Collins."

"He talked to you about me?"

"Sure. Now and then. Last winter."

Del smiled, and Tom looked at both of them, perplexed. "But he didn't even know me last winter."

"He did know you." And that, it seemed, would be that. The girl knitted her hands together and regarded him squarely. Despite what he had thought, she was relaxed. As slight and flowerlike as she was, she was a year older than both boys, and to Tom it was suddenly as if she were ten years older—she seemed massive and unknowable. But still her face with its full lips and high forehead broadcast vulnerability. The wet hair hugged her head. He realized that he envied Del, his closeness to Rose Armstrong. The girl seemed as perfect as a statue. *Living Statue.*

"He made me," Rose said with an air of bravery.

Now Tom's uneasiness increased.

"I never had a thought in my head until I met Mr. Collins," she said, and he relaxed. "I was nothing." That stabbing look of a wound deeply absorbed settled again in her face. "I would forgive him anything."

"Do you have to forgive him very often?"

"Well, he drinks a lot, and I don't like that. Sometimes he changes when he's had too much."

Tom nodded. He had seen the proof of that. He asked, "Why did you go out on that rock dressed up like it was winter? And open that smoke bomb."

"He told me to. He gave me the clothes."

"And that's enough?"

"Of course."

"Did you know that we were supposed to see you?"

"I assumed someone was supposed to see me. It wouldn't make sense otherwise."

"Does he forgive you too?"

"Why should he have to?"

"Because when I was coming up here, I met him in the hall. He was drunk. He said he was going to give Del a warning, but that I could do it for him. I guess it was about your being here."

She flushed. "I wondered . . . I guess I shouldn't be here. But tomorrow it'll probably be all right."

"You mean, when he's sober?"

She nodded. "But I shouldn't stay. Del, I . . . you know."

Tom felt the stab of envy or jealousy again. She had not once called him by his name.

"I guess so," Del said.

Tom watched as she stood up, glanced at him as if he had struck her—but was that just a part of her face, like Bobby Hollingsworth's smile? She peeled the shirt off. He jumped into the awkward silence. "Before you go, can I ask you something?"

She nodded.

"Are there some men staying here somewhere? Have you seen a bunch of men anywhere around?"

"Yes." She glanced at Del. "They haven't been here for a year or two. They stay in a cabin on the other side of the lake. They're his friends."

"Okay," Tom said.

"They used to work with him," she added. With another glance at Del, "I don't like it when they're here.

They're not like him." She was holding the shirt up before her, shielding herself. "They're dead."

This was totally unexpected. "That's ridiculous." He saw that it was something Collins had told her, and which she had accepted.

"You may think it is. He told me about it. About how it happened."

"It's still ridiculous." He heard the repetition, and thought he sounded nearly as stupid as the girl. "Did he tell you to say that to us?"

"No. I have to go."

Tom felt a burning impatience allied with an equally strong desire to keep Rose Armstrong in the room. "Where do you stay? In the house?"

"I can't tell you. I'm not supposed to." She dropped the shirt on the bed and smiled at Del. "I can tell it's your friend's first time."

"Could you carry a letter out of here for me? Could you mail a letter for me?"

"Nothing is supposed to leave here," she said, and began to move delicately toward the hall door. "But you could ask Elena."

"That woman? She doesn't speak English."

"I'm sure she understands the words 'post office.'" She gave her first smile. "I hope you're in a better mood the next time I meet you." Then she was at the door, sliding around it like a shadow. "Good-bye, Del." She turned the iridescent eyes toward Tom. "Good-bye, grumpy Tom." Then she was gone.

Del's face was rapturous. Tom heard the pad of bare feet moving down the hall in the direction he had chased the woman called Elena. Then the soft opening of a door.

Tom turned to the still-transfixed Del. "I saw the Brothers Grimm downstairs," he said. "I guess they're dead, too." Del simply smiled at him. "What is she, hypnotized or something?" Del did not speak or move. Tom walked away from him and went out the door. The hall was dark and quiet. In the woods, the lights burned like beacons. He went up to the glass and put his hands to his face to blot out his reflection. Rose Armstrong was padding over the flagstones; she began to descend the iron ladder.

He stood in the hall until the shaft of moonlight on the water illuminated a silvery, lifting arm; froth where her feet kicked.

"Now you know," Del said behind him.

Tom nodded. He heard the mistrust in his friend's voice.

3

War

"This is a true story," the magician said, "and its name is 'The Death of Love.' Ah, melodrama."

His thick white hair stirred in the light breeze. The three of them sat on the stony beach, Collins facing the sharp rise of land and the boys looking toward him and the glimmering deep blue lake behind him. To their right, the weather-beaten pier protruded out into the lake; beyond that the gray-boarded boathouse sat on concrete pilings. As Rose Armstrong had hinted, Collins showed none of his cold rage of the night before. He had placed a note on the boys' breakfast trays, asking them to meet him on the beach at ten in the morning. Each of them still turning over the encounter with Rose Armstrong in his mind, they had descended the shaky iron structure at a quarter to ten; Collins, a white sunhat on his head and a rolled blanket and a picnic basket under his arm, had come down the stairs twenty minutes later. He wore a long-sleeved blue shirt, gray lightweight slacks and sandals. The shirt and slacks were slightly too large, as if he had recently lost weight. "Good morning, apprentices," he said. "All parties have a good night's sleep after yesterday's exertions?"

Collins unfurled the blanket on the beach, set the wicker basket on it. He removed the hat and set it on the basket. "Sit down, boys. History lesson, if you are not too bedazzled by love to listen. Time for one of those stories I've been promising you. Face me, that's the way. If you get bored, you can always look at the water and daydream about Miss Armstrong." He smiled. "This is a true story.

* * *

"By now the two of you know more about the operations of true magic than ninety-nine percent of the population, including other magicians, and I want to take you back to a time when I was learning about these things myself—to the time when I first came into command of my own strengths. We are going forty years back, to just before the nineteen-twenties.

"In fact, we are going back to 1917, the year America joined the Great War. My name then was still Charles Nightingale—Del's father, my brother, was twelve years younger than I, still a boy for all practical purposes, and a stranger to me. I had trained as a doctor, and had supported myself as a magician during medical school. I was a good mechanic and card-cranker. Manual dexterity. I intended to be a surgeon. Magic was only a hobby then, though I had always felt in it something beyond the simple tricks I had mastered, something vastly powerful. Medicine seemed the only thing in the practical world that could approach that realm of responsibility and awe to which I aspired—I mean that world (only dimly apprehended by me) where the ability to make fundamental changes is so great as to automatically inspire awe. If I had been conventionally religious, I suppose I might have gone into the clergy. But I was always too ambitious for that. In 1917 I qualified as a doctor and was immediately given a commission and sent to France on a troop ship. My assignment was to a dressing station at Cantigny. I brought only a few things with me, clothes and cards and some books by a Frenchman named Eliphas Levi, a magician who had died in 1875. The books were the two volumes of *Le Dogme et Rituel de la Haute Magie,* rather wildly, verbosely written, but full of evocations of that power I was searching for. Levi helped me to understand that Good and Evil are earthbound distinctions—when you hear someone discriminate on that basis, he is invariably up to his ankles in mud. I also carried a book by Cornelius Agrippa, the Renaissance magician, who said when asked how man could possess magical powers— remember this, boys—"No one has such power but he who has cohabited with the elements, vanquished nature, mounted higher than the heavens, elevating himself above the angels. . . ." Vanquished nature. Doctors attempt that too, but with what clumsy weapons, scalpels and sutures!

"We landed in Brest on the *Seattle* and went immediately to the Pontanzen barracks for a few days of rest before being sent to the Gondrecourt area for some rudimentary training. We traveled as part of a section, with a motor truck, two ambulances, and a Packard car in which I and a few other young doctors rode. Our route was along the Beaumont-Mandres road. From Mandres we were meant to go to the Division HQ at Menil-la-Tour. It sounded easy, back in Boston, but back in Boston I had never seen a country torn to pieces by war. The only bodies I had seen were those on dissecting tables. And remember that my military training had been laughably brief. I don't even remember what I had expected to find: a tableau from a recruiting poster, I suppose, brave youthful soldiers brandishing German helmets like scalps. *And They Said We Couldn't Fight!*

"We had gone only a short way up the Beaumont-Mandres road when we passed an old battlefield. Great zigzagging rips torn through the ground, barbed wire looping over it all, and somehow a terrifying, claustrophobic feeling of death being all around—pressing its face toward us and blowing on us with its breath. The German trenches had been occupied since 1914 and ran parallel to the Flirey-Bouconville road. We could hear artillery going off in the distance. I had never seen anything remotely like it before—never seen anything like that destroyed snowy field, nor like the scale of death that it implied. To me, right then, what I saw looked like nothing so much as the shocking litter and mess you find at the bottom of a fireplace. Charred heaps of things, filthy little piles here and there, nothing orderly, nothing even recognizable except by an effort of the imagination. That was probably the last civilian image I would be privileged to have for two years. War refers only to itself—war is self-enclosed. It takes only the smallest exposure to make you know that.

"My first real exposure came in that five-passenger

Packard. Our convoy was shelled, and shelled very heavily. This of course was colossal bad luck, but the Beaumont-Mandres road was shelled day and night, and our superiors must have decided that it was a risk they had to take. If they had known that precisely one man of the entire convoy would survive, I suppose they might have decided otherwise.

"I could hear soldiers in the supply truck singing 'Glor-ree-us, Glor-ree-us! One keg of beer for the four of us!' That was a favorite, along with 'Snowy Breasted Pearl' and 'Say Au Revoir, But Not Good-bye.' Then over the singing I heard a whistling in the air. I knew immediately what that meant.

"Our driver muttered, 'She said there would be days like this,' and just then the truck in front of us blew up. '*Jee-sus!*' the driver yelled, and cramped the wheel. I saw a body sailing upward, as if a man had taken flight; the undercarriage of the truck rolled over, gouting fire, and metal pieces scattered all over the road. We fell into an old shellhole—everybody in the Packard was yelling something. Explosions went off all around us, deafeningly loud. I was vaguely aware of an ambulance bouncing into the air like a child's toy. Men were screaming and sobbing. An arm clad in heavy wool thunked down onto the hood of the Packard. All of us fought our way out of the car, and another shell landed very near.

"I came to in the field. My face and hands were burned, and I ached mightily all over and my head felt like it had been split apart, but otherwise I was all right. I had been fantastically lucky, and from that moment forth I knew that I had been saved for some great purpose. The shells were landing all over the road, and nothing rational, nothing sensible, was left of our convoy; in a few seconds, it had been altered into a scene from hell. The ambulances were destroyed. Dead men lay all over the road. A motorcycle wheel dragged a shredded litter into the wreckage of the truck. The rest of the motorcycle, which had been riding outboard of the convoy, was not even visible. The rear end of the Packard, jutting out of the shellhole, looked like an enormous gray cheese. I reached out and picked up my little satchel of books from a heap of snow. At first I thought I was the only man left alive in

the convoy. Almost unbelievable devastation lay before
me. Bodies and parts of bodies protruded from shellholes,
from the burning vehicles—and shells continued to fall for
some time, battering the broken ambulances and flinging
the dead about. It must have been one of the most
freakish accidents of the war, that routine shelling like
that destroyed an entire medical section. Then I saw
someone move, a man in the ditch between the road and
the field. I knew him.

"He had been in the Packard with me. His name was
Lieutenant William Vendouris, and he was a new field
doctor like myself. His guts had been opened up by
shrapnel, by a jagged piece of the truck—I don't know. I
saw him lying in the ditch in a lake of his own blood. He
was holding in his intestines with his hands. They flopped
like thick purplish ropes.

"'Give me something, for God's sake,' he hissed at me.

"I had nothing. Nothing except Eliphas Levi and a pack
of cards and Cornelius Agrippa. The supplies in the truck
had been blown to bits.

"'Jesus, help me,' Vendouris screamed. I knelt beside
him and felt around his wound, although I knew he could
not be helped. By all rights he should have been unconscious, but it had not taken him that way. I could feel his
blood beating against my hands. 'Settle down, old man,' I
said. 'There are no supplies. It all went up with the truck.'

"'Carry me to the HQ,' he pleaded. His eyes rolled,
and the whites were so red that they looked about to
explode. 'It's only another three miles. *God.* Carry me
there.'

"'I can't,' I said. 'You'd die if I moved you. You're
three-fourths dead now.'

"'*I'm falling out!*' he screeched. His intestines were
slipping out of his hands, bulging nearly to the frozen
ground. He almost passed out, and I wished that he had. I
recall that he had perfect, very white teeth which seemed
already to belong to someone else—those teeth should
have adorned another body.

"A piece of the snowy field shifted, and I jumped about
a foot—I was in shock, and I thought a dead man was
standing up out there in that terrible mess. Then it shifted
again, and I saw that it was a great white bird. A huge

white owl. I was to see it once more, in France during the war, but then I thought I was hallucinating. The owl beat its wings—four feet from tip to tip, it looked—and came toward us over the landscape of broken men.

"Vendouris saw it too, and began to rave. *'It's my soul, it's my soul,'* he screamed. Blood boiled out of him. The huge bird sat on a coil of wire and looked crazily at both of us. What with my shock and Vendouris' ravings, I almost thought I could hear it speak.

"*Shoot him,* it was saying. *It is the only way.*

"I touched the revolver in its holster on my hip.

"Vendouris understood the gesture. 'Oh, God, God, God, please, no,' he pleaded. So I put my hands under his shoulders and tried to lift him.

"He screeched more horribly than any sound I had ever heard in my life, and in the field I thought I heard the owl screech too, just as if it really were his soul. 'If I lift you up,' I said, 'half of you is going to stay here. It's not possible.'

"'Then get someone.' His head fell back, but he was still alive. Those perfect teeth which should have graced a tooth-powder advertisement shone in his gray face. 'You can't shoot me. I haven't even been here a month.'

"That weird rationality, an excuse like that of a third-grader. I could feel the presence of that perhaps hallucinatory bird behind me, and it was all of a piece with the stink of burned flesh I could suddenly catch from my own face, the smell of shit and intestinal gas coming from Vendouris—all of this was thrown into an odd relief by Vendouris' strange childish plea. Something in my mind moved: I was in the war, and the war referred only to itself.

"'It's not possible,' Vendouris said, and I knew he meant that it was not possible that this had happened to him. He was still a civilian mentally.

"Now, think of my choices. I could pick him up, as he wished, and kill him—give him an agonizing death. I could stay by him and let him die. He may have had another half-hour, or however long it took him to really understand his condition. In that half-hour he would have suffered every agony possible for man to know. Killing him by lifting him would have been more merciful. His pain was already burrowing through his shock. I could have left him, gone the three miles to the hospital, and left him to die alone.

"He began to breathe in sharp little pants, like an overheated dog.

"There was really only one solution. I took my revolver out of the holster. He saw me do it and his eyes widened, and for a second he was sane again. He tried to crawl back, and most of his insides cascaded out of him.

"Maybe he died then. But I do not think so. I think what killed him was the bullet I put into his forehead.

"A sink of odors surrounded me: my own burned flesh and sweat; Vendouris' horrible stinks of dying, blood; cordite. I picked up my things and walked along the edge of the road in the direction of the artillery fire. I should have been afraid. I should have felt like running back to the port and stowing away in the next ship for America. But instead I felt as though I were walking toward my destiny, for which poor William Vendouris and four other men had already given their lives.

"Now we move ahead a couple of months. The Field Hospital was desperately understaffed, the more so that Vendouris was dead, and two other doctors and I slept three hours out of every twelve, taking shifts on a camp bed in a little tent a few yards from the larger tent which was our operating theater. Which is to say that we breathed war, drank war and slept war every day. Our work was packing wounds, closing aspirating chest wounds, and controlling hemorrhages on soldiers brought in from the battlefields and trenches by the Norton-Harjes and Red Cross ambulances. When we had taken off a leg or put a Thomas splint on a fracture, the wounded were sent off to hospitals for more extensive treatment. The loss of the truck I had been on meant not only the absence of another doctor but also of three months' worth of morphia and other supplies due for the hospital—so most of our operations were done with little or no anesthetic. Often we worked under torches just like those you see in the woods out there, moving with the comings and going of the war in Les Islettes, Cheppy and Verennes. The troops we worked with were mainly men from New York, Pennsylvania, and Connecticut, boys of nineteen and twenty who'd wake up on the table and reach for their groins with the first movement of consciousness, just to make sure everything was there. It had not been a week before all of the medical staff and many of the troops knew about what happened to Vendouris. The other doctors, a tall red-headed Georgian named Withers and a smart, haggard, bald New Yorker named Leach, seemed to approve of what I had done, and so did most of the troops.

"But they gave me a nickname. Can you guess? They called me the Collector. That act of mercy toward a fatally injured man set me apart, even in conditions as cramped and abnormal as prevailed in Field Hospital 84. Sometimes when I walked into the mess, I could hear men whispering the name. And once when I was operating on a poor little rifleman from the Pennsylvania detachment, trying to put his stomach back in place, he opened his eyes—two orderlies were holding him down—and looked at me and gasped, *'The Col . . .'* and died.

"Leach told me, 'Don't worry about it. If I'm ever in that spot, I hope you'll do me the same favor. Most of the boys are so addled by war they no longer think right.'

"There was another reason for the name. For a time I made quite a bit of money playing cards with the line officers and other doctors. I assure you, I did not cheat. I just knew much more about the behavior of cards than they. But after a time I was no longer welcome in the games—I suppose I had won about a quarter of the regiment's money, most of it from Withers, who was a rich man. Withers had come to dislike and distrust me: after initially taking my side in the Vendouris business, he had begun to think that there was something fishy in it. By the time they had got around to bringing in the bodies, there was no money in Vendouris' pockets. And of course, being what he was, Withers distrusted all Northerners on principle. He hated Negroes the same way. And it is true that the work and the hours and the almost constant shelling had affected me too. I had lost forty pounds. When I was not on duty, I drank to put myself to sleep. And while I was still welcomed in card games, I played feverishly, recklessly—often I took large sums from Withers on the strength of a bluff.

"But after three or four months of those terrible conditions, I gave in to the strain. I began to imagine that I was poor William Vendouris. My destiny, which had seemed mysteriously near on the day I walked toward the front, had vanished with an equal mysteriousness. Unless Vendouris was my destiny. One day I saw him lying on a stretcher just taken from one of the Norton-Harjes ambulances—grinning in pain with his perfect teeth, holding in his purple guts with both hands. He looked toward me and said, 'My soul, Collector, my soul.' I staggered, and Leach saw me do it and took over my job.

"The next day it was clear to me: I *was* Vendouris. I had simply been given the wrong papers. I explained this to Leach and to Withers, and they sat me down and got the colonel. I explained to him too that my name was not Nightingale but Vendouris, and that Nightingale had been killed on his first day in France. When I looked into the mirror, I saw William Vendouris' face. When I dressed, I put on Vendouris' clothes. I asked the colonel if he could get me the address back home of my wife and family, because the war had driven it out of my mind.

"The colonel arranged for me to be sent to the Neurological Hospital at Tours, and after a week there I was evacuated to Base Hospital 117 at La Fauche, where I wasted my time with carpentry and woodcarving—they could have sent me home or sent me back to work, and they sent me back to work. To Ste. Nazaire.

"It was in Ste. Nazaire that my destiny and I finally came face to face. And it was my destiny that sent me there, for the day after I left, Field Hospital 84 got a direct hit from a German shell, and Dr. Leach and all the men there but one were killed on the spot. Only Withers, who was in the camp bed in the separate tent and who hated me, survived. And he was a part of my destiny too."

4

"I was quartered in a factory taken over by the army," Collins said, and Tom looked up to see that the air was

darkening. The sun was a red ball above the trees on the
other side of the lake. His watch said it was just past ten-
thirty. *It's a trick,* he told himself. *Relax and enjoy it.*

"Of course there was not much left to show what it had
been before the war—I think the Germans had used it
before we did. The lines had been dismantled and rows of
cots for the enlisted men filled three-fourths of the
enormous floor. Officers like myself had little cubicles
with doors you could lock. On the factory's second floor
were some staff offices—medical personnel also had the
use of a large gaslit basement filled with sprung couches
and exhausted chairs. The hospital was across the street
from the factory, and at most hours of day or night you
could find unshaven young doctors asleep on the couches,
breathing in clouds of third-hand pipe smoke. The idea
was, I guess, that I had suffered a temporary lapse and
could come to my senses away from the front, in a more
or less medical atmosphere. And if I did not—well, as
long as I was steady enough to operate in a week, it did
not matter what I thought my name was. We were short
of doctors, and nobody ever suggested sending me home.

"The orderly who showed me to my cubicle called me
Lieutenant Nightingale, and I said, 'That is an error. My
name is Lieutenant William Vendouris. Please try to
remember that, Private.' He gave me a rather frightened
look and faded out the door.

"I slept for about two days straight, and woke up
starved. I straightened my uniform, laced up my puttees,
and went across the street to the hospital canteen.

"Black attendants were dishing up the food and pouring
coffee, and I got in line, thinking that now things were
going to work out. Then I heard a drawling Southern
voice coming from one of the tables, saying, 'Waaall, the
Collector's here. The coin collector.' I turned around. Dr.
Withers was staring at me, exuding hatred from every
bristling orange hair on his head. He too had been
transferred to Ste. Nazaire. He leaned across the table
and began to whisper to the doctor eating with him. It
suddenly seemed that everyone in the canteen was looking at me. I put down my tray and left. Out on the street I
bought a loaf of bread, some cheese, and a bottle of wine
and went back to my cubicle. Later I went out for more

wine. I felt absolutely flat and useless. I knew Withers would be spreading terrible stories about me. I wanted to get back to work in order to prove myself, but my orders did not begin for another five days. Until then, I did not exist except as a name—the wrong name—on a cubicle door.

"Drink is a sacrament, you know. Any drink is a sacrament, and alcohol loosens the ropes tying down the god within. I reread some pages of *Le Dogme et Rituel*, and saw more in them than I ever had before. Then I ripped off a long piece of paper, lettered "Vendouris" on it and tacked it over "Lt. Nightingale" on my door. After that I rooted around in my case for my cards and did lifts and passes and shuffles for a couple of hours. If I did not exist in the Army's eyes, that was the perfect place for magic to flourish—an official limbo. And for five days I drank wine and ate cheese and bread and soaked myself in the practice of magic. It was a rededication—was I not a man risen from the dead? A man with secret power in his fingers? It was perhaps the most intense period of my life, and by the time it was over I knew that medicine was only a byroad for me, and that magic was the highway. I must have read Levi's book three times straight through, turning the pages with Vendouris' fingers, reading the type with Vendouris' eyes.

"On the sixth day I showered and changed my clothes and reported to the hospital. The major in charge of the administration admitted me and looked me over, knowing that I was crazy. He hated to be stuck with a mental case, if that was what I was, but no one had told him that I couldn't doctor with the best man on his staff. He said, 'I understand that you no longer acknowledge the name Charles Nightingale, Lieutenant.' All he wanted was for me to get out of his office and get to work, where my craziness would not be flaunted in his face. I said, 'That is correct, Major. But to avoid trouble until this matter is corrected, I have no objections if the staff want to address me as Dr. Collector.' He blinked. 'This is a nickname,' I explained. Of course by then he had heard it from Withers. 'Call yourself what you like, Lieutenant. Your performance records are excellent. I just don't want any trouble.'

"I could see his aura as I spoke to him. It was dirty, inflamed. He was a coward, an unhealthy man. Not like you two boys. You have wonderful healthy auras. Can you see mine?"

The red sun split into a brilliant haze behind the magician's head: Tom could look at Collins only by squinting. Glowing redness swam about him. "Yes," Del said beside him. Spears of blackness shot through the red.

"A month later, I met a remarkable man, whose aura was rainbowlike and seemed to blaze." Collins let this picture hang in the air before them a moment, then continued his story.

"There was a great deal of initial suspicion about me, but my behavior in the operating theater gradually put it to rest. It was a slightly more relaxed version of Hospital 84—most of the time we had morphia, and we did not actually have to tie up the wounds with bootlaces and fishing wire. But it was working nine or ten hours all day in the stink of blood, with the screams of the poor injured devils all about us. I knew that I was stronger than I had ever been in my life; I felt the beginnings of that power which I had always known would be within me, as fixed and steely as the light from a star. On the one morning a week I had off, I went through the bookstores which had survived the shelling and found French translations of the writings of Fludd and Campanella, the famous sixteenth-century magicians, and Mather's translation of *The Key of Solomon*. Even in the midst of the bloody, harried work of patching up soldiers so they could return to the trenches to be killed, I felt the strength of my other craft. I liked being called Dr. Collector. Eventually only Withers distrusted me—he still imagined that I had stolen his money at the card table, and he refused to work next to me or to eat at the same bench.

"Of course I had eventually begun to remember my own past, including the moment when I had shot Vendouris. To that extent the colonel's therapy had been successful. But I was the Collector: I had collected Vendouris, or he had collected me, and I kept his name on the door of my cubicle. It seemed to me that a portion of his soul had entered mine, and was a part of that which gave me strength.

"And the day after I remembered putting my merciful bullet into my dying fellow doctor and felt my repressed personality returning to me, I was sewing up a private named Tayler from Fall Ridge, Arkansas, after removing a bullet from his lung. To work on the lungs, you cut the ribs away from the breastbone and peel them back like a door to the chest cavity. I had the bullet out, along with a third of Tayler's lung, which had become nearly gangrenous with infection. I thought he had a fair chance for survival—these days, it would be a very good chance. It was in no way an exceptional operation, in fact I think it was my third like it of the week. But Tayler died while I was suturing him up. I felt his life stopping: as though I'd heard the sudden cessation of an unobtrusive noise, heard the absence of a sound. Then, though I had paid no attention to his aura before, since I never did when I was operating, I saw his go black and murky. Just then a great white bird flapped up out of his chest: a great white bird like the one I had seen in the field of dead men. It flew up without making a sound; the others looked but did not see. The owl sailed out through the closed window, and I knew it was going toward the man who had aimed the bullet at little Tayler.

"The day after that, I healed a man with my fingers alone.

"He was a black man, an American Negro named Washford. Negroes served in the 92nd Division, under their own officers; they were rigidly segregated. In the normal course of things, the only ones we saw were working as valets or kitchen help or orderlies in the hospital. They had their own meeting places, their own girls, their own social life, which was closed off to the rest of us. Well, Washford had caught a round in his ribs, and the bullet had traveled around inside him for a while, generally messing up his giblets.

"When the attendant wheeled him in, Withers had just finished with his last patient, and the man took Washford to his table. Withers turned away without looking, bathed his hands in the sink, and then came back to the table. He froze. 'I won't work on this man,' he said. 'I am not a veterinarian.' He was from Georgia, remember, and this was 1917—it does not excuse him, but it helps to explain him. His nurses looked at me, and the other doctors momentarily stopped their work. Washford was in danger of bleeding to death through his bandages while we decided how to handle Withers' defection. 'I'll exchange patients with you,' I finally said, and Withers stepped away from his table and came toward mine.

"'I don't care if you kill that one, Collector,' he said. 'But you'll be disappointed—he has no pockets.'

"I ignored him and went to Washford and pulled away the soaked bandages. The nurse put the ether pad over his nose and mouth. I cut into him and began to look around. I removed the bullet and began repairing the damage. Then I felt a change come over my whole body: I felt as light as if *I* had taken the ether. My mind began to buzz. My hands tingled. I trembled, knowing what I could do, and the nurse saw my hands shake and looked at me as if she thought I was drunk. My drinking was well known, but really all of us drank all the time. But it was not alcohol, it was the smack of knowledge hitting me like a truck: I could *heal* him. I put down the instruments and ran my fingers along the torn blood vessels. Radiance— invisible radiance—streamed from me. The mess the bullet had caused as it plunged from lung to liver to spleen closed itself—all of that torn flesh and damaged tissue; it grew pink and restored, virginal, as you might call it. The nurse backed away, making little noises under her mask. I was on fire. My mind was leaping. I jerked out the retractors and ran my first two fingers over the incision and zipped him up, welded his skin together in a smooth pinkish-brown line. Withers' nurse ripped off her mask and ran out of the theater.

"'Take him out,' I said to the astonished attendant, who had been half-dozing at the back of the room: he had seen the nurse run out, but nothing of the operation. Washford went one way, I went another—I was floating. I came out into the big tiled hallway outside the theater. The nurse saw me and backed away. I started to laugh, and realized I was still wearing my mask. I removed it and sat on a bench. 'Don't be afraid,' I said to the nurse.

"'Holy mother of Jesus,' she said. She was Irish.

"That miraculous power was ebbing from me. I held my hands up before my face. They looked skinned, in the tight surgical gloves.

"'Holy mother of Jesus,' the nurse repeated. Her face was turning from white to lobster pink.

"'Forget about it,' I said. 'Forget what you saw.'

"She scampered back inside the theater. I still could not comprehend what had just happened to me. It was as though I had been raised up to a great eminence and been shown all the things of this world and been told: 'You may have what you like.' For a second I felt my blood pressure charge upward, and my head swam.

"Then everything gradually returned to normal. I could stand. I went back inside the theater, where Withers was just finishing with the boy on my table. He looked at me in disgust, finished his sutures, and returned to his own table. I did five more operations that day, and never felt the approach of that power which had healed Washford."

The magician looked up. "Night." Tom, surprised, saw the lamps burning in the woods; lights on the beach pushed his shadow toward the lake. "Time to go to bed. Tomorrow I will tell you about my meeting with Speckle John and what happened after the war."

"Bedtime?" Del said. "What happened to . . . ?"

Both boys simultaneously saw the crushed sandwich wrappers, the paper plates laden with crumbs.

"Oh, yes, you have eaten," Collins said. His face was serene and tired.

"We've only been here . . ." Tom looked at his watch, which said eleven o'clock. "An hour."

"You have been here all day. I will see you here tomorrow at the same time." He stood up, and they dazedly imitated him. "But know this. William Vendouris, whose name I had taken for a time, *put a hurtin' on me*. Without Vendouris, perhaps I would have remained an amateur magician, locked out and away from everything I wished most to find."

5

Tom and Del climbed the rickety steps by themselves. Their minds and bodies told them it was late morning, but the world said it was night: the thick foliage on the bank

melted together into a single vibrant breathing mass.
They reached the top and stood in the pale, yellowish
electrical light, looking down. Coleman Collins was standing on the beach, looking out at the lake.

"Did you know he used to be a doctor?" Tom asked.

"No. But it explains why he didn't send for one when I
broke my leg that time. The whole story explains that."
Del put his hands in his pockets and grinned. "If I started
to heal wrong or anything, he would have fixed me like he
did with that colored man."

"I guess," Tom said moodily. "Yeah, I guess so." He
was watching Collins: the magician had extended one arm
into the air, as if signaling to someone on the other side of
the lake. After a moment the arm went down and Collins
began to stroll along the beach in the direction of the
boathouse. "Could we really have been down there all
day?"

Del nodded. "I was sort of hoping I'd see her today.
But the whole day vanished."

"Well, that's just it," Tom said. "It vanished. It was ten
in the morning, about an hour went by, and now it's
eleven at night. He stole thirteen hours away from us."

Del looked at him, uncertain as a puppy.

"What I mean is, what's to stop him from taking a week
away from us? Or a month? What does he do, put us to
sleep?"

"I don't think so," Del said. "I think everything just
sort of speeds up around us."

"That doesn't make sense."

"It doesn't make sense to say that you met the Brothers
Grimm, either." Del's tone was wistful, but his face
momentarily turned bitter. "*I* should have."

"Well, I never met Humphrey Bogart and Marilyn
Monroe."

"Uncle Cole said I had to watch out for your jealousy,"
Del blurted out. "I mean . . . he just said that once when
we were alone. He said that one day it would hit you, and
you would want Shadowland for yourself."

Tom fought down the impulse to tell exactly what
Collins had said about his nephew. "That's crazy. He
wants to break up our friendship."

"No, he doesn't." Del was adamant. "He just said—"

"That I'd be jealous. Okay." Tom was reflecting that Collins had after all been right: though it was not Shadowland that made him jealous, but Rose Armstrong. "Tell you what. Do you really want to meet the Brothers Grimm?"

"Right now?" Del was suspicious.

"Right now."

"Are you sure it's all right?"

"I'm not sure of anything. Maybe they're not even there."

"Where?"

"You'll see."

Del shrugged. "Sure. I'd like to."

"Come on, then."

Del gave a worried look down at the beach: Collins had disappeared into the boathouse. Then he followed Tom through the sliding doors into the living room.

"I guess we really ought to be in bed," Del said a little nervously.

"You can go to bed if you want to." Then he felt sorry for being so abrupt. "Are you tired?"

"Not really."

"Me neither. I think it's eleven-ten in the morning."

This was said in defiance of all the physical evidence. All Shadowland seemed put to bed, even if the principal occupants were still out of theirs. One lamp burned beside a couch; the carpet showed the tracks of a vacuum cleaner. On the end tables, the ashtrays sparkled. Tom marched through the dim, quiet room, almost hoping to see Elena silently buffing the furniture.

"Upstairs?" Del asked.

"Nope." Tom turned into the hall. One of the recessed lights gave a pumpkin-colored illumination.

"In the Little Theater?"

"Nope." Tom stopped where the short hallway intersected the main hall to the theaters.

"Oh, no," Del said. "We can't."

"I already did."

"And he saw you?"

"He was waiting for me when I came out."

"Was he mad?"

"I guess so. But nothing happened. You saw how he

was today. Maybe he even forgot it. He was pretty drunk. He wants us to see them, Del. That's why they're there.''

"Do they just sit there? Or can you talk to them?"

"They'll talk your ears off," Tom said. "Come on. I want to ask them some questions." He turned into the short hallway and pulled open the heavy door.

6

"Our young visitor again, Jakob," said the one with the seasoned, kindly face.

"And behind him, is there not another little *Geist?*"

"He has never been curious before, that one."

"He has never had his brave brother's help before."

Both of them laid down their pens and looked inquisitively at Tom, but Tom did not move forward. He was aware of Del stretching on tiptoe behind him, trying to see over his shoulder. Instead of the cluttered, cozy workroom in which he had seen them earlier, the two men in the frock coats and elaborate neckwear were surrounded by a more barren and purposeful but equally cluttered room. The walls were earthen, crumbling here and there; nails had been driven into the packed earth, and from the nails hung khaki jackets, peaked hats, and tin helmets. Complicated green-and-white maps hung on a wide board. A clumsy box with a crank and a headpiece sat on a trestle table which also supported rolled maps, bundles of paper tied with shoelaces, more military headgear, a fleece-lined jacket, and a kerosene lamp. Stark wooden chairs surrounded it. In this curious setting, the two men sat at their ornate desks. *A soldier's room,* was all that Tom could make of this. *Staff room?*

"Yes, little one," said Wilhelm. "They let us work here."

"For our work goes on," said Jakob, standing up and beckoning the two boys into the room.

Tom stepped forward and smelled the close loamy odor of earth; the trace of cigars. Del came alongside him. From far off, what could have been miles away, came the booming of big guns.

"And on and on. For the stories' sake."

"Where are you supposed to be now?" asked Tom.

"Shadowland," both brothers answered. "It is always Shadowland."

"I mean, France? Germany?"

"Things are getting dark," said Jakob. "We may have to move again, and take our work and our families with us. But still the stories continue."

"Even though Europe is dying, brother."

"The sparrows have given up their voices."

"Their choice."

Del was looking at the brothers with a rapt face. "Are you always here?"

Wilhelm nodded. "Always. We know you, boy."

"I want to ask you something," Tom said, and the brothers turned their faces, kindly and businesslike, to him. Outside, the shelling continued, far off and resonant.

"That is why you have found us," said Jakob.

Tom hesitated. "Do you know the expression 'put a hurtin' on' something?"

"It is not one of our expressions, but we know it," said Jakob. His expression said: *Follow this line, boy.*

"Okay. Did Del's uncle put a hurtin' on that train? Did he make it crash?"

"Of course," said Jakob. "Aren't you a bright boy? He put a hurtin' on it—he made it crash. For the sake of the story in which you find yourself."

Tom realized that he was trembling; two shells exploded very near, and dust drifted off the earthen walls.

"I have one more question," Tom said.

"Of course you do, child," said Jakob. "You want to know about the Collector."

"That's right," Tom said. "Is the Collector Skeleton Ridpath?" He saw the other one, Wilhelm, suppress a smile.

"For the sake of *your* story," said Jakob. "For the sake of *your* story, he is."

"Wait a second," Del said. "I don't understand. The Collector is Skeleton Ridpath? It's just a kind of a toy— kind of a joke—it's been here for years."

"Anybody can be collected at any time," said Wilhelm.

"But it's just a joke," Del insisted. "And I don't believe that my uncle caused that train to wreck. He wouldn't do a thing like that."

Wilhelm asked, "Do you know our story 'The Boy Who Could Not Shiver'? It too is a kind of a joke. But it is full of the most frightening things ever encountered. Many frightening things conceal jokes, and many jokes have ice in their hearts."

Tom suddenly felt afraid. The men were so large, and most of the friendliness had faded from their faces.

"As for your second remark," said Jakob, "do the two of you know the mouse's song to the rabbit?"

They shook their heads.

"Listen." The brothers moved together in front of their desks, crouched slightly at the knees, tilted back their heads and sang:

> *Way way way way down in the dump*
> *I found a tin can and I found a sugar lump.*
> *I ate the one and I kicked the other,*
> *And I had a real good time.*
>
> *Way way way way down in the dump . . .*

The lights suddenly died: a half-second later came the boom of an enormous explosion. Tom felt dirt showering down on his head. The whole room shook, and he momentarily lost his balance. A pair of rough hands shoved at his chest, knocking him back into Del.

He smelled sausage, smoke, sour breath beneath brandy: someone was whispering in his ear. "Did the mouse put a hurtin' on the sugar lump, boyo? Or did the mouse put a hurtin' on the rabbit?" The hands pressed him back. Del, stumbling behind him, kicked his shins. Rattling and banging: things were falling off the walls, the nails shredding out of the dirt. The hands, Jakob's or Wilhelm's, continued to push him back. The man's face must have been only inches from Tom's. "Way way way way down in the dump, I found a little boy . . . and nobody ever saw either one of us again."

Vacancy felt more than seen opened up before him: he heard a confusion of retreating footsteps.

"I'm getting out of here," Del said, sounding panicky.

Then the door was open and he was backing through it. Tom reached for the knob, but Del caught his elbow: the door slammed shut.

"You crazy?" Del said. His face was as green as an army blanket.

"I wanted to *see*," Tom said. "That's what this is all about. For once, I wanted to see more than he wanted us to."

"You can't fight him," Del said. "You're not supposed to."

"Oh, Del."

"Well, I don't want him to see us out here."

Tom thought that he too did not want Collins to see him outside the door. Del already was lost: fright glinted in his eyes. "All right. Let's go upstairs."

"I don't need your permission."

7

In the corridor outside their rooms, they looked out the big windows to see Coleman Collins just now reaching the top of the iron staircase. The lights pulled a long shadow out behind him on the flagstones.

"At least he was down there all the time," Del said.

"He knew where we were. He set off the sound effects, didn't he?"

"Then it was a mistake to go into that room. And I'm sorry I did." Del looked ferociously up at him, and Tom mentally braced himself for an attack. "You used to be my best friend, but I think he was right about you. You're jealous. You want to get me in trouble with him."

"No . . ." Tom started to utter some general shocked denial, but his dismay was overwhelming. Coming so soon after the threat from one of the "Brothers Grimm," Del's assault left him wordless. "Not now," was all he managed to get out.

Del spun away from him. "You sound like a girl." When he reached the door, Del turned to glare at him again. "And you act like you own this place. I should be showing you things, not the other way around."

"Del," Tom pleaded, and the smaller boy grimaced as if he had struck him.

"You want to know something, *pal?* Something I never told you? I guess you remember those times my uncle showed up in Arizona—at the football game and at Ventnor. Well, you wanted to know why I never talked about it with you."

"Because he confused you," Tom said, happy to be back on ground more or less solid. "Because I didn't ask about him enough. And he was here, not there, and—"

"Shut up. Just shut up. I saw you with him, dummy. You were right next to him—you were walking along with him, like something that was *going* to happen. I saw *you,* damn you. Now I know why. You always wanted him for your own. And he was trying to show me what you're really like." Del shook his balled fists at him, tears leaking out of the corners of his eyes, and disappeared inside his door. A second later Tom heard the slam of the sliding doors.

Glumly Tom went into his own room.

8

His dreams were instant, vivid, and worse than any that had appeared on the Carson School notice board. He was operating on a dead man in an impromptu theater, knowing that the man was dead but unable to admit it to the others around the table; he was supposed to be a surgeon, but he had no idea of what had killed the man or how to proceed. The instruments in his hands were impassively foreign. *Way way way way down in his guts,* whispered a nurse with blond hair and passive eyes. . . . *Collected. Wasn't he? Wasn't he?* Something stirred beneath his bloody hands, and the head of a vulture popped up like a toy, clean and bald, from within the open chest cavity. Great wings stirred in the mire. "I want to *see,"* Tom wailed to the nurse, knowing that above all, he did not want to see. . . .

Coleman Collins, wearing a red velvet smoking jacket, bent toward him. "Come with me, my little boy, come along, come along . . ."

and Skeleton Ridpath, no age at all, leaned forward in a chair and watched with a vacant avid face. He held a glass owl in his hands and bled from the eyes . . .

and a black man with a square, serious, elegant magician's face was standing in a corridor of light, holding out a real owl with both hands. The owl's eyes beamed brilliantly toward him. *Let him in,* said the magician; *let me in,* commanded the owl. . . .

He stirred, finally aware that a voice at his door was saying, "Let me in. Let me in." He remembered, in an unhappy flash of memory, that the man holding the owl had been Bud Copeland.

"Please," said the voice at the door.

"All right, all right," Tom said. "Who is it?"

"Please."

Tom switched on his bedside light, stepped into his jeans, and pulled a shirt over his arms. He padded to the door and opened it.

Rose Armstrong was standing in the dark hall. "I wanted to see you," she said. "This place is no good for you."

"You're telling me," Tom said, aware of his rumpled hair and bared chest. His face felt numb with sleep. Rose stepped around him and went into his room.

"Poor grumpy Tom," she said. "I want to get out of here, and I want you and Del to help me."

9

Now Tom was fully awake: his nightmares blew away like fluff, and he was aware only of this pretty girl with her half-adult face standing before him in a yellow blouse and green skirt. *The Carson colors,* he dimly noted. "I don't mean right away, because we couldn't," she explained. "But soon. As soon as we could. Would you help?"

"Would Del?" he asked. He knew the strongest reason for Del's refusal. "I don't know much about Coleman Collins, but I bet if Del sneaked out of here, he'd never be able to come back."

"Maybe he shouldn't ever want to come back. May I sit down?"

"Uh, yeah, sorry." He watched her go to the chair and neatly sit, looking at him all the while: she was relieved, he saw—or was that just her face again, meaninglessly recording the expectation of rejection? Having this girl in his room made him nervous; she seemed far more poised than he. And she had spoken the idea which should have been his, which he had been too anchored in Shadowland to have—the simple idea of escape.

"I thought you said you owed Collins everything," he said. He sat on the floor because there was nowhere else to sit but the bed.

"That's true, but he's changing too much. Everything's different this year. Because you're here, I think."

"How is it different?"

She looked at her small hands. "It used to be fun before. He wasn't drunk so often. He wasn't so angry and so . . . worked up. Now it's sort of like he lost control. He scares me. This summer, everything is so wild. It feels like a machine that's spinning around faster and faster, shooting off sparks, smoking away—ready to blow up. At least that's how I feel."

"What could I have to do with that?" He looked up at her as if she were an oracle: her shining knees, her glowing hair falling back from her high forehead. Even the way she spoke was full of little shocks for him, the clipped, slightly twangy Vermont accent. Suddenly his own voice seemed odd in his mouth, too slow and somehow dusty.

"I think he's jealous of you. He sees something in you—something he says you're too young to see yourself. You could be better than he is. He wants to own you. He wants you to stay here forever. From the time Del first mentioned you, he started talking about you. I heard him talking about you lots of times last winter and spring. He was going on about you and Del all the time."

She gave him a flat, unmeasured look that slid deeply within him, and he saw himself lifting a log with his mind alone, making it spin crazily, sickly, in midair. "Really, I think you should get out of here. I'm not saying that just because I want you to help me."

"Why do you need help?"

"Oh, because . . ." She looked into his heart again,

then tucked her hair back behind her ears. "Do you think you could get off that ridiculous floor and sit here?" She looked toward the bed; back at him.

He moved as if ordered.

When he sat on the edge of the bed, her startling face was only a foot from him. Her eyes, permanently wide and flecked with pale blue and gold and green, drew him in. "I need help because I'm scared. It's those men—you mentioned them that first time, in Del's room."

"Are they bothering you?"

"They might. They could. They wouldn't mind a bit. You know what they're like. They're animals. Mr. Collins used to watch them, but this summer they sort of run free. They have work to do—for him, you know—but I'm afraid that when they have a couple of days free . . ." She nervously tucked back her hair again. "They know where I'm staying. They drink a lot, too, and Mr. Collins didn't used to let them do that. I never liked them. But before, I was little. I was a little girl." She let the implication state itself.

"Why don't you just go?"

"I think someone always knows where I am. I can just sneak out sometimes and swim across the lake. They don't mind if I swim. Today I had to buy some things in town, so they let me go. They know I talk to Del sometimes. They don't mind that either. They laugh about it." Her face went smooth and hard and inward for a moment. "I hate them. I really do hate them. If Mr. Collins was the way he usually is, it would be okay, but . . ." The sentence died. "And I wanted to tell you what I was thinking. Do you want to leave here?"

"I'd have to trust you," Tom said.

"Why? Oh. You mean, maybe it's a trick?"

Tom nodded. "Everything's a trick, here."

"Well, do you trust me? What can I say to make you feel that . . . ?" She blushed. "Tom, I'm all alone. I like you. I want to know you better. I'm happy you came this summer. I just think that we can help each other."

"I guess I can trust you," Tom said. In truth, it was not possible for him not to trust her.

She smiled. "It would be terrible if you didn't. I want to help, Tom. I want to help *us*."

Us. The word seemed to fall toward his heart, along with the darting half-bold, half-sly glances into his eyes.

"Del thinks a lot of you," he said.

"I think a lot of Del." The sentence put Del at a cliché's distance from her.

"I mean, he cares about you."

"Del is really a little boy," Rose said, looking straight at him, and Tom felt the moral universe shift about him, expanding too quickly for him to keep track of it. "Physically he is a little boy. Mentally he has a lot of sophistication because of the way he was brought up, but actually you are a lot older than Del is. That was the first thing I noticed when I met you. Besides that, you were so grumpy."

"Grumpy? I was nervous as a puppy!"

She laughed; then, with her face turned fully toward him, she took his hand and leaned forward. She was blushing. "Tom, my life has been so funny. . . . I'm asking you to rescue me, I guess—and that sounds so dumb, like a princess in a story. I hardly even know you, but I feel like we're close already. . . . You're going to have to talk Del into leaving his uncle, and it'll break his heart. . . ." She leaned an inch closer, and in front of Tom her face filled the room, large and enigmatic and beautiful as a model's face on a billboard. When their lips met, Tom's whole being seemed concentrated in the few centimeters of skin that touched her mouth. By instinct but awkwardly he put his arms around her.

She pulled back. "You won't believe me, but the first time I saw you, I wanted to kiss you."

"I thought you and Del—"

"Del is a little boy," she repeated, and they kissed again. "We can meet outside sometimes. I'll tell you how. I'll arrange it. And I already know when we can escape. Mr. Collins is planning some big show—some big thing—in a little while. If you and Del will help, we can all get away then."

"But where can we go?"

"Into the village. From there, we can go anywhere. But we'd be safe in Hilly Vale."

"I have to get a letter out."

"Give it to Elena. She's the only one who goes to the village regularly. I think she'll mail it for you." Rose stood up and smoothed out her skirt. She looked tense and slightly drawn. "But be careful. And don't pay attention to anything you see me doing—I'm only doing it because I have to. Because he's making me do it. Just wait until you hear from me. Promise?"

"Promise."

"And do you trust me?"

"Yes. I do."

"We have to trust each other from now on."

Tom nodded, and she flickered a tentative smile at him and slipped away out the door.

A minute later he stood on the balcony outside in the warm fragrant air. He watched her disappearing into the woods down beside the lake, and stayed on the balcony until he saw her entering one of the circles of light. She turned and waved; he waved back at her slight, determined-looking figure.

10

After that he could not fall asleep again. He kept remembering her face swimming up before him, becoming more certain and beautiful the closer it came. That she had allowed him to kiss her was a blessing: it had not at all been like kissing Jenny Oliver or Diane Darling. Rose Armstrong was beyond his experience in a thousand incalculable ways. The unknown surrounded her, cast all of her words and gestures into relief—that yearning brooding uncertain beautiful face looming up before him, claiming him, not as much asking for trust as demanding it, had in some way been the essence of Shadowland. Certainly it was as unexpected as everything at Shadowland; as dreamlike, too, in its suddenness. And Rose Armstrong was much better at kissing than his earlier girlfriends. That, the sharp responsive physicality of her mouth, was anything but dreamlike.

He lay in his narrow bed, wondering. What was she

promising him? *Del is just a little boy.* He could not bear
to think of Rose Armstrong in the company of Mr. Peet's
brutes, but his mind perversely would not leave these
pictures be: as soon as he closed his eyes, he saw Seed or
Thorn pushing toward her, all belly and beard. Then he
saw her as he had with Del, pulsing through the dark
water.

After half an hour he threw back his sheets and got up.
He felt impatient, constrained by the room. With nothing
else to do, he decided to write to his mother. Sheets of
paper and envelopes were just under the flap of the desk.
Still in his underwear, he sat and wrote.

> Dear Mom,
>
>   I miss you lots. I miss Dad too, just
> like he was still alive and pretty soon I
> could go home and see him again. I
> guess I'll feel like that for a long time.
>   Del and I arrived safely, but the train
> before ours had a bad wreck. This is the
> strangest place anybody could be. Del's
> uncle is such a good magician that he
> can really mess up your mind. He keeps
> saying that I could be a good magician
> too, but I don't want to be like him.
>   I want to come home. It's not just
> homesickness. Honest. If I can get us
> out of this place, could you arrange to
> be back home? I guess I won't be able to
> get a letter back from you for about two
> weeks, but could you please . . .

That was no good. He balled it up and threw it in the
wastebasket.

> Dear Mom,
>
>   I'll explain later, but Del and I have to
> get out of this house. Can you possibly
> cut your trip short and come back
> sooner than you planned? Send me a

telegram. This is urgent. I'm not joking,
and I'm not just homesick.

Love,

Tom

This he folded into an envelope, wrote the address of the
London hotel where Rachel Flanagan was staying, printed
"AIRMAIL" and "PLEASE FORWARD" on it just in case,
and put the envelope on top of the desk. He stared at it,
knowing that it committed him to trying to get Del to
leave Shadowland. Now he was truly the traitor the
magician had said he was.

But he could be a magician without Coleman Collins,
and so could Del. You didn't have to lock yourself up in a
fortress and apprentice yourself to an alcoholic madman. . . . These thoughts bounced against an area in
himself which he did not wish to acknowledge, but which
was there all the same; part of him was fascinated by
Shadowland, and intrigued by the powers Coleman Collins might be able to find in him. *You are exactly the right
age. . . . Two and a half months isn't long enough.* This
was still tempting: after seeing Collins at work, any career
but that of magician seemed flat to him.

Tom dressed, knowing that he could not sleep. He put
the envelope in his wallet, the wallet back in his hip
pocket. For a time he paced around the austere room,
knowing that there was something he had intended to do,
something suggested by a comment made before Rose
Armstrong had sent everything but herself out of his
mind, but not remembering what it was.

He had wanted to look at something . . . That was as
far as he got.

Tom flopped down in the chair—the chair where *she*
had sat—and picked up his book. He willed himself into
Nero Wolfe's round of the orchid room, the kitchen, and
office, but read only ten pages before he gave up. That
orderly, talkative adult world was not his. His stomach
growled. He decided to go downstairs and see what was in
the refrigerator. Collins had not forbidden him that.

He closed the door behind him and slipped down the

hall. The magician's room was dark—what was it like in there, behind the swinging doors? As bleak as Tom's own room? Or would it look like Del's room at home, crowded with photographs and the apparatus of magic? He did not want to find out.

Down the stairs, around the corner in darkness into the long hall. Scattered ceiling lights dimly shone. This time he remembered to stop before the posters.

He was looking at one from the Gaiety Theater, Dublin. A NIGHT OF SPECTACLE AND ENCHANTMENT, it said in ornate type. Halfway down the list of names Tom found HERBIE BUTTER, *the Amazing Mechanical Magician and Acrobat*. Beneath that but in type of the same size was this line: *Assisted by* SPECKLE JOHN, MASTER OF BLACK MYSTERY. Beneath this, in slightly larger type: THRILL TO THEIR WIZARDRY, GASP AT THEIR OCCULT SKILLS. Far down the list of mainly Irish names Tom found *The Astounding Mr. Peet and the Wandering Boys—Music and Madness*. Tom searched the ornate poster for a date and saw it near the top: 21 July, 1921.

The poster beside it was in French, and featured a drawing of a black-hatted magician emerging from a puff of smoke. Was that where Del had got the idea for the beginning of their own performance? MONSIEUR HERBIE BUTTER, L'ORIGINAL. AVEC SPECKLE JOHN. This was dated 15 Mai, 1921.

Other posters were from London, Rome, Paris again, Bern, Florence. In some, Speckle John's name preceded Herbie Butter's. Mr. Peet and the Wandering Boys appeared on most of them. The dates of the performances spanned from 1919 to 1924. The last poster, from the Wood Green Empire in London, announced *The Last Appearance on any Stage, by the Beloved Herbie Butter. Farewell Performance. Thrills, Surprises, and Frights Guaranteed.* Here the illustration was of a smooth-faced young man in tails floating above an astonished audience, his arms out before him, his legs together like a man in the middle of a dive. Beneath the illustration was a line stating that Mr. Peet and the Wandering Boys would assist. *With an appearance by the Collector. Feats of mentalism. Defiance of gravity. Fire. Ice. The astound-*

ing Collector! Invisibility! Wizardry Unparalleled—Feats never before attempted on the English Stage. A Magical Extravaganza. The date on the poster was 27 August, 1924.

Then someone was moving, a shape was coming from the living room out into the hall. Tom gasped and whirled around to face it.

The old woman, Elena, was glowering at him. In a flash, she had disappeared back into the living room.

"Elena!" Tom called. "Please!" He ran down the hall and into the room. The woman was hovering by a couch, knotting her hands together before her. She looked very uneasy. Tom stopped running and held up his hands, palm out. "Please," he said. Her black eyes burrowed into him. "Letter? Post office?"

She dropped her hands, but her face did not change. Tom pulled out his wallet and showed her the letter. "Post office? Will you mail it for me?"

She glowered. Looked at the letter in his hands. "Post office?"

"*Sí. Da.* Yes. Please."

Elena stabbed her forefinger toward the letter. "Momma? You momma?"

He nodded. "Please, Elena. Help me."

"Is okay. Post office." She snatched the envelope out of his hands and buried it somewhere in her apron. Then she went past him without another word.

So now it was settled. He had two weeks at the most before he and Del and Rose would have to leave Shadowland.

11

Tom turned on the kitchen lights. Both the stove and the refrigerator were outsize and made of stainless steel—restaurant equipment. And when he swung open the refrigerator's double doors, he saw piles of steaks, cooked hams, heads of lettuce, bags of tomatoes and cucumbers, gallon jars of mayonnaise, rolled roasts of beef—as much food as he had ever seen in one place. All this, for one

man and his housekeeper? And a restaurant range to cook
it on? Of course—it was for Mr. Peet and the Wandering
Boys as well as Collins and Elena. Tom searched the
drawers for a knife, found a long bone-handled carving
blade, and cut a section of ham away from the bone.

Chewing, he remembered what he had wanted to do,
and the thought nearly made the ham stick in his throat.
Because of what the "Brothers Grimm" had said, he had
decided to take another look at the Collector in the
bathroom mirror.

For the sake of your story, he is.

Del had said the face just came forward until it was
near your own, and then retreated. It was a grisly joke, a
Shadowland joke. All he wanted to do was to see how
closely the horrible face actually resembled Skeleton
Ridpath's. That was all he wanted, but it still scared him.

Tom left the kitchen and walked slowly back down the
hall to the bathroom door. He jittered there a moment,
now thinking that the idea of inspecting Coleman Collins'
macabre joke was silly.

Not really, he thought. Because it would be better to
find that the Collector did not look any more like
Skeleton Ridpath than Snail or Root did—that way, he
could get rid of the feeling that he and Del were still in
some awful way linked to Skeleton Ridpath: that graduation had not taken Skeleton out of their lives.

But of course it did, he thought, putting his hand on the
doorknob. *He's gone for good.* Then Tom remembered
the day, years before, when an eighth-grade Skeleton had
knocked him down in the Junior School playground; and
knocked him down again; and then flurried his sharp fists
and shredded his lip. *Dirty little Irish nigger, dirty little
Irish nigger:* spitting that out mindlessly, his eyes showing
that his brain had switched off absolutely. Skeleton had
struck his face and slobbered with glee, and struck his face
again, making his nose bleed. Tom had fought back, but
Skeleton was three years older; he had never got close
enough to land a blow, and Skeleton kept chipping away
at his face. It might have gone on until the end of recess if
one of the teachers had not pulled Skeleton away and sent
him home.

The humiliation had been worse than the pain. The pain went away, but Skeleton Ridpath returned to school and the playground, a spindly, snaky eighth-grader who had only to look at Tom to tyrannize him. Long before Del's arrival at Carson, Tom had felt hounded by the coach's son. Tackling him, bringing him down hard again and again in the practice game between the varsity and the junior varsity, had helped him face down Skeleton during all the trouble with Del.

All right. He swallowed, reminded himself that it was just a joke and that Del had seen it a hundred times, and opened the door. He flicked the lights. His own face looked worriedly back at him from the mirror. The button, the one that brought the Collector, was just beside the light switch. *It just comes up close and then melts back down into the mirror.* He took a breath and pushed the button.

The yellow light instantly turned purple. That other face swam up from the mirror like something hidden in his own face. For a second, his own features obscured it. He knew in his stomach that he had made a mistake.

Then the avid, greedy face jumped into life. Purple, with distorted mouth and dead skin and flabby smudges under its eyes. Tom groaned, all but quailed back against the wall. It was Skeleton Ridpath's face, and no other: Skeleton blowtorched down to painful essence, skinned of whatever was human and pitying in him. Skeleton grinned at him and crawled forward.

Tom's knees turned to rubber. The figure was lifting its hands. *Mirror image,* Tom thought with weird rationality. Now the entire trunk was protruding out of the mirror, leaning toward him.

Tom backed away, in his panic forgetting all about the button. Skeleton's face was alight. He was holding himself up on the edge of the mirror, taking his weight on his arms in order to get his knee on the silver frame.

"Go back," Tom whispered.

Skeleton's knee appeared on the lip of the mirror. He opened his mouth in a wordless shout of rapture, and pushed his leg through the mirror.

"No," said Tom, barely able to get the word out.

The awful face homed in on the sound of his voice; the

distorted mouth began to drool. The Collector was blind. He grinned, showing purplish blackness instead of teeth. Balanced on the sink, he soundlessly dropped his feet to the floor.

Tom bumped into the door, moving sideways, then realized what the door meant. He opened it a crack, the Collector's face scanning brightly toward him, and jumped through the opening. He slammed the door shut and heard Skeleton's feet shuffle on the floor.

Bracing himself, Tom pushed in with all his strength: in an instant, the world had flipped inside-out and turned his mind to jelly. He felt a gentle push from the inside, then a harder push that nearly moved him. Tom laid his cheek against the wood and got his shoulder to the door. He heard himself making little whistling noises in his throat. Keeping the door closed was all he could think of. The next push wobbled him, but his feet held. When Skeleton came back for another attempt to escape the bathroom, he battered the door open an inch and a half before Tom was able to jam it shut again.

He saw himself standing there all night, bottling Skeleton up inside the bathroom.

The fifth blow knocked him back off his feet—he went sprawling in the corridor, and the door banged open. The Collector stood on the threshold, arms dangling, his face swiveling avidly from side to side. He wore the ancient black suit of the mural, and it too shone a faint purple. He shuffled forward.

Tom scuttled backward and got to his feet, making enough noise for the figure to focus directly on him. The Collector's face split open in a grin of empty radiance. "Great play," he whispered in a voice a shadow of Skeleton's.

He stumbled forward. "I told you to stay away from that piano. Take off that fairy shirt. I want to see some skin."

Tom ran.

"Flanagini! Flanagini! FLAAAAANAGINNNIII!"

Panting, Tom wheeled around the corner into the living room. Hide behind a couch? Behind a curtain? He could barely think: pictures of hiding places too small for him

rattled through his mind. From Rose Armstrong to this
. . . thing, as though a line were drawn between them.

Why, sure, Tom thought with bright panic: Rose
wanted out of Shadowland, Skeleton wanted out of the
mirror. Simple.

"I saw your owl, Vendouris," whispered a voice behind
him. "You are mine."

Tom spun around and saw purple Skeleton skimming
toward him. He uttered a squeak and dodged to the side.
Skeleton snaked out an arm and dug his fingers into his
shoulder. The thin fingers burned through Tom's shirt like
ice. "Dirty little Irish nigger!" Tom banged the side of his
fist against Skeleton's unheeding head, twisted in frantic
disgust to the side, and lost his balance. Skeleton lurched
nearer, Tom swung and hit a rock-hard chest, and when
Tom twisted again, he brought both of them down onto
the flowered couch.

"Great play," the Collector whispered. "I want to see
some skin." The icy hands found Tom's neck.

Tom was looking up at the inhuman face—the pouches
under the empty eyes were black. A foul, dusty, spider-
webby smell soaked into him. Lying atop him, Skeleton
felt like a bag of twigs, but his hands squeezed like a vise.

"Dirty little . . ."

Then sudden brightness stung his eyes; the frozen hands
fell away from him. He scrambled to his feet, flailing out,
and saw only the sliding doors and the lighted woods
where Skeleton should have been. The emptiness before
him momentarily felt as charged as a vacuum; then
ordinariness rushed into it.

Coleman Collins, in a dark blue dressing gown and
paler blue pajamas, limped into the room. "I pushed the
button, little idiot," said the magician. "Do not begin
things when you will get too flustered to remember how to
finish them." He turned to go, then faced Tom again.
"But you just proved your greatness as a magician, if you
are interested. You made that happen. And one thing
more. I saved your life—saved it from the consequences
of your own abilities. Remember that." He measured
Tom with a glance, and was gone.

12

Tom wobbled back out into the hall. Collins had vanished into one of the theaters or up the stairs to his bedroom. The house was silent again. Tom glanced in the direction of the hall bathroom, involuntarily trembled, and moved to the staircase. Up there he saw the dim pumpkin color—the single light that burned most of the night was still on. He went slowly up the stairs; near the top, he took a handkerchief from his pocket and wiped his face. Then, so tired he thought he would collapse on the stairs, he forced himself to the landing.

In a dark blue dressing gown like his uncle's, Del stood in the murky hall outside his bedroom door. He was looking rigidly out the window.

"Shhh!" Del commanded. "It's Rose."

Tom joined him, and Del moved a few inches away. When Tom looked down, his heart moved.

Rose Armstrong stood in the nearest pool of light, so near the house she was almost on the beach. Dirty rags covered her body; her hair blazed in the light. Nailed to a tree, crucified, hung the pale gray head of a horse. Two masked figures hovered at the edge of the light: a barrel of a man wearing a pale aristocratic young man's face, and a small woman with the hooked, sneering mask of a witch. Golden robes shone around both of them. Mr. Peet and Elena? Tom at first thought the horse's head was stuffed or plaster of paris, but after a second he saw lines of blood and gore rivering down the bark. "Oh, God," he said. He remembered the faint image of a gray horse in the darkness as Collins turned into his domain on the first night; the gray horse that had plunged through the snow, bringing him toward a burning school. Insects had summoned themselves to the edges of the wound, lifting and settling in little clouds. Rose pleadingly lifted her joined hands. The light above her suddenly died, and the two boys were staring at their own images in the window.

"Falada," Del said. "The Goose Girl. Remember?"

Oh, poor princess in despair,
if your dear mother knew,
her heart would break in two.

"Magic, Tom. This is what I live for. I'm on the side of *that*—I'm on the side of what we saw out there. I don't care what you get up to when you go slinking around at night, because I'm not on your side anymore. Remember that."

"We're all on the same side," Tom said quietly. Del gave him an impatient, disgusted look and went back into his room.

Part Three

"When We All Lived in the Forest . . ."

"Man is made in the image of God" and it has often been sardonically observed that "God is made in the image of man." Both statements are accepted as true in magic.

—Richard Cavendish, *The Black Arts*

I

The Welcome

The next day, if it was the next day, Del treated me like the Enemy, Satan himself come to destroy all his earthly arrangements. He began by eating alone in his room—I supposed he had gotten the same note I did on my tray, asking me to be at a certain point in the woods at nine in the morning. And sure enough, when I showed up, there he was. He wouldn't say hello; he couldn't even look at me any more than to let me know that our friendship was over. I felt struck by lightning, half-dead with guilt. Somehow Rose had managed to slip a second sheet of paper under my plate, asking me to be on the beach at ten that night. . . .

1

The designated spot was about half a mile from the house, near the hollow where Tom had seen Mr. Peet and the Wandering Boys at work on the first night. His directions had told him to start at the left of the beach and go straight ahead to the sixth light. The journey was much easier by day than it had been at night. When he reached the light he sat down on the grass and waited for whatever was going to happen. The note from Rose Armstrong, folded next to his skin inside his shirt, rustled and scratched—he was grateful every time he felt it dig at him. He could not have destroyed Rose's note: he wanted to pull it out and read it over again every few minutes. *Dear One: Beach near boathouse, ten tonight. Love, R.* Dear One! Love! He wished he could obliterate all the time between morning and night, and see Rose slipping out of the water to meet him. He wanted to ask her about the previous night's scene; he had a lot of questions about that: but far more than asking her questions, he wanted to put his arms around her.

Del came slouching into the little clearing five minutes later, in a starched blue shirt and jeans pressed to a sharp crease. Elena's work. A few burs clung to his cuffs, and after Del had glanced at Tom and dismissed him, he sat down to pick them off.

"How are you?" Tom asked.

Del lowered his head and twisted a cuff around to find a bur. He looked rested but tense: as though even the seams of his underwear were aligned. Comb marks furrowed his thick black hair.

"We have to talk to each other," Tom said.

Del tossed away the last bur, brushed at his cuffs with both hands, looked back toward the house.

"Aren't you even going to look at me?"

Without turning his head, Del said, "I think there's a dead rat somewhere around here."

"Well, I have to talk to *you.*"

"I think the dead rat should just go home if he doesn't like it here."

That shut Tom up—it was too close to what he had

been intending to say. They sat there in silence and heat, neither looking at the other. Coleman Collins startled them both by limping noiselessly into the clearing from deeper in the woods. He wore a slim black suit, a red shirt, gleaming black pumps, and looked as if he had just left the stage after a particularly brilliant performance.

"Gather round, children. Today we learn many things. Today we have a *son et lumière*. This is the second part of the story known as 'The Death of Love'—and I will require your close attention."

He smiled at them, but Tom could not smile back. The magician tilted his head, winked, and somehow produced a high black stool from the air; he sat. "Do I sense a little tension in the atmosphere? That is not inappropriate. If the first part of my unburdening could be subtitled 'The Healer Healed,' this part might be called 'The Undoing of the King of the Cats.'"

Collins propped his leg on a rung of the stool, looked up at a hawk cruising overhead, and said, "Rumors about my unorthodox surgical techniques on Corporal Washford had begun to circulate among the Negro soldiers.

2

"And I was not sure I welcomed that. The power I have spoken of to you marvelous boys was growing within me, but I had as yet no idea of its dimensions nor of its ultimate role in my life, and I had the impulse to nurture it in secret for a time. Even if I could have repeated my performance on Washford with some other poor devil, I do not think I would have—I wanted first to adjust to having done it once, and to refine my skills in situations where I was not under such intense observation. As you will see, I did not yet understand the nature of the gift, and I did not know how fiercely it would demand expression. And of course I thought I was alone. I was that ignorant. That there was a tradition, that there were many others, an entire society existing in the world's shadowy pockets and taught by one great hidden body of knowledge I had only barely skirted with my Levi and

Cornelius Agrippa, of all that I knew nothing. I was like a child who draws a map of the stars and thinks he has invented astronomy. When the Negroes who worked in the canteen and dispensary began to look at me in an odd, attentive way, what I felt was unease. I knew they had begun to talk. Maybe it was Washford himself—more likely it was the attendant in our operating theater—but however it had started, it was unwelcome.

"I have told you that the Negro Division had a life absolutely separate from ours—they fought nobly, many of them were heroic, but for most of us whites they were invisible. Unless one of us wandered into their off-hours clubs, where (or so I heard) it became evident that their off-duty lives were rather richer than ours. Many French-women were said to find the Negroes attractive—probably they just treated them like men, without regard to color. Some of those off-duty places were legendary, much as the Negro nightclubs became legendary in Paris right after the war. The difference was that a place like Bricktop's was heavily patronized by whites, while during the war, at least where I was, it was a rare white who dipped into the world of the Negro American soldier. The closest I ever got to it was one of my bookstore stops, when I browsed in a shop in an area where colored soldiers were billeted.

"I had been visiting this shop, Librairie Du Prey, for several weeks, and finally—after the Washford incident— I began to notice that another customer, a colored private, often appeared there when I did. I never saw him buy a book. Neither did I ever precisely catch him watching me, but I felt observed.

"A few days later, this same man appeared in the canteen. It took me a few moments to recognize him, since his uniform shirt was covered by a busboy's jacket, a garment which makes all men identical twins. He was picking trays up off the tables, and I tried to catch his eye, but he merely scowled at me.

"The next time I went to the Librairie Du Prey, another black soldier was browsing over the tables. He scrutinized me much more openly than the first man had, and when I had given him a good look in return, I was stopped dead in my tracks. He was a magician. I knew it. He was a noncom, a stranger, and foreign to me in a thousand ways: but when I looked at him I knew he was my brother and he knew that I knew. I wish for you boys a moment in your lives as wild with excitement—as wild with *possibility* —as that moment was for me. The man turned away and left the shop, and I could barely keep myself from running out and following him.

"The next afternoon in the hospital canteen, one of the messboys slipped a note into my jacket as I walked out. I had been anticipating some such thing all day, I knew it was connected to the magician I had seen in the bookstore, and I took it out and read it as soon as I was out the door. *Be in front of the bookstore at nine tonight*—that was all it said, all I needed. I washed up and went back to the operating theater in a mood of feverish anticipation. It was coming, whatever it was, and I wanted to meet it head-on. If it was my destiny, I no longer dithered and fought. I wanted that door to open.

3

"At nine sharp I was in front of that bookstore. I felt very exposed—I was the only white man in sight. In a closed-up shop down the street, someone was playing the banjo. It made a hot, vibrant, electrical sound. The night was humid and warm. The Negro soldiers who walked by looked at me with a kind of aggressive, aimless curiosity, and I sensed that one or two of them only just decided not to make trouble for me because of my rank. If I had been a drunken private with a week's scrip in my pocket . . . I remember feeling the metaphoric aptness of my situation: surrounded by the unknown, on the point of really entering the unknown.

"At nine-fifteen a Negro soldier came striding past, looked at me and nodded, and kept walking. It took me a second to realize what I was supposed to do. He was nearly to the corner by the time I started to follow him. When I got to the corner, I saw him disappearing around another sharp corner ahead of me.

"He led me up and down, around and around—a few times I thought I had lost him, those streets were so

narrow and twisting, and all around me the sounds of dark
voices, men singing or laughing or muttering to me as I
passed, but I always managed to catch a glimpse of his
boots at the last minute. Of course I was lost. I did not at
all know that section of Ste. Nazaire, and I recognized
none of the street names. He had led me into the colored
red-light district, and even a lieutenant was not safe there
after dark.

"Finally I rounded a corner, by now out of breath, and
a huge colored man in uniform stepped in front of me and
pushed me against the brick wall. 'You the doctor? You
the Collector?' he said. His accent was very Southern.

"'Thass him, thass him,' said another man I could not
see. 'Inside.'

"The giant astonished me by giggling and saying something I could not decipher—*Heez gon gew haid sumphum.*
Then opened a door in the brick and bundled me inside.

"It was a barren, sweat-smelling room. The magician I
had seen in the bookstore was standing before one of the
gray walls, wearing a battered uniform bearing his corporal stripes but no other identification. A man I thought
was the messboy peeked in, looked at me with huge eyes,
and slammed the door. The magician said, 'Lieutenant
Nightingale? Known as the Collector?'

"'I know what you are,' I said.

"'You think you do,' he said. 'You operated on a
soldier named Washford?'

"'I wouldn't call it operating,' I said.

"'Another doctor refused to attend to him because of
his race, and you volunteered to do the job?'

"*To do the job*—he was not a country boy like the
others, he had city stamped all over him, someplace
tough, someplace like Chicago.

"I agreed.

"'Tell me how you healed Washford,' he said. And I
could see the iron in him again.

"I held up my hands for answer. I said, 'You fellows
have been eyeing me ever since it happened.'

"'You have never heard of the Order? Never heard tell
of the Book?'

"'What I know is in these hands,' I said.

"'Wait here,' he said, and slipped out through the door. A moment later he reappeared, and nodded at me to follow him. I did. And I walked straight into Shadowland, which had been there all along, right under the surface of things, dogging me ever since I had set foot in Europe.

"The corporal gave me a glittering professional smile just as I was passing through the door, and it startled me, because it was the smile you give a target just before you pull the ace of spades out of his ear.

"I was going through an interior door, and expected to go into another room, but when I stepped through, I was in a sunny field—a mustard field. I turned around, and the house was gone. All of Ste. Nazaire was gone. I was out in the country, in the middle of a mustard field, those yellow blossoms under my feet, on a gentle hill.

"I whirled around, and before me a man was seated in a high, hand-carved wooden chair with carved owls' heads on the armrests and talons carved into its feet. He was colored, handsome, younger than I, with a smooth, regular face. He looked like a king in that chair, which was the general idea. He had just appeared out of nowhere. He wore an old uniform with no markings on it at all. This man who had conjured me out of the slum in Ste. Nazaire and conjured himself out of nowhere knit his fingers together and looked at me in a kindly, intense, questioning way. I could feel his power: and then I saw his aura. That is, he allowed me to see it. It nearly blinded me—colors shot out and glowed, each of them brighter than the mustard flowers. I almost fell on my knees. For I knew what he was, and what he could do for me. I was twenty-seven and he may have been nineteen or twenty, but he was the king. Of magicians. Of shadows. The King of the Cats. He was my Answer. And all the others, the ones who had watched me and taken me to him, were only his lackeys.

"'Welcome to the Order,' he said. 'My name is Speckle John.'

"'And I am . . .' I started to say, but he held up a hand and violent color seemed to play around it.

"'Charles Nightingale. William Vendouris. Dr. Collector, but none of those now. You will take a new name, one known to the Order. You will be Coleman Collins.

Only to us at first, but when this war finishes and we may go where we please, to the world.'

"I knew without his telling me that it was a colored name—the name of a colored magician who had died. It was as if I had heard the name before, but I could not remember ever having heard it. I wanted to deserve that name. At that second I became Coleman Collins in my heart, and wore the name I had been born with as a disguise. 'What do you want with me?' I asked.

"He laughed out loud. 'Why, I want to be your teacher. I want to work with you,' he said. 'You don't even know who you are yet, Coleman Collins, and I want the privilege of helping to show you how to get there. You may be the most gifted natural the Order has uncovered—or who has uncovered himself—in the past decade.'

"'What do you want me to do?' I asked.

"'Tonight you will stay here. Yes, here. It will be all night. And if you are welcomed tonight—don't worry, you'll see what that means—if you are welcomed, soon you will be able to repeat what you did with Mr. Washford whenever you wish.' He laughed out loud again, and his wonderful voice rolled out over the mustard field like the hallooing of a French horn. 'Of course, I cannot recommend that you do it every day.'

"'And after tonight?' I asked.

"'We begin our studies. We begin your new life, Mr. Collins.'

"He stood up from his throne, and the sunlight died. Speckle John stood before me in a vast starry night, really only an outline in the darkness. I could not make out his features. 'You will be safe during the night, Doctor, safer than you would be in our part of Ste. Nazaire. Tomorrow we begin.'

"Then he was gone. I moved forward, reaching out, and my fingers touched the back of his chair. The night seemed immense. I could hear only a few isolated crickets. The stars seemed very intense, and I fancied that I was looking at them with eyes made new by Speckle John.

"Well, there I was, alone on a hill in the middle of the night—the actual night I suppose, for the earlier daylight must have been an illusion. I had not a notion of where I was, and only Speckle John's word that the next day would find me returned to Ste. Nazaire and my work. His chair stood before me, and I was too superstitious to sit in it, though I wanted to. Even then, I wanted that chair for my own. I knew what it represented.

"I stretched out on the mustard, which was not very comfortable at first. 'If you are welcomed,' he had said, and I could not rest for wondering what that meant. Once it even went through my mind that I was the victim of a gigantic hoax, and that the Negro would leave me out in the wilderness. But I had the evidence of his extraordinary presence, and the care with which he had sought me out. And he had turned night to day and back again! What sort of 'welcome' could follow that?

"Even an excited man must sleep sometime, and so it was with me. I began to doze, and then to dream, and finally fell into a deep sleep.

"I was awakened by a fox. His pungent, musky odor; the sound of his breath; a jittery, quick, nervous presence near me. My eyes flew open, and his muzzle was a foot from my face. Terror made me jerk backward—I was afraid he'd take my face off. *Mr. Collins,* the fox said. I understood him! I said or thought 'Yes.'

"*You need not fear me.*

"'No.'

"*You belong to the Order.*

"'I belong to them.'

"*The Order is your mother and father.*

"'They are.'

"*And you will have no other loyalties.*

"'None.'

"*You are welcomed.*

"He trotted away, and I did not know if I had spoken to a fox or to a man in the form of a fox. For a long time I lay in the field consumed by wonder. The stars were dimming, and all I could see was blackness. I began to realize that I could float off the ground if I wanted to, but I dared not do anything to affect the mood of the night and myself as part of the night. That was floating enough. Finally I heard wingbeats. I could not see it, but I heard an enormous bird land some few feet away from me. I never saw it, but I thought, and I think now, that I knew what bird it was. Once again, I was terrified. Then it spoke, and I understood its voice as I had understood the fox's.

"Collins.

"'Yes.'

"Have you worlds within you?

"'I have worlds within me.'

"Do you want dominion?

"'I want dominion.' And I did, you see—I wanted to tap that strength within me and to make the duller world know it.

"The knowledge is the treasure, and the treasure is its own dominion.

"I suppose I muttered the words 'knowledge . . . treasure.'

"See the history of your treasure, Collins.

"Then a scene played itself out before my eyes. I was a child, an infant in arms. My father was carrying me. We were in a theater in Boston, one which had been torn down during my adolescence. Vaughan's Oriental Theater, it was called. A colored man in evening dress was performing on stage, exhibiting a mechanical bird which sang requests called out by the audience. My father shouted out 'Only a Bird in a Gilded Cage,' and everybody laughed, and the metal bird began to warble the saccharine melody. I remembered being moved by the music, and astounded by the ornateness of the theater. 'See his name, Charlie,' my father said, pointing to the sign on the side of the stage. 'His name is Old King Cole. Isn't that funny?' I remembered staring openmouthed at the man on the stage, wanting to smile because my father said it was funny, but too overwhelmed to see the humor. Then I froze. The magician, Old King Cole, was staring directly at me.

"So there it was—a buried memory, maybe the central memory of my life, and one that I think had guided me throughout my life even though I had consciously forgotten it. The man onstage was the original Coleman Collins. Or was there another Coleman Collins before him? And I knew that someday that would be me on the stage, though I would require a different professional name.

"You saw.

"'I saw.'

"And you know that the magician saw you.

"I remembered Old King Cole looking down from the stage, finding me there in my father's arms, a child perhaps of eighteen or twenty months, and . . . recognizing me?

"'I know.'

"*I have doubts about you,* the owl said.

"'But he saw me!' I said, now reliving the wonder of those few seconds as if they had happened only five minutes ago. 'He chose *me!*'

"*He saw the treasure within,* the invisible bird sighed. *Be worthy of it. Honor the Book. You are welcomed.*

"The huge wings beat, my interrogator flew off, and I was alone. Either I had been asleep all along or I slept again: I remember everything blurring about me, a feeling of wandering, drowsy bliss invading my every cell, and I slept solidly for hours. When I woke up, I was leaning against a wall back in Ste. Nazaire, only a block from the hospital. Withers was just walking past, taking an early-morning constitutional at a loafing Southern pace, and he saw me and snarled, 'Too drunk to get home last night, Dr. Nightingale?' 'You're welcome,' I said, and laughed in his face.

"Thereafter, I saw Speckle John almost every day. I received a note, usually from a messboy, waited outside the bookstore, and was led through the maze of slum streets until we came to that shabby, foul-smelling tenement which was more school to me than any university. I was taken back to that time when we all lived in the forest: I entered that realm which was mine by right since infancy. For a year Speckle John taught me, and we began to plan working together after the war. But I knew that the day would arrive when my growing strength would confront his. I was never content with the second chair.

"Open your eyes, boys. Watch carefully. This is to be your own night in the open. We are in the Wood Green Empire, London, in August of 1924."

4

The boys, unaware that they had closed their eyes, opened them. It was night, hot and vaporous. For a moment Tom caught the odor of mustard flowers: he felt drowsy and heavy-limbed, and his legs ached. Collins sat in the circle of light, but on a tall wooden chair, not the stool he had made to appear that morning. Over the black suit was a black cape fastened at the throat with a gold clasp. Tom tried to move his legs, and smelled mustard flowers again. "Oh . . . no . . ." Del said, looking into the woods, and Tom snapped his head sideways to see.

Dark trees funneled toward a lighted open space. A boy and a tall man in a belted raincoat were striding down the funnel. The boy, Tom sickeningly realized, was himself. He looked at Collins, and found him leaning back in the owl chair, legs crossed, smiling maliciously back. The magician pointed back to the scene: *Now!*

When he looked back, the man and boy were gone. The open space at the end of the funnel of trees was a theater. A crowd rustled on its chairs, fanned itself with programs. Plum-colored curtains swung open, and there they were, he and Del, Flanagini and Night. Very clearly, Tom saw Dave Brick sitting fat and ignored and alone at the back of the theater.

"Yes," Collins said. And a curtain of flame sprang up before the scene. *Wall of flame,* Tom thought: he heard the panicky, rushed sounds of many bodies moving, muffled shouts and commands.

Everybody out! Everybody out!
Stop in your tracks!
My bass!
They're hot! They're going to burn!
Get up off the floor, Whipple.

Just as Tom had been yanked back more than forty years while Collins had described his earlier life, just as he had *seen* Speckle John and Withers and the corporal with the professional smile, now he saw those moments again—the boys piling up first at the big outside doors, then at the door to the hall, screaming, clubbing each other, Brown yelling for his precious instrument, Del stumbling blind through piling smoke . . .

a young man in immaculate formal dress, white-face, and a red wig stood on the altered stage. The fire had whisked away like fog.

"No!" Tom shouted.

Herbie Butter waved his hands, and the light momentarily died, flickered red with a suggestion of flame, and returned to show a wooden hut deep in a painted wood. Up a trailing path came a young girl in a red cloak, carrying a wicker basket from which poked the heads of half a dozen blackbirds. . . .

The lights died and the stage disappeared into the funnel of trees.

"And one more," Collins said.

From one side of the narrow avenue before them a man in black cape and black slouch hat stepped out from between the trees. A moment later, a wolf came out to face him from between the trees on the other side. The wolf bristled, crouched. It looked starved and crazy, unwilling to do what it had to do. The man braced his feet; the wolf snarled. Finally it sprang. The man in the cape drew a sword from his side—he must have been holding it ready all along beneath the cape—and thrust it forward, impaling the wolf. With terrific strength, the caped man lifted the sword and held it straight in the air. The wolf's paws dangled over his hat. He stepped back into the cover of the line of trees.

Wolves, and those who see them, are shot on sight, Tom remembered.

"I put a hurtin' on Speckle John," Collins said. "I held him wriggling on my sword. *Ha hah!* He is still on my sword, children. In that sense, my farewell performance at the Wood Green Empire has not ended yet. But we will get to that in time. I want you to sleep outside tonight. A welcome may come, or it may not. You will find sleeping bags behind the second tree on the left side of the clearing."

He stood up and pulled the cape about him as if he were cold. "I must tell you that only one of you will prevail. Two cannot sit in the owl chair. But this is not a contest, and he who is not welcomed will lose only what he never had.

"But listen to me, little birds: the one who prevails will have Shadowland, the owl chair, the world. There will be a new king, whether it be King Flanagini or King Night."

For a second he was outlined in black, etched agains
the wood; then he was gone. Tom saw four square
flattened patches of grass where the chair had been.

"It won't be you," Del said. "You don't deserve it."

"I don't even want it," Tom answered angrily. "Del
don't you understand? I don't want to take anything away
from you. I only came here because I wanted to help you
Do you want to live like that—like him?"

Del hesitated a moment, then turned away to look fo
his sleeping bag. "You wouldn't have to. You could live
any way you wanted."

A hard and certain thought occurred to Tom. "If he'
let you. Why would he want to give up now? He's old, bu
he's still healthy."

Del was lifting something out of the leaves behind the
tree Collins had indicated. "Because he chose *me*. That'
why. You're just along for the ride. You never ever
wanted to be a magician before you met me."

"Aren't you my friend anymore?" Tom asked i
despair.

Del would not reply.

"I'm still your friend."

"You're trying to trick me."

"How can I? You're better than I am."

Carrying his sleeping bag back to the clearing, Del a
last looked at him. Pure triumph shone in his eyes.

"But, Del, no matter what happens, I don't think he'
going to . . . I think it's all a trick. On us."

"Get lost."

"Oh . . ." the letter from Rose, which Tom had forgot
ten, scratched him beneath a rib. He looked at his watch
It was ten-thirty. Half an hour late! He looked back i
agony at Del, and saw that he was trying to get into hi
sleeping bag. His eyes were clamped shut and he wa
crying. One of his heels had snagged on the zipper and he
could not free it without opening his eyes.

Tom went over to him and grasped Del's foot. He
moved it over the zipper and into the bag. "Del, you're
my best friend," he said.

"You're my *only* friend," Del said, almost blubbing
"But he's *my* uncle. This is where *I* come. You're onl
here *once*."

"I have to go away for a little while," Tom said, neeling by Del's side. "When I come back, let's talk, kay?"

Del's teary eyes flew open. "Are you going to see im?"

"No."

"Promise?"

"I promise."

"Okay." His face hardened for a moment. "You vouldn't even let me in to see the Grimm Brothers."

"I was just surprised—the room was different."

"But you saw. You saw you and him. Like I said."

"It's some kind of game. I was never with him. I would ave told you."

"I was feeling so alone," Del said.

"When I get back," Tom said, and turned to run across he clearing. *Hey, where are you going?* he heard Del vail; he did not answer.

5

Ie came pounding out of the edge of the woods and out f breath, stopped running. Sand moved under his feet. 'or a moment he wanted to remove his shoes. Far up the liff, the house shone from a dozen windows. He could ee Rose nowhere on the beach, which was a silvery nushroom gray beside the black smooth water. He hecked his watch again and saw that it was now ten-fifty. the had gone.

Tom trudged forward through the sand. Here was a urprise: a substantial part of him was relieved that Rose ad given up and gone back across the lake. Now he could eturn to Del.

But maybe just ahead, on the other side of the oathouse? He saw the slavering wolf pouncing toward er. If Collins had seen her waiting on the beach . . .

Now his mood had swung, and he desperately wanted o know if Rose Armstrong were safe. His mind was a umble of images: the wolf, held up with unbelievable trength, impaled on a sword; the badger being swung in a reat arc toward the pit; Dave Brick sitting on a metal

chair, waiting to be roasted. He banged open the door of
the boathouse. He walked in, and nearly fell twenty feet
into black shallow water.

Tom jerked himself back just in time. Inside the
dilapidated shell, the boathouse was chiefly water and
open space. A three-foot apron of concrete ran around a
wide hole open at the lake end. Most of this entire side of
the boathouse was open. Only six or seven feet down
from the top had been boarded across.

The door slammed shut behind him, and his heart too
slammed in his chest. Tom heard a metal bar sliding into a
brace. He hit the door with his shoulder. It rattled, but
would not open. He banged it again, beginning to settle
down from his original terror into ordinary fright. Who
was it? Collins? The Collector turned loose to get him?
One of the Wandering Boys? He would have to jump into
the water. He looked down, saw greasy-looking blackness, and then saw something else.

Then he heard giggles from behind the door: Rose.

"Let me out!"

"You stood me up three nights straight. Why should
I?"

"Three nights?" Tom's stomach fell away.

"I got your note this morning."

"No, you didn't, boyo. That was three days ago."

"Oh, God." He leaned against the creaky doors of the
boathouse wall.

"You didn't know?"

"I thought it was this morning."

"Likely story, but I'll let you out."

The bolt slid across. The door opened, and Rose stood
before him in a green 1920's dress. She was smiling
teasingly, and on her face it looked brave. She was the
best thing he had ever seen. The green dress made her
look more sophisticated than any girl he had ever known.

"I almost had heart failure in there," he said, "but I'm
so happy to see you, I guess I wouldn't mind dying."

She pouted, took a step back. "You almost had more
than heart failure. You know what I almost did to you? I
was so mad."

"Did to me?"

"Take a look at this and tell me about three days."

Rose stepped gracefully around him, and he saw that she was wearing high heels. "You were standing on the other side of the door, right? Okay." She bent down and tugged at a bar set in the sand beside the door. *Bang!* Iron rang against concrete. The apron he had been standing on had fallen in on a hinge. "It's like a kind of trapdoor. A long time ago, there was a boat, and a sort of winch fit in here . . . anyhow, I almost dropped you in the drink. The water's deep enough. You'd just have to swim out. I could have strangled you, boyo—three nights? I'm getting muscles from swimming across that lake!"

"You didn't swim tonight," Tom pointed out.

She turned away. "Of course not. I ruined my stockings. And this dress is full of gunk." She lifted the hem and brushed at dust and twigs. "I came all the way through the woods. Then I sat out on the pier. You walked by without even looking at me."

"I'll look at you now," he said, and made to embrace her. She looked as if she were going to back away, but stiffly submitted. "What's wrong?"

"This."

"Oh. I'm sorry." Chagrined, he dropped his arms. He could not read her face—she looked grown up in the green dress, far beyond his reach. "Really. The note came this morning. At least I thought it was this morning. That scene in the woods, that was just now, wasn't it? About half an hour ago?"

"Sure. Look, what day—?"

"I want to show you something. Something I want to look at again too."

"Oh?"

"In here." He pulled open the boathouse door and knelt. "Push that lever again." Rose stepped aside and tugged the rod back. The iron plate swung up on its hinge, clicked into place. Tom crawled out on it and peered down at the water.

"I was going to ask you what day you thought it was."

"I don't see it now. What day? I'm not sure anymore. Tuesday or Wednesday."

"It's Saturday."

"*Saturday?*" He looked up at her, standing just outside the boathouse on the sand. She looked very tall, very feminine. Though slim, her body curved.

"What month do you think this is? What week?"

"I'm trying to find something," he said. "Something I saw before." He looked down at the murky water. "Oh."

"Did you find it?"

"No." He scuttled backward.

"You did."

"What week is it, anyhow?" He stood up. "What month *is* it?"

"What do you think it is?"

"Early June. About the sixth or the seventh. Maybe as late as the tenth."

She rubbed her nose. "So you think it's the tenth of June. Poor Tom." Rose touched his cheek with the tips of her fingers. Tom felt as though new nerves had grown where her fingers had rested. "What did you see down there?"

"Tell me what day it is, Rose."

Her brave smile flickered in the moonlight. "I'm not sure, but it's at least the first of July. Or the second."

"It's *July?* We've been here a *month?*"

Rose nodded; her face searched his, sent out such sympathy that he wanted again to embrace her. "How can he do that?"

"He just can. One summer he made Del think that six or seven weeks went by in a day. It was the time Del broke his leg."

"And Bud Copeland came."

Her eyebrows lifted. "You know about that? Oh . . . Del told you. Yes, that summer. He didn't want Del to . . . I can't say."

"What happened?"

"The iron staircase. It broke away from the cliff."

"What can't you say?"

Now the smile was firmer. "Ask Del. Maybe he'll be able to remember by now. I can't, Tom."

She walked a little way up the beach and turned to him again. He saw that it was impossible: this was a secret that she would not give up. "I can't stay much longer, Tom," she said softly.

"I want to kiss you," he said. That she would keep her secret had made her even more desirable. "I want to hold you."

"I told you. It's wrong now. I have something to tell you and I don't want to get all confused, and I don't have much time. He'll want to see me again."

"Tonight?" He walked toward her over the gray sand. She nodded. At least she did not walk away.

"What for?"

"To talk. He likes to talk to me. He says I help him think out loud."

"But that's great. Then you can tell me and Del . . ."

"Right. That's why I gave you that note. I found out something. But now, after tonight, you probably know it anyhow."

"I don't know *anything*," Tom complained. And she reached out and took his hand.

"He wants to give his farewell performance over again. With you and Del in it. If we're going to get out, I think it has to be right before, when all they'll be thinking about is what they have to do."

Pleasurable impulses and sensations had been going all the way up his arm, and now she gripped him harder. "The important thing is that he's planning something big for this performance. Something dangerous. He said you'd have to choose between your wings and your song. Do you know what that means?"

Tom shook his head. "He said it to me once before. I don't know what it means."

"He said Speckle John chose his song, and he took his song away from him. So he didn't have anything left. I think we have to make sure we're out of here before . . ."

"Before I find out what it means," Tom said a little fearfully.

"That's what I think." Rose dropped his hand. Tom leaned forward and took hers and raised it to his mouth. He was trembling. He saw a girl in a red cloak carrying a wicker basket up a wooded path.

Rose said, "Tom, I feel so *terrible*—like I'm drawing you in deeper. But I have to do what he says, or he'll know something's wrong. Just trust me."

"God, I don't just trust you," Tom said. "I—"

Rose was suddenly upon him. Her face came down over his, blotting out the sky and the brilliant stars. Her mouth swam over his, and her teeth took his lips. Rose's legs nestled his, her breasts plumped against his chest. Tom put his hand in her hair and gave himself over to the kiss. His surprised erection grew straight into the softness of her belly; he groaned into her mouth, smelling a faint perfume and the fragrance of clean hair, tasting what she was. She was the girl in the window: it was knowledge he had not permitted himself before, but now he held two Rose Armstrongs, the girl in the green dress and the unattainable staggering girl who had raised her arms and shown herself to a frightened boy freezing in a wintry sleigh.

"You're going to break my back," Rose said into his mouth.

He put his hands again in her hair.

"We can't."

"We can't what?" Tom mumbled.

"We can't make love. Not here."

That nearly made him explode. *Not here!* He groaned again, jerked in an instant from a world in which he had feared he might be frightening or disgusting her with the evidence of his desire into one in which she could casually allude to its fulfillment. *"Where?"* he said, his voice out of control.

"Don't growl, I'm just barely . . . If you knew . . ."

"Oh, Jesus, I know," he said, and found her mouth again.

"It's not fair, is it?" She pulled her face away from his: in compensation, her hips tipped toward him. "Oh, you're so beautiful."

"Where?" he repeated.

"Nowhere. Not now. I have to go back and see him, Tom. And besides, I . . ."

She was a virgin. "I am too," he said. "Oh, my God." He pulled her tighter into him. "I want you so much."

"Pretty Tom." She grazed over his cheek, but she already felt distant. So much had happened to Tom, so many milestones had gone by in a blur, that he had no idea of what to do next. Despite what he had hinted to Del, Jenny Oliver and Diane Darling had stopped short even of French kissing. Rose's belly was somehow miraculously accommodating and accepting his erection.

"Pretty Tom," she repeated. "I don't want to be unfair to you. I want you, too." Her arms went around his neck, and he thought heaven had opened and taken him in. "I'm just afraid . . ."

"It's okay," Tom said. "Oh, Rose."

"The shadow of the boathouse," Rose said, and pushed him back with her body. They stumbled awkwardly back a few steps.

"There aren't any shadows, it's night," Tom said, and it seemed so funny to him that he laughed out loud.

"Dummy." She pinned him against the coarse wood and opened him up with her mouth again. She muttered, "Too bad I didn't drop you in the water, then you'd have to take off your clothes."

She was a cloud blessedly made of flesh, softly pillowing every part of him. Sexual urgency blasted him.

"It's okay, Tom," she whispered right against his ear. "I know. It's okay. Go on."

One of her hands left his head and lighted on his trousers. "Oh, no," he said. And she slipped her hand a layer closer to him. His whole body shook. Rose's fingers twined in, cupped and held—he felt a yard long. She said, "Oh, Tom," and he hugged her as close as he could and felt everything in him jump, an explosion seeming to happen in his spine and his head as well as where Rose was, and she *pulled*, and he thought he was turning inside-out. "Dear Tom," she said, and nuzzled his cheek, and he turned inside-out again. "We really shouldn't have done this," she said into his cheek, and he laughed until her hand left him. "Now you're a real mess."

"Thank God."

"You must think I'm terrible. I just could feel you . . . and you were moaning like that . . . I don't want you to think I'm . . ."

"I think you're amazing. Beautiful. Astonishing. Incredible. Fantastic." His heart was still thrumming. "You're even generous. I hardly know what happened to me."

"Well," she said, and her expression made him laugh again.

"How are you?"

"Fine. I don't know. Fine."

"Sometime . . ."

"Sometime. Yes. But don't start again." She stepped back on the sand.

"I love you," he said. "I'm just absolutely in love with you."

"Beautiful Tom."

"Not grumpy Tom."

"I hope not." Rose lifted her hands, bobbed her head self-deprecatingly. "I have to go. Really. I'm sorry."

"So am I. I love you, Rose." Tom was just beginning to return to earth. She blew him a kiss. Walked away down the beach, stopped to take off the high-heeled shoes, and blew him another kiss before she slipped into the woods bordering the lake.

"Hey!" he called out. "We could go back together! I have to . . ." But she was gone. Tom, still dazed, looked back at the boathouse and then followed her footprints toward the end of the beach. He remembered that he had to sleep in the woods that night, and wondered if he would ever find his way back to Del.

What could he say to Del? What Rose had done for him seemed an act of almost godlike charity.

When he reached the end of the beach, he took off his clothes and stepped into the cool water. "I love Rose Armstrong," he said to himself, and went in up to his neck. The moonlight made a path straight toward him, rippling when he moved. When he put his face in the water, he remembered what he had seen at the bottom of the boathouse, the severed head of a horse, tipping over slowly in murk.

Tom got out of the lake and dried himself hurriedly on his shirt. Then he brushed sand from his feet, got back into his trousers, pushed his feet into his loafers, and walked back into the woods, carrying his damp shirt under his arm.

6

Six lights: and there was the first, just ahead, near the place where Rose had enacted the scene from "The Goose Girl." After that Collins had simply dumped the horse's head into the water to rot. The magician would treat Del and Rose and himself the same way, Tom knew, if he had to. Now, if only he could make Del see that they had to escape before the climax Collins was planning for them. Tom knew in his bones that no matter what Collins said, he would not surrender his place in the magicians' world, whatever that was, to a fifteen-year-old boy. He would be more likely to do whatever he had done to Speckle John—and that, Tom knew in the same instinctive fashion, would not be told until the day of the performance.

Two. The second light, piercing a curtain of leaves. Daydreaming about Rose Armstrong, Tom parted the branches, stepped over a mulchy, rotting log; stopped. In the middle of the lighted clearing stood a huge man covered with fur. On his shoulders sat the giant head of a wolf. Tom stared at this hieratic figure in pure shock. He was not hypnotized, he was awake and his senses were all functioning. The man-wolf, more than anything else he had witnessed, seemed the embodiment of magic—magic personified, a guardian. Tom saw that the fur was sewn-together pelts. The man-wolf raised an arm and pointed deeper into the woods. Tom ran, plunging sideways into the trees until the man-wolf could not see him, and then slowly worked forward.

Three. Tom crept from tree to tree, trying to be noiseless. When he was close enough, he peered around a gigantic oak and looked over the marshy platform of earth beneath the light. Cautiously he stepped onto the spongy ground. The forest around him began to melt. *"No!"* he shouted. And tried to jerk himself backward to escape the transformation. His back struck something metal. In an instant the air cleared: he was in a parking lot. A wide, low city lay around him in early morning, with soft humid air and a rising sun beginning to tint the buildings to his left. Was this where he was to be welcomed? None of the few cars in the lot looked familiar—though not new, they were newer than any cars he had ever seen.

"Where?" he said aloud—there were no landmarks. Then through the sun-tipped buildings to his right he saw a line of pale blue. An ocean. California? Florida?

He stepped up on one of the concrete dividers. The

metal thing he had banged into was a parking meter.
What could come to him here, in a city?

Then he noticed the battered green car before him. A
series of drops hung at the bottom of the doorframe,
filled, and splashed on the concrete. The drops were red.
Tom looked at the driver's window, and saw a man's head
propped against the glass. Curling blond hair flattened
against the window. The red drops were the man's blood.
Tom nearly threw up. He could not look at those drops
gathering and falling. He jumped off the divider and
walked fearfully around to face the front of the car.
Florida plates. Was he supposed to see the man's face?
Through the windshield he saw broad unknown features.
It was the face of a man in middle age. Some stranger,
some visitor. Where his parting should have been, his
head was horrible. Then for an instant he thought he
knew the face—he felt small and helpless, turned away in
moral anguish, rejecting the terrible half-familiarity of the
dead man's features.

An old man in a Harry Truman shirt and a baseball cap
was at the far end of the lot, walking toward him and the
green car. *"Mister!"* Tom shouted, and the old man
peered up at him in fright. "Hey . . . I need . . ."

The old man was waving his fists at him, and the
revulsion and disgust and fear on the old man's face made
Tom step backward. The old man screamed something at
him, and Tom turned around and ran.

When he reached the end of the lot and was just about
to pound along the sidewalk, he felt like he had fallen
over a cliff: his legs went out from under him, the city
whisked away, and he rolled over onto wet leaves. It was
night again, and the air smelled different. He was back in
the woods. When he picked himself up he saw that he was
on the other side of the marshy clearing. He had to go on.

Not *Marcus*—that was not lazy, cheerful Marcus
slumped in the green car. That man was too fat, too old.
He shook his head, not believing it but knowing that the
man had been Marcus. A moment later he turned away
from the empty clearing.

A worn little path led toward the fourth light; roots
stubbed his feet, black arms reached toward him. The
woods now were filled with gibbering and leering faces. A

branch rustled, and an eye winked at him. Then fireflies, a series of little eyes, danced up and whirled around. Between these flickerings, darting observations, he saw the next light.

Four. Only two more to go.

Tom approached the light nearly on tiptoe. He remembered. The torch was hung over a wide flat shelf of rock, the most stagelike of all the little arenas in the woods. Here it was where Rose had enacted the fable about the beginning of all stories on their first night in Shadowland.

Here too something waited for him.

He crept toward the rock shelf. Yes, someone waited for him—he caught a glimpse through the branches of a cannonball head. Snail; or Thorn, with his Halloween face. Tom edged sideways, trying to see the face. A red ear came into sight, pink flesh under a stubbly haircut. At last he saw the rest of the ponderous, studying face.

Oh, God.

He stepped on a stick, and it snapped as loudly as a bone. Dave Brick lifted his head and uncrossed his legs. He was sitting on a metal school chair. "Tommy?" he said; his voice was plaintive and lost. "Please, Tommy."

Tom stepped out onto the rock. Brick sat facing him twelve feet away, wearing the old tweed jacket Tom had lent him. "You left me, Tommy," Dave Brick complained. "You chose flight. You should go back and find me."

"I wish," Tom said. "But it's too late now."

"I'm still there, Tommy. I'm waiting. But you chose wings. Go back and find me. You saved a bass fiddle and some magic tricks. Now it's my turn." Brick sounded forlorn and slightly peevish.

"It's too late," Tom said. He thought he might be losing his mind; thought of his mind giving up and walking away.

"You can do magic. Save me. I want to be *saved*, Tommy. Something fell on me . . . and somebody hit me . . . and Mr. Broome told me not to move . . ." Brick looked ready to cry; then he was crying.

"Oh, don't," Tom said, "I can't take it. I can't handle it. It's too much."

"Del took the owl," Brick said through his tears. "I

saw. He made everything happen. Ask him. After you go back and save me, Tommy. It's all his fault, Tommy. Because you're supposed to get the owl chair. Ask him."

"You're not Dave Brick," Tom said. There were wrinkles in the face; the hands were huge and powerful. He ran across the edge of the slab, and the thing in the chair began to howl. *"You can be saved, Tommy! He can save you! Like you can save me!"*

Tom ran from the voice deep into the forest. He was crying himself now, whether from shock or outrage or horror he did not know. Was Coleman Collins telling Rose about this right now, chortling? Or had she known it was going to happen when she blew him a kiss? No—that could not be true. Running, he grazed a tree, staggered and stopped. Where was he? Dave Brick's look-alike howled far off to his left.

Tom struck out blindly through the moonlit forest, going in the direction where the trees were least dense. He still saw faces in the patterns of the branches, but now they looked at him in horror. Leaving Dave Brick behind, he had become a monster.

Five. There it was, just as he had known it would be. A flaring torch, not an electric light; not the same fifth light, but the one he was supposed to find. He felt like crying again. Then he had a premonition. He would see Rose standing on the dark grass, petting a wolf . . . Rose with her teeth sharpened . . .

All those nightmares, back at school, all those dreadful visions: they had come from him. Beginning in him, born in him, they had spread out to infect everyone he knew. Even back then, when he had thought magic was a few deft card tricks, he had been on his way here. The torch flared, visible between giant black growths. Tom shuddered and stepped forward.

First he saw the dead wolf. The sword wound in its belly gaped. Tom suddenly smelled mustard flowers, smelled Rose's faint perfume lacing delicately through. The wound in the wolf's belly gaped because the wolf had been nailed to the tree by its paws, and gravity was trying to haul it earthward. It hung just below the torch. "Rose . . ." he said. "Please . . ."

A man in black stepped out of the woods. Black cape, black hat shielding his face. He carried a bloodied sword and pointed it across twenty feet of open space at Tom's chest.

Have you worlds within you?

"No." He did not want these worlds.

Do you want dominion?

"No."

He saw the treasure within you, child.

"And he hated it."

Honor the Book.

"I don't even know it."

You belong to the Order.

"I don't belong to anything." Tom feared that the man with the invisible face would run him through, but instead he said, *You know what you are, child.*

The sword burst into flame. The man swung it to one side and pointed the way he must go. The way led straight to the sixth light, now extinguished.

7

In the dark glade Del lay curled on the ground in his sleeping bag. His hands pillowed his head. When his own sleeping bag was unrolled and he had slipped in, Tom lay on the ground, feeling every hump and depression fail to fit his body. He heard a cricket's *chirp-chirp*, a sound of mechanical and idiot joy. Tom rolled on his back, adjusting his body to avoid the most prominent bumps, and looked up at a full moon. It looked damaged, a battered old hull. *You know what you are.* He turned his head, and his eyes found a tree split in half by lightning.

Help me, Rose. Get me out of this.

8

An animal was breathing on him, bathing his face in warm foul air. He shuddered into wakefulness; the animal retreated. Tom could smell its fear of him. Now it was hours later: the moon was gone. He could see only the white oval of Del's face, ten feet away. But though he could see nothing, he felt around him the presence of a hundred alien lives—animal lives. In the invisible trees was a drumfire of wingbeats. *"No,"* he whispered. He closed his eyes. *"Go away."* Something rustled toward him. No fear came from it, only a cold self-possession. In the invisible trees, the hundreds of birds moved.

You know what you are, boy.

Tom shook his head, clamped his eyes shut.

There are treasures within you.

He tried to stop his ears.

What is the first law of magic?

The snake waited patiently for him to answer. He would not.

We have no doubts about you, boy.

Tom shook his head so hard his neck hurt.

You will learn everything you need to know.

Then something else approached, some animal he could not identify. The snake furled rapidly away, and Tom clamped his eyes shut even more firmly. He did not at all want to see it—the same searching, grasping feeling came from it as from the little figure down on Mesa Lane, back at the start of everything. This animal had about it an air of irredeemable wickedness; not cool and insinuating and impersonal like the snake, it was deeply evil. But it spoke in a thin and graceful voice which hid a hint of a chuckle. It was a mad voice, and the animal was no animal, but whatever the man with the sword had been pretending to be.

You will betray Del.

"No."

You will stay here forever, and drive Del away.

"No."

You are welcomed, boy.

At once all the birds left the trees. The noise was huge and rushing, almost oceanic. Tom covered his face: he thought of them falling on him, picking him to ribbons of flesh. Del sobbed in his sleep. Then the birds were gone.

Tom rocked himself down into his bag.

9

When he woke up, it was with a realization. If Rose had been right about the date, his mother must have had his letter for at least a few days. Very soon it would be time to run. He rolled over and saw Del sitting on the grass at the far side of the glade, leaning against a tree. "Good morning," Tom said.

"Morning. Where did you go last night? I want you to tell me."

"I just walked around. I got lost for a while."

"You didn't see my uncle."

"No. I didn't. I told you."

Del shifted and rubbed his hand over damp grass. "I don't suppose anything happened to you last night. I mean . . . anything like he was telling us about?"

"Did it happen to you? Were you welcomed?"

"No," Del said. "I wasn't."

"I wasn't either," Tom said. "It was probably the dullest night of my life."

"Yeah, me too." Del beamed back at him. "But I thought I heard something—really late, it would have been. A big noise, like a billion birds taking off at once." He looked shyly at Tom. "So maybe I was welcomed? Maybe that was it?"

"Let's go brush our teeth," Tom said. "There'll be food back at the house."

Tom put on his shirt, which was wrinkled as a relief map. They rolled up their sleeping bags and left them in the glade.

"You look different," Del said.

"How?"

"Just different. Older, I guess."

"I didn't get much sleep."

They were walking through the woods, going beneath big high-crowned trees. In minutes they reached the clearing where the man with the sword had told him that he knew what he was.

"Maybe we'll see Rose today," Del said.

"Maybe." Tom walked straight through the clearing toward the barely visible path, no more than a few trampled weeds, which led to the rock shelf.

"Tom, I'm sorry I got so mad at you. I thought you were trying to ruin things—you know. That was nuts. I'm really sorry."

"It's okay." Tom pushed aside ferns and went back into deep woods.

After a while Del spoke again. "You know, I think we've been here a lot longer than it seems. He did that once to me before."

"Yeah, I think so too."

"The sun's in a different position. Isn't that neat? It's like he can move the sun."

"Del, I have a headache."

"Oh, that's probably why you look different. Look, what did you think of Rose? I know you only met her once, but what did you think? I hope you liked her. I think you did."

"I liked her," Tom said. This was unbearable. He thought of a way to stop Del talking about Rose. He turned around on the narrow indistinct path. Now they were within sight of the rock shelf. Spangled pale light fell on them. Del looked up at him, purged of his doubts and friendly as a puppy. "I want to ask you something," Tom said.

"About Rose? You can be my best man, if that's what you want."

"That time you broke your leg. That was the time you were here longer than you thought?"

"How did you guess that?" Del looked at him in amazement. "Yes. You're right."

"Can you remember anything about what happened? When Bud came for you?"

Del's amazement altered to perplexity. "Well, it's like I was asleep for a long time or something. Why do you want to know about that? Sometimes I remember little pieces of what happened—little things, like you remember dreams."

Tom waited.

"Well, like, I remember Bud arguing with Uncle Cole. That's mainly it."

"Arguing about you?"

"Not really. Bud wanted me to come home right away,

I remember that. And Bud won. I did go home with him. But I can remember Uncle Cole sort of taunting him. He said he hoped Bud wasn't waiting to be included in my will. I know that was a terrible thing to say, but he was mad, Tom. That's about it. Except . . . well, I can remember Bud sitting on one end of the living room and Uncle Cole sitting on the other end. I must have been lying on my side of the couch. They were just staring at each other. It was like they were fighting without words. Then my uncle said, 'All right. Take him, you old woman. But he'll be back. He loves me.' And Bud went upstairs to get my stuff. When he came back down, we all went out to the car, and Bud said, 'We don't want any repeat performances, Mr. Collins.' My uncle didn't say anything."

" 'No repeat performances.' "

"Right." With the light falling on him in disks and shafts, Del seemed a part of the forest, camouflaged to blend in as easily as a squirrel. "But that was silly. I was never going to break my leg again. I guess Bud was being extra careful."

"Okay," Tom said. He began to walk toward the rock ledge.

"I sure wonder if we'll see Rose today," Del said behind him.

You will betray Del: that had already happened. The rest of it, Tom swore, never would.

II

Flight

1

Shadowland's windows reflected the sun. Milky soap bubbles between the flagstones picked up the brilliant light. Del pushed open the sliding windows, and the two boys walked into the living room. Grooves in the carpet were vacuum-cleaner tracks; a smell of air freshener and furniture polish lingered. The ashtrays sparkled. Tom felt immediately that they were alone in the house. It felt empty and up for sale, open for viewing.

"Isn't this a beautiful place?" Del said as they walked through to the hall. More furniture polish. The banister gleamed. "I almost think . . ."

"What?"

"That I'd be happy here. That I could live here. Like him. And just work on magic. Go into it deeper and deeper. Never perform, just get it perfect. It's really pure."

"I see what you mean," Tom said. "You think breakfast is in the dining room?"

"Let's see, master."

Del chirpily crossed the hall and opened the door to the dining room. Two places had been laid on a vast mahogany table. A series of covered serving dishes sat on a sideboard. There and on the table, brilliant freesias lolled in vases.

"It sure is," Del said. "Wow. Let's see what we have here." He raised one cover after another. "Ah, eggs. Bacon and sausages. Toast in the toast rack. Kidneys. Chicken livers. Hash-browns. I guess you could call that breakfast."

"I guess you could call it six breakfasts."

They piled food on their plates and sat, on Tom's part a little self-consciously, at the immense table. "This is wonderful," Del said, beginning to attack his food. "Some coffee?"

"No, thanks."

"It's like being a king, but better. You don't have to go out and tax the masses, or whatever kings do. But I guess he is a king, isn't he—from what he was saying yesterday?"

"Yeah."

"You really don't want it, do you?" Del asked shyly.

"No, I don't. You're welcome to it."

"And I wouldn't be alone, like he is. I mean, I wouldn't have to be alone."

"I have a headache," Tom interrupted. "The kidneys seem to be making it worse."

"Oh, I'm sorry," Del blurted. "Tom, I feel like I have so much to apologize for. I guess I got a little crazy. I know there was no reason to be jealous, but he was spending so much time with you. But that just means that you'll be a fantastic magician, doesn't it? I'll always want your help, Tom. I know he chose me, and all that, but . . . well, I was thinking you could have a wing of this house all your own, and we could do tours together, just like he did with Speckle John."

"That would be good," Tom said. He pushed his plate away. "Del, just be careful. Everything isn't settled yet." He could not talk to Del about escape while Del was mentally crowning him kinglet.

"We'll have to pick new names. Have you thought about that yet?"

"Del, we don't know what's going to happen yet." Del looked sulky for a moment. "All I'm saying is, take it slow. There's a lot we have to find out yet."

"Well, that's true," Del said, and went back to work on his eggs.

Tom plunged in deeper. "I never asked you this before. How did your parents die?"

Del looked up, startled. "How? Plane crash. It was a company plane. My father was flying it—he had a pilot's license. Something happened." Del set down his fork. "They couldn't even have a funeral because the crash was a kind of explosion—there wasn't anything left. Just some burned-up parts of the plane. And my father put in his will that there wasn't to be any kind of memorial service. They were just . . . gone. Just gone." He rattled the fork against his plate.

"Where were you? How old were you?"

"I was nine. I was here. It was during the summer. I was in a boarding school in New Hampshire then, and it was a rotten hole. I knew I was going to flunk out after that. And I did. If Uncle Cole hadn't been so good to me, I probably would have . . . dropped dead. I don't know." He looked uncertainly up at Tom, who had his chin propped in his hands. "Uncle Cole kept me together that summer."

"Why didn't you live with him after that?"

"I wanted to, but my father's will said I had to live with the Hillmans. My father didn't know Uncle Cole very well. I guess he didn't trust him. You can imagine what bankers think about magicians. Sometimes I had to really beg my father to let me come here in the summer. In the end, he always let me, though. He always gave me what I wanted."

"Yeah," Tom said. "Mine did too."

After a time Tom said, "I think I'll go lie down or something. Or take a walk by myself."

"I'm really tired too. And I want to take a bath."

"Good idea," Tom said, and both boys left the table.

Del went upstairs, and Tom went back into the living room. He sat on the couch; then he lay down and deliberately put his feet on it. A water pipe rattled in the wall. The big house, so flawlessly cleaned and polished, seemed vacated; waiting. If he dropped a match and burned the carpet, would the carpet instantly restore itself? It felt like that—alive. His feet would never dirty the fabric of the couch. And Del wanted to live here; in his imagination, he already ruled Shadowland.

Tom jumped off the couch and ran up the stairs. The bed had been folded down for a nap. He threw his clothes on it and went into the bathroom to shower.

The cold sparkling tub said: *You can't.*

The fresh towel said: *We will beat you.*

A new tube of toothpaste on the sink said: *You will be ours.*

After he dressed in fresh clothes, Tom dropped his stiff underpants into the wastebasket and covered them with balled-up sheets of paper from the desk. This minimal act of defiance cheered him. At least a few inches of the house were less immaculate. He left the room. Through the big windows in the hall he looked down at the boathouse: Rose in her green dress and high heels. If he looked different, it was because of the astonishing thing that had happened there, not because of the magical hoops he had been put through on his way back to the clearing.

He could feel the house around him like a skin. Without hearing a single noise, he knew that Del was already in his bed, nearly asleep, a dot of warmth in the cold polished perfection. If Rose Armstrong were in the house, he would feel her like a fire.

Tom left the window and went downstairs. It seemed to him that he could visualize every inch of the house, every curve of the stair posts, every watermark in the kitchen sink.

He would not stay in this house a day longer than he had to.

He could see it bare of furniture, stripped to walls and floors, gleaming with new paint: awaiting its new owner. And he thought that Shadowland, an ugly name for a house, was anywhere secretive and mean, anywhere that deserved shadows because the people there hated light. Shadowland implied dispossession. And Coleman Collins seemed a man lost within his own powers, a shadow in a shadow world, insubstantial. An old king who knew he would have to suffer at the hands of his successor.

2

At least that is what the thirty-six-year-old Tom Flanagan told me—he would not have used those phrases at fifteen, and I am more or less improvising on his words as it is, but the fifteen-year-old boy who stood at the bottom of the staircase and felt the house claiming him experienced the despair and pity that the adult man described to me. For he knew that he had been elected, though he had refused it; he knew that he was to be the new King of the Cats, though he would refuse that too, if he were able. And the adult Tom told me that at fifteen he had known that the Florida parking lot in which he had seen a battered car containing a dead man was the truest image of Shadowland. He could not get that picture out of his head.

3

So he left the bottom of the stairs and aimlessly went down the hall toward the front door. It was not locked. In a dazzle of sunlight, Tom let himself out onto the top step. The bricks shone like freshly polished cordovans. Squinting, Tom went down to the asphalt. Water lay in slanting streaks on the drive.

What would happen if he were to walk up the drive and take a look at the gate? A grown man couldn't get through the bars, but he and Del and Rose could do it easily. From there they could walk to Hilly Vale in less than an hour, through the woods and fields if they had to. Maybe the physical act of leaving Shadowland would be the simplest aspect of their escape; persuading Del would be the hardest. But Rose could do that, he realized. Hot sun warmed his shoulders, the top of his head. Del would listen to Rose.

The drive curved up around the bank of the hill. Halfway up, he could see the tops of the gateposts.

Why do you light up the forest like that?

So I can see what's coming and what's going. And what big eyes you have, Grandmother.

Through trees he could see the brick wall fanning out from the gateposts. They might even be able to get over that, if he hoisted Del on his shoulders. He walked closer, and saw that the bars in the gate were about nine inches apart. It would be easy to squeeze through an opening like that. And if men were chasing them, they would have to stop to punch the code to open the gates.

He went up to the gates. The spikes on top of each bar looked more than ornamental. And the brick wall, he could now see, was topped with thick jagged pieces of glass embedded in concrete. Barbed wire snaked over the glass. So it had to be the gate. He looked through it at the narrow brown dirt road which would lead them down to Hilly Vale.

Whenever you're ready, Rose, he thought, and put his arm experimentally through the bars.

"What do you think you're doing?" a thick voice shouted behind him.

Tom jumped—he thought he must have gone a foot into the air—and turned around, unsuccessfully trying not to look scared. Thorn and Snail came lounging out of the trees. They looked more than ever like dwarfs. Thorn wore a dark blue hooded sweatshirt covered with stains. He drained the last of a beer bottle and tossed it into the woods behind. Snail wore an ordinary gray sweatshirt. The sleeves had been cut off, and his tattoos showed on the thick pasty arms like brilliant medals.

"I asked, what the hell are you doing?" Thorn said. "You don't go out there. Nobody goes out there." His

jack-o'-lantern face, Tom saw, was the result of surgery.
Welts of scar surrounded the eyes and mouth.

"I wasn't going out. I wasn't doing anything," Tom
said. The two men came up to the edge of the drive and
stopped. Snail put his hands on his hips. The gray
sweatshirt bulged across his chest and belly.

"La-di-da," Thorn said. Snail tittered. "You're the one
saw us before," Thorn said. The ugly sewn-together face
bit down on itself. Tom felt aimless, stupid violence
boiling off both men—mad dogs who had found themselves in temporary possession of the kennel.

"Maybe he's looking for his girlfriend," Snail said,
grinning.

"You looking for your pretty little girl, sonny boy?
Think she came up for air?"

Snail tittered again.

"I wasn't looking for anybody," Tom said. "I was just
walking around."

They looked at each other with a quick, practiced
surreptitious movement of the eyes. *Prison,* Tom thought,
they've been in—

They were coming toward him. "You can't get out of
here," Thorn was saying. Snail was grinning, holding one
fist with the other and pumping up his arm muscles.

"Maybe he's looking for that badger yet."

"Maybe he's the badger," Snail said.

Tom backed up into the bars of the gate, too scared to
think.

"Ain't he somethin'?" Thorn said. "Gonna shit your
pants before we get there, or after?"

*Do not begin things when you will get too flustered to
remember how to finish them.* Tom smelled coarse, dirty,
smelly skin, stale beer. He closed his eyes and thought of
his shoulders opening and opening. His mind flared
yellow, and he saw Laker Broome shouting orders from
the smoky stage: just before they got to him, he saw a
ceiling where a huge bird screamed down at him. *Yes.* He
floated three feet off the ground, straight up. The bars
scraped against his shirt. *God, yes.* He went up another
three feet and opened his eyes. He laughed crazily.

Thorn and Snail were gawping up at him, already
backing away.

"*Uhh*," Tom grunted, unable to speak, and pointed toward a twenty-foot birch growing near the wall where they had come from. The veins in his head felt ready to burst. *Now, damn you.* A crack flew across the ground: snapping sounds like gunfire came from the trees. The birch heeled over to the left, and a root broke off with a thunderous crack.

"Freak!" Snail screamed.

Tom moaned. The birch swung up out of its hole, trailing a four-foot-long ball of crowded roots and packed earth. It hung in the air, parallel to him, and Tom almost heard the birch howling in pain and shock. He dropped it as he would a dying mouse or rabbit, some small life he had injured; self-loathing filled him. Not knowing why, he mentally saw an uprooted dandelion, and imagined blood pouring across his hands.

Thorn and Snail were disappearing back into the woods when he fell to the asphalt. *That's what Skeleton wanted,* he thought. He wobbled, his spine taking the shock, and then rolled over onto elbows and knees. Wet asphalt dug into his cheek. *That sickness.* If the dwarfs had come back, they could have kicked him senseless.

4

Eventually Tom picked himself up and tottered back down the sloping grass. Shadowland gleamed at him, burnished by the strong light. The house looked utterly new. The brick steps beckoned, the doorknob pleaded to be touched. Tom's head pounded.

An unmistakable rush of welcome warm air and fragrance washed over him.

Tom went down the hall, took the short side corridor, and threw open the door to the forbidden room. No wise, spectacled face looked up at him; the room was neither a crowded study nor an underground staff room. It was bare. Silvery-gray walls, glossy white trim around the windows, a dark gray carpet. Empty of life, the room called him in.

*Everything you will see here comes from the interaction
of your mind with mine.*

An invisible scene hovered between those walls, waiting for him to enter so that it could spring into life.

Tom backed away from the invisible scene—he could
almost hear the room exhale its disappointment. Or
something in the room . . . some frustrated giant, turning
away . . . Tom closed the door.

And continued down the hall to the Little Theater. The
brass plate on the door was no longer blank: now three
words and a date had been engraved on it:

*Wood Green Empire
27 August, 1924*

Tom cracked the door open, and the audience in the
mural stared down at him with their varying expressions
of pleasure, amusement, cynicism, and greed. Of course.
Just inside the door, he was so close to the stage as to be
nearly on it. He backed out.

He went a few steps down the hall and let himself into
the big theater. It too shone; even the banked seats were
lustrous. Tom walked deeper into the theater. The
curtains had been pulled back from the stage. Polished
wood led to a blank white wall. Ropes dangled at varying
heights above the wood.

Tom went halfway up an aisle and sat in one of the
padded seats. He wished he could lead Rose and Del out
of Shadowland that afternoon: he did not want to see
anything of Collins' farewell performance. That would
contain more than one farewell, he knew. He knew that
the way he knew his own senses.

These too seemed to have taken part in the general
change within him. It was as if his senses had been tuned
and burnished. All day, he had seen and heard with great
clarity. Since he and Del had returned to the house, this
intensity of perception had increased. Ordinary, almost
inaudible sounds needled into him, full of substance.
Oddest of all had been his awareness of Del, sleeping in
his bed: that dot of warmth. He was still conscious of it.
Del shone for him.

Then Tom felt some shift in the house, a movement of mass and air as if a door had been opened. The house had rearranged itself to admit a newcomer. Tom could half-hear the blood surging through the newcomer's body; his muscles began to tense. He knew it was Coleman Collins. The magician was waiting for him. He was somewhere in the theater, though nowhere he could be found by ordinary search.

Tom left the chair and walked down the aisle toward the empty stage. What was it Collins had said about wizards, in the story about the sparrows? They gave you what you asked for, but they made you pay for it.

He crossed the wide area before the stage and went toward the farthest aisle. Tom remembered seeing those green walls forming around him, flying together like pieces of clouds. The white columns reminded him of the bars of the gate—solid uprights between open spaces. Then he knew where the magician was.

Feeling foolish but knowing he was right, Tom pressed his palm to the wall. For an instant he felt solid plaster, slightly cooler than his hand. Then it was as if the molecules of the plaster loosened and began to drift apart. The wall grew warmer; for a millisecond the plaster seemed wet. Then only the color was there, solid-looking, but nothing but color. His hand had gone inward up to the wrist. On the other side of the wall of color, his fingers were dimly, greenly visible. Tom followed his hand through the wall.

5

He was in an immense white space, his heart leaping. Coleman Collins sat in the owl chair regarding him with an affectionate sharpness. He wore a soft gray flannel suit and shining black shoes. A glass half-filled with neat whiskey sat on the arm of the chair beside his right elbow. "I knew when I first heard your name," Collins said, propping his chin on laced fingers, "and I was certain when I first saw you. Congratulations. You must be feeling very proud of yourself."

"I'm not."

Collins smiled. "You should be. You are the best for centuries, probably. When your studies have ended, you should be able to do and to have anything you want. In the meantime, I want to answer whatever questions you may have." Collins lowered his hand and found the glass without looking at it. He sipped. "Surely even an unwilling bridegroom has a query or two."

"Del thinks he was chosen," Tom said.

"That's of no consequence to you." Collins tipped his head and looked purely charming. It was like looking at Laker Broome trying to be charming; Tom read the magician's tension and excitement, half-heard the drumming of his pulse. "In fact, I suggest that you can no longer afford to worry about matters like that. One of the perils of altitude, little bird—you can't see the lesser birds still trying to find their way out of the clouds."

"But what's going to happen to Del when he finds out? I don't want him to find out."

The magician shrugged, sipped again at the whiskey. "I can tell you one thing. This is Del's last summer at Shadowland. It will not be yours. You will be here often, and stay long. That is how it must be, child. Neither of us has a choice." He smiled again at Tom, and took a familiar envelope from a jacket pocket. "Which brings me to this. Elena gave it to me, as you should have known she would. I couldn't let it go out, you know. I am still considering the insult to my hospitality."

It was the letter to his mother, and Tom looked at it with dread. Collins was still smiling at him, holding the letter upright between two fingers. "Let's dispose of it, shall we?"

A flame appeared at the envelope's topmost corner. Collins held it until the growing flame was a quarter of an inch from his fingers, then tossed the black burning thing upward; it vanished into the flame, and then the flame itself vanished, disappearing from the bottom up.

"Now that is no longer between us," Collins said. "And there shall be nothing like it in the future. Understand?"

"I understand." Tom had gone very pale—somehow

the letter had been proof to him that he would escape Shadowland.

"This is far more important to you than your schooling, boy. This is your real schooling. And in fact I want to show you something you are bound to ask me about sooner or later." He bent down and retrieved a slim leather-bound book from beneath the chair. There was no title on cover or spine. "This is the Book. *Our* book. The book we are pledged to honor."

The magician's excitement was almost palpable. Beneath his cool exterior, Collins was seething.

"Speckle John gave it to me. In time it will be yours— you will have read it a hundred times by then. The original was lost for centuries, and may have ended its existence on an Arab's fire—the mother of the man who discovered a cache of unknown gospels used them for fuel before they discovered their black-market value. But we have had our copy for centuries, passed from hand to hand. A watered-down version, known as *The Gospel of Thomas,* has been known to scholars for something like thirty years. But that weak document does not reveal our secrets. What is the first law of magic?"

"As above, so below," Tom said.

"Do you know the meaning of that?" Collins waited; Tom felt the gravitational pull of his tension. "It means that gods are only men with superior understanding. *Magicians.* Who have found and released the divine within themselves. Jesus shared this knowledge with only a few, and the knowledge became our secret tradition." He ran his fingers lovingly over the leather binding. "The Book will be in the room I forbade you to enter. After my performance, go there and read it. Read it as I read it forty years ago. Learn the real history of your world."

"Does it talk about evil?" Tom said, remembering the final creature that had approached him in the night.

"God, in the orthodox view, causes famine, plague, and flood. Was God evil? Evil is a convenient fiction."

Tom looked into the magician's powerful old face. What he saw blazed so fiercely he had to look away.

"You avoid examining what you saw last night. So I will not force you, boy—it will come. But you must know that every boy at your school was touched by our magic, some beneficially, some not. It could not have been otherwise, given that you and Del were there."

"I knew the nightmares were from me," Tom said out of the full awareness of his guilt.

"Of course. From what was hidden in you, from what you were too stupid to know you had. From your treasure."

"My treasure."

"Any treasure locked away in a dark room will begin to fester and push its way out. An untreated body in a coffin will do that. It is in the Book: *If you bring forth what is within you, what you bring forth will save you. If you do not bring forth what is within you, what you do not bring forth will destroy you.*"

"Is that what happened to Skeleton Ridpath?" Tom asked.

"He did not thrust the power away from him, like another in your class, but begged for it—for its cruelest aspects—when he was unready for them. That boy wanted me to come for him, and so I did come for him. With Speckle John, I had already invented the Collector. He was originally a thing of cloth and rubber, a toy to frighten an audience. I saw that he could be a vessel. There are many candidates for collection. There are many volunteers."

Collins' hands were trembling. "I gave him what he asked for." He looked up at Tom with a look of wild challenge. "Come with me. You'll see what I mean."

He began striding away from the chair. Afraid to be left alone, Tom hurried after him. The magician's tall gray-suited form was already deep in white mist. It gathered around Tom as he got nearer to Collins, and for a moment was thick enough—a freezing cloud—to hide Collins altogether. Then Tom saw broad gray shoulders ahead, and rushed forward.

He walked out of the mist onto dry sandy grass. They were in Arizona again, he recognized before he recognized anything else. Cars stood in rows about them. In the distance, a tinny cheer went up. "Hurry," Collins said, and Tom gasped: the magician was wrapped within a long trench coat, his face shadowed by a wide-brimmed hat.

Tom drew near and saw where they were.

At their feet the land fell away to a flat limed plane—the football field. Across it, the stands were crowded with parents and boys. Two football teams clashed and grunted on the field. Collins said, "Two things called me here. That disturbed boy on the bench who is looking at me this very minute—and you. Look."

Tom saw Skeleton's face go rapturous and unhinged over the padded frail chest and shoulders. With his newly burnished senses, he could feel what was happening inside Skeleton, a sick thrilled wave of passion. Then he heard a noise of love mingled with fear, and saw Skeleton's head snap around to look up into the stands. And there was Del, trying to get on his feet in the last row, staring with wild eyes straight at him. The feelings which surged from Del were too dense for him to fully take them in, love and terror and the horror of betrayal and confusion wretched in its magnitude. He saw himself, with an uncomprehending and innocent face, hauling Del back down into his seat.

"Enough," Collins said. He whirled around and marched back through the rows of cars.

The grass had become springier and the cars were gone. Collins strode on beside him, going into the green vale. It was Ventnor. The disastrous football games were over. "An interesting thing is happening today," Collins was saying. "I want you to see it."

As they walked along, Tom glanced over his shoulder and looked at a wandering path on which stood a handful of boys, himself among them. Del raised his bandaged arm as if to ward off a blow. A second, almost subdued shock wave of betrayal. He was visible to no one else—he was merely Collins' shadow. "Of course this is the day of the famous theft," the magician said.

They were proceeding down a long green distance, and Tom remembered seeing this in a dream, long ago—he knew that Skeleton Ridpath was standing rigid with joy near the Ventnor gym.

"When we all lived in the forest," Collins said, "we could turn into birds at will." They vanished around an edge of concrete—Tom was sweating, on the edge of

collapse—and the magician rose off the ground, beating
great gray wings. He was an owl.

Tom beat his own wings; he too had become a bird.
Below and behind him, Skeleton howled. The transforma
tion had been instant and painless; putting on feather
was easier than putting on a shirt. Inside the small bird he
was, he was still Tom Flanagan; and when he looked at
the owl, he could see Coleman Collins within it. The
magician smiled, his hair flattening against his head. The
owl wheeled overhead and sailed back toward the Vent
nor buildings. Tom turned beneath him and followed
From what he could see of himself, he was a falcon.

"A peregrine falcon," Collins said. "I see you are
curious." There was laughter in his voice.

Tom looked out over the landscape, and for a moment
was transfixed by its beauty and strangeness—trees and
glinting lake and long stretches of green. It looked like
Eden, a place shining with newness and promise. Beyond
it lay a network of curving roads and straight roads, a
cluster of houses, desert. Miles away, mountains reared
and buckled. Geologic tensions and muscles underlay it
all, churning with life. Small things scurried in grass and
sand. He was seeing through falcon's eyes.

Collins interrupted his reverie. "Child."

Tom looked down and saw the magician sitting on a
roof by a wide tilting pane of glass. He reluctantly
descended. When he landed on the roof, he was just Tom
again, and that miraculous insightful vision was gone. He
walked toward Collins, leaning against the pitch of the
roof.

"You see, it's not all bad," the magician said. "Could a
simple-minded morality give you anything like that?" He
looked down through the skylight. "But here comes our
moment. Watch."

Tom saw himself and Del in a sea of heads, alone in a
crowd near a woman pouring tea. Then Marcus Reilly
approached, dogged by Tom Pinfold, and Tom saw
himself turn away to speak to them. He stared at the
wheaten top of Marcus' head as if he could see into it and
find whatever wayward germ had put his friend into the
bloody car.

"You're wasting your time," the magician said with
brutal suddenness. "Look across the room."

Tom shifted his glance. Skeleton was mooning along the far wall. His face foreshortened but visible, Skeleton looked like a robot on automatic pilot. Tom looked back down again and saw that Del had moved a few feet away from the Tom Flanagan down there: Del was standing by himself, and his nose was pointing directly at Skeleton.

"My nephew is weaker than Speckle John," the magician said. "You see, he feels threatened, he doesn't know if he can trust his eyes, but they seem to tell him that his best friend is in secret complicity with his idol. He cannot ignore or reject his best friend. But he must strike out somewhere. And he has begun to admit that the person he fears and hates most in the world might also have a secret relationship with said idol."

Del was rigid with concentration. The air around him seemed to darken. Tom saw or felt Del's strain with his lingering bird senses.

"Don't want to be a great man," said the magician, "be a great donkey."

On the other side of the room, Skeleton drifted near the shelves. He let his hand float over the glass objects. The hand dipped and closed. He slipped something into his pocket and grinned blankly.

Below Tom, Del relaxed. That was proof of a kind. Tom grieved for Del, for Dave Brick (who was gripping his slide rule and gaping at Skeleton), for himself too: so much misery, so much turmoil, from jealousy.

"That was your strength he used," Collins said.

"And the levitation . . ."

"Again your strength." Collins stood up, and Tom stood too, blinking. "Come."

The huge gray owl lifted itself out over the skylight and the roof, making for the clouds; Tom staggered, raised his arms and found they were wings. Again that instantaneous translation. White clouds gathered around him, the owl was gone; he found himself on hands and knees crawling toward a pane of green.

When his mind cleared, he was sprawled out before the first row of seats in the big theater.

6

Tom crept into bed and tried to rest. He could not sleep. Whenever he closed his eyes, he was either flying or falling.

Eventually he got up and went downstairs, to find lunch set for one in the dining room. Cold sliced ham and beef, a wedge of Stilton, sauerkraut. An icy glass of milk. Tom ate as unreflectively as an animal, then returned his dishes to the kitchen and deposited them in the sink.

For some time Tom coasted through the living room and looked at the paintings. Then he drifted to a cabinet with glass doors. On the topmost shelf an ancient revolver lay on velvet in an open leather case. Beneath it was a porcelain shepherdess with a crook. Other porcelain figurines stood a little distance from it, a boy with a satchel of schoolbooks, a fat Elizabethan gripping a beer mug, a cluster of drunken men with misshapen faces holding songsheets. He looked again at the shepherdess, and saw that she had Rose's face—high vulnerable forehead, full lips, widely spaced eyes. She looked embarrassed to be thrust forward from the others. Tom's hand went to the catch on the glass door; stopped when it touched the metal. He had a superstitious fear of touching the porcelain figure. Finally he turned away.

He confronted Del that evening, after he had taken a long nap.

The pocket doors had been pushed halfway back into the walls, opening an arch between his room and Del's. Tom went through the opening and heard water drumming in the bathroom. He sat on the bed.

In a little while Del emerged from the bathroom, a towel around his neck like a cape, his glossy wet hair skimmed close to his head. Then Tom realized that Del looked like a child to him, frail as a nine-year-old. "I feel great! I must have slept all day!" Del beamed at him.

"I did too," Tom said.

"If we keep this up, we'll be on magician's hours before long—up all night, asleep all day. But that's neat. I like night, don't you?" Del began rubbing his hair with a towel, completely unselfconscious about his nakedness.

"I prefer daylight."

Del peeped out from under a fringe of towel. "You in a bad mood?"

Tom shook his head, and Del's face vanished beneath the towel. "You feel like working with some cards after I get dressed?"

"Sure."

"We have to practice more—I haven't touched a pack of cards in weeks. You have to keep up with it or you get rusty. I could even show you that shuffle I was reading about."

"Sure."

Del pulled the towel off his head and wiped his legs. His hair fluffed at his temples, still clung damply behind his ears. He dropped the towel and began to dress in clean white underwear. "Pretty soon, maybe tomorrow, we'll hear the rest of my uncle's story."

"I guess so."

Buttoning a yellow Gant shirt, Del looked up almost shyly at Tom. "I hope that both of us can spend the summers here from now on. We could learn together. Right?"

Del paid no attention to his silence, but went to his desk and got a fresh pack of cards and slit the cellophane seal. "Here, pull a chair up to the desk," Del said, fanning the cards in his hands. He manipulated them in some complicated fashion Tom could not see, involving much palming and ending in a two-handed riffle. "Okay. Look." He spread them out in a fan on the desk. The four twos were together, the threes, and so on up to the aces. "Pretty good, wouldn't you say? You can do just about anything with that triple shuffle. In a couple of months I'll be able to do it so well that—"

"Del," Tom interrupted, "tell me about the Ventnor owl."

His friend looked up at him with big alarmed eyes. He scooped the cards together and shuffled them again. "There's nothing to tell."

"I know better than that."

Del looked down at his hands. "The funny thing is that everybody thinks that speed is what counts, and they're so

wrong. Nobody's hand is quicker than the eye. It has a lot
more to do with feel—with finesse. Speed hardly counts.''

"Tell me about it, Del."

Del fanned out the cards: two red kings glared from a
sea of black. "I wanted to hurt Skeleton," he mumbled.
"I wanted to get him kicked out." He glanced at Tom in
agony. "How'd you know, anyhow? How'd you find
out?"

"Your uncle told me."

Del's face whitened. He tipped the cards into a stack,
cut them, did a conventional shuffle, and cut them again.
He lifted the top four cards: four aces. He shuffled the
pack again and lifted the top four: kings.

"You're stalling," Tom said.

Del tried the trick again: three queens and a seven lay
face up on the desk. "But it was because of him . . ." He
stopped—he was trying not to cry. "Even *Skeleton*
seemed like he was stealing Uncle Cole away from . . ."
Del wiped at his eyes. "I wanted to get him into trouble."
He looked down at the botched trick. "I was looking at
him, and I was thinking about him—and you started
talking to Marcus Reilly—I was feeling so terrible about
what Bobby Hollingsworth had said after the game—and
right after that I saw you with him, Tom, I did see you,
and you looked right at me, but nobody else could see
you—and it was like that day I broke my leg—I hated
everything, and I couldn't talk to you . . ." Del put his
hand before his eyes. "So I thought, I'll get *rid* of
Skeleton. I thought Mr. Broome and everybody would
know right away it was him, I never thought it would go
all crazy like it did. . . ." He snuffled, looked up at Tom.
"So I made him take it. I did magic on him. I never did
anything like that before, but all of a sudden I knew I
could do it. I concentrated so hard I thought I'd blow up.
And I made him do it." He glanced down, then again at
Tom. "So I guess I caused all that trouble afterward. The
fire, and Dave Brick, and . . . everything."

"No, you didn't," Tom said. "*He* did."

"Skeleton?"

"Your uncle."

"Why would he?"

"Look, Del," he said. "The things he does are

like . . ." He laid a hand on the cards. "Like this. He shuffles them around, forces one, palms one, shows you a deuce when you expect an ace—see? A fire, a life, they're just two more cards to him. He doesn't believe that he can commit wrong. He doesn't believe in evil or good."

"But I made Skeleton do it," Del protested.

"And you just told me why."

"You're talking this way because you're not a good enough magician," Del said, beginning to turn resentful again.

"I'm not going to argue about that with you." He stared angrily at his friend. "Del, Rose thinks we should leave Shadowland. She thinks that your uncle is losing control. She is afraid for us. For herself, too."

That reached him. "Rose is afraid?"

"Afraid enough to want to leave. And to take us with her."

"Well, maybe I'll talk to her about it. If you're telling me the truth."

On they talked—it was talk that progressed to no conclusion, so we may leave them here, but Tom was grateful that Del was willing to go as far as he had without demanding that their discussion end. In fact, they stayed up talking until dawn, and at one point Del got up to get a candle; he put a match to the wick and turned the lights off, and the two of them sat three feet apart over the little desk, at first with wariness on one's part and guilt on the other's, later with an unspoken recognition of the importance of their friendship in their lives, talking within the warm envelope of candlelight, talking about magicians and cards and school. And about Rose. Despite the undercurrents on both sides, it was the last, best night of their friendship, at least the last night when they would be able to talk in the warm rambling manner of an old friendship, and both of them understood that this was so.

7

A week passed, the week before Tom became ill and met the devil, and it was an odd limbo in which they met

chiefly at the lavish breakfasts and at dinner. Breakfast-
time moved from eight to ten to nearly noon, and
replaced lunch. Both boys stayed up until one or two
every night, but they talked little, as if the all-night
conversation had dried their tongues. Del often went into
the big theater to practice with the props crated in the
wings. When the call came, his friend saw, Del wanted to
be ready.

While Del shuffled and manipulated cards, Tom swam
in the lake, floating on his back with his ears under water
and the sun beating down on him. He found he could
swim across the lake if he relaxed and sidestroked for long
periods. At the far end of the lake was a beach only five
feet wide. The first time, he stretched out naked on the
sand and fell asleep. When he woke it was with the feeling
that Mr. Peet's trolls had come upon him and left without
waking him. Then he saw that the sand around him was
full of footprints.

The next day he walked through the forest in the early
afternoon. At the clearing by the funnellike narrowing
avenue of trees, Tom came upon Del sitting on a white
stump. "Oh . . . hi," said startled Del. "I'm just . . . ahh
. . . sitting. Took a walk." "Me too," Tom said. "Guess
I'll go on a little farther." Each knew that the other was
hoping to see Rose Armstrong. Tom waved and faded
backward into the trees. On Del's face he saw that he was
an intrusion.

The ground dropped at a gentle grade, and half an hour
later it was flat, at the level of the water. He kept seeing
blue from time to time, shining between the trees; then he
saw a golden strip of sand.

Because he was curious, he walked through brush to get
there. When he emerged out onto the little bright tan rug
of beach, he saw the pier pointing across the water like a
finger toward him, the boathouse like an open mouth;
Shadowland high up on the bluff threw back light from all
its windows. It too seemed living. Glare swallowed up the
rows of windows of fiery yellow: the eyes of a god too self-
absorbed to attend to earthly matters.

The footprints still marked the sand.

Tom scuffed over them to walk away from Shadowland,
went through feathery tall grass, and soon found himself

in a parklike area of sparse poplars and mown grass. Ahead of him, winding gently to the left, was an overgrown little road.

A minute later he saw a frame building with a ripped, bulging screen tacked over a sagging porch. A summerhouse: it looked as though it had stood vacant for years. Trees arched over it. Tom went slowly, cautiously toward the ramshackle building. He peered in through a rip in the screen. Two battered chairs sat on the porch, one of them with an overflowing ashtray on its arm. Splayed open on the boards of the porch was a magazine with a cover of a naked woman raising thick legs into the air. He listened: no noises came from the house.

Tom opened the screen door and went onto the porch. He glanced into a window. A bed with a sleeping bag and pillow, an open closet where shirts hung on wire hangers. Pictures of naked women had been tacked to the walls. He left the window and went to the half-open door.

Tom stepped just inside. The living room was filled with broken furniture and the stink of cigars. Doors at the sides of the room must have led to the kitchen, smaller bedrooms. Empty beer bottles lay on the floor, as did bottles of other kinds. White ticking foamed from a rip in an armchair.

Then he heard a door close, and footsteps came toward him. He froze for an instant, too frightened to run, and then backed toward the front door.

Rose Armstrong, wearing rolled-up jeans and a blue sweatshirt, walked through an arch. When she saw him, she dropped the towel she was carrying. "What are you *doing* here?" Her mouth remained open.

"Looking around." He watched her pick up the towel. "Is this yours—where you live?"

"Of course not. Let's get out of here." She walked toward him through the mess. "I don't have a bathtub, so I have to come over here to use theirs when they're out. Come on. Being here gives me the creeps."

"You could take a bath in the lake."

"And have them all watch? Ugh." Rose took his hand and led him out of the house, across the porch, and out onto the grass.

Rose's face was shiny and pale: she looked younger and

smaller than she had the last time he had seen her. She
also looked tougher. Her rather ethereal face was anchored by taut little lines at the sides of her mouth. He
realized that this was the first time he had seen her in
daylight. "Over here," she said, and led him across the
overgrown road into the shelter of a group of poplars.
"Okay. It's nice to see you, but you have to go back. You
can't stay here. They'll tear you to pieces if they catch you
snooping. I mean it."

"I love you," he said.

The little lines tucked into the corners of her mouth. "I
love you too, sweetness. But we hardly have any time . . .
and I'm kind of embarrassed about . . . you know."

"Don't be," Tom said. "I could never think anything
bad about you."

"You don't know me very well yet," Rose said. He
could not read her face. "Well, I was going to try to get
across the lake pretty soon. I would have come today, but
I felt so dirty."

"Where do you stay?"

She pointed deep into the "park," to the right of the
overgrown road. "That direction. We can't go there.
What I wanted to tell you is that everybody is waiting for
some things to arrive—fireworks and some other things
for his show. The men are cutting firewood and stuff like
that. Sometimes they go into Hilly Vale and drink at the
tavern. That's where they are now. But they could come
back any minute. I took the fastest shower on earth."

"Do you know any more from Collins about what he's
going to do during the performance?"

She shook her head.

"But you still think we should go."

Rose said, "Tell me something. Would you still try to
get out if you had never met me?"

"Yes. Now I have to get out. And I have to get Del out
too."

She raised her eyebrows. "Okay."

"But you'll have to talk to Del. He's even thinking
about living here someday."

"Oh, God," Rose said. "Sometimes I hate magic."

"Why don't you just get out by yourself? What's over
there?" He pointed away from the lake.

"A big wall. With glass on top. I couldn't get over. I need your help."

"Well, I need you," Tom said. "I think about you all the time. I really love you, Rose." He felt imbecilic, uttering these banal words: the vocabulary of love was so tired.

"And I really love you, beautiful Tom," Rose said, beginning to back away and giving sidelong glances over her shoulder at the trolls' house. "I should be able to come over in a couple of nights. That's when I'll talk to Del." She stopped momentarily and looked at him in a shaft of light. "You won't ever hate me, will you?"

"*Hate* you?"

"I still have some work to do for him."

He shook his head, and she blew him a kiss and faded back through the cluster of poplars. Tom waited a few minutes, aching for her and puzzled by her, and then went back through the empty forest to the beach.

Dinners, during this period of waiting, were at eight. Elena never appeared; when Collins came downstairs, the three of them went into the dining room and uncovered the chafing dishes. Beside Collins' place was a decanter of whiskey and another of wine; he was already drunk when he sat, and proceeded to get drunker. Del got a glass of the wine, which made his cheeks flush. The rest went to the magician. While they ate, Collins stared fixedly at each of them in turn, saying little. Apparently Del was used to this, but Tom looked forward to dinners with dread.

Del asked questions. Tom squirmed in his seat and tried to ignore Collins' glassy stare.

"Did you ever do any more healing by magic in the army, Uncle Cole?"

"Once." The glassy eyes on Tom. "Once I did five in a row. Didn't give a damn if anyone saw. Knew I was going to leave soon—go to Paris to meet Speckle John."

"Five?"

"Ordered the nurses to look away. Impatient as a blister. My mind on fire. Little Irish pudding damn near lost her lunch. I could have done a hundred. Lightning."

"Are you going to work with us some more?"

"Any day now."

That was two days after Tom met Rose in the run-down

summerhouse. The next morning he swam across the lake
and stood on the beach in dripping undershorts, thinking
that Rose would materialize out of the air and water.
Hours later, when a man shouted something deep in the
woods, Tom waded back into the warm water and swam
toward the pier.

He put on his dry clothes over the wet undershorts and
went up to the house. Del was nowhere in sight. Tom
went into the living room—it was to be another afternoon
of dullness, another terrifying dinner. He felt as though
the tension would make him ill. Whenever Collins fixed
his devouring eyes on his at dinner, he thought that the
magician knew all about him and Rose. Then he *did* feel
ill: his whole body grew hot. It passed; came back in a
giddy rush—he might have been standing in front of a
blast furnace. His head swam. Again the illness receded
for a moment, and Tom, suddenly aware of the sensations
of his body, felt a burning at the back of his throat, a
stuffiness in his head; his stomach sent a signal of burning
distress.

He went to the nearest tall surface to lean against it, put
his hands on the glass of the cabinet. He looked in. The
figurines were moving. He saw the porcelain boy sprawled
on the polished wood of the shelf, the drunken men with
misshapen faces kicking him again and again. The
bearded Elizabethan holding a beer mug looked on and
smiled. They were killing the boy, kicking in his ribs and
head. The boy rolled over, exposing the pulp that had
been his face. Blood pooled on the wood. "Oh, yes,"
Tom said. "Oh, yes. Shadowland." The blast of heat
returned with triple force, and he staggered out toward
the hall bathroom.

8

He was feverishly ill for three or four days: he did not
know how long. His body felt as though it would crack
and fissure like a salt flat—so dried out—and even the
softest sheet chafed and burned against his skin. People
appeared and talked incomprehensibly; like mirages,

disappeared. Del moved in front of him, looking very worried. "Don't fret," Tom wanted to say. "I'm just being punished, that's all." But when he said it, he was speaking to Rose, who held his hand. "No, you're just sick," Rose said. "You're wrong," he said to Elena. She scowled at him and pushed soup into his mouth. Then: "You didn't mail my letter." Old King Cole gazed down at him with false sympathy. "Of course I didn't," he said. "I burned it in front of you. Like this." He held up his right hand, and flames coursed along his index finger. "Make me better," Tom pleaded, but he was talking to startled Del and glum Elena. His only coherent conversation during the illness was with the devil.

"I know who you are," he said, and was troubled by a recollection: hadn't he said the same thing to someone else, when he was still new to Shadowland?

The devil sat on the edge of his bed and smiled at him. He was a short ginger-haired man with a thin, intelligent face—the face of a nightclub comedian. "Of *course* you do," the devil said. He was dressed like a prep-school teacher, in a light brown tweed jacket and gray wool slacks. When he drew up one foot to cock it on his knee, Tom saw that he wore Bass Weejuns. "After all, we've met before."

"I remember."

"I'd introduce myself, but you would never remember my name. If you like, you can call me by my initial, which is M."

"Was it you who made me get sick?"

"It was really the only way I could speak to you directly. And I wanted to get a better look at you than I could the other night. You fret too much about things, you know. You fight against the natural course of events. You'll just wear yourself out. If I hadn't made you ill, you would have done it to yourself quite soon. In short, Tom, I worry about you."

"I wish you wouldn't," Tom said.

"But it's my *job*." M. brought his hand to the area of the tweed jacket that represented his heart. "My job is to care about you. To care *for* you, if you like." The hands opened like a sunburst. "There is so much we could do for each other. All you have to do is stop fretting. You have a

large and remarkable talent, after all. And I must point
out, my boy, that you and your talent are at a crossroads.
I'd hate to see you waste yourself. So would your
mentor."

"He's not my mentor," Tom said, and saw the devil's
face shine forth his frustrated greed.

"Well, you see, there are only two ways to go," said the
devil. "You could take the high road, which I definitely
recommend. That way, you become the master of Shadowland—or not, as you choose. But the option is open to
you. You become stronger and stronger as a magician.
Your life is full, varied, and satisfying. Everything you
could want comes to you on a high tide of blessings. Or
you could take the low road. Not advisable. You run into
trouble almost immediately. You endanger your happiness. Whatever happens, I can offer you very little help. I
really think that's the way it is, Tom. You see why I had
to talk to you. I want you to spare yourself a considerable
amount of nastiness."

"I'll have to think about it," Tom said. The devil's
conversation was making him very thirsty.

"Now you're being reasonable," M. said. "I know
you'll make the right decision."

Was it because he not only dressed like a teacher but
also talked like one? Why would that make him thirsty?

M. winked at him.

"Did you make those porcelain things come alive?"
Tom said. But M. was gone. He groaned and lay back
against the pillows, and when he opened his eyes, Del was
before him.

"You look a lot better today," Del said. "But I still
don't understand what you're talking about."

"Could I please have some water?" Tom asked.

Del went into the bathroom and returned with a brim-
ming glass. "Rose was here a lot," he said, giving Tom
the glass. The water had the ripest roundest most satisfying taste Tom had ever known—it was astonishing that
something so delicious came out of a tap.

"I could see that she likes you, Tom."

"Yes. I like her, too."

"She saw how worried I was about you. I couldn't
figure out what happened—you got sick so fast."

"It was . . ." Tom began, and did not finish. "It was because I got tired. I picked up some bug while I was swimming."

"I guess so. Anyhow, I talked to Rose." He said no more, but his mood rang like a clarion.

"That's good."

"I guess we do have to get her out of here. And I was thinking—I bet if I come back and explain everything to Uncle Cole, he'll let me keep on working with him. He'll understand. Are you well enough for me to be telling you this?"

Tom smiled. Del was so impatient to tell him that trying to stop him would have been like holding up a hand before a tidal wave. "I feel better already," he said.

"Well, see, he's my uncle. He'll be mad at me, but it'll work out. He's my uncle."

"We're going to take the low road," Tom said, grinning. "You fret about things too much."

"Is there a low road?"

"Never mind. I have to sleep, Del." He closed his eyes and heard Del tiptoeing away.

9

As soon as Tom was able to get out of bed, he went to the cabinet in the living room. The china figures stood in their old places, the girl with the crook, the boy, the Elizabethan, the revelers. The boy's face was undamaged: that horrific vision had been inspired by his fever, a hallucination forced on him by the same tension which had made him ill. Tom's legs felt like those of a baby, unused to carrying his weight. Muscles he had never noticed before grumped and ached.

At dinner that night the magician complimented him on his recovery. "I feared we might lose you, my boy. What do you think it was? Touch of the flu?"

"Something like that," Tom said. And shied from the magician's glowing eyes.

"Would have been a terrible irony if you died, don't you think?"

"I can't see it that objectively."

Collins smiled and sipped at his wine. "At any rate, you look splendid now. Don't you think he looks splendid, Del?"

Del mumbled assent.

"Simply splendid. Has a look of the young Houdini about him, wouldn't you agree? Bursting with strength and health and craft. Unassailable. Do you feel unassailable, Tom?"

"I feel pretty good," Tom said, hating that Collins could make him feel like a fool.

"Superb. Wonderful." The last of the wine went past his lips. "Since you have been resurrected to us, tomorrow you shall have the penultimate episode of my life story. Do you feel up to it, little bird?"

"Sure," Tom said.

"Tomorrow, then. Not at the regular time. Ten at night, I think. By the sixth light. I'll look for you there."

10

Tom tested and strengthened his muscles by swimming; besides the exercise, which he needed, it gave him solitude. Collins was nearing the end of his unburdening. As the story neared its end, so did their time at Shadowland. Tom hoped every hour for a message from Rose. He prayed that she would not actually delay their escape until the day of the final performance. Now that Del was at least theoretically prepared to desert his uncle, the sooner they left, the better.

The weather was still warm, but the moisture in the air had concentrated and darkened. Fog hung over the middle of the lake and stole out of the forest. The air seemed to melt indivisibly into cloud. Against his skin, the water was almost bath-warm.

Sounds of hammering came to him: *tock-tock-tock*: each blow of the hammer threatened to nail him into Shadowland.

Knowing it was in vain, he hoped that Rose would get word to them this afternoon.

Instead of that, he saw her. She came alone out of the

woods in a curl of fog, unbuttoned a plaid shirt which engulfed her like a serape, and in the black bathing suit waded into the water like a doe.

He swam toward her, his heart half-sick with love.

Rose heard him splashing—emotion made his swimming even less expert—and retreated into water shallow enough for her to stand. Tom plowed toward her through heavy warm water. Only her head and neck were visible above the surface.

"Thanks for coming to visit me," he said. "I remember seeing you there a couple of times."

"Well, I would have been there all the time, but I didn't want to upset Mr. Collins." Rose was looking directly into his eyes with a quiet, deadly frankness.

Tom pushed his way through the water closer to her. "It's so good to see you," he said, and her face tightened down into itself again. She said, "Me too."

"Can't we get out of here soon? Today, maybe? He's going to tell us some more of his story tonight—it kind of makes me nervous."

"They'd catch us today," she said. "Those men are all over the place. It's too early. Anyhow, you're okay until the big performance. Just be patient. I'm doing what I can."

"I trust you, Rose," he said. "It's just that I'm getting . . . I don't know. This waiting is driving me crazy. I think that's why I got sick."

Her hands, warmed by the water, lifted and rested on his shoulders. She linked her hands behind his neck. "You won't be foolish when you see me tonight, will you?"

"Tonight?"

"During his story. I'm supposed to do some work then."

"Oh. One of those scenes."

"Sort of. But don't . . . you know. Say anything."

"I won't," he said. He was trembling.

Her face swam closer; the touch of her mouth extinguished his words. Then she spoke again. "Tom, don't listen to anything he says about me. I think he knows I love you. You can't hide anything from him. But if he talks about me, it'll all be lies. Everything here is a lie."

Rose hugged him tightly, and then gave him a comradely little pat on the back. "Be patient," she said. "I have to go now." Her head went under water, her body jackknifed, and she executed a smooth strong stroke which carried her away from him.

Tom turned around, his heart full, and saw a tall lean figure standing on the pier looking straight toward him. Coleman Collins. He glanced back to find Rose, but she was still under water. Tom felt a sudden unreasonable terror, as if the tiny figure on the dock had overheard what he and Rose had said. Collins was beckoning to him. He began to sidestroke back to Shadowland through the warm water.

Collins motioned him toward the pier, chopping with his hand. When Tom was only a few feet from the pier, he looked up at the magician's steely face. "So you know our little Rose better than any of us realized," Collins said. "Come up here."

"I just met her by accident," Tom said.

"Get on the pier."

Tom dog-paddled nearer, and Collins bent and reached down. Tom raised his own hand, and the magician lifted him onto the pier as if he weighed nothing. Dripping and frightened, Tom stood before him.

"I cannot recommend any distractions for you at this time," Collins said.

It took Tom a moment to understand what he meant.

"In fact, excessive distraction from your task could prove dangerous, Tom. Do you understand? I will need your entire concentration."

"Yes, sir."

"'Yes, sir.' Like a little schoolboy. Is it possible that you still do not understand the seriousness of what you are involved in?"

"I think I understand," Tom said. The magician appeared sober but very angry.

"You *think* you do. I hope you know that you cannot put any credence in any word Rose utters. She is not—repeat—not—to be trusted. If you allow yourself to be led astray by that girl, you will be ruined. Is that clear?"

Tom nodded.

"I see you still do not understand. So I will tell you one

of my secrets. That delightful child you were embracing in the water has never seen the town of Hilly Vale. She has no grandmother, and she never had parents. She is my creation. She has no notion of morality, and less of love."

Tom looked at him sullenly, hating him.

"Oh, dear me. I see I better tell you a story," the magician said. "Sit down and listen."

11

"The Mermaid"

Many years ago, when we all lived in the forest and nobody lived anywhere else, a lonely old king lived by the side of a lake in a drafty castle which had seen better days. Once it had been the most beautiful castle, and he the most powerful king, in the entire forest, which covered half the continent. Once tapestries had glowed from the walls, gold plates had shone from the table, and all of the castle had seemed to sparkle with a light which was the image of the great king's glory. But the queen had died, and the princesses had married princes from lands far away, other kings in the forest had taken territory in battles, and the old king lived alone and bitter, without glory or affections. His army had died of old age or been taken from him or simply faded into the forest, and so he could not increase his treasury by conquest. Only a few woodsmen and hunters remained to pay his taxes, and they paid chiefly out of loyalty to what had once been.

One of the old king's few pleasures was to walk at evening along the shore of the lake near the castle. The water was deep and blue, and from time to time he could see a bass jump, disturbing the gloomy quiet with a splash loud as cannon fire and causing ripples to spread all the way to the shore. At such times, the king would mourn, remembering when his own power was such that its rumors and effects rippled and widened a hundred miles in every direction. The old times of love and power—how he ached for them!

One night, taking his melancholy walk beside the lake,

he saw a mighty bass leap out of the water, and was so moved by longing that he mumbled quietly to himself, "Oh, I do wish . . ."

Then he heard a voice as ancient and cracked as his own. "Do wish for what, your Majesty?"

The king whirled about and saw a wrinkled old man with a crafty face and a threadbare robe seated on a fallen log half-concealed by overgrown vegetation. He did not immediately recognize the old man, for he had not seen him since the days he had just been mourning.

"Oh, it's you, wizard," the king said. "I thought you were dead."

"I die fresh every morning," said the wizard. "Coughing brings me back."

"Tricks and confusion, that's all I ever had from you," said the king, turning away from the lake in irritation. In truth he was pleased to see the wizard again, despite the accuracy of what he had just said.

"Halvor is very important now in the north," said the wizard, as if to himself, "and Bruno has made a name for himself in the south, and Lester the Ambitious in the west, and—"

"Shut up," grumped the king. "I know all that. I suppose you sold yourself to them, like everyone else. I suppose you work your evil tricks for reptiles like Lester, who gained power by poisoning most of his relatives." The great bass rose out of the water again, smacked back down with a silvery thrash of his tail, and the king's heart folded with loss.

"They have their own wizards—upstarts who think only of money. If I worked for them, wouldn't I at least have new robes?"

"Umph," the king said. "You do look rather seedy, wizard."

"No more than I feel. But didn't I hear you wishing a moment ago? For old times' sake, I'd be pleased to help you."

"And bamboozle me the way you did everyone else you aided."

"Wizards must be paid, like everyone else," said the ancient creature on the log. "What were you wishing for? A vast army? A treasury full of gold?" Then he gave the king an extremely shrewd look, and all his wrinkles seemed to smooth out for a moment. "Or was it a beautiful young wife to warm your bones? A young wife, perhaps, with the power to restore your kingdom and return to you all that you have lost?"

The king's face darkened.

"I think I could find a wife for you," mused the wizard, "who could bewitch the armies of Halvor and Bruno so that you could subjugate the territories that were once yours, then raise enough treasure to invade the province of Lester the Ambitious—and who, though incapable of giving you children, would give you the illusion of love."

"Only the illusion," said the disappointed king.

"Look at it from my point of view," said the wizard. "All love is illusion to a wizard. And to possess this great blessing from which the others would flow, you need only tell me that you would sacrifice your gray hair and wear a beard instead. It is a better bargain than I gave the sparrows. It is a bitter truth, your Majesty, that you have less to surrender than they."

Though old, the king was still vain, and he hated the thought of baldness. "Will it be a full beard?" he asked.

"A very noble beard," the wizard said. "Need I point out that you do not require your hair to enjoy the fruits of love? And the wife I shall give you will make you a young man again."

"Where will you get her from?" asked the king. "Some foul contraption of wax and bear grease?"

"Not at all." The wizard smiled. "I will get her from there." He nodded to the lake, and on the instant the great bass again broke the surface. "She will be as beautiful as beautiful, with the power to enchant armies, but she will have the cold heart of a fish. Yet as long as you are king, you will believe in her love."

"A strong back and firm flesh," said the king. "And the power to enchant armies." He trembled on the edge of his decision for a moment, fearing that he was about to make a great mistake, but then thought of a woman as beautiful as beautiful, with the power to turn the armies of Halvor and Bruno against them, and his blood stirred, and he whispered, "I take your bargain, wizard."

"You must be on this spot at midnight," said the

wizard, all his wrinkles deepening as he grinned and disappeared.

At eleven o'clock the king stood by the lake. By eleven-thirty his bones were aching and he sat on the wizard's hollow log, burning with hope and impatience. Fifteen minutes later he saw a great bubble burst on the surface of the lake. He stood up in the moonlight and went to the very shoreline. He rubbed his aching hands together. He sucked his teeth. He felt years younger already.

At midnight something broke the surface of the water in the center of the lake. Terrified, the old king stepped backward just as the head of a beautiful young woman appeared. Her shoulders lifted from the water, then her whole upper body, as well as the neck and head of a horse. The old king backed up until he felt bushes pressing against him. The woman emerged entirely from the lake, dressed in a long white gown and astride a magnificent white charger. Her hair was golden-red; her face was beautiful as beautiful, and the king saw that she could indeed enchant armies. "Come, my husband," she said, and reached down to him a hand which, when he touched it, was as cold as if no blood ran there. With the strength of a giant, she pulled him up onto the saddle with her, and they went on the white horse to his castle. And that night, with the horse stabled outside, the king knew the delights of the marriage bed as thoroughly as any twenty-year-old prince.

The next day they went north to Halvor's land, and met his army, which was going to kill them until the soldiers looked into the face of the queen. Instantly the soldiers dropped their weapons and swore their allegiance to the old king. Then they proceeded to Halvor's castle and found that Halvor had already escaped and fled farther north, to where only reindeer and wolves lived.

That night, the old king knew again the joys of love. Though his bride was fish-cold to the touch, she had beauty to break his heart and swore she loved him. And the king again felt his youth restored as half his kingdom had been restored.

On the second day, he and his bride and Halvor's army went south, where Bruno's soldiers fell to the ground and wept, welcoming them. Bruno himself fled farther south, to the land where alligators and giant lizards crawled over black rocks and slipped into stinking rivers.

The king rode back to his palace dazed with happiness. In two days he had recaptured all his old kingdom and more, and he had an army to take any land he wished. Lester the Ambitious would fall in a day. His new bride gave him glances sweeter than maple sugar, and he knew that the wizard was mistaken about her ability to love.

When the king and his wife and the joined armies had reached the palace, the king saw the wizard sitting on a broken pediment by the gates. "Hail, great king," said the wizard. "Are you satisfied with your bargain?"

"I am satisfied with everything, friend," said the king, feeling very grand astride the great white horse. He and his nobles went inside to feast on beef and roast pig and gallons of ale; and during the feast the king saw with pride how his nobles, the bravest and strongest men in three lands, paid court to his queen; and saw how like a queen she treated the nobles, giving a word to this one and a smile to that one, but reserving the best of herself for him, so that all knew that her heart was his alone.

When the king and queen left their guests to go to the royal bedroom, the king locked the door behind him and advanced toward his bride.

"Hold a moment, your Majesty," said the wizard, who was seated in a window casement.

The king swore, and made to push the trespasser out of the window, but the wizard held up his hand and said, "Since you are satisfied that I have kept my word, now I will ask you to keep yours."

"Take my hair . . . give me my beard . . . but leave!" bellowed the king. The queen, who had begun to disrobe, continued to do so.

"It is done," said the wizard, snapping his fingers, and a great agony overtook the king, an agony greater than any he had known, pain that threatened to split him apart and burn his eyes from his skull. He fell howling to his knees.

Before the queen, who concluded her undressing as if nothing of any importance were happening, and before the wizard, who merely smiled as coldly as had Lester the Ambitious when the last of his relatives had been poisoned, the old king was transformed into a goat. The hairs of his head became coarse stubbly goat fur, and long goat whiskers sprouted from his chin. He bleated and kicked, but could not bleat and kick himself back into human form. The wizard joined the queen in the bed, the goat was sent down to the kitchen, and the entranced nobles continued their feast. Thus the wizard ended his many days with a beautiful wife, a great army, and the possession of kingdoms.

12

"And what's the point of that?" Tom asked, shivering on the pier.

The magician smiled at him: smiled as coldly as the wizard in his story. "Need I really say? Rose can never leave Shadowland. Kiss her all you want, Tom, but don't believe a word she says, for she has no idea of the truth."

"That's a terrible . . . ridiculous . . . *lie.*" Tom began to walk away from Collins down the pier.

"I don't blame you for being angry with me," the magician called out into the fog between them, "but whatever you do, don't forget my warning. Don't take her too seriously." Tom was now at the iron ladder. As he set his feet on the first rung, he heard the magician call, "Our lives take many different turnings, Tom, and today's king is tomorrow's goat. Don't be fool enough to think it cannot happen to you."

III

Two Betrayals

1

At night the fog still hung over the lake and in the forest swirled around the trees. The lights above the clearings were glowing yellowish disks. "Let's not get separated," Del said, and took his hand as they slowly made their way through the trees.

When they came into the clearing of the sixth light, Coleman Collins was waiting for them. He sat in the owl chair, his legs crossed at the ankles.

Tom swallowed, knowing that he would see Rose down in the funnel of trees before this part of the story was done.

"The sorcerer's apprentices," Collins said, turning his head to greet them. His voice was blurred. Both boys had seen the bottle clamped between his thighs. "Just in time, yes, and wandering lone through the mists like orphans. Sit down in your accustomed places, boys, and attend. We have reached the next-to-last chapter of my unburdening, and the weather is appropriate.

2

"First of all, it was a foggy day when I deserted the armed forces of the United States. It was the first week of December, and the war had been over for three weeks. I was in England, waiting for my discharge papers. Speckle John had been discharged a week earlier, and was already in Paris. I could see no reason why I should not leave immediately, but for the strict interpretation the government puts on such things as premature departure from its service. At the time, I was not serving anyone, in fact. I was waiting out the period before my papers came in a country house which had been turned into a hospital and convalescent home—Surrey, this was—and I was more or less being kept out of sight. The patients there had been on what was called Blighty Leave, a term I suppose you boys are too young to understand. Nobody knew when the papers would come through. Some of the men had heard rumors that they might not be discharged, or demobbed, as the English soldiers said, for a year. Don't think these were idle rumors, either; some men were still in France eight months later.

"I don't suppose you boys know Surrey? Physically, it is quite a beautiful county. Before the war and for the well-off, it must have been a sort of paradise. But the weather, at least while I was there, was miserable, cold and misty—the most expressive weather I've ever known, somehow speaking of blasted hopes and dead expectations. The English had lost nearly an entire generation of men, and in those villages in Surrey I think they felt the loss especially keenly. When Speckle John's letter came, I felt I simply had to get out.

"So in the first week of December I just left, carrying only a hand valise with a few books and my razor and toothbrush. I walked two miles into the village, waited a couple of hours at the station, and caught the Charing Cross train. From the moment I walked through the gates of that house, I was a criminal and a fugitive, traveling on forged papers I'd had the foresight to buy on the black market just before we left France. The next day I took the boat train to Paris. The name on my false papers was Coleman Collins. I let the hunt for Lieutenant Charles Nightingale go on without me.

"For there was a hunt, and that was the reason I had been sequestered away in Surrey. At dinner I told you boys about that day I did five magical cures in a row. Reckless, even stupid—certainly arrogant. I was *on fire* with impatience. Austria-Hungary had just surrendered after the Italian victory at Vittorio Veneto. Everybody knew that Germany was exhausted. Finished. I wanted *out*. So I let rip, boys, I let rip. Five in a row. Spuds-and-Guinness, the Irish nurse, thought the devil had appeared. Of course my display caused an uproar. Withers saw what I was doing, and after finishing up his own work, tore out faster than any Georgian has ever traveled before or since. To see the colonel, I was sure. I did not give a damn. Anyhow, to make a long story short, before I got to England, there were new rumors about me. Not just among a handful of Negro soldiers, but among the general public. Reports had begun to appear in the English and French papers. *Miracle on the Battlefield*. That sort of thing. First in one place, then in another. By the time I left Yorkshire, the English papers were conducting their own search for the "miracle doctor." If I had wanted that sort of thing, I could have had it in a minute, boys—if I had wanted to be a performing monkey the rest of my life. But what I wanted was in Paris, working on our act and looking for theater bookings. What I wanted had secrets and knowledge to make a faith healer look like a dogcatcher.

"I set foot again on French soil on December 5, 1918, hung-over, unshaven, in a cold rain. My phony papers had never been questioned, not even looked at twice. I did

see, after a few weeks in Paris, that a newspaper had
managed to identify the 'miracle doctor' as one Lieutenant Charles Nightingale, who had unreasonably vanished
from an English village shortly before his release from the
army and was now AWOL. But by then the doings of
Lieutenant Nightingale were no more important to me
than those of General Pershing.

"Speckle John was living in rooms in rue Vaugirard,
and I took a room directly below him. You entered the
building through huge wooden doors on the street and
came into an open court surrounded on all sides by high
gray brick walls. Smaller doors let onto staircases. To
your right was the concierge's office; straight ahead, the
stairs to Speckle John's rooms. This building was so run-
down it was moldy, but to me it looked beautiful. Now I
can almost see it before me. And so, I think, can you."

The boys looked down the funnel of trees and saw the
suggestion of high gray walls in the fog. Dark windows
stared down at a tall figure in a hat and Burberry. Then a
black figure, his face in shadow, emerged from a door in
the brick.

"My mentor, my guide, and my rival was waiting for
me."

The man in the hat and long Burberry walked through
the swirling fog toward the black figure. Then another
door opened, and a slender girl hurried past both men.
Rose.

"On that first day, I saw a girl walking past us but did
not look closely at her. Later I found that she was named
Rosa Forte, that she was a singer, and that her rooms
were on the ground floor just below mine."

Rose had disappeared into the trees; the two men had
vanished too; the scene at the end of the tunnel of trees
went black.

"At first I thought that she was the most enchanting girl
I'd ever known, brave and intelligent, with a face that
delighted me more than any painting. Within weeks I had
fallen in love with her. Once I saw a shepherdess that had
her face in a provincial antique shop, and because I had
no money to buy it, I stole it—slipped it into my pocket
and took it home. When Speckle John and I toured, I
took it with me. Stared at it; stared *into* it, as if it knew
mysteries Speckle John did not."

Down in the narrow space between the trees, Rose Armstrong appeared, dressed in a long white garment of indeterminate period. She held a shepherd's crook, froze like a statue, and looked at Tom with unfocused eyes.

"Mysteries, yes. Mystery is always duplicitous, and once you know its secret, it is twice banal. In time I came to think that Rosa Forte was like some maiden in a fable, blank to herself for all her surface charm, the property of anybody who listened to her tale." Collins lifted his bottle, and Rose Armstrong disappeared backward into fog and trees.

"Ah. Speckle John and I began working almost immediately. We booked ourselves into theaters and halls all over France. I was afraid to stay long periods in England because of the 'miracle-doctor' business, but we did cross England several times to perform in Ireland. We proceeded to invent an entirely new kind of performance, using the skills we had, and eventually worked our way up toward the top of the bill. What we were after was extravagance, and we could twist an audience around so that they could not be sure by the end of the performance exactly what had happened to them. When they saw us, they knew no other magician could come near us. One of our most famous illusions was the Collector, which began almost as a joke of mine. It was not until eighteen months later that I decided that I had the necessary power to use a real person as the Collector."

Del gasped, and the magician raised his eyebrows at him. "You have a moral objection? So did Speckle John—he wanted to stick with the less successful toy I'd invented earlier. But once it had occurred to me that I could fill up my toy, so to speak, with a real being, the toy began to look inadequate. The first Collector was a gentleman named Halmar Haraldson, a Swede who came upon us in Paris and wanted nothing more than to be a magician. He saw it as an avenue of revenge against a world which had not welcomed his abilities; and Halmar saw in us something more powerful than the usual run of stage magicians. What he saw, quite rightly, in magic was that it was antisocial, subversive, and he hated the world so badly that he hungered and thirsted for our power. Haraldson dressed always in cheap anonymous black suits above which his bony Scandinavian peanut-shaped head

floated like a skull; he took narcotic drugs; he was th
most extreme exponent of the postwar nihilism that
knew. Consciously or not, he resembled one of thos
apparitions in Edvard Munch's paintings. So I met hir
one night and collected him, and thereafter my to
glowed with a new life. Halmar lurked inside it like :
genie."

"What happens to the person you use?" Tom asked
"What happened to Halmar?"

"I released him eventually, when he became a liability
You will hear, child. Speckle John would have insisted o
abandoning the Collector altogether, but I had gaine
control of the act. After all, I was his successor, and m
powers were soon the equal of his. He could not insis
with me, though I could see him growing unhappier an
unhappier as we toured together. I am talking abou
something that happened over a period of years.

"It's a commonplace irony, I imagine. Partners wor
together and achieve success, but fall out personally. H
began to make it clear that he thought I was a mistake–
that I should never have been chosen. Speckle John, t
my disappointment, was not large-minded. His ambition
were small, his conception of magic was small. 'The tes
of a mature magician is that he does not use his powers i
ordinary life,' he said; and I said, 'The test of a tru
magician is that he has no ordinary life.'

"Rosa joined our act after a time. Her singing ha
never led to anything, and she needed a job. Speckle like
her, and because she had performed, stage fright did no
cripple her. We taught her all the standard tricks; she wa
adept at them, and her *gamine* quality was effective wit
audiences. My partner took a paternal attitude towar
her, which I thought ridiculous. Rosa was mine, to d
with as I wished; but I did not object to their having talk
together, for it helped reconcile her to her position. Th
other reason I did not object was that my partner's car
with the girl proved to me that it was he, not I, who ha
been the mistake. My little shepherdess was porcelai
through and through, beautiful to look at, but only :
reflector of borrowed light."

Wind pushed at the fog, swirled it. A deeper chi
entered the clearing.

"When you travel as we did, you begin to know a community of all the others who play the same theaters. Jimmy Nervo and Teddy Knox, Maidie Scott, Vanny Chard, Liane D'Eve . . . One group interested me, Mr. Peet and the Wandering Boys. There were six 'Boys,' tumblers and strongmen, rough characters. I think they had all been in prison for violent crimes at one time or another—rape and robbery, assault. Other performers left them alone. In fact, their tumbling was only adequate, not nearly good enough for them to be headliners, and they broke it up with comic songs and staged fights. From time to time they let the fighting wander offstage. I know of a couple of occasions when they beat men nearly to death in drunken brawls. They were rather like an unevolved form of life. I wanted to hire them, and when I approached their leader, Arnold Peet, he immediately agreed—better to be second stringer in a successful act than to wither on your own. And he agreed also that his 'boys' would work as my bodyguards when we were not performing. Eventually they feared me—they depended on me for their bread—they knew I could kill them with a glance and they did anything I wanted them to do. Our act immediately became stronger, too, wilder and more theatrical, because it took its direction from me.

"For a time, boys, we were the most famous magicians in Europe, and titled and well-known people everywhere sought us out, gave parties for us, came for advice. I met all the surrealists, all the painters and poets; I met the American writers in Paris; I met dukes and counts, and spent many afternoons telling fortunes to those who wanted the help of magic in planning their lives. Ernest Hemingway bought me a drink in a Montparnasse bar but would not come to my table because he thought I was a charlatan. I heard that he had referred to me as 'that dime-a-dance Rasputin,' a description I did not mind a bit. The real tinpot Rasputin was an Englishman who fancied himself a demon. I met Aleister Crowley in England, and knew at once that he was a sick, deluded fraud—a blubbery ranter whose greatest talent was for mumbo jumbo.

"Crowley and I met in the garden of a house in Kensington belonging to a rich and foolish fancier of the

occult who supported both of us and wanted to know what
would happen if we met. I was already in the garden when
Crowley oozed through the scullery door. He was
sluglike, thoroughly repulsive; wore a black caftan; dirty
bare feet; shaven head. His face was crazy and ambitious—there was a kind of crude magnetism to him.
Crowley looked me in the eye, trying to frighten me.
'Hello, Aleister,' I said. 'Begone, fiend!' he shouted, and
pointed a fat digit at my face. I turned his hand into a
bird's claw, and he nearly fainted on the spot. 'Begone
yourself,' I said, and he shoved the claw under the caftan
and exited with great haste. Later I understand he
displayed the claw to a female admirer as proof of his
satanic abilities, and worked over spells for months before
he was able to change it back.''

Something moved into the fuzzy light down in the trees.

''From what I've said already, you know that I had
grown careless about spending time in England. By
1921, we traveled freely back and forth across England,
playing theaters in towns from Edinburgh to Penzance,
though most of our work was in London, especially at
the Wood Green Empire. I thought the world had forgotten the mysterious Dr. Nightingale. But one person
had not, and I met him one summer night after a
performance. He was waiting by the stage door of the
Empire, and I saw his red hair and knew who he was
before I saw his face.''

A light in the trees showed a flight of steps, a brick wall,
a suggestion of a narrow alley. The figure in the Burberry
and hat came down the stairs. Tom saw Rose hovering
behind him. The magician lifted his bottle as if toasting
his former self, but did not drink. With the magician's
next sentence, Tom knew that it was not himself he was
toasting.

''There she is, Rosa Forte, my porcelain shepherdess,
my enchanted fish. I was glad she was there—I wanted her
to see what I could do. I wanted her to know that nothing
in her code or Speckle John's could hinder me for a
moment. And I want you boys to know that too. I will not
be hindered.''

The little scene down in the trees was obscurely,
inexplicably sinister: Collins' surrogate in hat and long
coat, the fragile girl behind him on the stairs. Savagery

seemed to flicker about them—a hopeless violence curled in the fog.

Another man stepped out of the fog; red hair shone.

"'I knew it was you,' Withers said to me. 'I should have known you'd wind up like this—a worthless parasite.' Except that he said it *wuthless pa'site*. 'Call yourself Coleman Collins now, do you, murderer? Well, you put on a pretty good show, I'll say that for you. I hope they'll let you perform in the stockade.' *Puff-oahm.* He stood there, beaming hate at me, hate and satisfaction, because he thought he had me. This little racist Southern doctor, traveling through Europe on undervalued American dollars, piling up anecdotes to wow them with back in Macon or Atlanta.

"I asked, 'Are you threatening me, Withers?'

"'That I am,' Withers said: he was simply gloating. 'You went AWOL. Somewhere, somebody's still looking for you. I'm going to see that you're found.'

"So I called up Halmar Haraldson and sicked him on Withers."

The Collector lurched into the fuzzy light, his face glowing with moronic glee. The red-haired man backed up. On the stairs behind Collins' surrogate, Rose could not see why the man playing Withers was frightened. She stared at the man, confused and beginning to be alarmed.

"Hey!" the red-haired man shouted. "Hey, Mr. Collins?"

Tom's stomach tightened: this was not just a scene. The Collector stumbled forward. Rose saw him and screeched.

"'No, *you* are found, Withers,' I said. And now observe how well your friend Mr. Ridpath fulfills his role."

"Oh, my God," Del said, and began to stand up. Rose screamed again, and Collins' stand-in gripped her arm.

The Collector flew at the red-haired man, who shouted, *"Stop him! Stop him!"* The Collector knocked him down.

"Collins! Help me!" A red furry thing flopped from the man's head, and Tom saw that he was the man on the train, the aged Skeleton Ridpath. The Collector had him pinned to the ground and was battering his face. "Found you! Found you!" he keened.

Del was on his feet, screaming; Rose, unable to move, screamed too.

"Shut up!" Collins ordered, and Del silenced.

One blow; another; the monster's bony fists smashed away again and again into the man's head. Rose turned away and shielded her face against the brick of the staircase.

"Yes, as I did, you're going to see it happen," Collins said calmly. "You have to see it. The poor devil didn't know it, of course, but that was the only reason he was here. To be Withers' stand-in."

Skeleton was humming tunelessly, battering in the old man's head.

"An entirely expendable character—a failed actor named Creekmore, no better than a skid-row bum." Collins gave a snort of amusement. "He answered an advertisement, can you believe it? He sought me out. So did Withers. Withers *knew* I'd stolen Vendouris' money— as if taking the money of the dead were a crime." Collins lifted the bottle and drank.

Down in the fog, Skeleton was doing something vile to the actor. Blood gushed from the head—Tom saw the skin leaving the bone, and stood up and turned away.

"Don't even think of running," Collins said from his throne. "Your friend would catch you in seconds. And then all this would be real."

Tom looked back down to where the awful scene had taken place. The Collector was gliding back into the fog. The body was gone; Snail and Thorn and Pease stood beside the staircase with their arms locked over their chests.

"It wasn't real?" Tom said.

"Not now, child. Withers was no more. Don't worry about Creekmore. He has a few scratches, no more. I'll pay him tomorrow and send him off. He will think of me with gratitude, I assure you."

Del gradually ceased quivering. "That *was* Skeleton," he mumbled. "I saw him ripping . . . that man's face . . . all that blood."

"A few bloodbags concealed in the mouth. Creekmore is already in the summerhouse washing his face and wondering where to find his next bottle."

On the staircase in the fog, Rose slowly lifted her head.

Collins waved the bottle, and the scene went black. "For me, the horror was still to come."

Shivering, the boys sat back down on the damp grass.

3

"Even I was surprised by Haraldson's savagery. What you boys saw was a little pig's blood and the hint of something grotesque—what I saw was a man being slowly dismembered and kept alive in absolute agony until the last possible second. I had been thinking of the Collector as a sort of toy, as it had been when I had invented it. Of course, the power was mine, not Haraldson's. He was only a tool, a doll filled with my own imagery. And because Haraldson was now a liability, I realized that he could be replaced by any number of our hangers-on— even with one of the Wandering Boys if necessary. I released Haraldson from the Collector as quickly as possible, after I was sure Withers was dead. The police found him almost immediately: the Swede was in such a daze that he was put away in a mental home and convicted but never executed for Withers' murder. There was a little stir in the papers for a bit; then it died away, and we were far out in the country, working the provinces; no one connected Withers or Haraldson to myself.

"The other thing I had realized while the Collector gathered in poor Withers was that I had no real need of the Wandering Boys anymore. The Collector was bodyguard enough. This was just a seed in my mind, understand. I thought about it while I gave the Wandering Boys their one amusement, badger-baiting. Whenever we were out in the countryside, they arranged for a couple of dogs, and we went out in the middle of the night with our shovels and tongs and put paid to a couple of badgers. The night after Withers had been dispatched, we were in the countryside west of York, and I looked at those six trolls and their ringmaster working for the moment when they could witness the slaughter of a few animals, and I thought: *Are they really necessary?* I filed the thought away: there was a great deal on my mind at the time.

"Rosa Forte, for one. She had become distant and
sulky, and this infuriated me. I often beat her when I was
drunk. I could not tell if she loved or hated me, her
manner was so contradictory. Speckle John, who by 1922
was definitely my second fiddle, used to try to advise me
about her, and his advice was an old woman's. Be nicer to
her, treat her better, listen to her, that sort of thing.
She would go to him and weep. I despised both of
them. Money was also on my mind. Though we were
as successful as any magicians were in those days, I
constantly felt pinched for extra money. Even with
what I made reading fortunes and doing prognostications
for the wealthy, I wasn't satisfied. I wanted to live
well, I wanted a lavish act; even then, I think I had
the germ of my farewell performance in my mind. A
good climax is important to any performance, and I
knew that when I tired of touring—of dragging nine
other people around the world with me—I would want my
final show to be the most spectacular performance ever
seen.

"That would be very expensive; and indeed my own
tastes had become costly. We were already charging as
much as we could ask. So I adopted other means, and
here the Wandering Boys were useful to me.

"I went unannounced to that rich fool in Kensington,
Robert Chalfont, late one night. When he opened the
door to me, I saw on his big-jawed public-school face that
he was both flattered and unsettled, even a little frightened. That was perfect. He knew what I had done to
Crowley in his garden earlier that summer. Chalfont
invited me in and offered me a drink. I took some malt
whiskey and sat down in the library while he paced up and
down. He had invited me for dinner several times and I
had not come; now that I was there, he was nervous.
'Nice of you to drop in,' he said.

"'I want money,' I said unceremoniously. 'A lot of it.'

"'Well, look here, Collins,' he said. 'I'm afraid I can't
just give you money on demand, you know—there are
ways of doing things.'

"'And this is my way,' I told him. 'I want three
thousand pounds a year from you. And I want you to sign

a paper stating that you give it voluntarily, in recognition of my work.'

"'Well, dammit, man, no one respects your work more than I do,' he said, 'but what you're asking is pre-posterous.'

"'No, *you* are preposterous,' I told him. 'You wish the privilege of associating with great magicians. You want intimacy with their secrets; you want to witness displays of their power. Now it is time to pay for the privilege.' And I reminded him of what I could do to him if he refused me.

"He asked me for time to think. I gave him two days—I could see on that stupid well-brought-up face that he wished he'd stuck to shooting and fishing.

"The following day I sent Mr. Peet and his trolls around to his house, and they did some damage there. Chalfont came straightaway to my hotel suite and agreed to what I'd demanded. But by then I had decided I wanted more—all of it, in fact. And he gave it to me, everything he had."

"He just gave you all his money?" Tom asked. "Just like that?"

"Not exactly." The magician smiled. "I invited Chal-font to participate in our act."

"You collected him," Tom said, horrified.

"Of course. Once he'd had a sample of that, he signed everything over to me. I kept the trolls with him every day while he made the arrangements. And when I had his name on the papers and his money in my account, I collected him again. As he should have had the sense to expect. He gave a new dimension to the Collector, a sort of poignance. In fact, I began to think it was a pity I'd never put Crowley in the Collector. Imagine what a Collector he would have made! But we made do with Chalfont for as long as we stayed together. And I had no other Collector until I heard the pleas of your school-friend and saw how helpful he would be to us this summer."

Down in the trees, a faint light began to glow, teasing the fog that moved slowly across it.

"But pay attention now, boys. We are coming to the next turning point in my life—one of those great reversals, like the death of Vendouris or my first meeting with Speckle John.

"The money question had been solved, for many of my wealthy admirers had half-suspected the kind of thing that had happened to Chalfont, and gave over large sums whenever I wanted them. But I was growing tired of Europe. Europe was dead. I sensed new life in America—life that did not stink of corpses. Europe was really a graveyard, and in America my family had enough money to keep me for the rest of my life. I took a month off, sailed to the States, and looked for a suitable place to set up my compound. For that was how I thought of it: a guarded place, remote from any city, where I could extend magic as far as it could go; without the third-party trappings of an audience. I found this place and bought it and hired workmen to make the improvements I had in mind. The price was too high originally, but I persuaded the owners to let it go reasonably. And my methods ensured that no one would come prowling around in my absence."

There was an immense, terrifying beating of wings: a huge white owl came to life in the dim light. Both boys froze. The owl looked predatory, more purely savage than the Collector; it beat its wings once more, then blew apart like smoke, becoming part of the fog.

Still the light glowed, promising visions to come.

"I landed again in France in the autumn of 1923. It had been only five years since my first landing, but imagine the difference! Now I knew who and what I was: Coleman Collins had found and developed the power which Charles Nightingale had only dared to dream existed within him. I was rich enough to do anything I wished, and I was famous enough to draw large audiences wherever we appeared. Now I owned a house and extensive grounds in New England. And beyond all else, of course, I was King of the Cats, famous throughout the occult world. This was a position I intended to hold as long as I could—at least until I sensed the arrival of a magician whose powers were as much greater than mine as mine were than Speckle John's. Then, I thought, we'd see what we would see."

The white owl flickered again down the funnel of trees; its eyes blazed. The great wings rustled the leaves. Then it was gone again.

"We drove, Mr. Peet and I, he actually driving the Daimler and I relaxing in the backseat, down through western France toward Paris. I looked forward to seeing Rosa Forte and Speckle John—most especially, Rosa Forte. I thought of bringing her back to America with me—she could not survive without me, I knew, and she would have her uses in my new life. As yet, all of that was only a vague dream. I wondered what new bookings Speckle John had managed to get for us; I wondered how long the trolls would go before they required another badger-baiting; I wondered what invitations had come, which women would be waiting for me with their palms extended and their checkbooks out; I wondered too if Rosa would be as amorous in her greetings as she usually was when I returned from long trips. So down we drove, going at the dazzling speed of perhaps thirty miles an hour through village after village, each with its obelisk inscribed with the names of those who had died in the war. The light was heavy, and the chestnut trees were turning red and orange; the dust rose up from the road; I thought of all the blood in those fields, which were just ripening into harvest time. I remembered what I had done to that poor ranter Crowley, and laughed out loud—also I thought about the attacks recently made against me by Gurdjieff and Ouspensky, names important in the occult field at the time but now utterly forgotten. That heavy light . . . the orange, blood-soaked fields . . . Rosa waiting with her porcelain skin and open thighs . . . that feeling of time itself dying with a beautiful melancholy about me . . .

"Ten kilometers outside Paris I saw a peasant smile at my car with white flawless teeth, and I thought of Vendouris screaming in the frozen muck—thought of him for the first time in years, and it seemed to me that it really was time to get out when all of a beautiful European autumn seemed epitomized to me by the gleam of a dying man's teeth.

"We entered Paris from the northwest, throwing up plumes of dust behind us, and crossed the Seine at the Pont de Courbevoie and worked our way through the streets to the Ranelagh Gardens, where we lived in a splendid building on Avenue Prud'hon. We drew up before the splendid building. I could hear children's

voices in the heavy air. The trees in the Ranelagh
Gardens were brilliant gold, I remember, and the grass a
very powerful dark green. Still the beautiful melancholy. I
invited Peet to join me for a drink in my sitting room,
which eventually cost him his life. We mounted the stairs,
me carrying a small bag and Peet the two large suitcases
from the Daimler's trunk. The interior of the building
smelled of sandalwood. I opened the door of my apart-
ment and let Peet enter. He went in a few steps and
dropped the bags—they made a particularly loud thump. I
followed and saw his face, which was both embarrassed
and terrified. Then I saw them. Saw what any schoolboy
would have suspected long before."

The light blazed up in the trees, and Tom saw Rose
lying naked on what looked like an oriental carpet. About
her was the suggestion of a large room with oyster-colored
walls. Rose's unmistakable body was sideways to him, her
blond head turned away. A thick naked man with heavy
arms and thighs lay atop her; his face was buried in her
shoulder. Tom went rigid with shock. Beside him, Del
gasped. The heavy hands kneaded her breasts, the brutal
body thrust and thrust, moving itself blindly toward
climax; and Rose clung to his hips, accommodating and
moving with him. Shock spread so definitively throughout
Tom that he could feel its progress, freezing him as it
went. He could not even think of how Del was responding
to this sight. *You won't be foolish when you see me
tonight, will you?* That was what she had said, linking her
hands behind his neck as they stood in chest-high water.
And before that, *You won't hate me, will you? I still have
some work to do for him.* This is what she had meant.
Everything here is a lie.

He seized at that straw until the girl tilted her face
toward the sky and he saw the wide high brow, the mouth
that had said she loved him. He felt as though he had
been blowtorched. The man quickened, trembled,
clutched at her. Rose's arms and legs clamped on the
plunging man. Then the light died again, and they were
alone with the magician. Del's eyes were dull. He was
breathing heavily, almost panting.

*You won't be foolish when you see me tonight, will you?
Everything here is a lie.*

He could not see his way out of it.

"Of course it was not Root who was enjoying my Rosa, but my partner, Speckle John. I merely wanted you boys to feel my shock and outrage—and I see that I have succeeded. Arnold Peet fled. I left on his heels. When I returned half an hour later, Rosa was still there, dressed now, feigning contrition. She pretended that it had been the first occasion, but I knew better. I let her lie to me, and thought of all the consoling Speckle John had done for my poor Rosa. She expected me to beat her—she *wanted* to be beaten, for that would have been forgiveness. I did not beat her. I did not shoot her, either, though I had my service revolver with me—I always carried it in those days. I just let her plead and weep. And when I met Speckle John the next day, neither one of us mentioned what I had seen on the floor of my sitting room. I began to plan my final performance."

Collins stood. "Tomorrow night you will see how I wrapped up all the strands; how I removed Arnold Peet, who had witnessed my humiliation, along with his trolls; how I revenged myself against those who had humiliated me; and how I gave the gaudiest performance of my life." He looked down at the two stricken boys. "And stay in your rooms tonight. This time I will overlook no disobedience."

The magician tilted his head, looking as if he were enjoying himself, and put his hands in his pockets, his amused eyes finding Tom's; vanished.

To hell with you, to hell with you, Tom said to himself. He leaned down and helped Del to his feet. "Will you do whatever I ask?"

"Whatever you ask," Del said. He still looked semi-catatonic.

"Let's go back now. We'll get out of here as soon as we can tonight. I don't know how, but we'll do it. I'm through with this place."

"I feel sick," Del said.

"And listen. You were never going to be invited back anyhow. Get me? Shadowland was over for you anyhow. He told me. You weren't going to be chosen—he said this was your last summer here. It was over anyhow. So let's get out now."

"Okay," Del said. His lip trembled. "As long as you're coming with me." He wiped at his eyes. "What about her? What about Rose?"

"I don't know about Rose," Tom said. "But we're getting out of here late tonight. And nobody's going to stop us."

He led Del back through the wood to the edge of the lake.

"You were chosen," Del said. The moonlight lay a white cap over his black hair. A frog croaked from the side of the lake. Whiteness hung over the surface of the lake like a veil, and ghostly wisps trailed from the edge of the lake. The iron staircase rose up out of a pocket of gray wool like a ladder set in a cloud. "You were the one who was welcomed," Del said. "Weren't you?"

"But I didn't welcome them back."

"I was sure it was going to be me. But inside, I knew it wasn't me."

"I wish it *was* you."

They trudged across the sand. Del put his hands on the flaking rungs of the ladder; went up six rungs, stopped. "I think everybody lied to me," he said, as if to himself.

"Tonight," Tom said. "Then it's all over."

"I want it to be all over. But I almost wish this ladder would fall over again and kill both of us."

As they went through the dark living room, Tom thought of something. "Wait." Del drifted out into the hall and stood like a man on a gallows. Tom went to the cabinet in the corner and opened the glass doors. The porcelain shepherdess had been broken in two—Collins had done it. It was a joke, or a warning, or like the last moralizing line in a Perrault fable. The broken halves lay separated on the wood, a little fine white powder between them. All the other figurines had been pushed to the back of the cabinet. They faced him. The boy with the books, the six drunken men, the Elizabethan. Their eyes were dead, their faces. Then Tom understood. It was they who had murdered the shepherdess. That was a message straight from Collins to him. He took his eyes from them and picked up a piece of the broken figurine and put it in his pocket. On an afterthought, he took the pistol too and stuck it inside his shirt.

He followed Del upstairs. They walked down the hallway past a black window. "Look," Del said, and pointed. Tom should have seen it for himself: all the lights in the woods had been extinguished. There were no more stages, no more theaters in the woods. They could see only their own faces against solid black.

Del vanished around his door.

Tom went into his own room. The pocket doors were shut. He sat on his bed, heard rustling. He patted the bed and heard the whispery crackle again. Tom put his hand under the coverlet and touched a sheet of paper. He did not want to see it.

No: he did want to see it. He wanted with his whole damaged heart to see it. When he pulled it out and allowed himself to read it, it said: *If you love me, come to the little beach.*

So she too wanted to escape tonight. Tom saw Coleman Collins as a huge white owl swooping savagely toward them all, gathering and crushing them in his talons. He saw Rose squeezed in those claws. He folded the note and put it between the revolver and his skin. Then he touched the broken figurine in his pocket. "Okay," he said. "Okay, Rose."

Tom went to the doors and pushed them aside. Del lay on his bed in the dark. His shoulder twitched, one hand stirred babyishly. "What?" he asked.

"We're going now," Tom said, "and we're going to meet Rose."

The porcelain figures, lined up at the back of the cabinet, staring out with dead faces at their handiwork. Rosa Forte had been murdered by the Wandering Boys, and Collins wanted him to know it.

"I just want to get out," Del said. "I can't stand it here anymore. Please, Tom. Where do we go first?"

Tom led the way down the stairs, through the living room, and out onto the flagstones in the cool air. "We're going back through the woods," he said. "All the way this time."

"Whatever you say, master."

IV

Shadow Play

1

Tom took the gun out of his shirt and put it in his waistband at the small of his back. "What's that?" Del asked. "That's a gun. What do you need a gun for?"

"Probably we won't even need it," Tom said. "I took it out of the cabinet. I'm just being careful, Del."

"Careful. If we were careful, we'd still be in our rooms."

"If we were careful, we'd never have come here in the first place. Let's find Rose." He started down the rickety iron ladder. It moved away from the bluff a half-inch. Tom swallowed. The ladder had felt wobbly every time he had climbed it. "Anything wrong?" Del called out. Tom answered by going down the ladder as fast as he could. He started to walk across the beach in the darkness. He could hear Del's feet hitting the sand as he ran to catch up.

"He wanted to keep you here, didn't he? Forever."

"He was going to do worse to Rose," Tom said. "We have to get to that beach on the other side of the lake. That's where she'll be."

"And then what?"

"She'll tell us."

"But what'll we say to her, Tom? I can't even stand . . ."

Tom could not stand it either. "Do you want to try to swim across or walk through the woods?"

"Let's walk," Del said. "But don't lose me. Don't lose me, Tom."

"I'm not going to. Not losing you was the real reason I came here," Tom said. Curls of fog still leaked from the woods. He slid between two trees and started toward the first platform.

"Maybe we could bring her back to Arizona with us," Del said.

"Maybe."

"Hold my hand," Del said. "Please." Tom took his outstretched hand.

Rose was waiting for them on the little beach. They saw her before she noticed them—a slender girl in a green dress, high-heeled shoes dangling from her hand. They padded toward her, and she turned jerkily to face them—frightened. "I'm sorry," she said. She glanced at Del, but her eyes probed Tom. "I didn't know if you'd come."

"Well, I saw this," he said, and took the broken shepherdess from his pocket.

"What is it? Let me see." Tentatively, as if she were afraid to stand too near him, she came a few steps closer. "It does look like me. That's funny." Rose probed his face again: gave him a taut, bitter half-smile. "Don't you think that's funny?" Because he did not smile back, her eyes moved again to the broken shepherdess. Something in her posture told him that she wanted to step away. Then he understood. She was afraid that he would hit her.

"You don't think it's funny," she said. "Oh, well."

"Hey, I'm here too," Del said.

. Instantly more at ease, Rose altered the set of her shoulders and turned to him. "I know you are, darling Del. Thank you for coming." Her eyes flicked at Tom. "I wasn't sure if . . ."

"You had to, right?" Del said. His voice trembled. "He's crazy, that's all. Not half-crazy, all crazy."

"Everything here is a lie," Rose said. "Just because you saw it doesn't mean it really happened."

Tom nodded. He was curiously reluctant to take up this hope she offered. If he reached out, it might bite his hand. Del, however, had not only reached out, but embraced it. His face was glowing. "Well, we're here, anyhow. Now, where do we go?"

"Where you were before," Rose said. "This way." She led them back into the woods.

"Where he was before?" Del asked. "Where's that?"

"An old summerhouse," Rose said, walking through fog and night but needing no light to see her way. "The men were living there, but they're gone now."

"Wait a second," Tom said, stopping short. "*That* house? What's the point of going there?"

"The point is the tunnel, grumpy Tom," she said. "And the point of the tunnel is that it takes us out of here. I spent the whole day getting this ready—you'll see."

"A tunnel," Tom said; and Del repeated, "A *tunnel*," as if now they were truly on the way home.

"I've never gone all the way through it," Rose said, still moving ahead through the fog, "but I know it's there. I think it goes almost to Hilly Vale. We can stay in it all night. Then in the morning we can get out, walk to the station, and get on a train. There's an early train to Boston. I checked. They won't even miss you until late in the morning, and by then we'll be out of Vermont."

"What about your grandmother?" Tom said.

"I'll call her from wherever we get to." Her eyes rested questioningly on him for a moment.

2

Like wary animals, or like the ghosts of animals half-visible in the fog, they stepped away from the last of the woods. When Del saw the parklike area with its manicured lawns and artfully placed trees—here too the cold fog floated and accumulated in the hollows—he said, "I never even knew this was here!"

Rose said, "I think other people used to live here, a long time ago, but Mr. Collins made them leave."

Tom nodded: the huge shining owl had driven them away.

"I think it used to be a resort," Rose said. "And I think the big house used to be a sort of nightclub and casino."

"But why did they need a tunnel?" Tom asked.

"I guess it had something to do with bootlegging," Rose told him.

"Sure," Del said, suddenly knowledgeable. "This side must be close to a little road. It wouldn't all have been walled in then. If they heard of a raid, they could hide the booze and wheels and stuff in the tunnel."

"Only if the tunnel went back to Shadowland," Tom pointed out.

Rose said, "Del's right. There is more than one tunnel. You'll see in a minute." The shabby house was even more run-down in the fog. The rip in the porch screen gaped like a hungry mouth.

The three of them went toward the house. Tom kept seeing it in the past Rose and Del had drawn for him, in a postwar summer, surrounded by a few other houses like it—now fallen in—inhabited by men in blazers and boaters, women in dresses like the one Rose wore. There would be canoes, a man somewhere would be practicing the banjo, and ice cubes would chime in martini pitchers.

Good stuff. Prewar. Came in from Canada.

Nick, why don't we cross the lake and go up to the lodge tonight?

Good idea, sport. I want another fling at that wheel.

Say, you haven't heard anything about that owl Philly claims he saw last night?

No—that would have been later. "Sweet Sue" was what the banjo was playing, ringing out *chinga-chink-chink, chinga-chink-chink* through the summer air.

Yes, let's try our hand at the lodge tonight. I feel lucky. Waft some gin this way, sport, if you'll be so kind.

"You daydreaming?" Rose called out. "Or are you just afraid to come in?"

Tom went up on the porch with the other two. Rose led them into the house and switched on a single lamp. The old building looked as though no one had been in it since the magician's winged emissary had sent them all packing. Dust lay on all the ripped chairs, on the blurry carpet.

"Those men are set to go after tomorrow night," Rose said. "All their things are either thrown away or back at the house. Or maybe in one of the other tunnels."

"Wait a second," Del said. "How many are there?"

"Three. Don't worry, I can find the right one." She smiled at Tom. "I put some sandwiches and a thermos and some blankets down there. We'll be all right tonight."

"So where is this tunnel?" Del asked. "Hey, if there are rats down there, you can shoot them."

"I didn't see any rats," Rose said, and gave Tom a speculative look.

"Well, I brought his gun," Tom admitted. "It's about a hundred years old. I don't know how to shoot it, anyhow."

"The tunnel's this way." Rose moved a dusty wicker table and pushed back the rug. A trapdoor lay flush against the wood. She bent down, put her finger through the ring, and swung the door up. "Used to be how you got to the little cellar." Wide concrete steps led down into blackness. "They made the tunnels later."

"Boy," Del said. "As simple as that."

"You waiting for something?" Rose asked, and Del looked at both of them, uttered "Oh" in a squeaking voice, and began to go slowly down the steps. "There's a flashlight on the bottom step."

"Found it. Come on, you guys."

3

The tunnel was high enough to stand in. Packed earth made the floor and walls; timbers shored up the roof. When Rose shone the flashlight down its length, they could see it going deeper into the earth at a slight pitch, falling and falling. Where the light began to die—a long way off—it seemed to turn a corner.

"Well, you said you were going to take the low road," Del said. "This is really cool. Look how big it is! I thought we'd be crawling on our hands and knees."

"Not a chance," Rose said. "Would I do that to you?" She gestured with the light as they walked along. The air changed, became colder and drier in the total blackness around the spreading beam.

At the juncture of the tunnel's three branches the flashlight picked out a little heap of things. The juncture was a circular cavern slightly taller than the tunnels themselves. The ceiling was rounded and intricately buttressed by a lattice of two-by-fours. "Here's our bedroom," Rose said. "And blankets and food and stuff like that." She knelt and lifted the blanket off the magician's wicker basket. "I didn't think he'd miss this. Is anybody hungry?"

Tension had made the boys ravenous. Rose stood the flashlight on end in the center of the vaulted cavern and handed them ham sandwiches wrapped in wax paper. Collins' ham; Collins' wax paper, too, probably. Each of them ate leaning against a different wall, so they were only half-visible to each other. Enough of the light filtered out and down to dimly touch their faces.

Del asked, "Which one of these tunnels do we take, Rose?"

"The one next to Tom." Tom leaned over and turned to peer down it. A wave of cold air washed toward him from out of impenetrable dark. "One of these used to connect to another summerhouse." From the cold darkness of the tunnel Tom heard:

chinga-chink-chink, chinga-chink-chink of the banjo and an amateurish but sweet voice singing

There's a moon a-bove
Dum da dum-dum
Sweet Sue,
just you.

"I think we ought to try to go to sleep," he said. "Toss me one of those blankets, please, Rose." Her face blazed into color as she bent forward, throwing a plaid blanket toward him. "Good idea," she said. For a time they arranged the blankets on the hard floor.

"I don't suppose the rest of you hear anything," Tom said.

"Hear anything?": Del.

"Just my imagination."

Rose came forward into the center, her head and trunk floating in the light like the top of the woman sawed in half in the old trick. She gave him a liquid, molten message from her pale eyes—*Forgive me?* Then the beam of the flashlight dipped like a flare along the curving walls and momentarily dazzled Tom, shining directly into his eyes. His shadow spread gigantically up the wall behind him. The beam swung away, and he saw Rose's body outlined against it—a wraith from the twenties in her green dress, wandering down here on whatever errands brought the resort people below ground.

Who was that lady I saw you with? Nicholas?
Just a lady who can be in two places at once.

Those captured voices.

The beam found Rose's blanket already spread. Her shoes dropped gently to the packed ground. "Good night, my loves."

"Good night," they said.

The flashlight clicked off, and seamless black covered them.

"Like floating," Del said. "Like being blind."

"*Yes,*" Rose breathed. Tom's heart went out to both of them.

He sprawled out on his blanket and covered himself against the chill. *Like being blind.* When he heard those captured voices drifting in the tunnels, he knew that nothing would be as easy as Del thought—that nothing had ever been that easy—and fear kept his eyes open though he too was blind.

(splash of water: canoe paddle lifted and dripping, the gleam catching your eye from clear across the lake)

Two places at once, very handy, Nick.

Summers are for dalliance, dear boy.

Wife sick again, is she?

Something in the water, she says. Foolishness. Something in the gin, more likely.

Or something in the air. Philly saw that owl again last night.

There is no owl, dear boy. Trust me.

Don't trust him, Tom said to himself; there is, there is an owl.

Philly's darling wife is the only reason we tolerate him, after all. . . .

Then voices from later in the summer: he could hear the coming chill, the promise of dead leaves and gray freezing water.

Joan can't be moved. Can't figure it out—doctors can't either. Going crazy with this thing.

And I saw the owl over your cabin, Nick . . .

Can't get her out, can't stay . . .

And Philly's wife dead—something in the air or something in the water . . .

Heard they sold the whole place. The devil must have bought it.

Waft the gin this way, Nick. Keep having these terrible nightmares.

The other two slept in the perfect blackness. Tom lay rigid in his blanket, listening to their even breathing as the captured voices lilted from the tunnels, moving and changing until there was only one voice left.

Good-bye, all, good-bye . . . All alone. Just me, chicken inspector number 23. Better waft myself some more of this gin and keep the boogies away . . . all alone, all alone . . . with the moon a-bove, da da dum dum . . .

He knew that if he looked deeply enough into one or another of the tunnels, he'd find a skeleton. Twenties Nick, with a supply of prewar gin and something going with Philly's wife while his own wife sickened and died and while a plausible but sinister young expatriate bought up the resorts where he had come for a pleasant summer of gambling and lovemaking. Twenties Nick, who had stayed on until it was too late and now was never going to leave . . . Crooning "Sweet Sue" in the tunnel that had allowed him and his mistress to be in two places at once.

Collins had killed them off, the ones that couldn't be scared away. Then he had taken the old resort and perfected himself, toying with Del Nightingale in the summers when he thought that Del might be his successor: later, just sharpening his skills, waiting for the successor to come, fending off anyone who tried to invite himself, knowing that in time the only person in the world who meant danger to him would appear.

And when his extorted money had run out, he had killed Del's parents. Brought their plane out of the air and claimed his share of the inheritance and bided his time, keeping his ears open—knowing that sooner or later he would hear about some young fellow who still didn't know what he was.

Waft myself some more of that good stuff, sport.

Plenty of wafting went on over the years. Here's to you, Nick.

And to you, Sweet Sue.

He heard it as though someone had spoken from the very mouth of the tunnel nearest him. Tom turned over inside his blanket—or was this too a dream?—and felt a chill breeze advancing toward him.

The devil, M., emerged wrapped in the breeze from the mouth of the tunnel. He shone palely, as if lit by moonlight. M. was no longer dressed in the uniform of a private-school teacher, but in a blazer and high stiff collar. Above the collar his face still radiated sympathy and intense but misdirected intelligence. He knelt down before Tom.

"So you took the low road after all, and here you are."

"Leave me alone," Tom said.

"Now, now. I'm offering you a second chance. You don't want to end up like our friend back there, do you? Salted away like a herring? That's not for you."

"No," Tom said. "It's not."

"But, dear child, can't you see that this is hopeless? I'm giving you your last chance. Stand up and get out. Leave them—they're of no use to you. Take my hand. I'll put you back in your room." He held out his hand, which was black and smoking. "Oh, there'll be a little pain. Nothing you won't get over. At least you'll save your life."

Tom shuddered back from the awful hand.

"Reconsider. I promise you, that creature you think you've in love with is going to sell you out. Take my hand. I know it's not very pretty, but you have to take it." White curls of smoke hovered over the extended hand. "Mr. Collins has explained it all to you. She's not your way out, boy."

Tom saw the inevitability of it: a final betrayal, like Rosa Forte's. "Even so . . ." he said.

M. retracted his hand, which was now pink and smooth. "I wonder where you will end up. Down here? In the lake? Nailed to a tree to be eaten by birds? I'll come back and remind you that I tried to help."

"Do that," Tom said: *I told you so* must have been one of the devil's favorite sentences.

M. sneered and flickered away.

"Not like that," Tom said to himself.

4

"What time is it *now?*" Del asked several hours later.

The flashlight flared out light: illuminated Rose's wrist and bare arm. "Twenty minutes later than the last time you asked. Six-fifty-one. Is everybody awake?"

"Yeah," Tom said, jolted out of deep sleep. Rose played the light around the vaulted chamber, shining it in his face, then in Del's. Finally she turned it on herself. She was sitting against the wall, and unlike Del and himself, did not look disheveled. Her hair was in place; Tom saw with astonishment that she was even wearing lipstick. "There's still coffee in the thermos, and I've got some hardboiled eggs. We can have breakfast before we start."

"I have to pee," Del said, sounding embarrassed. "So do I," Tom said.

In pitch darkness they stumbled into the first tunnel and splashed the walls; came back guided by the light to eat the hardboiled eggs.

"Now, which tunnel do we take?" Del asked.

"That one." Rose stabbed the light toward a gaping hole in the curving wall. She walked to the entrance of the tunnel and played the light on a white chalk line. "I made this when I brought everything down. This is the one."

"Didn't you say the one next to me?" Tom said.

"This was the one next to you," Rose said. "You got mixed up walking back here. This is the one I marked."

"How far does it go?" Del asked.

"Long way," Rose said. "We'll have to be in it about half an hour."

"You're sure this is the right one?" Tom asked.

"I marked it. I'm sure."

. . . sell you out. Just an unhappy dream: but had it not been from this tunnel that he had heard the lost and captured voices spinning through their eternal and terrible summer? "Shine the light on your face," Tom said. "Humor me."

Rose lifted the flash and pointed at her face. She squinted in the glare, but her hand was steady. *That creature you think you love.* She was the girl in the window; she was the girl in the red cape carrying a basket down the wooded path. He wrapped his fingers around the broken figure in his pocket.

Farewell, Nick.

Come back anytime, Sweet Sue.

In the lake? Nailed to a tree to be eaten by birds?

"Let's get started," Tom said.

5

The light bobbed before them, touching timber after timber. Their feet hushed on the dirt. An unrecognized image, almost a sense of *déjà vu,* troubled Tom. But it was not *déjà vu,* because he knew he had never been in this place before. Still, the sense of a parallel experience hung in his mind—something that had led to . . . what? A taste of unpleasantness, a hint of wrongness, of things being not what they seemed.

"What did you think you heard back there?" Del asked quietly.

"I guess I was just nervous."

"So was I," Del confessed.

Down they went, feeling as much as seeing their way. The air in the tunnel grew damper and colder. Rose's flashlight picked out beads of moisture on the wall.

"Did you really come here this summer to . . . you know. Protect me?" Del could ask this because of the darkness which hid his face.

"I guess I did." Tom's voice, like Del's, went out into pure blackness.

"But how did you know I'd need it?" Del's piping voice seemed to hang in the air, surrounded by charged space. How could he answer it? *Well, I had this vision about a wizard and an evil man, and then later I saw that the evil man had overtaken the wizard. Bad things were coming for you, and I had to put myself in their way.* It was the truth, but it could not be spoken: he could not send out his own voice into the waiting blackness if it were going to say those things.

"I guess it was that 'towers-of-ice' night—remember?"

"When I didn't know if you were taking Uncle Cole away from me or not," Del said.

"God."

Del actually giggled.

Then he had it, the memory: Registration Day: walking down the headmaster's stairs after filling out forms in the library, following Mrs. Olinger's flashlight and fat Bambi Whipple's candle. Going toward their first sight of Laker Broome.

For a long time they walked in silence as well as darkness, going always down, down, as if the tunnel led to the center of the earth instead of Hilly Vale.

6

A long time later, Tom felt the ground changing. The drag forward which had tired his legs had become a drag backward. They were going uphill now: muscles on the tops of his thighs twanged like rubber bands.

"Was that halfway?" Del asked.

"More," Rose said. "Pretty soon we get out."

Thank God, Tom said silently: the constant darkness had begun to prey on him.

A face sewn together like Thorn's, a jigsaw of flesh and scars, floated up through the air and winked.

"Something wrong?" Del asked.

"Tired."

"I felt you jump."

"You're imagining things."

"Maybe *you* are," Del said slyly.

"Remember when you said you heard something?" Rose asked.

"Sure."

"Well, now I think I do. Stop talking and listen."

That surge of fear again: unavoidable. The flashlight clicked off, and for a moment its afterimage burned in Tom's eyes.

"I don't . . ." Del began. He stopped: he, and Tom beside him, had heard it too—a complicated, rushing, pounding noise.

"Oh, God," Del breathed. "They're *after* us."

"Hurry, hurry, hurry," Rose pleaded. The light went on, blindingly bright, and searched past them. The long tunnel snaked down and away, empty behind them as far as they could see. "Please."

Carrying the light, Rose started to run. Tom heard the pack behind them—it could have been two men, or four, or five, and they sounded a good way off—and then he too ran after Del and Rose. He heard Del sobbing in panic, making a trapped witless noise in his chest and throat. The flashlight bobbed crazily ahead.

"They knew where to look," he shouted.

"Just run!" Rose shouted back.

He ran. His shoulders knocked painfully against a wooden support. He almost fell, pain shooting all the way down his arm; scraped his hand against a rock protruding from the wall and righted himself.

As soon as he got back into his stride he ran straight into Del. Del was still making a sound of utter panic.

"Get up and run," Tom said. "Here—here's my hand." Del caught at him and pulled himself up. Rose was twenty feet away, jerking the flashlight impatiently, shining it in their eyes.

Del sprinted away like a rabbit.

"Gotcha!" a man yelled from far back in the tunnel.

Dogs and badgers; the bloody greasy pit. Had Collins known even then that they would end like this? Tom pushed himself forward.

"Gotcha!"

"The stairs!" Del screamed. "I found the stairs!"

A huge bubble of relief broke in Tom's chest. They could still escape; there was still a chance. He pounded on, panting harshly. Over all the other noises he could hear Del scrambling up the steps to the outside.

"Tom." Rose touched his arm and stopped him.

"We can make it," he panted. "They're far enough back—we can do it."

"I love you," she said. "Remember that." Her arms caught his chest and her mouth covered his. Sudden light flooded into the tunnel.

"Rose," he pleaded, and stepped toward the light, half-carrying her. Her face was wild. He twisted her around to see the steps, the open door.

Something wrong. Some detail . . . His heart boomed. A huge roulette wheel, so dusty that red and black were both gray, tilted against the side of the steps. Del's legs abruptly soared up and out of the opening as he was grabbed from above.

In the next instant, Del screamed.

"What. . . ?" He still could not believe what was happening. Del screamed again. "Rose. . . ?" She was out of his arms and walking toward the broad concrete stairs. "You'd better come," she said. "It has to be like this."

He was numb; he watched her mount the first of the steps and turn to face him. Straight in her green dress and high heels, walking away from him; her job done.

Don't hate me.

"You brought us back," he said. His lips and fingers had lost all feeling. "What are you?"

"It has to be like this, Tom," Rose said. "I can't say any more now."

Del's screams had broken down into ragged animallike groans. Tom turned his head to look back down the tunnel. Root and Thorn, not running, came dimly into sight. They paused at the very edge of the penumbra of brightness from the open trapdoor, waited for him to act. He looked back at Rose, who also waited, her face expressionless. Thorn and Root were a wall of crossed arms and spread legs. Rose mounted another step, and he went toward her.

Coleman Collins gaily sang, "Come out, come out, wherever you are," and before Tom got to the steps, a sudden fearful clarity visited him and he thought to tug his shirt out of his trousers, hiding the gun.

As soon as he reached the steps, he looked up and recognized the ending of the tunnel: it was the forbidden room. Then he knew how the "Brothers Grimm" had come and gone.

"So the birds have come home once again," Collins said.

7

Tom came up into the crowded room. Rose was standing next to Coleman Collins, and the magician was gazing at him with a gleeful, deranged impishness, gently massaging his upper lip with an index finger. The other four Wandering Boys stood off to one side, dogs on the leash. "Dear me, what a face," Collins said. "Can't have that sort of thing, not for our stirring finish—not for the farewell performance. Tears, perhaps, but never scowls."

Just behind Collins, Mr. Peet was gripping Del by the bicep, squeezing hard enough to hurt. Del's face was gray and rubbery with shock. Mr. Peet, dressed in the old-fashioned clothes from the train, grinned maliciously and shook Del—jerked him like a doll.

"Why does it have to be like this, Rose?" Tom asked. She looked back at him as from a great distance. Collins smiled, stopped caressing his lip, and took the girl's hand. *"Why does it have to be like this?"*

Del began to weep from terror.

"I'll answer, if you don't mind," Collins said. He was still smiling. "It has to be like this because you are unfit to be my successor. As you have just proven. I am afraid that the world will just have to wait for another gifted child to appear—there's no hope left for you, Tom. You have just been sent back to the ranks. Spectator-participant. Good, here are the others."

First Root, then Thorn, emerged from the trapdoor. Thorn was breathing hard: the run had tired him. Their shoulders nearly filled the opening.

"I could have been your salvation," Collins mused. "And how I tried. But even the best potter cannot work with inferior clay." He shrugged, but his eyes were still dancing. "Now, let us check our schedules." He raised both his hand and Rose's and looked at his watch. "We have several hours before the final act." He bent down and brushed Rose's hand with his lips. When he gently let go of Rose's hand he turned to the lounging men. "Thorn, Pease, and Snail. You'll bring this boy along to the big theater. Rose, darling, I want you to wait in my bedroom. You others, take my nephew outside and play with him for a couple of hours. If he whimpers, punish him. He is of no use anymore."

She was his girlfriend, Tom thought. His mistress. Betrayal upon betrayal sank into him like lead. Two of the trolls roughly grabbed his arms. He looked into Rose's eyes.

Don't hate me.

"Get along, Rose," the magician said. But she hung by his side for a moment, answering Tom's gaze. *Don't hate me for what I had to do.* "I said go." Rose turned and walked away. Collins' mad eyes snagged and held him.

"Do you understand?" the magician said. "I had to see if you'd really try to leave. You don't deserve your talent—but that is academic now, for you won't have it much longer. When it came down to it, you chose your wings."

"You killed all those people," Tom said. "You killed Nick. And Philly's wife. All those people from the summer cabin."

"And Nick's wife, for that matter," Collins said.

"You killed Del's parents too," Tom said. "For your share of their money." He saw Del reel back, be brought sharply upright by Mr. Peet.

"I thought I'd get Del's share too, you know." Collins smiled. "At one time I thought he might be my successor. It would have been better if he had been. I could control my nephew. But there you were, shining away like the biggest diamond in the golden west."

As Del began to wail, Tom again caught the resemblance to Laker Broome. Collins was smiling, pretending calm, but his nerves were on fire—he was burning with anger and crazy glee. "Stay behind, Mr. Peet. You others, take that squalling boy outside. I don't care what you do with him."

Root, Seed, and Rock moved toward Del. Seed was grinning like a bear. He clamped his paw on Del's elbow and tore him away from Mr. Peet. "You needn't worry about bringing him back," Collins said. Seed began hauling Del toward the door, Root and Pease crowding after. "Mr. Peet, I want you to open the wall between the two theaters. We'll want all the space we can get."

Mr. Peet nodded and followed the others through the door.

Now only the three trolls—Thorn, Pease, and Snail—the magician and the boy were left in the room. The trolls too wore the four-button suits and Norfolk jackets from the train, and looked balloonlike, stuffed into the hot tight clothes. Thorn's sewn-together face was dripping. The three moved in closer to Tom.

"What are they going to do to Del?"

"Oh, it won't be as interesting as what happens to you," the magician said. "You're going to be crucified."

"Is that what you did to Speckle John?"

"Why, no. I gave him a lifelong punishment, didn't I tell you that? I made him a servant. He was a son of Hagar, after all, or is that too biblical for you?"

"I know what it means."

The magician smiled and glanced at the sweating trolls. "Take him now."

Snail put hands the size of footballs on Tom's shoulders. With those hands he could have broken both of Tom's arms; and Tom felt an intention like this in the man's touch, which was more than brutal. It was utterly without human feeling. They were going to hurt him, and they would enjoy it, the more so because he had humiliated them earlier. Snail lifted him off the ground, gripping hard enough to bruise, and carried him out of the room. The other two laughed—hoarse braying barnyard laughter.

She never told him about the gun, he realized. *She knew but she didn't tell him.* It kept him from passing out.

8

Snail's fingers were steel bars thrust into his muscles. As the man carried him like a weightless doll down the corridor to the theaters, he bent his head forward and whispered into Tom's ear. "My daddy used to whup me— my daddy used to near take the skin off my back—oh, how my daddy whupped me—" he made a coarse oily noise Tom realized a second later was a chuckle. Then he put his lips on Tom's ear. "—and I didn't have skin near as white as yours." He bellowed with laughter.

Tom kicked backward and hit Snail's legs with his heels. The troll responded by shaking him hard enough to break his neck.

"Play pretty, now," Snail said, setting him down outside the door to the little theater. The brass plaque still read:

Wood Green Empire
27 August, 1924

Collins opened the door and Snail hauled Tom in.

One whole wall was gone. The two theaters were joined into a single massive space. Mr. Peet was up at the back of the pitched seats, looking at his picture in the mural.

"Hey, this is pretty good," he called down to Collins. "That guy looks just like me." He sounded almost childishly, egotistically pleased.

"Are you an idiot?" Collins barked. "Get away from there."

Mr. Peet looked surly and insulted, then lounged down the bank of steps.

"Take him up to the back," Collins said. "Once we get started, I want him to be able to see. And turn the lights off."

"Hey, you're not really—?" Tom began, but Snail slapped him, stinging a whole side of his face. "Used to whup me real good," he said, grinning. "Damn near *ventilated* me." Like Seed, he too was missing some teeth. He jerked Tom across the smaller stage and into the larger space. The overhead spots died, and only faint amber light from the stage showed Tom the rows of empty seats. Snail pulled him forward and up.

"What's going to happen to me?" Tom asked.

"I just work here," Snail said. "But what do you think Root's doing to your buddy?" Tom hesitated, and Snail said, "Don't try any of that crazy stuff. You do, and I pull your legs off."

That crazy stuff—Snail meant levitating. But that area in him was lost anyhow. He was too frightened to find that key. They reached the last row of seats. *Crucified?* He remembered the dream from long ago, the vulture hopping forward and rending his hands with its yellow beak.

A wooden frame in the shape of a large X had been screwed to the wall. It had a temporary, provisional look, the look of something thrown up in a hurry, easily dismantled after it had been used. From the center of the X hung a leather cinch. On the carpet beneath · lay two long nails and a wooden mallet.

"He can't really do that," Tom said.

"As long as he don't do it to me, he can," Snail said.

"Stop talking and pick him up," Collins ordered. "He'll fight, so get a good grip."

Tom jumped sideways and tried to run back down the stairs, but Thorn put an arm around his chest and yanked him backwards. He kicked, and Thorn hit him on the top of his head with his knuckles.

"Get a grip on him, I said." Collins bent over to pick up the nails. When he touched them, they shimmered on the carpet, and when they were in his hands, they glowed a pale silver, as if lit from within.

Pease grabbed a leg with each doughy hand. Snail took

his wrists, and he could not move: Tom strained against their touch, but Thorn increased the pressure on his chest and drove all the breath out of him. Mr. Peet wandered off and sat down on the aisle seat, where he twisted around to watch. Thorn's sour breath washed directly over Tom's face.

"Observe the nails," Collins said. Now he held the mallet in his right hand. The long nails had turned a molten golden-red, and seemed to pulse in the magician's hand.

"Good trick," said Thorn.

"You stink," Tom said, and Thorn rapped him on the head again; a sharp jarring pain. With only half his strength, Thorn could break his skull.

"This boy is a magician. We need something extra to hold him." Collins held the nails in front of Tom's eyes. "Understand? You'll never coax these out of the boards. I think you'll be content to wait for the performance." He turned to Pease and Snail. "Hoist him up."

The three trolls carried Tom to the frame, Thorn walking backward. "Keep a hold on those arms," Thorn said, and freed his arms so that he could grip Tom's waist with both hands. "Come along with me—I'll belt him in." He lifted Tom, and pinned him with one hand stuck hard into his belly while he worked the cinch. Tom wriggled, but Thorn's hand pushed his stomach against his spine.

The belt closed around his belly. The men sprang away. He was firmly held and four feet above the ground. The clasp bit at his skin; the old pistol chewed the small of his back.

Collins held the nails up again. They shone out bands of color, like prisms. "All right. We will proceed. Thorn, kneel down and hold his feet against the wall." Thorn bent down and rammed Tom's heels against the green.

"Snail, you hold the right arm. Pease, you take the left. Palm out against the brace."

They seized his arms and pulled them out, stretching them until his elbows threatened to turn inside out. Tom howled, "You can't! You *can't!*"

"That is your opinion," Collins said, and approached, one shining nail between thumb and forefinger, the mallet already lifted in his right hand.

"NOOO!" Tom bellowed. Pease flattened his fingers back, exposing the palm.

"The pain won't be as bad as you anticipate," Collins said, and pressed the point of the first nail into Tom's left palm.

Tom clamped his eyes shut and fought against everything—the men holding him spread-eagled, the buckle sawing at his skin.

Collins hammered the mallet against the head of the nail. There was a grunt immediately before the impact: and then incredible pain, as if not just the nail but the mallet itself had thrust itself through his palm. He screamed, and heard the scream in a disembodied, hallucinatory way: it was as visible as a flag.

"You ain't paying us enough," he heard Pease say.

"Now you, Snail. Get those fingers back."

Tom's right fingers uncurled by themselves. My *hands*, he thought. *Will I ever. . . ?*

The pinprick of the nail's point: the muffled grunt of effort of concentration; the rape of his right hand.

My hands! They seemed the size of his whole body, and burning. He saw his own screams rippling away from him.

"Not too much blood," Collins said with satisfaction.

Tom went out of his body and floated among the bright screams.

9

Sometime later the pain in his enormous hands brought him back. Sweat dripped down his nose, itching like a dozen ants. His throat had been sand-blasted. His muscles screeched; his ears pounded. At intervals a loud *crump!* from the outside rattled the frame on which he was suspended, and he deliriously thought that bombs were falling, that Shadowland was being shelled, and then realized that the explosions were fireworks. One after the other, single explosions, double and triple explosions, like wordless sentences commanding and insisting and insisting again.

Ka-bang! Ka-bang whamp!

He was afraid to look at his hands. The three trolls lay across the seats in the last row, now and then looking at him without curiosity, as if he were a picture they found wanting. One of the nails kept a bone from being where it wanted to be, and the pressure, which faded in and out, made all the other pains increase. He tried to push his hands flatter against the wood, and for as long as he could hold them there—not a long time—the agony lessened.

When his hands sagged, the fire returned. Pease and Snail glanced up at him with real interest. "Sings good," Pease said, and Thorn snickered.

"The kid's right," Pease said. "You do stink."

"Kiss my ass," Thorn said.

Tom risked a peek at his left hand, and was relieved that he could see no farther than its heel. A little drying blood crusted the strap of his watch.

You're a magician, aren't you?

I never wanted to be.

But you are?

Yes.

Then use your mind to pull out the nails.

I can't.

That's what you thought when he told you to raise the dog. Just try.

He tried. He saw the nails slipping out of the wood, gently easing from his hands, sliding out easy and slow . . .

and it felt like wires had been suddenly thrust into the wounds; he could *see* the nails glowing, turning gold and blue and green . . . he uttered a high floating falsetto wail, and saw that too, a thin rag ascending to the ceiling.

"Kid sounds like a female alcoholic," Pease said.

See the odd things you learn? If you hadn't tried that, you'd never have known that Pease is the trolls' wit.

"We ain't gettin paid enough for this," Pease said, as he had before. "Badgers is one thing, this is something else."

"You tell me how," Thorn growled.

"Blow your mouth some other way when you talk at me."

Tom sagged against the cinch.

When he looked up, M. was sitting beneath him, his knees drawn up, his back resting on Thorn's seat. He was

back in the prep-school costume. "Did I call it, or did
call it? Give me a little credit."

Tom closed his eyes.

"I can't save you from this, obviously, but I can sav
you from the rest," M. said. "Open your eyes. Aren't yo
at least prepared to admit that you've been had?"

"Leave me alone," Tom said.

"It talks!" Pease roared.

"I can still do you a lot of good," M. went on calml
"Those nails, now—I could slip those out for yo
Wouldn't you like that?"

"Why?" Tom asked.

"He wants to know why," Pease said.

"Because I'd hate to see you wasted. Simple as tha
Your mentor has done us a fair amount of good over th
years, but you—you'd be extraordinary. Should I t
those nails? It's a simple matter, I assure you."

"Go away," Tom sobbed. "Get out of here. I turn m
face away from you. I *revile* you. I can't stand the *smell*
you—you *are* these nails." His voice broke down. Swe
burst from every pore of his body. He was freezing
death. M. disappeared, still smiling up.

"Kid gets on my fuckin' nerves," Thorn said.

"Give him a break," Pease said, "he's in a tough spc
Ain't you, kid? Let's go farther down."

"What the hell, he's crazy," Snail said. "He's out of h
gourd." He stood up. The three of them loafed down th
stairs to the first row. Tom closed his eyes and let his he
loll back against the wall.

"Look, we can even go outside, hey?" he heard Tho
say. "Who's to say we can't?"

Tom passed out again.

When he came around again, he thought it was night. I
was alone in the vast dark theater. A plum-colored glc
emanated from the curtains. He was soaked in sweat,
was ice-cold, and his hands were soaring and sobbing. T
bone fought the pressure of the nail, lost, and bounced
his hand. Hundreds of nerves sang.

"Tom," came a velvety voice he knew.

"No more," Tom said, and rolled his head back to lo

own the aisle in the direction of the voice. Bud Copeland
as standing like a deeper shadow in the dark aisle.
That's not really you," he said.

"No, not really. I can't really do anything but talk to
ou."

"I guess you're Speckle John," Tom said. "I should
ave known."

"I used to be Speckle John. But he took my magic
way. He thought that was worse than death." Bud drew
earer. Tom realized that he could see through him, see
ie line of seat backs and the dark wall at the end of the
isle through Bud's snowy shirt and gray suit. "But I had
nough left to hear Del when the little boy was born. Just
ke I had enough to know you when I saw you for the first
me. And to hear you now."

"Am I going to die?" Tom said; wept a few stinging
ears.

"If you don't get down," Bud's shade told him. "But
ou're *strong*, boy. You don't know yet how strong you
re. That's why they make all this fuss about you, you
now. You're strong as an elephant—strong enough to
etch me here. Only wish I could do more than talk." Bud
iifted uncomfortably, and his transparency grew cloudy.
He did the Wandering Boys just like he did you—in the
ellars of the Wood Green Empire. Mr. Peet and all . . .
ll those stupid men who thought they'd get a free ride for
fe off him. Oh, he gave a show: he gave a real show,
oy. He's still proud of it. Made a scandal big enough to
rive him out of Europe."

"What did he do to Rose?"

"Rosa? Don't bother with that, boy. Just get yourself
ff that brace. Outside, they're fooling with Del. They're
able to kill him if you don't get down."

"I *can't*," Tom wailed.

"You got to."

Tom screamed.

"That's not the way. There's only *one* way, boy. You
ot to use that strength. You got to pull your hands off.
hat's the way it works."

"*Nooo!*" Tom screamed.

"You do it with one hand, the other one will come

easier. You got to choose your song—you got to choo
your skills. You already tried wings, and that didn't wor
You can't run from him."

Tom leaned his head back against the wall and look
at Bud through red eyes; asked a silent question.

"*I* tried song, Tom. But he was stronger than me. Aft
that the most I could do was try to keep Del safe fro
him. I knew he wanted that boy—until he heard abo
you, he wanted him anyhow. Now it's your turn. And yo
have to do more than save Del. You know what you ha
to do."

"Kill him," Tom said weakly.

"Unless you want him to kill you. Do what I say, no
Push your left hand forward. Just keep on pushing. I
going to hurt like blazes, but . . . shit, son, doesn't it hu
already? When you get that one free, push with your ri
hand. Those nails can't stop that. They can only stop yo
doing it the easy way."

"Just push."

"Push with all you got, son. If you don't, worse th
that is going to happen to you. And there won't
enough of Del left to worry about. Hear that? You he
him?"

Then Tom did hear Del: heard a piping, anguish
eeee, like a sound he had made himself not long before

He concentrated on his left hand; and pushed.
hundred mallets hit a hundred nails, and he nearly faint
again.

You're strong.

He pushed as hard as he could, and his hand flew free
the nail in a spray of blood.

"Sweet Jesus, son, you did it! Now, push the other o
. . . please God, boy, push that other one . . . push t
hell out of it . . . don't even think about it, just slam it o
of there."

Tom filled his chest with air, unable to think about t
agony in his left hand, opened his mouth with the fu
force of his lungs, arched his back as the yell began, a
jerked his right hand forward.

It flew. Blood spurted out over the row of seats befo
him.

. . . now you know why I took that job, boy . . . Bud's
voice faded; the rest of him was already gone.

Sobbing, Tom slumped over the cinch. The buckle: the
buckle worked on a catch. It was trying to saw him in half.
And for my next trick, ladies and gentlemen . . . He
raised his left hand and pushed the base of the thumb
against the catch. Blood smeared on his shirt, soaked
through to his belly. *My next trick is the never-before-
attempted the Falling Boy.* He urged the base of his
thumb around the catch. His hand pounded, but his
thumb rested against the catch. He shoved, blood gouted
from his hand, and he tumbled out of the strap and fell
like a sack to the carpet.

10

Del. That was where he had to go. Del was outside, being
killed by the trolls. Tom crawled toward the steps, using
elbows and knees, ignoring the blood streaking down his
arms. Could he flex his fingers? When he reached the top
of the stairs, he tried the left hand, and the pain made his
eyes mist, but the fingers twitched. How about you, right
hand? Mr. Thorpe: chapel on a sunny morning: raising his
right hand: *boys, that brave young man took out his
pocketknife and carved a cross in the palm of his right
hand!* Bet he did too, the jerk. Tom clenched his teeth
and made his fingers move.

And for my next trick . . . the Amazing Falling Boy will
now attempt to go down a flight of stairs.

Tom crawled to the edge of the steps. Facefirst? He saw
himself falling, knocking his head against the metal sides
of seats, rolling on his hands . . . he turned over, sat up,
put his legs over the edge and went down like a one-year-
old, on the seat of his pants.

Now do something really difficult, Tom, old boy. Walk.
His feet were on the floor, his bottom on the second step.
Well, don't rush into it—stand up first, do it the easy way.
He flailed out with his dripping arms, his back knotted
and ached, and he was on his feet. Immediately his head

went fuzzy, and he leaned his shoulder against the wall for
support. Funny how much pain your body can hold—it
can be just like a bucket filled up with pain. You'd think
you'd spill some of it along the way, but the bucket just
gets bigger.

*Come outside now, boys, we are going to witness a
miracle.* Skeleton hiding at the back of the stage, waiting
for the piano player to leave so he could check his stolen
exams, take a look at the Ventnor owl and see if it had
anything special to say to him today. . . . *It just broke,
Mr. Robbin. Yassuh, just up and broke on us.*

Gee, you monkeys are clumsy.

*That's us, sir, clumsy all over today, all we can do just to
stand up . . .*

He made himself go forward, pushing the door open
with his shoulder. Yeah, the old bucket just keeps on
getting bigger. Tom staggered out into the darkened
corridor, knocked into the opposite wall with his shoulder, and paused to rest.

This is not an easy school. Not! Not an easy school!

You had to admit they weren't liars.

He leaned forward, and his feet followed him down the
corridor. As long as he rested his right shoulder on the
wall, he could keep moving and stay upright. Blood
dripped steadily down his fingers and onto the brown
carpet. Past the forbidden room, past the kitchen.

He heard Del screaming again—repeated, hopeless
screams, the screams of someone who knows he is lost.

Tom wobbled into the living room. He mentally
charted his path to the glass doors. Chair to table to
couch, then a long unsupported walk.

No princes and no ravens. Del's despairing, injured
cries floating upward. Tom put his left hand delicately on
the back of a chair and hobbled forward: two steps to the
coffee table.

Bud Copeland was sitting on the couch, and Tom could
see the delicate green-and-blue pattern through his suit.
"You made it this far, Tom, you're going to make it all
the way. Remember there's a safety catch on the gun,
you'll hang yourself if you forget that."

"No repeat performances," Tom said.

"That's the way, son."

By instinct, Tom turned his head to look at the glass-fronted cabinet in the corner. His stomach flipped over. Blood splashed and spattered on the inside of the glass—spattered again, obscuring the entire shelf behind a screen of red.

Ka-whamp! went the fireworks outside. *Whamp!*

The prelude to the performance.

"You gonna make it all the way," Bud said.

Tom listed over to the left, put a bloody palm print on the coffee table, sucked in air because of the pain, and reeled toward the glass doors, still bent over and unable to straighten up.

He crawled up the glass of the sliding doors.

Whamp!

Through the mist of blood his hands left on the doors he saw the sky: an orange flower drooping and dying, going blue at its edges . . . *Whamp!* A red column grew through its center and spread throughout the gray air.

Soon it would be night.

Ka-whamp! Whamp! Whamp! Beside the spreading column of red, an owl made of white light was drifting down, its wings wide and awesome, burning down out of the darkening sky.

"Get that door open—you *got* to," came Bud's voice.

Tom pushed his slippery hands along the glass. Del shrieked somewhere off to his left, and Tom used his forearms to move the glass sideways.

The aluminum riser caught his foot, and he fell forward onto the flagstones. Shock vibrated up to his shoulders from his elbows; his hands flamed. He groaned. Rolled onto his back and swung his legs out. His heart almost stopped in terror. The fireworks owl, silvery light in the gray sky, dropped toward him with its claws out, sailing down to get him.

Tom closed his eyes. *All right. I can't beat that. Carry me away, do what you want. Just get it over with.*

Another explosion took place above him. He looked up and saw that the owl was dying, turning to cinders and shredding apart, becoming something meaningless. Tom got to his feet.

Then went back to his knees again, because he had a glimpse of them, just around the side of the house. The

Wandering Boys were on the sloping lawn about thirty yards away, just before the start of the woods and the bluff. He had seen Snail and Root, who were looking upward for a moment, watching the last seconds of the owl before they went back to their work.

Del whimpered.

All right, get the gun out. You think you're a hotshot? Then get the gun out of your pants. He went prone on the flagstones, face down, and tried to reach behind his back. The index finger of his right hand brushed the lump of metal under his shirt; the same miraculous finger twitched up the tail of his shirt.

Little more, there, Buck Rogers.

Another twitch. Now the grip of the pistol was exposed. He forced his hand back and touched what he thought was the trigger guard. Sweating again, he hooked the index finger around it and tugged.

Whamp! Spreading brightness about him, but with his face pressed into the rough flagstones, he could not see what figure the fireworks were making. He tugged again at the trigger guard, and his hand yelled at him.

He heard the sweetest sound, the pistol clunking on the stone, then heard himself sob with relief.

Tom twisted on his side and scooped the pistol toward him with both hands. The grip and trigger guard were bright red. *Safety*. He did not know what it looked like, and turned the gun over in his fingers, looking for anything that might be the catch. Finally he saw a little knurled button, pushed it forward.

Walking on his knees, he came around the side of the house and off the flagstones and onto lush grass. The six men stood in a circle at what seemed an impossible distance away. Root and Snail were joking—he saw Snail's mouth open in a gap-toothed grin. Thorn was wiping his broken face on his sleeve. Seed, whose shirt was bubbling out between his pants and vest, was prodding something with his foot.

Del squeaked, nearly invisible in their midst.

Tom flattened out in the grass and tried to take aim. But it was no good. The pistol trembled in his fingers. If he were to shoot, the bullet would go off into the woods; into the lake; dig itself into the ground.

"Stop it," he said. But his voice was only a whisper. The gun fell out of his hands. He hooked his index finger through the trigger guard again and crawled forward several yards. It seemed he was going with unreal, impossible slowness. A cricket sang. The saw teeth on the side of a blade of grass jumped into focus directly before him. He inched forward.

"See what you can do to his ribs," Snail said. "Ten bucks you can get him that way."

"Stop it," Tom said. He sat up on the grass. "Stop. I said stop." Seed, who was facing him, looked up in puzzlement. Tom fumbled for the pistol and pointed it vaguely at the men. He saw Snail grinning at him, Thorn rubbing his chest. He wondered if the old pistol would actually work.

Here goes nothing. Trying to hold the gun level, he pulled the trigger.

At first he thought his whole arm had been blown off. The sound was much louder than he had anticipated, deafening him for a moment. The pistol had dropped from his fingers again. Both of his hands were balloon size.

The trolls were looking at him with great concentration, moving out of their cluster.

An explosion turned the sky pale green.

Tom picked up the gun, twisted it so that it faced the men again. Snail was coming toward him, a small worry line carved between his eyebrows.

"Hey," Thorn yelled. "Watch yourself."

"He's got holes in his hands, he can't do nothin'," Snail said. Still there was the look of almost delicate worry on his face.

Tom swung the gun to the center of his chest and held the grip with the fingers of his right hand while he prodded the trigger with the index of his left. Again the recoil tore the gun from his hand. His ears rang.

A spot of redness appeared in Snail's chest. It looked like a boutonniere. Snail's feet flew out from under him.

Tom picked up the gun again and stood. He was crying, not entirely from pain, but despite his fears and the agony of his hands and arms, he felt a great nervous concentration.

Ka-whamp! All the air turned yellow. He saw Del curled up on the grass. He awkwardly lifted the pistol and aimed it at Pease.

Pease broke away, running for the iron ladder to the beach.

Tom swung the gun back and shot at random into the men. This time he managed to keep the gun in his hands. Thorn jerked backward and fell down heavily. A bubbling sound came from his throat.

Del rolled over on his side and stared at Tom with dull eyes. Redness covered his face.

The others were already tearing into the woods, going for good, Tom knew. They were just employees. They weren't paid enough to be shot at. He swayed sideways and watched Pease reach the top of the ladder. He remembered the man bending back his fingers so that Collins could drive in the nail. He dropped the gun, and it fired and jumped when it hit, zinging a bullet harmlessly into dark air. He remembered Pease twisting in his seat, looking at him as if he were an inferior painting.

Ladder, he thought. *Bolts. Loose bolts.* He saw them: saw the rusty threads, the iron going into the clips. He began to trudge toward the ladder. He could hear Pease banging his way down. Two rungs, three, four . . .

A ground-shaking explosion. A red orchid bloomed in the sky.

He let his hatred of Pease bloom. *Out. Out.* In his mind the bolts were beginning to stir, crushing their threads, rattling free . . . he saw them flying out of the clips, tumbling down the bluff.

Pease screamed. In the silence between fireworks, a sudden popping noise of shattered metal stood out as sharply as a color. Tom made his legs go faster and reached the edge of the bluff in time to see Pease sailing far out and down, still clinging to the iron ladder. He seemed to fall dreamily for whole minutes, still trying to climb down the rungs. In time his feet fell out beneath him; then his hands let go, and he and the ladder were tipping back in tandem. There was a noise of splintering wood when Pease hit the pier. A hole instantly opened up in the wood. A second later the ladder sliced it in half.

Pieces of the pier flew upward. Then water gouted up.

Now there was only one way out.

11

He trudged back to Del and half-fell, half-sat on the grass beside him. Del was wiping the blood away from his face with his sleeve. They had hit him in the face before deciding to kick him to death.

"How do you feel?" he asked.

Del's eyes swam up. The lids fluttered.

"Did they break anything?"

"I hurt all over." Red froth appeared on Del's lips. He looked dully at Thorn's body; at Snail's, facedown, closer to the house. Thorn was muttering something.

"What did they do to you?" Del said. "Did they beat you up too?"

"Sort of," Tom said.

The sky shook: after the thunder, an ice-blue fountain shimmered in the air.

"They're coming back!" Del shrieked.

"No," Tom said. "We're through with them."

"Oh." Del closed his eyes and put his head down on the grass.

"Can you move?"

"I want to go home."

"Who doesn't?"

The lights in the forest flicked on; the house blazed. Tom could see the red smears on the window wall. Then he heard a car starting, heard the tires whisper on the drive. Could Collins have given up so easily?

Thorn's breath rattled and chugged in his throat. Tom turned to him in horror. "Ah," Thorn said, and died. No white bird lifted from his chest, but Tom knew that he had seen his life go.

"Car . . ." Del said. "He left, Tom. He *left!* We can go—we can get out."

"I don't think so. You see all those lights? The show changed theaters, that's all."

"Oh, my God," Del said. He was looking at Tom's hands. "How did you. . . ?"

"I was lucky," Tom said. He looked up at the house. "He's still there, Del. I think we really just started."

"But *we* can't fight him." Del shrank back into himself.

"We'll do whatever we have to." It was not a strong statement, and Tom did not feel strong—he felt emptied of his resources, capable of doing nothing more than lying on the lawn and waiting in despair for Collins to produce his special effects.

Suddenly the sky was filled with fireworks, layer after layer of explosions in the night air. They would not have to wait long for the rest of it.

12

"WELCOME TO THE WOOD GREEN EMPIRE!" The amplified voice echoed from the trees, from the side of the house: as if the trees and boards themselves were speaking. "WE PRESENT AN EVENING OF SPECTACLE AND THRILLS UNPARALLELED ON ANY STAGE ANYWHERE IN THE WORLD. THE FINAL PERFORMANCE, THE FINAL PROFESSIONAL APPEARANCE OF THE BELOVED HERBIE BUTTER. IS HE ONE OR IS HE MANY? DECIDE FOR YOURSELVES, LADIES AND GENTLEMEN. THESE FEATS OF CONJURY AND PRESTIDIGITATION ARE FAR BEYOND THE POWERS OF ANY OTHER LIVING MAGICIAN.

"FOR YOUR OWN PROTECTION, DO NOT ATTEMPT AT ANY TIME TO LEAVE THE THEATER."

Del was crying again, his wet face illuminated by the brilliant flashes of fireworks.

"PRESENTING . . . MR. HERBIE BUTTER!"

The explosions in the sky doubled: a roll of snare drums from the loudspeakers. Whole areas of the sky blasted into white, fitting themselves together like a puzzle around eyeholes and an open, grinning mouth. *Kawhamp!* Glowing red lay atop the giant face, and Herbie Butter stretched across the sky, grinning down at them. It was like a cartoon face, sharply etched and two-dimensional.

"THE AMAZING MECHANICAL MAGICIAN AND ACROBAT! THE KING OF THE CATS!"

Collins seemed too powerful to Tom, too tricky and experienced. He watched the enormous cartoon sift down through the air, seeking them out. Then he looked back at the house. All those blazing windows: he remembered his first full day at Shadowland, Collins a figure with the face of a wolf, pointing across a gulf and showing him that he could have anything he wanted . . . then he felt as though Collins were nailing him to the air behind him, pounding a spike through his chest. Rose Armstrong was looking down at him from the window where he had seen her that day. It was his bedroom. Even on that first day, they had been taking part in the magician's repeat performance.

It has to be like this. This is not an easy school.

Rose looked down with a stricken face. She motioned for him to stay where he was: that she would come down. Stupidly, he shook his head. Rose turned away from the window. He looked up again: Herbie Butter still sifted down toward them.

Tom saw the gun, a black lump in dark green. He could not imagine how he had lifted it. Very little fresh blood came from his wounds, but both hands had swollen. They felt like gloves.

"Rose is coming," he said to Del. Fear had stolen the color from his friend's face.

"Oh, no," Del wailed.

"MAY WE HAVE TWO VOLUNTEERS FROM THE AUDIENCE, PLEASE?"

"I think her part is done," Tom said. His heart was as numb as his hands.

"STEP UP, STEP UP SMARTLY—WE REQUIRE THE ASSISTANCE OF YOU BRAVE YOUNG PEOPLE."

Rose burst out of the living room onto the patio and started running toward them. The green dress shone in the light. Whiteness flickered in her right hand—she was carrying white rags.

"Leave us alone!" Del screamed at her, and she stepped on the grass. She looked fearfully at the two bodies. "Go back inside, you Judas!"

"I had to do it," she said. "I didn't know what he'd . . . I thought it was just part of his show. . . . Tom, I'm so *sorry* . . ." She held out her arms. "He would have killed me otherwise, but I wish he had. . . . I brought some handkerchiefs for your hands, they're all I could find, please let me tie them on for you. Please, Tom."

"Who was in the car?" Tom asked.

Del screamed, "Don't let her touch you!"

"Elena," Rose answered. "She ran off. She saw the blood . . . she left him. I want to help you, Tom. Please. I have to."

"Because he told her to!" Del screamed. "Get away!"

"He wanted me to wait in his room," Rose said. "You weren't supposed to see me anymore. But I thought it was just going to be a performance, Tom. If I'd known . . . we could have hidden in the woods . . . I wouldn't have brought you back."

"You liar!" Del shouted.

"No, it's the truth," Tom said. "She didn't know. She was tricked too."

"Can I help your hands?"

"Come on," he said.

She stumbled forward.

"AND WE PAUSE TO REMEMBER OUR HEROINE OF THE CRIMEAN . . . THE ANGEL OF THE BATTLEFIELD . . . FLORENCE NIGHTINGALE!"

Ka-whamp! Rockets sailed up, making red tracers in the sky and—*whamp!*—exploded into the British flag.

"He's going to get us," Del said. He wiped more of the blood from his face with his sleeve. "There's no way . . ."

"Get it as tight as you can," Tom said.

Rose was folding the first handkerchief over his hand and twisting the ends together to knot them. "Who's left, Rose? Who's left in the house?"

"Just Mr. Peet. They were both upstairs when we heard the shots. At first they thought they were rockets. Then they went downstairs." She began to fold the second handkerchief around Tom's right hand. "And he said something about the ladder."

"What happened to the ladder?" Del asked. "The ladder's gone!" He was slipping into panic again. "We can't get down!" He turned his head toward the house and went quiet. Coleman Collins stood at every window they could see, far enough from the glass for the light to show him clearly.

Six, seven. . . ? It didn't matter how many, because it could be any number. Identical Coleman Collinses, caressing their identical upper lips with identical index fingers.

"We have to go in there," Del said, a little awe showing through his voice.

"That's what he said about the ladder." Rose tied the ends together. Red circles had already appeared in the centers of the two handkerchiefs. "That you'd have to go in. And he said you'd want to go in."

"But that's just a trick," Del pleaded. "There's only two of them, really—and Mr. Peet will run like those men."

"Maybe not," Tom said, trying to move his fingers. "But there's someone else. He wanted two volunteers, remember? He had the other one all along."

The images of the magician vanished from the windows.

"I'm on your side, Tom," Rose said. Her voice was desperate. "I told you I didn't know what he was going to do—you know I'm telling you the truth. I left him."

"I didn't mean you," Tom said with more calm than he felt. "He still has Skeleton."

"HAVE WE ANOTHER VOLUNTEER?" the speakers boomed. "HAVE WE? HAVE WE? AH! THE HANDSOME GENTLEMAN IN THE BLACK SUIT!"

13

A shadowy figure appeared on the lawn behind them: or had it been there before, unnoticed? Rose grabbed Tom's arm. Del stepped backward. "It's Skeleton," he said, his voice way above its usual register, high enough to be birdsong: but Tom saw that it was not Skeleton.

The figure stepped forward, and tortoiseshell eyeglass frames turned red in the light from the house.

"This school has been unwell," Laker Broome said, "and now it is time to cut back the diseased branches." He moved closer to them. "Pruning, gentlemen . . . pruning. Time to clean up our garden." Tom could see the lights down in the woods through his glen-plaid suit.

"We'll get you! We know who you are and we will get you!" He raised a transparent fist, and Rose and the boys stepped back.

"We have had indiscipline, smoking, failures, and theft—and now we are cursed with something so sick, so *ill*, that in all my years as an educator I have never seen its like.

"NEVER!"

He stepped forward again, pushing them back to the flagstones and the light.

"A guilty mind and soul are dangerous to all about them—they *corrupt*. All of you boys have been touched by this disease."

Another mad, threatening step forward. "You, Flanagan. Did you steal that owl?"

"Yes," Tom said. For that was the final truth.

The index finger stabbed at Del. "You. Nightingale. Did you steal that owl?"

"Yes," Del said.

"You will report to my office immediately—we will rid ourselves of you, do you hear? You are to be expunged, a word meaning erased, omitted, cast away . . . *Mala causa est quae requirit misercordiam.*" His face seemed the size of a billboard. Rose, still gripping Tom's arm, was whimpering. "And I see you have brought a girl into this school. That too will be dealt with, boys. I very much fear that you will not be allowed to leave these premises alive. Theft, failure, smoking, indiscipline—and ingratitude! Ingratitude is a capital offense!"

Tom felt the rough fieldstone flags under his feet, and Laker Broome looked with transparent eyes at a transparent watch and said, "And now I believe we have some magic from two members of our first year."

Del goggled at him: the bruises were starting to come up from his face, purple across his temples and green on his cheeks and jaw. In a couple of hours he would look like a mandrill.

Animal faces: he was suddenly aware of a cramped room about him, gloomily lacquered with photographs—a crazy quilt on the walls and ceiling, horrible faces leering at him as in the wizard's house in the dream, leering but stationary, fixed on the wall so they could never float away . . .

("To-o-o-o-m," Del wailed.)

. . . but what was floating was him, going up off a strange fetid bed straight toward the ceiling. Rose's arms held him back, then broke away, and he was going right toward those pictures, toward a dead man in his car with his brains all over the windows, some dripping car in an empty parking lot. *Scene of the Murder. The former Miami lawyer was discovered at 7:10 yesterday morning. Miami resident Herbert Finkel, threatened by a loitering youth described as wearing blue shirt and tan trousers . . .*

toward a picture of Coleman Collins in his Burberry and a wide-brimmed hat, his face only a blank white oval . . .

toward the Carson School, a black-and-white aerial photograph crayoned with red—crayon flames, drawn over the field house and auditorium, a red crayon smear obliterating the little tree in the court. Closer to it, closer, the crayon flames seeming to leap, seeming to warm his face.

Rose's fingers grasped his right hand, torturing the wound, and he yelled just as the crayon flames grew up around him.

They were back at Carson. Del and Rose were on either side of him, standing on the solid wooden floor of the auditorium, Mr. Broome at the podium, his face a lunatic's, mouthing gibberish. A hundred boys twisted and howled in their seats, many of them bleeding from the eyes and nose. Noise like a foul smoke rose from them, and Mr. Broome screamed, *"I want Steven Ridpath! Skeleton Ridpath! The only graduate of the class of '59. Come up here and get your diploma!"* He held out a burning document, and Tom felt himself sailing up, his limbs spidery, all of his skin so tight it felt it might split open . . .

down below him—a photograph? It moved. The dead boys twisted and howled. A teacher dressed in a Norfolk jacket moved across the blackening floor and took Del's arm, twisted it savagely around his back, and yanked him away. It had the quality of a photograph, a moment stopped in time so that you could look back and say, yes, that's when Uncle George ripped his pants on the bob-wire fence, that's when Lulu looked down the well, wasn't

that funny, sorta like an omen cuz that's when things
started to go bad and wrong and just see how happy we all
were . . . but Del's face was turning purple and green and
Rose was screaming and the man wasn't a teacher, he was
Mr. Peet . . . he was still above them all, floating toward
Laker Broome, who held out his burning hand and
fastened it around Tom's wrist, scorching his flesh,
grinning at him and saying, *I said there'd be a little pain,
didn't I? Should have taken my hand back in the tunnels,
boy. Don't you agree things would have worked out a little
nicer that way?*

The burning hand clamped harder on his wrist. *Don't
make the fool's mistake of thinking this ain't happening,
kid. Even though it ain't.* Tom felt his wrist frying in the
devil's grasp. *Mr. Collins has your pal. You chose your
song.*

So sing it.

Beneath the white of the magician's handkerchief, his
wrist was blister red.

"To-o-o-m!" Del cried again. His voice was getting
smaller. "Tom! Tom!"

He shook his head, trying to clear out the fuzz—almost
as if he had been Skeleton Ridpath, seeing what Skeleton
had chosen to see, had wanted with all of his messed-up
heart to see—

"They *moved* us, they *moved* us," Rose wailed, "oh,
Tom come back—you like died for a second."

He opened his eyes, and was looking up at Rose's
scared face. She was not even pretty anymore. Her
forehead was wrinkled like an old woman's, and for a
second she looked like a witch bending over him and
shaking his arms. "Oh," he said.

She stopped shaking him. "That man touched you and
it was like you died. Mr. Peet came out and carried you in
here and pulled Del along—and I just followed, I hit him
on the back, but he never even blinked at me. He took
Del away, Tom. What are you going to do?"

"Dunno," Tom said. He did not know where he was.
Artificial stars, friendly lights, winked down at him.
Wasn't there a color wheel? Wasn't there a band?
"'*Polka Dots and Moonbeams*,'" he said. "Fielding went
off the wall over some saxophone player. Six cups of

punch. Everybody went outside and looked at a satellite, but it was really just an airplane. Skeleton was there, and he looked really creepy. All in black." Tom looked perplexedly up at the friendly lights. Where the color wheel should have been, only a spaghettilike pipe ran through the distance, joining another thin pipe at a T-junction.

"What are you talking about?" Rose had her witch face again.

"Carson. Our school. When Del and I . . ." He shook his head. "Mr. Peet? I saw him."

"He carried you here. And he took Del."

Tom groaned. "Our headmaster was a devil," he said. "Do you suppose he actually could have been? And maybe he was the man on Mesa Lane last summer—it was only his first year, you know? The new kids never realized that. They thought he'd been there forever. No wonder we all had nightmares."

"Are you all right?" Rose asked.

"He's a talent scout," Tom said, smiling. "Good old M."

"Tom."

"Oh, I'm okay." He sat up. "Where are we, anyhow? Oh. Should have known." They were in the big theater; because of the removed wall, he could see into the smaller theater. The figures in the mural watched him with their varying expressions of pleasure, boredom, and amusement. And of unearthly greed.

"Collins is right, you know. He did give Skeleton what he wanted. Skeleton wanted exactly what happened. He even drew pictures of it."

"But now what?" Rose said. "Tom, what do we do now? I don't even know what you're talking about."

"Do you know what I think, Rose? I think I still love you. Do you suppose Collins still loves his little shepherdess? Do you really have a grandmother in Hilly Vale, Rose?"

The worry lines in her forehead puckered again.

Tom got to his knees. The mural, a real audience, watched with sympathetic interest. "For my next trick, and this has never before been attempted on the continent, ladies and gentlemen . . ."

"Are you crazy? Did that man do something to your mind?"

"Be quiet, Rose." The entire mural blazed at him: he could almost see their hands carrying food to their mouths, see them talking to each other: *I'll miss old Herbie, say what you like, he was the bloody best. Turned a man's hand into a claw, now, didn't he? In Kensington it was.* The folks in the shilling seats, looking forward to having their brains turned inside-out at Mr. Butter's last show.

In the mural, the Collector turned his head to beam his glee toward Tom Flanagan.

I say, that girl's a smasher. French she is.

"Stay quiet," he said. "Go somewhere—go hide on the stage. Find a corner and hide in it and stay quiet."

"What. . . ?"

He waved her off, hoping she would find the safest corner in all Shadowland. Now there was no reassuring button to push and turn the awful thing back into a joke.

A loudspeaker crackled: "AH, THERE YOU ARE, SIR! YES, YOU—THE GENTLEMAN IN THE BLACK SUIT. LADIES AND GENTS, WE HAVE OUR SECOND VOLUNTEER. A GENEROUS HAND, PLEASE!"

Ghostly clapping, applause from the year 1924, splashed from the walls.

The Collector slid down from the wall, grinning blind and toothless at Tom.

Now, Mary, don't carry on—that bloke's in on it, do you see? He's part of the show. He's what you call a stooge.

The Collector was stumbling to the end of the aisle in the smaller room, still focused entirely on Tom. A face without any personality at all. Dr. Collector. It was what they all looked like, really: Skeleton, Laker Broome, the magician, Mr. Peet and the Wandering Boys, so warped by hate and greed that they would steal and kill, cheat and tyrannize anyone less powerful. Collins had even stripped a dead man's pockets. Yes. Dr. Collector. They offered their own kinds of salvation. *Want to be a man? I'll make you a man. I am your father and your mother.*

"Here I am, Skeleton," he said. Disgust, loathing, flooded through him. He stood up. His hands felt like molten lead weights, held together only by the knotted handkerchiefs.

"Come on, Skeleton," he said.

The Collector lurched eagerly down the stairs.

14

The truth is, Tom does not have any idea of how he is to fight the Collector. As he hears Rose's high heels clattering into the wings of the stage, he remembers the scene in which the actor Creekmore impersonated Withers, and the impulse which led him to face this dreadful representation of Skeleton Ridpath begins to look like a fatal mistake. The Collector was the magician's best bodyguard—he had said that himself. It suddenly seems very likely to Tom that he is going to die—die none too pleasantly—in the Grand Théâtre des Illusions, just as Withers had died in an alley outside a stage door.

"Vendouris!" the Collector calls. "I saw your owl, Vendouris."

Tom edges away as silently as he can, wondering even now if he can get out of the theater and somehow snatch Del from Collins . . . leave the Collector wandering and calling inside the theater—

but the Collector is a magic trick.

"I want to see some skin," the Collector whispers. "Where are you, Vendouris?"

He is a magic trick, and Tom is a magician. In the hallucinatory scene which had played out when Laker Broome had touched him, there had been the flicker of a clue, the smell of an answer strong enough to make some part of him know that the Collector could be made harmless.

"Some skin," the Collector says, opening his mouth to show purple blackness. His empty eyes shine with delight. He is stumbling over the little theater's stage, going by a blind man's radar to the Grand Théâtre.

Tom moves quietly down the front of the big stage, backing away. What is the clue, the answer? He can remember the auditorium filled with dead boys, himself floating over it in Skeleton's body.

It is there somewhere, the answer. He has to think. But how could you think, with your mind turning to jelly? It's just magic, that's all, he says to himself, getting as far as the wall and straightening his back against it and watching the Collector step off the little theater's stage. Two more steps would bring him into the larger room. The Collector is drooling, reaching out, and Tom remembers how it was to be inside Skeleton, feeling all that hate which was love knocked on its head, Skeleton's helpless, dumbstruck love for Collins and what he could do.

"I'm not Vendouris," Tom says, still feeling his loathing for Skeleton lying like a weight in his chest.

"Aaah," Skeleton moans, and focuses his ecstatic head toward Tom. He is shuddering with pleasure. He begins to stumble into a row of seats.

"Your name is Steve Ridpath," Tom says. "And you cheated on your exams. You're the unhappiest boy in the whole school. You're supposed to go to Clemson in the fall. Your father is a football coach."

"Burn that ball back," whispers Skeleton.

"Stay away from me," Tom says.

"Burn that ball back!"

"You set a fire in the field house," Tom says, searching frantically for the key which will find whatever remains of Skeleton inside the Collector. "You wanted to see everybody die."

"Get away from that fucking piano," the Collector whispers. He is now at Tom's end of a row of seats, and about a dozen steps up toward the back of the big theater. Behind him and to the left, Tom can see the X of the wooden brace, irregularly stained with red.

But why was I Skeleton? Tom wonders. The awful toy is coming down the steps, brightly scanning for a sign of motion. "Stay away," he says, half-pleading.

The Collector descends another two steps: Tom is by now really almost too scared to move; and he knows that if he tries to run, Skeleton will gain on him effortlessly, and bring him down as happily as a lion brings down a zebra.

"Oh, Flanagini," the Collector whispers, only four

steps up from Tom. "Not to hurt Mr. Collins, Flanagini—
not to hurt Mr. Collins."

"I will hurt him," Tom says, and raises his useless
hands.

"I can fly, Flanagini," Skeleton whispers, and is nearly
on him.

"You're a joke, Skeleton," Tom whispers too, for he is
unable to make his voice louder. Then his mind twists and
he sees the interior of that room again, the gloom and the
lacquered pictures. It is as if they paper the interior of his
skull.

He's what you call a stooge.

Skeleton howls in pain or joy, lurches off the last step,
and his hands find Tom's throat. The empty eyes glow
before Tom, shine directly into his brain, and while the
hands tighten about his throat, Tom can hear a mad
babble of voices. *Owl Dr. Collector see some skin skin owl
out to stay now pictures window knew he was there FIRE!
owl owlfire takes this life too, you too, Vendouris, coming
from where? joy foxhead OWLFIRE FLANAGINIFIRE
wolfhead baby on a spear light shining through blood glass
thing moving in my pocket . . .* an unending spool of
gibberish which is Skeleton's soul and mind and is more
purely frightening than even the hands around his throat.

Then Tom's mind twists again, and he raises his useless
hands, defending himself from the pictures and knowledge there: *Flanagini fire,* Skeleton's melted consciousness sings to him, and the crushing hands continue
to do their work.

15

Rose had scrambled through the strange assortment of
props in the wings of the stage, knocking over tables and
spilling loose packs of cards. One deck flattened out on
the floor beside her, and she saw that it contained only
aces of hearts and twos of spades. From the center of the
spilled deck a joker who was a devil popped out of a box
and grinned, raising a red pitchfork. Her only thought was
to get out. She had seen Tom die once, when the

transparent man jabbed his finger forward and touched him, and now she knew he was going to die again. She brushed against a tall structure that looked like a gate or a stanchion, and a shiny slanting blade came hissing down to thwack against the bottom of the frame.

She heard faint applause echo from behind the curtains, out there where Tom was. *Applause?* It was true, what she had said to Tom long ago. Mr. Collins had been out of control all summer, drinking even more than usual and screaming in his sleep, so that she knew his mind was in that other time, the time which was mythical to her, with Speckle John and Rosa Forte and the original Wandering Boys—Tom Flanagan was the cause of that. . . .

Rose too was in pain. Rose is always in pain, and only Mr. Collins knows this. For as long as she has walked, she had walked on swords, broken glass, burning coals; the ground stabs her feet. Only Mr. Collins knows how when she walks on her high heels, nails jab into her soles, making every step a crucifixion like Tom's. . . .

She wished she were on a train with him, her feet on the seat before her, going away and away and away. Tom would be stunned by the joy she could bring him, and the reflection of that joy would stun her too.

Her hand found the edge of the stage door. Behind her on the other side of the curtains, the Collector howled, and she knew there would be no train, no sweet Tom beside her in a sleeper—only Mr. Collins knew how to get inside the Collector and talk to the twisted boy who lived there.

Rose groped for the knob. It moved under her hand, and the door swung open onto the dark corridor.

"Dear Rose," Mr. Collins said, and she gasped. He was standing in the hall, leaning against the wall with his arms crossed over his chest.

"Please," she said. Then she saw—it was not Mr. Collins, but one of his shadows, one of those that had appeared in the window just before that satanic creature in the eyeglasses had come shouting and pointing his finger. She could always tell the shadows from the real thing, thought it was one of his best tricks. Del, who had seen it many times, could sometimes tell too.

"Where do you think you're going, dear one?" the image asked.

"Nowhere," she said sullenly.

"That's true, isn't it? You are not going anywhere. You cannot go anywhere. You remember that, don't you, Rose?"

"I remember," she said.

"Thinking about running away with him? Did your little playacting make you wish it could be real?"

She just looked at the shadow, which smiled back at her.

"Did you talk to him about Hilly Vale?" it taunted her. "Oh, I'm being mean to our pretty little Vermont Rose. I mustn't be mean to someone who has helped me so much."

"No, don't be mean," she said. She was nearly in tears.

"If your boyfriend escapes from my toy in there, which is really very unlikely, we will have to lead him a dance, won't we? We'll make him choose again. And he will make the wrong choice. Because he will think it is the only choice he can make. And then you will help me, won't you, Rose?"

"I won't," she said.

"Defiance—from someone I have aided so often? Are you telling me that you would like to go back home, little Rose?"

He was so calm. She knew he would win. Mr. Collins always won. But she shook her head anyhow.

"Of course, it is an academic question," the shadow said. "Because you will always live here with me and be my queen. The darling boy will be found at the bottom of the cliff, along with my nephew, and next summer perhaps there will be another adorable boy. Next summer or in five summers—a boy with strange stirrings in him, a boy who does not know who he is. A few more voices in the tunnels? I shall be in better control next year, I promise you."

"I hate the tunnels," Rose said.

"Better control next year," the shadow promised, fading away. "And more control over *you*, dear one. . . ."

16

"Hang on to him, Mr. Peet," the magician said. "Hold him tightly, and very soon we will know if we will need him to play his part. Need I say that your men did not play theirs very well?"

"If we're up here by ourselves, except for *him*"—Mr. Peet yanked savagely at Del's hair with his free hand—"except for this little shit, that is, do you have to call me by that name?" Mr. Peet was actually a glasshouse marine named Floyd Inbush, who had earned a dishonorable discharge from Korea for removing the ears of a Korean: a South Korean. In his civilian life, Inbush had spent five years in Joliet state prison for assault with a deadly weapon. This "Mr. Peet" business was getting on his nerves, like his employer's references to the failure of the men he had recruited.

"While you are in this house or on these grounds, you are Mr. Peet," the magician said. "You understood our terms when I hired you."

"I understood, did I?" Inbush growled. "I didn't understand a lot about this lousy job, and you know I didn't. Take a look at this kid. Is that what we're supposed to be guarding you against?" He jerked Del back and forth by the hair, and Del's limbs moved like a marionette's. His eyes were wide and glazed, his face a sickly gray color under the natural olive cast. Inbush had seen a dozen men go that toadstool color when they had realized that their lives were going to be taken.

"His friend acquitted himself very well against six adult men," Collins said.

"He was *armed*," Inbush shouted. "Arm a baby, he's as good as a combat soldier. Goddammit, if he's armed he *is* a combat soldier."

"I must conclude you are inadequate for the job I hired you to do."

"You calling me inadequate, you old juicer?" Inbush took a step toward Collins, who was sitting in the owl chair and regarding him in a detached but regretful manner.

"I must also conclude that you would be happier leaving my employ."

"Damn right I would. Three of my men are dead—two of 'em ran off, the chickenhearted scum—and you want me to guard you against this little zombie?" Another savage shake for Del. "I'm ready to go right now."

"And so you will, Mr. Peet. You have definitely outlived your usefulness."

"Hold on. You looked pretty good when we dug for that badger, I'll say that for you, you're in good shape for your age, but I can take you. I can take you good. I'm walking out of here."

"You are an offense, Mr. Peet." Collins sat up straight in the owl chair. "You are going to leave my way. Watch this, nephew."

Del whimpered as Inbush cast him away and began to move toward Collins.

"Watch carefully," Collins said, and closed his eyes. A shadow line of black appeared around him, outlining him for a second. Inbush stopped moving. A line of red joined the black, and both lines became a single thick line of vibrant blue.

Inbush screamed.

Collins' aura blazed for a moment. Inbush's scream went up an octave in pitch, and the man's hands flew to his scalp. A smell like gunpowder invaded the room, and Floyd Inbush blew up as if there had been a bomb in his guts.

Both the old man and the boy were splashed with red. A wad of something that looked like pink dog food struck Del's chest with the force of a line drive and adhered wetly to his shirt. Del slowly looked down at it, and his mouth fell open and his eyes shuttered and his ears sealed. Del was safe: he stood in the bloody room and he heard nothing and he saw nothing.

17

Tom is looking into Skeleton's blank shining eyes. In part because of the mad babble coming from Skeleton's molten mind, in part because he can see Skeleton's history as clearly as if it were a movie playing in those dead eyes, he knows Skeleton thoroughly—knows him too well. He sees Chester Ridpath walloping young Skeleton, sees spittle flying from the coach's mouth, hears his curses. He sees Skeleton's hands as if they were his own, opening the lid of the Carson piano as the glass owl rattles itself against the wood; sees the pictures going up, one by one, onto the walls and ceiling.

Skeleton's thumbs are pushing into his windpipe; Skeleton is drooling and humming to himself.

I was in your room, Tom thinks, and the pressure of the thumbs miraculously eases a bit.

Skeleton, I was in your room: I saw the owl at the window: and he does see it, he hears it battering the glass, whapping its great wings. Then another picture takes hold of his mind, and he says to Skeleton: *I rode those wings and heard the voice.*

Do you hear me in there, Skeleton?

Beneath the lunatic flood of gibberish, there is a small voice which says: *Yes.* The Collector's hands hang loosely on Tom's neck now; the Collector's torched-down elemental face is frozen like paint on a wall.

I stole the owl, Tom thinks into Skeleton's rushing brain. *I set fire to the field house. I was the one you wanted, Skeleton. Not him. Not Del. Tom Flanagan.*

"Flanagini fire," the Collector whispered.

Flanagini fire—you tied into my battery, Skeleton, before I even knew I had it. Tom hates these thoughts, they violate everything he once had known about himself, everything he had wished to be. *My fire, my room, Skeleton: I wasn't just in your room, I was your room.*

I was your room. This is the worst thought of all, worse even than the certainty that he alone had seen Skeleton hanging like a spider from the auditorium ceiling because t that moment Skeleton was a broken-away and unvanted piece of himself: that Skeleton's cave of horrors, ovingly clipped from magazines, was a depiction of some oarded-off area of his mind, the area to which Coleman Collins had thrown open the gates in his own soul in the arly 1920's.

I am your room, he sends into Skeleton's mind, taking esponsibility for it all. His mind and Skeleton's are nearly ne—*your room is me*—and Tom knows with true and ertain finality that in saying this he has finally become a nagician: not just a low-grade psychic, but a magician, he black figure with a sword. He has welcomed himself.

After that, after he has sickened himself, he knows how o free Skeleton Ridpath from the Collector. He looks nto the grotesque parody of magic before him and sees a igh-school boy way down there, with wax Dracula teeth n his mouth and a frightwig on his close-cut hair; a highchool boy who had wanted in the most pathetic way to be cary; and he reaches for him. *Come on out, Skeleton,* he ays. *You can come out now. Get out of the Jar.* There is a ittle tug at his mind, a tug like a headache: it will work.

Tom reaches inside, extending a long probe, and this ime Skeleton twines around it. *OUT!* Tom pulls back, ind it is like trying to pull a swordfish out of the ocean; gravity tries to drag him down in there with Skeleton, he eels he is bench-pressing twice his own weight. *OUT!!* He early blacks out with the effort of pulling.

The snap of release knocks him backward, and a hot vind blasts him against the wall. A limp thing like an pright sack is before him; beside it stands a tall thin boy vith purple-black eyes. The sack flutters down, and a noment later the thin boy collapses.

Tom goes to his knees. He glances at the Collector just o see what it is when it is empty. A rubbery face, a thing f cloth and wire. Beside it, Skeleton is moving his fingers ike an infant, his face drenched with sweat. His eyes are hut. Skeleton groans. "Flanagini. Uh. Fire," he says.

"That's all over," Tom says, bending over. The odors f an unwashed and unhealthy body are very strong. Skeleton is wearing filthy jeans and a T-shirt which is oddly scorched. "Do you understand me, Ridpath? It's over. You're free."

"Um," Skeleton says into the carpet.

"Can you move?"

Skeleton opens his bloodshot eyes. "Flanagan?"

"Yeah."

Skeleton's face scrunches up. "I met him," he says. "I did. I finally met him."

"Can you move? You're going to have to get out of this house."

"What house?" Skeleton asks, and his eyes look normal for the first time—eyes the color of thin mud in a roadside ditch. Tom does not want to touch him.

So he forces himself to touch him. He shakes a shoulder that feels like putty covered with grease. "It's not important for you anymore. Just get up and get out. You'll find the door. Go up the driveway, slide through the bars, and turn left. We're in Vermont. A town called Hilly Vale is about an hour's walk away."

"You're like him, aren't you?" Skeleton is trying to get up on his hands and knees, and he is wobbly as a colt, but he makes it. "You don't have to answer. I know."

Tom looks at the bruised hateful face and sees—this is a shock!—repugnance equal to his own. Skeleton spits at him. Yellow phlegm slides across Tom's jaw. "You're like *him*," Skeleton says.

Tom flicks the wet gobbet off his chin. "Get out, Skeleton. Otherwise he'll kill you." A crazy voice in his own mind, wholly his, is clamoring that he use his powers to pick Skeleton up and throw him against the wall, break his bones, grind him to dust . . . he sees the aerial photograph of Carson School crayoned over with red childish flames.

Skeleton looks into Tom's face and shudders backward, banging into the first row of seats. "Get out," Tom says, and Skeleton goes unsteadily toward the door. Tom's hands are burning weights.

18

Applause, gentlemen? But the figures in the mural had frozen into place again. Even the Collector was back on

e wall of the little theater, staring toward Tom as if still
angry for him. No need for that anymore: you've eaten
e already. Tom felt again the terrible gravitational pull
side the Collector. If he had been a shade weaker, he
ould be in there now, sharing eternity with Skeleton
idpath, their minds a couple of hundred-watt bulbs.

He went to the stage, and did not have the strength to
all himself up onto it. "Rose?" She did not answer.
Rose?" Tom walked as quickly as he could to the side of
e stage and trudged up the little flight of steps. Behind
e curtain he was in an underwater world. Dim rosy
ght: heaps of things like banks of coral, shining from
explicable edges and corners, as if fireflies nested on
em. A fanned-out deck of cards on the floor showed a
evil popping up and grinning at him. *Do you like the low
ad, my boy?* One of the undersea fireflies was light
inting from the top of a guillotine blade. "Rose." A
ble had been knocked on its side and lay with its legs
raight out like a dead animal. He moved past and saw
e stage door.

He was in the dark corridor, leaning against the wall.
om came quietly out of the stage door and saw her for a
ng moment before she noticed him: she was forlorn in
er outdated green dress, like a little girl abandoned at a
rthday party, and for an instant it seemed to him that
e too had come up against what she was, some
keleton's room of her own. Then she recorded that
meone else was in the corridor, and she jerked around
face him. Her face instantly recorded disbelieving joy.
You did it," she said quietly, but her voice rang like a
ell.

Tom nodded. "Are you all right?"

"I'm fine now," Rose answered. "As long as I can see
ou, I'm fine." There it was again—that flicker of kinship,
brotherhood in unhappy self-knowledge.

"Why are you looking at me like that?" she asked. It
ccurred to Tom that he could probe her mind as he had
e Collector's—just send a little question mark into her
d see what that kinship was.

He almost did it: started to do it, in fact, but something
ade him stop as soon as he had begun. Not just the

certainty that to do so was like raiding a friend's desk
read his mail; but the uncanny feeling even the delicat
feathery first touch had given him, a sense of airlessne
of suffocation, of being in an alien place. His mind made
sudden shocked withdrawal, having touched for the brie
est moment a world in which it knows no landmarks and
queerly cold and lost.

"Del is upstairs. With him," Rose said.

For a moment a sick, scared worry passed betwee
them, perfectly shared, as if they each knew what th
other was.

"Something happened to you—while I was in there
Tom suddenly knew; and knew he should have seen
from the first. "What was it?"

"Mr. Collins was here—not really him, one of h
shadows. Like we saw in the windows. He talked to me
Rose tilted her head bravely back. "He said I could nev
leave him."

"Is he going to hurt Del?"

Rose blinked. "Not until you make him."

"I'm getting that gun I dropped," Tom said, and beg
to go down the corridor. "I'm not going to give him
chance to hurt Del."

He had gone only a short way down the dark corrid
when she came up beside him and wedged a supporti
hand under his arm.

19

The patio lights limned two vague heaps out on the si
lawn, and Tom let Rose guide him in that direction. Th
night had deepened while they had been in the house, an
stars filled the sky, gleaming like smaller, colder refle
tions of the myriad lights blazing again in the forest o
either side of the lake.

"Can you find it in the dark?" she asked.

"Got to," he said. He tried to remember where he ha
been when he had dropped it. Had it been before he ha
gone toward Pease and the ladder, or had he carried th
gun for a while? He saw himself dropping the gun, saw

re into the grass, flipping over with the force of the
ecoil.

"Stop, Rose," he said. "I was about here. I stood up
omewhere around here. I never got very far from the
ones." He saw it all rolling on before him, Del with his
loody face, the knot of men going seriously about their
usiness, Snail with his delicate look of worry walking
orward right into the bullet. He looked down and did not
ee the gun, and panic started up in him again. He
hispered, "I don't see it! I don't see it!"

"Let's go ahead a little bit," Rose said.

They went five feet forward.

"No, this is too far," Tom said, seeing Snail's body
ing slantwise on the grass. Snail looked like an exhibit in
wax museum. The other body, Thorn's, was a surprising
ay off.

"Did Snail get that close to you?" Rose asked.

"I don't think . . . I don't know." Again he saw Snail
almly coming for him, keeping his almost kindly eyes on
om, that little wrinkle dividing his forehead.

Tom stepped backward, remembering how they had
ood. He moved a foot sideways and when he looked
own he saw the gun black against the near-black of the
rass. He went to his knees and collected it up with both
ands. The barrel was still warm. He stood up and
isplayed it like an offering. "Two bullets left," he said.
I'm going to shoot his eyes out."

When he looked at Rose he saw only a fuzzy aureole of
air outlined by the patio lights. "Help me," he said.
He's a fiend, and I'm going to shoot his eyes out."

Ie still cradled the pistol in his joined palms. He would
e able to lift it in the proper way only once, and
manipulate the trigger with his left index finger. Then he
ould shoot the magician's eyes out.

Rose helped him toward the patio, then across it. They
ame into the living room, which was daubed here and
here with Tom's blood. No rush of ecstatic air greeted
im, as on the morning after his welcome. Shadowland
vas waiting, he realized. Shadowland was neutral. He
ulled the gun toward his chest. It smelled like explosions
nd oil—it smelled like a burned trombone. Holding it
loser like that helped the ache in his forearms.

"We just go up?" Rose asked.

"We just go up. Very quietly."

They left the living room and went softly to the big
staircase. It rose from gray darkness into dim light
Outside Collins' bedroom, the recessed lights tinted the
top of the walls and the swinging doors.

Rose went onto the first step, looked back at him
Hugging the gun into his chest, he nodded, and she wen
noiselessly up another step. He could do this by himsel
Tom put his feet where she had, trying to walk exactl
where she had walked—sometime while he had bee
trying to get his fingers under the gun, Rose had remove
her shoes, which she now carried in her left hand. As h
set his feet where her bare feet had been, what he sti
thought of as his new senses sent him the impression c
. . . *knives. Fire.* He looked up, startled, almost feelin
sharp points and flames working in his feet, and saw Ros
slowly and silently and slowly going up one step afte
another. Tom moved his foot two inches to the side: mut
ordinary carpet. When he moved his foot back again, th
impression was still there—*knives*—but fading. He wen
farther away from the railing and crept up after her.

She stood on the landing, waiting for him to climb th
last tread. Again he had that sense of kinship, as strong a
love but different from it, of something in her that wa
like the magician in him, hidden away. *He said I woul
never leave him.* Did he say you would always walk o
knives, Rose?

"Oh, Rose," he whispered.

She shook her head, either telling him to be quiet o
that she could not answer the question she knew he wa
going to ask. Rose looked anxiously at the swinging door
set off the landing; back at him. Keep your mind on th
job, Tom. He adjusted the gun in his hand and got it s
that the barrel pointed out from his chest, his right han
on the grip, his left supporting it.

Rose gently pushed one half of the swinging doors, an
it noiselessly opened. Tom slipped through into darkness
and saw light outlining Collins' bedroom door. It wa
chinked open, and all he had to do was burst in.

One final adjustment of his hands: he took the whol
weight in his right hand, and wedged his finger into th
trigger guard.

Just go in and shoot, he told himself. Don't even stop to think. Just push back the trigger. Then it's over.

He gathered himself, consciously made himself still. He raised the gun so he could sight down the barrel when he was in the room. His heartbeat surged and pounded. When he was ready, he stepped forward and kicked open the door and ran into the bedroom.

What he saw stopped him cold. A gigantic blood-smeared skull grinned at him, its mouth the size of a shark's. *"Del!"* he screamed, and the barrel of Collins' pistol went wavering blindly as his left index finger involuntarily jerked the trigger back.

20

The pistol jumped, but his right hand went with it and clung. The explosion rocked his head: his ears felt as though he had dropped fifty feet in a roller coaster. A bit of the blood-spattered ceiling shredded away. All of the room was covered in gore. Directly opposite him the blown-up photograph of a skull was dappled in blood; gouts and puddles of blood covered the bed and other furniture, blood ran and dripped from the ceiling, which had been covered with photographs of owls. *"Del!"* Tom howled, and saw on the floor where he had been about to set his foot a partial upper plate from which a single white tooth protruded like a fencepost.

"We are over here, Tom," Collins' voice said from his right. "I trust you want to save your friend's life."

He swung around toward the voice—he heard his breath hissing in his mouth. The gun felt like a barbell. Collins sat in plain view on the owl chair, and Del was on his lap. They too were dappled with red.

"There's one bullet left," Tom said, trying to steady the gun on the magician's amused face. Del stared at him without recognition. "Del, get off his lap."

"He can't hear you. He won't, I should say. He's given up. He's gone inside and locked the door. Now, put down the gun."

Tom frantically tried to fit his left index finger into the trigger guard.

"I could melt that gun in your hand in a second," Collins said. "Or I could kill you by making it explode when you fired. If you had a chance to do it that way, you've lost it. It's time for you to make a sacrifice, Tom. It's time for you to choose. As Speckle John had to choose. The repeat performance isn't over—in fact, it has hardly begun." Behind him Tom gradually took in another blown-up photograph: Rose Armstrong dressed as a porcelain shepherdess, her high-browed face not a contemporary, not an American face at all, but of another century and place.

Tom lowered the gun.

"To save my nephew's life, will you sacrifice the pistol? Del is in traumatic shock, I must point out. He might die anyhow. But if you do not sacrifice the gun, I will stop his heart. You ought to know that I can do that."

"Then why don't you just stop mine?"

"Because then I would cheat myself out of the performance. But you have to decide." He smiled again. "I will give you yet another choice. The choice of giving up your song. Leave Del. Leave Rose—you will have to do that anyhow. And leave magic. Let me have your gifts. You could just walk out of Shadowland, and be precisely the boy you thought you were when you came here." Collins spread and lifted his hands: simple. "That is the best choice I can give you. Sacrifice your song, and use your legs to depart Shadowland for good."

"Del dies, and you keep Rose here. I leave unharmed, if I can believe you."

Del sagged on the magician's lap. His face was gray, and he scarcely seemed to be breathing.

"And the other choice?"

"You throw away the gun. Your song against mine. The performance continues until Shadowland has an undisputed master, the new king or the old. What do you say, boy?"

Take my magic and let me out of here, Tom shouted inside himself. He heard movement behind him and snapped his head sideways. Rose stood in the open door. *Knives.* How often, how many nights, had she been in this room where the owls screamed down from the ceiling? She silently pleaded with him, but she could have been pleading for either choice.

"Song," Tom said, and flipped the pistol toward the smeared bed. From the side of his eye he saw Rose slipping back out the door. The pistol landed with a squishing sound far out of his reach, and Tom's viscera curled around a block of ice. *I fooled you, I fooled you;* Lonnie Donegan's mocking chant to the inspectors on the Rock Island line went through him like a spear, and he knew that he had been forced, had forced himself back into the magician's game.

"Good. But of course you remember the salient point about wizards," Collins said.

I fooled you, I fooled you . . . got all pig iron!

"They get the house odds—they use their own decks. You should have walked, child." Collins stood up, his eyes flashed, and the owl chair was empty.

A dazed bird fluttered along the floor, its wing feathers painting the blood into delicate Japanese calligraphy.

21

Tom knew. Collins had carefully prepared him to know: he had foretold it, planted the seeds of this final betrayal in his mind. *They once were birds, but were tricked by a great wizard, and now they are still trying to sing and still trying to fly.* This dazed sparrow scrawling Japanese letters with Mr. Peet's blood on the polished wooden floor was trying to stand and move like a boy so that it could shutter up its mind again and be safe. The sparrow cheeped, and Tom knew that Del was screaming. In horror Tom watched as it fell on its side and fixed him with an eye like a madman's: a panicked black pebble.

The fairy tales had blown into each other and got mixed up, so that the old king had a wolf's head under his crown, and the young prince in love with the maiden fluttered and gasped in a sparrow's body, and Little Red Riding Hood walked forever on knives and sword blades, and the wise magician who enters at the end to set everything right was only a fifteen-year-old boy kneeling on bloodied floorboards and reaching for the transformed body of his closest friend.

"I can't change him back, Rose!" he wailed. The

sparrow-heart beat, a thousand times faster than his own, against the tips of his fingers.

"I don't know how to change him back!" He heard his voice as he had when the nails had gone in, sailing up high enough to freeze. The sparrow quivered in his hands. A wing feebly struck his thumb.

"Then you'll have to make Mr. Collins change him back," Rose said. She stood just inside the door, looking down at Tom with the stunned bird in his wrapped hands. *"Make* him do it," and her voice was fierce.

22

He came out of the bedroom holding Del as he had held the gun, and Coleman Collins was lounging against the top of the banister. "Welcome to the Wood Green Empire," the magician said. "Front-row seats? Excellent."

"Change him back," Tom said.

"Sorry, no refunds, no exchanges. You'll have to take your seats now."

"That's not him," Rose said at his shoulder. "It's a shadow."

"Oh, you told on me," the image said, and flickered away into dozens of dancing flames.

"WELCOME TO THE WOOD GREEN EMPIRE!" boomed the metallic voice. The bird trembled in Tom's hands, cheeping frantically, twisting its neck to look up into his face. The flames died before they fell, like fireworks, leaving them in darkness. Down the hall to Tom's side, moonlight cast panels of silver on the floor and folded halfway up the wall; otherwise Shadowland was as dark as the tunnels beneath the summerhouse.

Del went utterly still in his hands, and Tom feared that he had died. Then he felt a high regular throb beneath his fingers, the sparrow's heart thrilling away, and he opened his shirt and tenderly put Del next to his skin. He buttoned his shirt up halfway. Feathers rustled against his chest.

Outside, the fireworks began again with a thumping

explosion that rattled the windows down the hall and sent shooting rays of red and blue across the silvery pane of windows. Soft against his skin, Del made almost a human cry.

A beam of light at the bottom of the stairs: Herbie Butter outlined in light, dressed in his black tails, red wig, and white face. "We have a volunteer, ladies and gentlemen—the brave Tommy Flanagan, all the way from sunny Arizona in the United States of America! Are you ready, Tommy? Can you sing for us?"

"Change him back!" Tom shouted, and Herbie Butter rolled over in a backflip and landed on his feet, an index finger pointed to the sky.

"Change? Easier said than done, boy—but that's magic for you." He too dissolved into dancing, lilting flames.

"THE OLD KING! THE ONLY KING!"

Tom felt his way down the stairs in the dark.

. . . *Philly's wife looks a little peaked this summer, Nick* . . .

. . . *what you get from being in two places at once* . . .

Voices from the tunnels, come out to play in the dark. And voices from the other place that had been Shadowland.

. . . *if a senior drops his books on the floor, pick them up. Carry them where he tells you to carry them. Do anything a senior tells you to do* . . .

He came down from the last step and nearly stumbled, expecting another.

. . . *got that? You will be doomed to destruction, DOOMED TO DESTRUCTION, if you do not learn the moral lessons of this school.* . . .

He smelled the biting aroma of gin.

"Change him back!" he shouted: felt the crippling hysteria bubbling in him and knew that too could destroy him.

"You have to find the real one," Rose said. "He wants you to find him, Tom."

Tom cupped his hands around Del's shivering body. The sparrow had drawn up his feet and clamped up his wings, and was small and warm inside his shirt: small and warm and terrified enough to die of shock. That terror made his own insignificant. He looked down at the

pregnant little bulge in his shirt, and saw two circles of
blood where his palms had rested. His hysteria, something he could not afford, eased. "I want it too," he said.

23

They turned back into the main body of the house.
Sudden light stabbed his eyes, and Coleman Collins was
standing in a column of flame beside the row of theatrical
posters. Orange light danced on the opposite wall, on the
ceiling. "That was your shortcoming, you know," the
shadow said. "You simply were not capable of learning
the moral lessons. The Book would have been useless to
you. It never did Speckle John much good, either, as far
as I could see."

"You perverted the Book," Tom said. "You perverted
magic. Speckle John should have left you to die on that
hillside. The fox should have torn out your throat."

The elegant figure in the flame chuckled. "Now you
sound like Ouspensky." He mimed yawning and then
grinned. "You know, they were afraid of me, Ouspensky
and Gurdjieff. That is why they carried on so. Afraid of
me, like that ranter Crowley." The flame had begun to
consume itself from the bottom up.

Outside, fireworks battered in the sky.

The flame was a teardrop hanging in the air; only
Collins' head was visible in it. "And he was stronger than
you, dear boy. . . ." The flame and the head vanished
together.

He stood in the dark with Rose, feeling Del palpitating
against his belly. "You know, he's right. I can't do any of
those things he does. He's bound to beat me, and he
knows it." He felt shock radiating out from her and he
said, still with that fatalistic clarity, "It doesn't mean I'm
not going to try, but I can't do those things. I just can't."

"Have you ever tried?" came her voice.

"No—not projecting myself like that."

"Then try it."

"Right now?"

"Sure."

"I don't even know how to start."

"But haven't you been getting better—haven't you been learning?"

"I guess."

"Then just start. Try it. Now. For the sake of your confidence."

It would not do his confidence much good if he failed, he reflected, but tried anyhow. It had to be like all the rest, he thought. It had to be a place in his own mind and all he had to do was find it. Suppose there were a mirror in front of you, Tom. Suppose you could see yourself. Suppose the mirror-Tom could speak.

"You're better than he is, Tom," Rose whispered.

Del tucked himself together even more compactly against Tom's skin, and Tom remembered flowing down into Skeleton's mind, how that had felt . . . that feeling of gaining and losing control simultaneously, of flowing out . . . his eyes fluttered, and a key turned within him as he thought of Skeleton's gibberish unreeling out toward him, and a ball of light momentarily flickered in the corridor.

"Oh, do it, do it now," Rose pleaded.

Tom released it.

The Collector stood down there moving toward him with frustrated eyes and a foolish mouth—

KA-WHAMP! A rocket exploded over the house, big enough to send darts of light shooting in the window above the front door.

His mind jolted, and the Collector fell over. "Sorry," he said. He even laughed. "But did you see? It was harmless that time. There was nobody inside it."

"Put Tom down there," Rose insisted.

Tom reached toward the key again, and imagined not a mirror but himself on the day he had met Del, and felt the flowing, the letting go, and another Tom Flanagan took shape in a ball of light down the hall. He was pulling a beanie down to two fingers balanced on his nose. He smiled, opened his mouth, and a paralytic croak issued from him. He disappeared.

"You see?" Rose said.

Then light poured out from the entrance of the living room and showed them the collapsed rubbery bundle which was the Collector, and Tom knew that he had

moved it from the big theater just by thinking about
Skeleton. He heard a whirring noise, as if machinery had
been switched into life.

A second later, Humphrey Bogart walked into the hall
from the living room.

24

"You goint to do some tricks for us, kid?" Bogart asked.
He wore a slim black tuxedo, and a cigarette smoked in
his fingers. "Little more of the old razzle-dazzle before
the curtain comes down?"

"Del told me about some summer when he was
twelve—the whole thing was like a movie . . ." Tom
muttered these not very coherent remarks to Rose as he
watched the actor impatiently toying with his cigarette.
Tom looked sideways, but Rose had gone somewhere into
the darkness behind him.

"Come on, we got some people who are interested in
you," the actor said, and snapped his fingers. "Yeah, this
way. Come on in and join the party."

Tom went toward the entrance of the living room.

All the lights burned. A gathering of men in tuxedos, of
women in dresses, filled the living room. The smell of gin
invaded his nostrils again. "Hey, sonny," a bluff-faced
man Tom recognized as William Bendix shouted, "how
you doing!"

"*Oooo, Tom,*" crooned a platinum-blond woman with
very red lips and a playful face that made a delicious,
sensual joke of its own beauty. . . .

"Bird lover, are you?" Bogart said, and made to strike
Del cushioned in Tom's shirt. "Got a couple little dogs
myself."

"That monkey music—I can't take that monkey music," William Bendix snarled, though all Tom heard was
the chattering of dozens of voices and the whirring sound.
Bendix wore a porkpie hat on the back of his head and
was slamming a beer glass down on a bar.

"Aw, leave him alone—poor bastard has a plate in his
head," Bogart said, tugging Tom deeper into the party. "I

guess you never met Mr. and Mrs. Nightingale. They came here just to have the pleasure."

A man with a face like a run-over dog and a woman whose head was a charred stump were standing up from the flowered couch, holding out their hands and struggling to speak through mouths that had been seared shut. Tom gagged and stepped backward. Their clothes were smoking; curls of flame sprouted from the man's collar.

"Can that monkey music!"

"Never mind them, kid," and a hand spun Tom around. "They're too fried to talk straight—you remember those other people I mentioned?"

Snail and Thorn were standing beside the table, Tweedledum and Tweedledee all dressed up to go dancing (now he could hear the music, a trumpet lead over strings like a hundred make-out albums, *Jackie Gleason Plays for Lovers Only*).

"Can't stand it!" William Bendix hollered, smashing his beer glass against the bar.

Snail and Thorn bled from holes in their foreheads, though that was not where he had shot them, and their faces were blameless and bland, washed of emotion . . .

"Take a drink—aren't you a man?" Bogart sloshed something that smoked and bubbled from a decanter into a glass. He winked, and half his face jumped in a tic. "Just get this down into you, it'll chase away the snakes."

Tom was looking for Rose, and Humphrey Bogart was putting the smoking glass into his hand, which was whole and unharmed. Rose had disappeared.

Then a red-haired woman in a low-cut black dress leered at him—*she's . . . she's . . .* a face from a hundred movies, an uptilted nose and perfect mouth—and her face suddenly had needle teeth and a long red-furred snout—

and all the well-dressed people at the party had animal faces, monkeys and apes and foxes and wolves, and they were leering at him, chattering now over "Moonlight Becomes You." Tiger eyes set in glowing tiger stripes blinked toward him.

A creature with a pig's head was clamping his hand around a bubbling glass and forcing it to his lips, and Bobby Hackett was using his cornet to tell a girl that she certainly knew the right things to wear and across the

room a man named Creekmore was stumbling forward
with half his face dangling like a flap over gleaming bone.
Damp weeds dripped from his shoulder.

"Rose!" Tom called, but the party noises screwed up
loud enough to deafen him and a boar chuckled in his ear
and Bobby Hackett's spring-water tone had turned coarse
and blasting . . . something bitter and burning touched his
lips.

AWAY! he shouted with his mind. *GONE!* He closed
his eyes and mouth, and something burningly spilled
down his chin . . . and then silence, as if all power had
died.

Rose touched his face. "You're scaring me."

"Did you see them?" They were alone in the darkened
room. Moonlight pouring in through the glass doors
showed silver furniture, immaculate and dead.

"See what?"

A trace of gin—juniper and alcohol—lingered in the
air. Del's body thrummed against his skin.

"What scared you, Rose?"

She too was touched by the moonlight: her face hung as
white as a sail before him. "You were talking to yourself—you were acting funny."

His heart gradually slowed.

A blast of fireworks turned the room and her face
violently red: rose-red.

25

"I can't describe it," Tom said. "I think he almost got me.
I think he damn near killed me just now. You didn't see
anything?"

"Just you."

"You didn't even see that actor—Creekmore?"

She shook her head.

"He's dead. It wasn't just bloodbags and a few
scratches. He died like I was supposed to." Another
explosion outside rattled the windows and touched her
face with pale blue. "Rose, what did you think would
happen when you brought us back here?"

She shook her head. "Nothing like this." Her face worked: she was going to cry. "I thought he'd put on a show. And I thought I could get you and Del out in the middle of it." Now she was crying. "I'm sorry, Tom."

"You thought you would get me and Del out? Not yourself too?"

Whitened by the moonlight, her face altered and the tears stopped. She wiped her eyes. "Of course. Of course myself too."

"But we have something in common, don't we?"

Rose turned away from him and began to go back toward the hall.

"Why did he say you couldn't leave?"

Rose looked over his shoulder at him, slipped into the blackness beyond the doorway.

"Why does it. . . ?" *Why does it hurt you so to walk?* He gingerly put his right hand a few inches into his pocket and touched one of the sections of the broken shepherd-ess. He tweezed it out. The top half of a girl.

The top half of a girl.

Like . . .

Tom went toward the door and out into the corridor, following her. "Rose?" He threw the broken thing aside.

A thunderous noise from outside—*WHAMP! WHAMP!*—as if, yes, just as if a gigantic bird, a bird larger than the house, were battering it down with its wings.

"Rose!"

"AND NOW, LADIES AND GENTLEMEN, THE FAMOUS WINDOW OF FLAME!"

A blast of heat rocked him backward, and he shouted her name again. A second later, the point at which the corridor entered the other wing of the house flared into bright flame. Rose was running back toward him, cover-ing her face with her hands. Inside the solid flame, something was writhing and turning, twisting into itself like a hundred snakes.

Rose ran until she careered into him, and then she put her arms around his chest. Black stains spread along the ceiling; the glass on one of the framed posters shattered with a loud cracking noise.

"It *is* snakes," Tom said, watching the writhing forms within the solid flame.

"No. It's me," Rose said into his shirt.

He saw. Vines curled and twisted, the heads of roses flailed, impaling themselves on the thorns, stabbing themselves so they bled . . . the glass over another poster exploded.

BANG! Another gigantic wing beat from outside. Inside Tom's shirt, Del quivered and tried to flatten himself into nothing.

The blood was petals, dropping away and being consumed. But the whole flowers would not be consumed, they would twist in agony until the flowers died or disappeared.

"AND THE WINDOW OF ICE!"

As the heat had preceded fire, an intense chill poured through the corridor a moment before the fire froze into place, turned gray-white and monumental.

The orange light disappeared with the fire, and a single white spot glowed down from the ceiling on a version of Coleman Collins. He was leaning against the glacial wall in an open-collared chambray shirt. "You could have gone that way, you know, but that would have been too easy—especially since you escaped your drink in the living room. I rather expected you to work your way out of that one, you know. Congratulations!"

"Change Del back," Tom said.

"For that, you'll have to speak to the original," the shadow said. "He's still waiting. He wants to see the end of the performance, too. It's been a long time, you know. Over thirty years." The shadow smiled. "In the meantime, did you enjoy the picture of little Rose's plight?"

Behind him, the impaled and twisted blossoms hung half-visible in the ice.

"The rose that wounds itself," the shadow mused. "Poignant, isn't it? But not half so poignant if you know she wanted it. Prayed for it. Begged for it. Perhaps not unlike how your old friend Mr. Ridpath begged to be fitted into that contraption." He nodded at the collapsed and singed Collector, which lay heaped against the wall.

Another gigantic wingbeat pounded at the house, and this one was followed by the unmistakable noise of the glass doors in the living room shattering beneath the blow.

"We are all getting impatient with you, Mr. Flanagan," the shadow said. "Why don't you locate the old king and settle the issue?"

"I'm trying to do that," Tom said. "*Damn* you."

The shadow clapped his hands, and the wall of ice slid out of existence, becoming so transparent that the frozen roses blazed out a moment before they too faded into transparency. "Your friend should be able to help you distinguish the real from the false. Or don't you remember your old stories?"

Then he too was gone, leaving behind him the impression of a smile and the smells of singed carpet and blistered paint.

"What old stories, Rose?" He turned on her. "Tell me. What stories did he mean? If you knew all along . . ."

She stepped backward, alarmed. "Not me," she said. "He didn't mean me. He couldn't have."

Tom could have screamed with frustration. "There isn't anyone else. He did mean you."

"I think he meant Del," Rose said.

26

"Think," Rose said. "You know, and he knows you know. Remember it, Tom."

"Del?" It was an almost fantastically cruel joke. "It can't be." He fumbled with two shirt buttons, working them with thumb and index finger until the flat white disks found the holes. Del flopped out onto his palm; the wings feebly stretched. "Oh, my God. Oh, Del."

"Think about what he said," Rose pleaded.

Another pane of the glass door exploded into the living room.

"We read stories in English class," Tom said, frantically trying to remember . . . a sparrow? "We read 'The Goose Girl.' We read 'Brother and Sister.' We read . . . *shit*. It's no use. 'The Fisherman and His Wife.' 'The Two Brothers.' It's no good." What he remembered was how

birds had plagued him: how a robin on the lawn had
looked in through a window and drilled him with its eyes;
a starling in a Quantum Heights tree quizzing him as the
world revolved and witches filled the sky.

"It's no good," Tom said. "Our teacher said . . . ah, in
'Cinderella,' he said a bird was the messenger of the
spirit. A bird gave her pretty clothes. Another bird took
out the stepsisters' eyes. Oh, wait. Wait. It's 'Cinderella.'" He held Del out from his body. "Birds tell the
prince that the stepsisters are not to be his bride. They
make him find Cinderella. The birds make him find the
right bride."

In the darkness Rose was looking up at him with
gleaming eyes. Del stirred on his bandaged palm.

"Find him," Tom whispered, feeling half-exalted, half-
sick with the impossibility of both his task and Del's.
"*Find* him."

Del's head lifted; his wings unfurled. And Tom's heart
loosened too, and overflowed. On his bloody, aching
hands the bird opened its wings and beat them down.
Once. Twice. *Go, little bird. Go, Del.* A third time the
wings opened and beat down, and the sparrow lifted off
Tom's hands.

The messenger of spirit swooped into the air. *Find him.
For us, for you. Find him.*

The messenger circled in the dark air above them, then
settled once on Tom's shoulder—a gesture like a pat on
the head, a gesture of love—and took off down the
corridor.

27

They followed it, stumbling past the abandoned Collector
in the dark, past the entrance to the forbidden room, past
the door to the Little Theater. Del flew in rapid, excited
circles before the Grand Théâtre des Illusions, darting
again and again at the door.

Rose reached the door before Tom.

Another gigantic wingbeat rattled the entire back of the
house. Tom heard the case in the living room toppling

over, breaking the glass doors and splintering the wood. Inside it, the porcelain figures would be smashed and crumbled into each other.

"What is that outside?" Rose asked.

"An owl. Another messenger."

"It's not him?"

"No. It means someone is going to die," Tom said. "It means someone should have died already. The performance was supposed to end a little while after they . . ." He almost swooned, remembering precisely how Collins had held the glowing nails and used them to rape his hands. "Stay out here," he said.

"I'm coming with you," she said, and pushed open the door. She took two steps in and halted.

The sparrow sailed inside, into light and noise. A crowd filled the seats.

28

"You have front-row seats," three Herbie Butters said from three owl chairs. "Please take them."

Tom looked at them, scarcely bothering with the audience that had transfixed Rose. People from another age stared at the three magicians, peeled oranges, stuffed candies into their mouths, smoked. Unlike their painted images, which were visible at the rear of the Little Theater, they moved in the seats, raised their arms, applauded, and called out inaudible comments in a general din.

"You see, they like my little illusions," three Herbie Butters said in unison. "And now my volunteers will attempt to distinguish reality from its shadow. Failure to do so will bring a penalty, ladies and gentlemen."

Cheers: catcalls.

"Change Del back," Tom said, pitching his voice to go under the uproar behind him.

"Ah! The boy wants me to work magic on his pet—a sparrow, ladies and gentlemen! Our volunteer is very droll." He held up his palm. "But he is more than that, my friends. The young man is an apprentice magician. He thinks he could entertain you as well as I."

More cheers; derisory shouts. Tom looked over his shoulder, saw Rose just turning away from the audience with a stricken, horrified expression. In her face was the conviction that they could not win. Up in the middle of the twentieth row, Del's parents, with their smashed heads and burning clothes, were politely applauding. Around them, visible behind Rose, men and women with animal faces screamed down at them and the stage.

"You see what audiences are, my little volunteer," said the three Herbie Butters in unison. "All audiences are the same. They want symbolic blood—they want *results*. You cannot trifle with an audience. Are you ready to make your choice?"

Zoo noises erupted from the thrashing audience. Tom glanced back and saw that everyone, even Del's parents, wore the heads of beasts. Dave Brick writhed there too, stuffed into Tom's old jacket, with a sheep's head on his shoulders.

"You see, you must never . . ." said the Herbie Butter on the left.

". . . make the fatal mistake of thinking . . ." said the Herbie Butter in the center.

". . . that any audience is friendly," said the Herbie Butter on the right. "Are you ready to make your choice? You will be severely penalized if you choose wrong. I PROMISE YOU THAT!" he shouted to the audience, who screamed back in a thousand animal voices.

Tom looked up. Their messenger of spirit was circling in the vastness overhead, frantically trying to find its way out, like any bird.

Is there any Del left in you? Tom thought: his mind was fraying apart, shredding under the onslaught of noise from the audience of beasts. *Or are you lost, just a sparrow now?*

The sparrow came to rest on a pipe and was almost invisible, far up above him. He saw its head twitching from side to side.

"We're waiting," said three voices.

Find him, Tom thought. *Find Collins.*

"If you do not make your choice, you will be sent back," said three voices. "You will be part of the audience forever. For they are each important, and each adds to the whole."

Find Collins.

"Your pet is not a bird in a story," said the Herbie Butter on the left.

"He is only a pestilential sparrow," said the Herbie Butter in the middle.

And that would be right, Tom knew. No angels were looking after him and Del. The messenger of spirit was no longer a messenger of anything. Del's mind had guttered out in the frantic, restless little body.

"Del!" he shouted.

"One of a hundred lost pets," said one of the magicians.

The sparrow left the pipe and swooped down over the audience, causing an uproar of shouts and curses.

Find him. Find him. Whatever you are now.

The sparrow curved in flight, and went for the stage. Tom's heart paused: his blood slowed in his veins. The sparrow flew in a straight line over the three figures on the stage, circled back and flew over them again. It came down suddenly, and as it went toward the lap of the magician on the left, Tom screamed, "That's enough! Leave him! He's going to—"

The sparrow came to rest on the knee of the magician on the left.

"The young man *is* a magician, ladies and gentlemen," Collins said through the mask of Herbie Butter. "This part of the performance is concluded." He tenderly reached forward and closed his fingers about the sparrow's body, and his companions faded into dark pools cast on the stage by opposed spotlights. "My friends in the audience, this young man's pet has given his life so that his master may advance another stage."

He's what you call a stooge, someone whispered behind Tom. *You'll see. It's all part of the act.*

Collins stood up from the owl chair, gripping the sparrow in his right hand and holding it out, brandishing it. "You see before you a real bird," he caressingly intoned. "You have seen it fly. What is it? A boy's pet, a winged rodent, or a messenger of spirit? You have heard how magical birds aid their masters in quests and divinations, you know how they roam widely and freely in the world, bringing rumors of goodness here and there, soaring above what holds us to our earthly existences—

ladies and gentlemen, aren't birds our very image of the
magical?" He thrust forward the bird, and it—Del—
poured out a cascade of melody unknown to any sparrow,
as though its whole body had been filled with leaping
song.

Oh, Del. That's you. And you're not afraid.

"You see—a special bird. Does it not deserve a place in
the eternal?"

Still the heartbreaking cascade of melody erupted from
the captured sparrow.

"Do I need my fiddlers three?"

"NO!" bellowed the audience of beasts.

"Do I need my pipe and my bowl?"

"NO!"

"No. You have it, ladies and gentlemen. You comprehend. The singing bird is magic itself. It is indeed the
messenger of spirit. And it could sing, I assure you, any
melody you called out—but it has already surpassed such
vulgar tricks. So I propose to give this living spirit
messenger, with your permission, ladies and gentlemen of
the perfect audience, its final form. Its ultimate form."

"No!" Tom shouted, echoing the roars of the audience.

"Yes." Collins smiled down at him and released the
bird. The song cascaded fully out, spearing Tom with
what Del was bringing forth from his trapped soul, the
liquid and overflowing song which was Del's only speech.
Del ascended an inch above the magician's hand and

no no no no—please—

froze, shooting out a spray of refracted colors, was
silent, the miraculous song cut off in the middle of an
ascending note; the ghost of the note sailed into the
ceiling; and a glass bird fell back into the magician's
hands.

Del.

"You are in Shadowland, boy," Collins said. "You are
part of the performance. You cannot leave." He bent
forward, and Tom stepped up to stand before him, afraid
that he would drop what Del had become as Del had
deliberately shattered the Ventnor owl. The audience
ceased its roaring. Tom vaguely saw Rose coming toward
him with an expression of total dismay—*We can't do it,
Tom, I thought we could but I was wrong, we'll always be*

here—and tremblingly took the glass sparrow from Collins' hands.

"Now for your own conclusion," Collins said. "You know it's over, don't you? Look. Our audience has gone home."

Tom did not have to look. He knew the seats were empty now, waiting for the next repeat performance and the next after that.

"Rose is already mine," Collins said. "And so are you, but you don't know it yet."

The lights snapped off. Collins' fingers brushed his own, and the glass sparrow was filled with glowing many-colored light.

29

Tom stepped backward in the punctured darkness, aware after a moment of blinding pain that the magician had healed his wounds. In the moment of pain, the glass sparrow had jumped out of his hand and landed safely on the carpet before the stage, where its inner light darkened and died.

The handkerchieves fell from his hands.

"Tom?"

"Wait," he said, and picked up the glass sparrow. No light was left in it.

"Now it is your time, apprentice," Collins whispered.

"Why did you heal me?" Rose found his waist, her arm circled him, and they both backed in lockstep into the first row of seats.

"I want you as you came," Collins said. "Aura. I don't want you to have the aura of a wounded fawn. I want the original Tom Flanagan, complete in every aspect—the shining boy."

Tom pushed Rose sideways, toward where he remembered the door was placed.

"You can see me, can't you?" Collins whispered. "Even in the dark, boy? I can see you perfectly well."

And he could see the magician, for he was wrapped in a dazzling, rippling band of color.

"Del was not enough. The other messenger demands you."

"Or you," Tom said. He held up his right hand. It was in darkness, but ribbons of light ran about it. Rose sucked in her breath, terrified.

"You've frightened our dear little Rose. She's never seen you in full dress before. Never seen your choir robes. But then, you haven't either, have you?"

"I'm as good as you are," Tom said, knowing he was not.

The magician ripped off the wig and sent it sailing toward the stage, where first it glimmered and then dimmed like a cheap lightbulb.

"Speckle John thought so too."

CRASH! Another deafening, destroying wingbeat.

"The owl wants to be fed."

Tom made sure of his grip on the glass sparrow with one hand; clamped Rose's wrist with the other and gave a signaling tug; and ran.

30

Behind him in the empty theater Collins started to laugh, and Rose went only a few steps before she said, "I can't. I can't run. You go. I'm his anyway."

"You won't stay." He yanked her along behind him and pulled her through the open door.

"We can't get away."

He looked past Rose and saw a flickering outline coming calmly, inexorably toward the door.

My little girl is right. Collins was feeling inside his mind as he had felt inside Skeleton's. *You cannot. Look at me.*

The outline blazed like a lightningbolt, so strongly that purple and red radiance flashed through the door and made the wall opposite momentarily gleam like a neon sign.

You will be at home in Shadowland, Tom. I am your father and mother now.

"Just come on," he said, and dragged her down the hall. She had begun to cry: not from fear, he knew. From pain. "Hurry," he commanded.

They had exactly one chance, Tom thought. An impossible chance, but their only one. If Collins could send a fishing line into his mind, he could send one back. Burn that ball back—Skeleton had said it, dredging up what must have been some miserable childhood memory. Okay, I'll burn that ball back. I'll take off his head with it.

Rose sobbed with every step.

"Only a little more. Only a few more feet." He felt for the light switch on the wall outside the kitchen, and his fingers ran over ribbed plastic. "There." Yellow light fell on them.

The curled posters, the shattered glass. The carpet had been singed into black popcorn. Big oval blisters bulged from the walls, surrounded by meteor showers of smaller, round blisters.

No need for shadows now.

Rose jerked in pain or surprise beside him, and he thought it was because of Collins. But she was looking in the wrong direction for that—behind him, in the direction of the living room and front door.

"You're going to need a little help, Red," came a velvety voice. In the same moment, Tom whirled around and the scarred receptacle from which he had pulled Skeleton Ridpath shuddered to its feet.

Climb in, boy? Or do I have to push you?

"Just remember you got a great big battery," Bud Copeland said. "You found out a lot of things about yourself today, but you got to forget about that now. You have to think about the job, son."

The Collector dangled in the hall, knocking itself against the blistered and discolored walls. Its empty head swiveled toward Tom; toward Rose; back to Tom.

Bud moved up beside them, and there was the shock of seeing right through him again, to the blisters on the wall. They looked like stains on the fabric of his suit.

"I'll give you a big, big shove. You'll have a real good time. Way way way way down in the dump."

Tom's mind felt a sudden wrench, followed by an enormous flaring pain.

"Remember what you heard, Red. Anybody can be collected at any time."

Collins went fishing in his mind again, and the hook snagged on the picture he had of himself and Skeleton

down in there, trapped inside the Collector. He stepped
back, more afraid of that picture than he'd been of
anything at Shadowland; more afraid of that than death.

"You don't want to run, do you, Red? You want to stay
near where you got to stay."

Yes, he thought. Where I got to stay. He felt Collins
jerking him like a fish, and he blasted, *Out!*

"I'm what you know, Red," Bud told him. "That's all I
am now. *You* brought me here—so I could tell you. I'm
just your shadow. That's your battery working, Red.
Crank it up as high as it can get."

But I don't know how to crank it up, Tom thought
despairingly: sometimes things just come.

"Like you did on the wall with nails through your
hands," Bud's voice whispered. Or was that his own
voice? "It's not going to be any easier than that. But I
helped him long enough—now I'm going to help you." He
vanished, and Tom felt suddenly abandoned.

Collins appeared at the corner of the hallway, surrounded by a prismatic light.

If I made you come, Tom said inside himself, *then come
back. I need you. Now.*

"Now," Collins echoed, and the force of his mind
jerked Tom forward to him. "Now, little bird."

31

It was like being caught in a typhoon. Invisible wind
pushed him, tore all but his helplessness from his
thoughts—he forgot Bud and Rose as he struggled to stay
on his feet. He fought to stay away from Collins and the
Collector, but the typhoon swung him irresistibly forward.
The wind whipped him sideways, and his head cracked
against the wall. Smell of burning: the smell of Carson
warping toward destruction. Strong hands were inside his
head, a hook was in his brain, tugging and tugging.

Strong little bird, aren't you?

The glass sparrow in his hand turned glowing red. *No!*
his mind shouted, and the pull of the hands weakened.
The typhoon dropped him.

Collins' face hovered a foot from his own—the sneering mouth, the powerful nose. The Herbie Butter makeup was dripping down his cheeks, streaking away, as if being burned off from within.

It's work for him too, Tom realized.

He shot an impulse from his own mind straight into Collins' eyes, aware of Rose screaming back there by the living room—she had been screaming since he had been torn away from her. Collins reared back, and he tried to follow his impulse into the magician's head.

Revulsion checked him: not the blind, lost feeling when he had probed Rose's mind, but the instinctive holding back of touching something repugnant, a cancer. . . . Collins' mind slammed against his like a crossed sword.

Not that way, brat. It's your bedtime.

Collins pushed into his mind with terrific force, and he reeled among images of lacquered birds, steaming bodies, one great bird swooping down to carry him off. Circuits in his brain smoked and flamed . . . *locked in that room for good, boy, that's where you'll be. . . .*

In his hands, the glass sparrow turned black.

Hands, fishhooks, metal clamps like those that had held the squalling badger—all this poured into Tom and grasped something that seemed like a white bird.

Bedtime, child.

Collins started to haul him out. The whites of the magician's eyes burned red.

Tom summoned up Bud Copeland with the last of his flickering energy. *Come back, Bud, now . . . now . . .*

"You again," he heard Collins say, and the cruel machinery opened and loosened within him; and for Tom there was a drift of a thought—*You betrayed me, bird . . .*

"You are the traitor," he heard Bud say. "Not the boy. Let him go, Doctor."

"You lost! Leave me!" Collins shouted. "I sent you into insignificance!"

Tom looked sideways, falling back out of Collins' grasp. The glass sparrow flashed yellow light, and the warmth of it went through his hand, burning a little on the fresh scar tissue.

"You told the boy everything here came from the meeting of your mind with his," Bud said. "And that's all

I am. Guess you gave him a weapon, Doctor, without knowing you were doing it."

And then a sidling, sly, sidestepping voice in his own mind and nowhere else: a voice he knew was his own, though it came wrapped in Bud's gorgeous rumble. *You waitin' for the next train, child?*

"NO!" Collins screamed. "You helped him! Traitor!"

The wings shook the entire house, reminding Tom of the vastness of the powers just under his tongue and just behind his eyes. "Look at me, killer," he said. "I'm going to feed the owl."

He knew the glass bird was gold and red, knew that he was broadcasting an aura to fill the entire house.

"TRAITOR!" Collins screamed, and his eyes locked into Tom's: but Tom was already pouring in, grasping Collins as he had grasped Skeleton Ridpath, going past pictures of dead men with their faces ripped apart and exploding airplanes, going into the swamp of Collins' being, where nothing could hold him now, going as invincibly as if he wore white armor and feeling Collins melt beneath him. A bolt like lightning shivered him, but he grabbed and held, gripped the stuff of Collins' being and ripped backward. *Get those fingers back.*

The secret did lie in hating well.

"The pain won't be as bad as you anticipate," he whispered. He pulled with everything in him, feeling the power blossom out and engulf Collins, feeling it wrapping about a squirming, wriggling, finally helpless force; and broke it; broke free.

Something invisible and screaming was held suspended in the air: something treacherous and furious, something that would have been pure if it had not been so fouled by misuse.

Tom groaned, and stuffed it deep down inside the Collector. "Slam dunk," he muttered.

Rose tottered back, mumbling in fright, not knowing what had happened. In front of Tom, Collins' body lay in the corridor in what appeared to be deep coma. Beside it, the Collector, a threat again, whirled toward him with its unappeasable hunger.

"This time I can remember how to finish it," he said. Tom stepped to his side, the Collector tracking him brightly, and reached inside the bathroom and slammed the button home.

32

The whole purple body, damaged by the earlier flames, flowed past Tom, howling wordless sounds of disbelieving shock, and was pulled through the door. It grasped the frame with its fingers. The melted eyes found Tom, and the boy saw what he had not wanted to see: Collins far down inside, scrambling for release, still enough himself to think he could escape and trying to fight his way out of that awful room with its pressing horrors, the very grease of human misery. *You made it,* Tom thought. *It's yours.* The fingers weakened, and the Collector flowed out of sight.

Tom stepped into the bathroom. He turned on the light. The mirror showed a roiling, smoky confusion. He switched the light off and tottered out.

"You did it," Rose breathed. "I was hardly . . . I didn't think that anybody . . ."

"Yeah," Tom said. He sat down. Bud was gone; but Bud had never been there. "Fine. Got one more thing to do."

Rose hovered in the dim light. "One more. . . ?"

"Ladies and gentlemen," he pronounced, almost enjoying the sight of Rose's tremulous uncertainty. "Come over this way, Rose. I don't want you to get hurt. Ladies and gentlemen . . . the amazing Wall of Fire."

He had strength enough to reach down inside himself and find the key that had to be there. *Fire,* he thought, and a feeble little row of flames sprang up along the carpet directly before him. Rose stepped nearer to him. "Not much of a wall," he said, and giggled with exhaustion. "More of a picket fence. Let's improve it."

And through his headache thought it into being. The row of flames mounted the wall and began to lick at the ceiling. Tom sat slumped in the hall and watched the fire grow. It ate the frame of the bathroom door, and looked as beautiful as a rose garden to him. He heard it spreading down the hall, feeding on the carpet, going toward the living room. It would love the staircase. Get it all, he thought, swallow every inch of it, and did not have to reach for more of his strength because the fire would swallow everything anyhow.

He dully watched it spring up along the frames of the posters. Through the opening between the burning carpet and the fire spreading across the ceiling, he saw the flames speed into the living room.

He giggled again. "Forgot to think about a way out, Rose. Sit down and enjoy the pretty fire." He picked up the glass sparrow and cradled it on his lap. "Did you hear him singing, Rose? Did you hear that? That was the most beautiful thing . . . it sounded like he was so happy. It sounded better than that." The fire moved toward his shoes. "I'm sorry there isn't a way to get out, Rose."

"Of course there's a way to get out," she said.

"As a barbecue. Sit down and let's be barbecued together. I don't know what you are, but I love you anyhow."

She reached for him, and he raised his hand. The heat was starting to cook him now, and he imagined that there might be a minute or two of pain, only a little worse than the pain he had already suffered. But instead of sitting beside him and holding his hand, she pulled. "I can't," he said, and she pulled again, and he staggered up.

"The tunnels, you dummy," she said. "We can go back under the lake."

She pulled up the trapdoor, and he looked around for a last time at the forbidden room. "You know," he said, "he really was a great magician. Del was right about that. And at the beginning, it's hard to believe now, but at the beginning it was even fun in a way. I kept trying to figure out what it was all about."

Rose looked at him with cautious but almost maternal curiosity.

"There's something in this room," he remembered. "Rose, I can't leave until I find it."

"There's nothing here," she said. And that seemed true.

"Something he said he was going to leave here for me—

when he thought I might stay with him. I have to find it."

"We don't have any time."

"I don't think it'll take any time."

He woozily looked over the silvery gray walls. There had been a moment, the day after his "welcome," when he had paused at the door and sensed the presence in here of some invisible scene: Shadowland had wanted him to read the Book.

"Hurry!" Rose said. The noises of the fire were advancing down the hall.

"It's here," he said dreamily. He turned about, still amazed that he could stand. He was looking at the wall opposite the door. Tom walked past the entrance to the tunnels and ran his hands over the wall. It was already warm. He gently moved his hand over the silvery paint.

A panel swung open onto a little recess. The Book lay on a wooden stand, opened in the middle and surrounded by plush. If he had perverted the Book, Collins had at least kept it reverentially. Tom reached in and took the leather-bound volume off the stand. He reached behind his back and slid it under his belt where he had kept the old pistol. "All right," he said. "I'm ready now."

Rose led the way down into the tunnel.

33

The way back, as it always is, was easier than the way forward. Tom heard no voices, no Twenties Nick sang "Sweet Sue" and wafted himself another pull of prewar gin; the only noise they heard, and it followed them for half an hour, was the whooshing of the fire that consumed Shadowland: as if that were all Twenties Nick needed to hear before he could go back to his long sleep. The owl had been fed.

"I'm so tired," Tom said. Rose moved steadily on before him, playing the flashlight on the wooden supports and flaking walls.

Soon he saw their sleeping bags unrolled in the vaulted cavern. "Please. I'm going to fall down."

"The house is only about ten minutes away," Rose

said. "I have a better idea. You can sleep on the beach. In fresh air."

He followed her back to the summer house.

34

Rubbing his eyes, he came up into the dark living room. The sparrow weighed like a heavy suitcase in his right hand. Rose glimmered before him in the green dress: he realized that she had come barefoot all the way from the house. "You must want to lie down too," he said. "Aren't there beds here? I just have to . . . I could take a nap." His eyes were burning.

"Whose bed do you want," Rose said. "Thorn's or Snail's?"

"Oh, my God." He could not sleep in those beds. "But why the beach?"

She put her arm around him. "It's so close, darling Tom. Just a few steps more."

She took him out of the room and onto the porch. The moon made all bright with a magical silvery light which transformed all it touched. The world was a place of wonders. The edge of the sky before them burned a faint orange-red.

"I like that little beach," Tom said. "I used to look for you there sometimes. The week before I got sick."

"I was always looking for you," Rose told him. "I was looking for you long before you came here."

"Come back to Arizona with me. Could you do that, Rose?" She was leading him down the steps. The grass was that leaning ocean, breathed upon by moonlight, he had seen once before. "Del wanted that. He said it to me once. We could find you somewhere to live. I guess we could."

"Of course we could," she said.

"We could get married when I'm eighteen. I'll work. I could always work, Rose."

"Of course you could," she said.

They were walking down the overgrown roadway. Each

leaf on the trees about him shone with silvery light. The trunks were made of silver and pitchy onyx. "So you'll marry me?" he said.

"In eternity we are married."

"In eternity we're married now," Tom said. That seemed overwhelmingly delightful and overwhelmingly true. "It's just a little way now, isn't it?"

"Just a little way."

They came through delicate brush onto the beach, also silvered by kindly moonlight. Across the water Shadowland gouted flame. The smoke pouring from the burning roof was darker than the sky. They stood on the sand a moment, watching it engulf itself. Tom saw flames moving behind the upper windows where Collins' temptations had been arrayed before him. "The funny thing is, he was great," Tom said. "He was just what he said he was."

"Lie down," Rose said. "I don't want to look at that anymore. You need to sleep." She stretched out on the pewter sand. "Please lie down next to me."

"Hey . . . how do we get out? The wall . . . the barbed wire . . . we'll have to go back—"

"No, you won't. Follow a path behind the summer house. It leads to a wooden gate."

"Clever Rose." He lay down beside her on the sand, put the book beside him, and set the glass bird on top of it. Then he turned to Rose and took the perfect girl, the magic that seemed no magic but earthly bounty, in his arms.

35

They did not make love. Tom was content to hold her, to feel the petal skin of her shoulders, the curve of her skull beneath his hands. He could have sung like Del, in his friend's last moments, of the perfection of such things. Radiant moonlight, warm sand along his side, Rose's quiet breathing swinging him toward sleep.

In eternity they were married.

"Rose?" he muttered, and she made an interrogatory

mmm? "He told me a story—he told a story he said was about you."

"Shhh," she breathed, and put her fingers on his mouth, and he swung all the way into oblivion.

36

Did she say anything before she left? We do not know. She would have spoken to him, I think, whispered a message into his sleeper's ear, but that message would have joined his bloodstream like Del's final song and would have been impossible to reconstruct into ordinary flawed human speech. And again like Del's song, which was an expression of completion and the end of change, it would have spoken of, would have hymned a further and necessary and unforeseen transformation: it is like saying that the message would have been the heartbeat of magic.

In his sleep, he heard her go; and heard the rippling of the water.

When he awakened it was to warm cloudless day, the sun already high. He saw that she was gone, and called her name. He called it again.

Across the lake Shadowland, a smoking hole in the landscape, fumed like an old pipe.

"Rose?" he called again, and finally looked at his watch. It was eleven in the morning. "Rose! Come back!" He stood up, looked into the trees and did not see her, and for a moment was sick with the thought that she had returned to the house.

But that could not be: the house no longer existed. Rubble would have fallen into the entrance of the tunnel and blocked it off for good. A few boards jutted up, one chimney stood in a blackened column. Everything else was gone. Rose was freed from that.

As was he. For the first time he looked at his hands in daylight and saw the round pads of scar tissue.

He sat down to wait for her. Even then, he knew that if he waited until his beard grew to his waist and men danced on the moon and stars, she would never come back. He waited anyhow. He could not leave.

Tom waited for her all day. The minutes crawled—he was back in common time, and no one could fold the hours together like a pack of cards. He watched the lake change color as the sun crossed, changing from deep blue to paler blue to light green and back to blue. In the late afternoon he gently moved the glass sparrow onto the sand and opened the leather-bound book. He read the first words: *These are the secret teachings of Jesus the son of God, as told by him to his twin, Judas Thomas.* He closed the book. He remembered what Rose had said to his frantic speculation that they might have to go back through the destroyed house. *No you won't.* Not: no we won't. She would not go down the path to the gate with him: she would not trek into the village, holding his hand, or stand at his side while they waited for a train.

Tom waited until the brightness drained from the air. Shadowland still smoldered, and a few sparks drifted down the bluff, falling toward a thin layer of ash the rain would take in the fall. When the falling sparks glowed like tiger's eyes, he stood up.

He walked toward the water, carrying the glass sparrow and the book. He went to his knees on the damp sand just before the edge of the water. He set down the sparrow and looked at it. At its center hung a deep blue light. He wanted to say something profound, but profundity was beyond him: he wanted to say something emotional, but the emotion itself held his tongue in a vise. "Here you go," was what came out of him. He gave the sparrow a push into the water. It glided an inch or so along the bottom, then a ripple passed over it on the surface of the lake and the sparrow seemed to move against the motion of the ripple, going deeper into the lake. The blue in the glass was identical to the blue of the water. Another unseen ripple took it with it, and the sparrow went— flew—so far ahead under the water he could not see it.

Tom stood up, pushed the book into his belt, and walked back across the beach. Soon he was parting the delicate brush.

The End of the
Century Is in
Sight

The end of the century is in sight and Tom Flanagan's story was about events more than twenty years back in time. I listened to it here and there about the world, and wondered what sort of story it was and how much of it was invention. I also constantly wondered about what Tom had been reading. His imagination had surely concocted those radical illusions—the speeding of time, the transformations and the sudden dislocations of space, also the people with animal faces, which were straight from the works of symbolist painters like Puvis de Chavannes—and I thought that he had been steeping himself in lurid and fantastic novels. He had wanted to give me good value.

The idea that Laker Broome had been a minor devil was a ripe example of this. It was true that I, like all the new boys, had assumed he had been at Carson for years. Yet Broome had been the Carson headmaster for our

freshman year only—when we returned in September a
capable man named Philip Hagen had his job, and we
assumed that Broome's breakdown and his conduct during the fire had blessedly got him out of the way.

I wrote to the Association of Secondary School Headmasters, and found that they had no information about
Laker Broome. He was not in their files. One night, still
trying to find what had become him, I called up Fitz-
Hallan and asked him if he remembered what had
happened to Broome. Fitz-Hallan thought he had managed to get a post at . . . He named a school as obscure as
Carson. When I wrote to the school, I got back a letter
saying that they had had the same headmaster from 1955
to 1970, and that no one named Laker Broome had ever
been on their staff. However, a penciled note at the
bottom said that a Carl Broome had come to them in 1959
as a Latin teacher and had stayed only one year; might I
have the wrong name? Why was Carl Broome released
after a year? I wrote back on a long shot, but was
informed that such matters "are a part of the confidence
which any school of repute must retain with respect to
former employees." This was very fishy—didn't they give
recommendations?—but it was clear that they did not
wish to tell me what I wanted to know; and anyhow, I was
fairly certain that Laker was not Carl Broome, so there
was no point in continuing. Lake the Snake had lost his
job and disappeared. That was all I knew about him.

Tom's story had abandoned Steven Ridpath as he
(presumably) crept out the front door and wriggled
through the bars of the gate, and I imagined that a
conversation with Ridpath would immediately tell me
how much of Tom's story had been fiction. Here I had
much more luck than with Laker Broome. Skeleton had
gone to Clemson, and universities keep wonderful records. The Alumni Office told me that one Ridpath,
Steven, had graduated near the bottom of his class in
1963. From there he had gone to a theological college in
Kentucky.

A theological college? A Kentucky Bible school?

It seemed impossible, but it was true—the Headley
Theological Institute in Frankfort told me that Mr.
Ridpath had attended from 1963 to 1964, when he had

converted to Catholicism and left them for a seminary in Lexington. The Lexington seminary, run by an order of monks, eventually wrote me that Steven Ridpath had become Brother Robert, and had been placed in a monastery near Coalville, Kentucky.

I drove from Connecticut down to Coalville to see if he would talk to me.

Coalville was a run-down hamlet—no other word would fit—of three hundred people. Unhappy buildings sat in an unhappier landscape. Wherever a stand of trees grew, behind it was a wasteland of slag heaps and abandoned mining buildings. There was a motel, but I was the only guest. I sent a note to the monastery. Would Brother Robert agree to discuss with me whatever had led him to this unlikely destination? I let the assumption stand that I was doing an article or a book about the decision to enter the church.

Come if you must, came a note by return mail. *I expect you have made a useless journey.*

I appeared at the monastery gates at the time he had named. It was still early enough for roosters to be crowing within the grounds—there was a farm there, and the brothers raised their own food. I swung the clapper in the big bell and waited and shivered in the early chill.

Eventually a monk pulled open the gates. He wore a coarse brown robe and the hood shaded his face. "Brother Robert?" I said, startled by this apparition.

"Brother Theo," he said. "Brother Robert is waiting for you in the garden." He turned about without another word and preceded me up a stony path.

We went around the side of a red brick dormitory. "Our farm," Brother Theo said, and gestured with a flap of his sleeves. I looked to the left and saw a red barn disgorging cows after their morning milking. It still seemed impossible that Skeleton Ridpath was in such a place. "The chicken coop," said Brother Theo. "We have sixty-eight hens. Good sound layers."

At last we came to another gate. Over a brick fence I could see massed rosebushes. The brothers would soon have to begin pruning, for the roses were crowded together, fulsome and blowsy. My guide opened the gate. A gravel path led between banks of roses. "Follow the path," he said. "In fifteen minutes I shall see you out."

"Fifteen minutes?" I asked. "Can't I have a little more time?"

"The time was specified by Brother Robert." He turned away.

I set off down the path. It led me around a corner, and when I turned into the garden proper, I nearly gasped. It was set out like a medieval garden, parceled into small plots where varying herbs and flowers grew, and it was a place of great order and serenity, much larger than I had expected. A monk sat on an iron bench before another bank of the overgrown roses. Beside him on the bench something glinted in the early sun: secateurs. When he heard my footsteps on the gravel, he looked up and swept the hood off his head.

It was Skeleton: no one could have mistaken him for anyone else. His hair had been cropped down to graying bristle, and a little wire-brush beard filled out his cheeks, but he still was Skeleton Ridpath. "Do you like our garden?" he asked.

"Very much," I said. "It's beautiful, in fact. Do you tend it?"

He ignored the question. "I must get occupied with the roses. They are in a sorry state." He picked up the secateurs and nodded gloomily, indicated that I could be seated. "I can give you fifteen minutes," he said, "but I must tell you now that you are wasting your time."

"I'd better decide that," I said, "but in any case, I'd better also plunge right in, if you don't mind. Why did you decide to attend Headley Theological Institute after Clemson? It can hardly be what you had in mind when you started college." I took out a pen and notebook.

"You would not understand," he said, and clicked the secateurs shut.

"Since you've given me fifteen minutes, why not test me?" I asked. "Otherwise your time is wasted too. I understand at least that you are a talented gardener."

He scowled at me, refusing the compliment.

"Was there a crisis—a spiritual crisis of some kind?"

"There was a crisis," he said. "You might call it spiritual."

"Could you describe it in any way?"

He sighed: he was really itching to get back at the roses.

"You could do some of your work while you talk to me," I said.

He promptly left the bench, mumbling "Thank you," and began on the roses. *Snick-snick:* a thick brown rope laden with heavy blossoms collapsed, and petals showered on the bench.

"In my second year at college," he said, and for some reason my chest tightened, "I nearly dropped out. I had a disturbing vision. One that subsequently was shown to be prophetic."

"And what was that?" I asked.

"The vision was of one of our classmates." He turned to glare at me. "I had a vision of Marcus Reilly. I saw his death. Not once, but many times." I think I stopped breathing. "He was in his car. He removed a pistol from his pocket. He placed the pistol beside his ear. Do I have to go on?"

"No," I breathed. "I know how Marcus died."

Snick: another cluster of roses flopped. More petals drifted to the bench.

"That is what I have to tell you. You would not understand the rest. I'm sure the rest was all conventional anyhow. I accepted Christ first, and later I accepted the Church. It is unusual only in that I am a converted Catholic."

"You gave up your wings, didn't you?" I asked.

"I will never leave this place. And I will never want to. If that is what you mean."

He suddenly seemed very agitated.

"Brother Robert, what happened in Vermont?" I dared to ask; unwisely.

"I'm sure our time is up," he said, not looking at me. "I am sorry I ever agreed to speak to you." Now the roses were tumbling all over the bench, lolling over and rolling onto the path.

"If I brought Tom Flanagan here, would you agree to meet him?" That suddenly seemed to me a brilliant solution.

Brother Robert stopped pruning the roses. He stood stock-still for a second, with his arm frozen where it had been when I had uttered Tom's name. "Under no circumstances whatsoever. Also, I will never see you again, under any circumstances whatsoever. Is that clear?" He lopped off another tangle of roses, and our interview was ended. He would not let me see his face.

"Thank you for what you've told me," I said, and went back to the gate, where Brother Theo waited. He had the air of a man who wished he had been eavesdropping; he asked me if I had enjoyed my visit.

Later that year I visited friends in Putney, Vermont, and before I left them I looked up Hilly Vale on an old Sunoco map and made a hundred-and-ten-mile detour on my way home.

The town was much as Tom had described it. Few changes had happened to Hilly Vale in twenty years. I parked on Main Street and went into a health-food shop— it must have been one of the changes. A young man with shoulder-length hair and a striped apron stood behind the counter eating a carob bar. He put the final touches to my theory about change in Hilly Vale. "I'm looking for the site of the old Collins place," I said. "Can you help me?"

He grinned at me. "Been here only a year and a half," he said. "Maybe Mrs. Brewster knows it." He nodded to a fiftyish woman in a down jacket lingering over a display of purses in plastic bags.

"Mrs. Brewster!" he called. "This guy here wants. . . ?" he raised his eyebrows at me.

"The old Collins place, Mrs. Brewster," I said. "Where they had the big fire. In 1959, it would have been. At the end of the summer."

"Why, sure," she said, and again I felt that tightening of the chest. "Nobody even knew about it until the whole place was gone. We didn't even know for weeks after. Terrible thing. Mr. Collins died there. He was a famous magician once, you know." She gave me a sly look. "You wouldn't be Mr. Flanagan, now, would you?"

"Why, no," I said, startled. "Why do you ask?"

"Thought you'd know. That's the Flanagan place now. 'Course, it isn't a *place,* not that way. And that's a shame, too. Valuable land sitting like that—some folks here would like to buy some of that land. You're not from the real-estate people, are you?"

"No," I said. "I'm just a friend of Mr. Flanagan's. But I didn't know he owned it."

"All of it," she said. "Right clear around the lake. He never comes here. Probably thinks he's too good for the likes of us. He's a magician too—oh, you know that. But he's not the equal of Mr. Collins. He's not like Mr. Collins. Lived here from 1925 on, Mr. Collins did. And he kept to himself." She nodded firmly.

"No, I gather he's not like Mr. Collins," I said.

"Couldn't hold a candle to him, in my opinion."

"Did you actually see Collins perform?" I asked her, barely able to credit it.

"Never even met him," she said. "But I can tell you how to get to the place, since you're so curious."

I followed her directions out of town, and soon found myself in the peculiar position of being in a landscape I had written about without ever having seen. Here was the fork in the road; here was the ascending unpaved track through the trees; and here was the pasture where Tom had seen the horses. It was overgrown with chicory and burdock: it needed Brother Robert's talents.

And here, finally, was the loop of a drive.

I parked my car and walked down. It had once been paved. Now weeds and grass had pushed aside and broken the asphalt all the way to the gates. Someone, probably a party of teenagers, had broken them open, and they had rusted over the years. Vines trailed through the bars. The wall around Shadowland still stood, though, and other vines twisted happily through the brick, clumping and blossoming where the top layer had broken off. The barbed wire was long gone—I supposed some thrifty farmer had rolled it up and trucked it off.

I walked down the broken drive, slipping a little on the loose stones, wondering when I would see the house. I left the treacherous drive and walked into tall grass. It was a lie, I saw—all of it a beautiful and whopping lie. There was no house. There never had been.

Then my foot connected with a brick, and I realized with a great thumping shock that I was actually standing in the house. Mossy bricks lay scattered randomly through the grass; after a little more prowling, I came across the ruin of a brick fireplace tipped over on its side, its opening

half-filled with dirt and rubble. O. Henry and Snickers
wrappers; a beer bottle poking out through weeds; an old
comic book gone to pulp. I was standing in Shadowland's
basement, where everything had fallen. Now it was just a
little dip in the land—it could have been a glacial hollow.
I bent down and picked up a brick and brushed off ants. It
was discolored: fire-blackened.

But the bluff was still there, and so was the lake. I went
through the tall grass, pursued by the eerie feeling that I
was walking with Tom Flanagan and Rose Armstrong as
they fled the burning house, and came up out of the
hollow. The land fell away spectacularly for a hundred
yards or more, dropping down a thickly overgrown cliff.
The lake winked back sunlight. Tom's woods blanketed
the sides. I'd had no idea of the scale, that it was all so
large and the woods so extensive—they looked forbid-
dingly thick—and the lake so long. It must have been
nearly a mile across.

Rose Armstrong, I thought, and then I saw a tiny strip
of gold at the lake's far end and my heart stopped. I
nearly fell down the bluff. At that moment I believed
everything Tom had said to me.

I could almost see them there, Tom and his Rose,
curled together on the tiny strip of sand beside a book and
a glass bird; could almost see her whispering whatever she
had whispered into his ear before she . . . what? Slipped
into the water and left all that was human behind her,
welded into Tom Flanagan's memory?

A warm wind came from nowhere: mustard flower; gin;
cigar smoke. I could have told myself that I caught all
those odors. The surface of the lake darkened and belled
under the shadow of a cloud, and I turned back to walk
across the ruins of Shadowland to my car.